THE BEAUTIFUL
BLUE

THE BEAUTIFUL BLUE

Lucinda Hart

PRESS

Published by Vulpine Press in the United Kingdom in 2023

ISBN: 978-1-83919-495-5
Cover by SL Johnson

www.vulpine-press.com

For Chris Hart (Paddy), 1946 – 2017
I miss you and love you every day

"She's there with him now. I saw them."

The line goes dead; with a rattle and a tinny clang a coin drops into the tray. Amy gropes for it, still holding the greasy receiver. The light in the phone box illuminates the graffiti scratched into the shelf, the Bombay Mix packet on the floor, the cigarette butts, tissues. She fumbles the twenty-pence piece back into the slot, dials the number again. It rings out and out and out, but no one picks up.

Guy and Heather shove through the throng at the door of the village hall out into the night. Rain slices the corona of the street lamp, splatters into the deepening puddles. There's a crowd round the phone box. Guy recognises the girls, the two boys. The smell of cigarette smoke, Lynx deodorant, sweet perfume, and tension. The thrumming in the air before a fight.

Guy sees this in some weird slow-fast time frame. Behind him the bass beat from the disco thuds his blood faster.

He finds his voice at last. "Hey, you lot! Everything OK?"

The faces swing round to him, the girls dark-eyed with kohl; one of the boys has zombie make-up, the other's wearing an eye-patch.

"Mr Lovell," they chorus. Just over a year ago he was still teaching them English.

"Is everything OK?" he asks again.

"It's Amy."

"He's cheated on her."

Guy scans the group. He can't see Amy Langford anywhere.

"Should we go after her?" someone asks.

"Where's she gone?" Guy demands.

"Home?" one of the girls asks.

"I thought she was going to Olly's. That's Penzance."

Guy hesitates. He still feels responsible for this gang, who suddenly look so young in the rain and the pale street-lamp glow. But Heather's with him, just a few steps away, her hood covering her lovely chocolate-coloured hair. Hovering uncertainly, probably wondering if she's done the right thing leaving the disco with him.

"Aren't her brothers here?" Guy says. "I thought I saw Pete inside."

"Yeah," says eye-patch. "They're both in there."

"They can go after her," one of the girls says, breaks away, runs into the village hall.

As she opens the door the thump of the music swells, and pulsing light bleeds out. Guy just hears her bellowing *Pete Langford, Dave Langford!*

"Thanks, Mr Lovell," says eye-patch.

The rest of the group move towards the door too. Guy turns, half-expecting Heather to have disappeared into the night, but she's still there, wrapped in her padded coat.

"Sorry, sorry," he says. "I thought there was trouble."

"What was it? Someone run off?"

"Someone's boyfriend has done the dirty. Come on, let's go."

~

Rain cascades down the dark windscreen. Amy shivers. She's left her coat at the disco. She fires the ignition, juggles the pedals

2

with shaky feet, and the car lurches onto the road. The Hallowe'en scarecrows loom unsteadily in the rain: a flapping arm,
a carved pumpkin head, an eyeless mask.

People shouting on the pavement, a hot-potato stall. Past the
pub, past the church; Amy misses a gear change, and the car
splutters.

So that's why the house was dark when she called round earlier.

Amy's mouth tastes foul: beer and cigarettes. Her heart-rate
thunders. She must not cry, not now, not when she's driving,
not in this rain, this storm. There's water all over the road. Only
five minutes to home. If she's going home. Or is she going into
Penzance to find them? She doesn't know what to do. She is
suddenly alone, just a girl in a car, on a country road at night,
with the wind, and the rain, and the water. She's so alone.

Dark trees crowd the road, dripping more storm-water.
White chevrons glow in the distance. The road falls away to the
Bends. She races down to the first right-hander far too fast.
There's always water there when it rains, gushing out of the
craggy rockface, across the road, and over the edge to join the
stream in the gully below.

Trees, bend, rain, dark, water, water, water.

~

"Have you told your friends where you are?" Guy asks.

"Yes."

"And that I'll run you back to Helston later?"

"Yes," Heather says again.

3

~

"You what?!" Vicky said later, when Heather told her she was going for a drink with Guy at the Archangel, and that he'd drive her back to Helston.

"Heather Read!" Carol whooped. "Fast worker or what?!"

~

She'd met him when the three of them had run into Guy on their way from the carpark to the disco. He was studying a scarecrow – a mummy whose damp bandaging was adrift and fluttering – and Carol had called out to him because she'd known him for years.

Heather smiled and said hello to the rangy man in front of her. In the half-light it was hard to see the exact colour of his hair – pale brown, she guessed. He had a neat beard, and was wearing a waxed jacket. Older than her, probably forty-something.

He had the most beautiful voice.

Heather stood there on the pavement, like a lemon, just listening to his rising and falling cadences as he talked to Carol about some mutual friend while trick-or-treat kids shrieked past. And then, suddenly, somehow, he was walking with them, through the village, past pumpkin lanterns, past a little stall selling toffee and parkin and chestnuts, past a hot-dog stand, drifting with the breath of onions, towards the village hall.

"Do you teach at Helston too?" Guy asked Heather.

"Yes. Art. Same school as these two. You're at St Michael's?"

The bottoms of Heather's jeans are soaked with puddle water. The rain is angry and jabbing. But she doesn't care, except that once they're in the warmth and light of the pub, she'll look a mess because her hood keeps blowing off, and her make-up is probably smudged.

Just as they arrive at the Archangel two motorbikes roar past.

"Amy's brothers, I think," Guy says, and opens the door for her.

~

Sunday morning. The first of November. The end of half-term. Heather never expected to start this day in St Michael.

Guy's burgundy Fiesta is splattered with raindrops. There are puddles on his drive, thick viscous water, clotted with mud. He unlocks the car door and she slides in. The car smells of cigarettes; the ashtray is open, full with stubs. Heather's mouth tastes too minty from the toothpaste she applied with her finger. She couldn't remove her make-up with water in Guy's bathroom, and now her eyes are dark and scratchy. Perhaps there are girls who carry a toothbrush and pot of Nivea with them just in case. Heather wouldn't know. She's never done anything like this before.

Guy is forty-four, eleven years older than her. He teaches English at the comprehensive in St Michael. He loves Shakespeare, Elvis, and Walter Sickert. He was married once, a long while ago. Heather cannot understand why no girl has snatched him up by now.

He reverses out of the drive onto the road. A gunmetal sky. Everywhere is wet; there is rain in the air, more drifts of water than the slashing needles of the previous night. There are scarecrows still standing, lopsided and sagging from the storm. One has collapsed in a drunken heap. A car parked at the roadside is splattered with broken eggs.

Guy snaps his lighter at a cigarette as they pass the village hall and the red telephone box. As they pass, Heather glimpses the blackened orange of a pumpkin head that has rolled up against the hall door, and a few beer bottles on the pavement. Across the road a huddled group of people are talking, wrapped up in their raincoats.

"Shall we have some music?" Guy turns up the radio. Ocean FM playing Queen.

They drive through the village without talking. It's not awkward, it's comfortable. Past the Archangel, where Guy kissed her over their beers. More people, too many people, close together, talking urgently, shaking heads.

The news comes on at midday. Guy's saying something about a series they're both watching on the telly; the newsreader says *fatality* and *St Michael*, and Guy twists up the volume. *Notorious bends on the B road to Penzance…Flash flood.*

The driver has been identified as an eighteen-year-old woman from St Michael.

~

Chloe Johnstone's Golf bumps down the lane towards the cliff edge. The driveway for the Headland Hotel is on the right, between two pale stone pillars. It's dark; ahead of her the sea falls away to the horizon, sparkled with lights from three boats. Mount's Bay curves into the sodium lamp chains of Penzance and Marazion and the distant Lizard peninsula.

Chloe's tuned to Ocean FM as usual. Guy Lovell's Sunday night show. Even though he's been a radio presenter for years Chloe still thinks of him as her English teacher. When she moved back to St Michael with eighteen-month-old Evie, Guy was one of the first people she ran into in the post office. He recognised her, hugged her awkwardly, welcomed her home, and tickled Evie under the chin. Chloe could hardly believe the frail man with long straggly greying hair was Mr Lovell, who'd read *Macbeth* with such passion. Her eyes kept sliding back to the tube coming from his nose, hooked over his ear. *Oesophageal cancer*, he'd said. *Feeding tube. Radiotherapy; chemotherapy; surgery in a few months' time.*

Tonight he sounds like he's getting a cold, Chloe thinks, killing the engine. Guy's hoarse voice disappears.

She opens the door, and smells the breath of the sea. Waves break with soft splashes far below. She shoulders her new sports bag and starts across the carpark to the chunky building embedded in the cliff behind the hotel.

She's written the entry code on the back of her hand. The door releases with a hiss, and she steps inside. Immediately, another smell.

7

I can still go home, she thinks, I don't have to go on. But she climbs the stairs. Then, a huge blue abstract painting on the wall. Blue painting; blue smell.

The stairs turn, and there's a glass door leading into a foyer. Chloe opens it. Heat surges around her, and there, through floor-length glass panes, is the pool. The blue, blue pool.

Beguiling and terrifying.

Someone's sliding through the water, stirring the surface into choppy troughs. Heather watches his head swoop up, like a seal's, then down again.

A woman's echoey voice through the glass. "Legs, legs."

The man stops halfway to the shallow end, shoves his goggles onto his forehead. The woman standing on the edge snaps her arms together in the air.

"Like this."

There are two more guys up at the deep end. One starts swimming down, slowly, carefully. The other, who looks younger, is floating on his back, all that water beneath him.

There's a girl sitting on a beanbag at the poolside. A girl with spiky red hair, in a black and pink swimsuit, knees drawn up under her chin, a dark tattoo on her upper arm. A pair of goggles dangles from her hand.

The instructor looks up, sees Chloe hovering beyond the glass panes, and waves at her. Too late to turn and flee now. Chloe follows the sign for the changing room. There's a dull clang, then the slap-slap of someone walking in flip-flops across tiles. Chloe nearly collides with the woman leaving the changing room.

"Oh, sorry," she mutters, inhaling with surprise.

The woman with a blue towel slung around her shoulders is someone she knows. Someone from St Michael. Heather, Guy's wife.

~

Heather glances over her shoulder at the girl going into the changing area. Yes, she's from St Michael. She's got a little one in a buggy. Been past the gallery a few times. She looks terrified, Heather thinks. She must be the new girl.

Heather opens the glass door to the pool, and the heat slaps her in the face like she's opened a wet oven. Kat's sitting on the beanbag, watching the three men in the pool. Or rather, watching Jason.

Heather's been swimming with Kat and Jason for some months now. Only a few days ago, Christa, the instructor, texted them all to say she was moving Jason to the earlier group with the two other men, as she had a new girl starting. Heather knew Kat would be disappointed.

~

Evie, Evie, I'm doing this for Evie, Chloe reminds herself as she struggles to shove her hair inside her brand-new swimming hat. The changing room is so hot and damp, she imagines that if she opened her mouth she could drink the air like water. Her hands shake as she tugs goggles over her head. She feels next to naked in her plain black swimsuit.

She hadn't thought to bring flip-flops; the tiles are wet and clammy under her toes. She shoves her stuff in a locker, almost drops her towel as she fiddles with the pound coin and the key.

Evie, Evie, she thinks as she pads towards the pool. Evie, who turned three just a few days ago on New Year's Day, and who wants to know why she can't go swimming like her cousins Zac and Luca.

Because Mummy's too frightened to swim is the answer. But Chloe won't give that answer. Instead, she's here tonight to learn to swim, aged thirty-nine.

~

Kat stands up as Heather hangs her towel up on a hook. The three men are all floating now: Rob and Tim, the older ones, on their backs, their hands stirring the water to stay afloat; Jason's on his front like a starfish, thick auburn hair darkened like seaweed. Kat really likes Jason. But Jason doesn't seem to have room for anyone.

"How are you?" she asks Heather.

"I'm OK. Just a bit…worried."

Kat watches Jason haul himself up the metal steps. He picks up a white towel and ruffles his hair dry. She tries not to look at the droplets sparkling on his beautiful shoulders, the scattering of freckles on his back. The names intertwined in ink on his forearm.

"What you worried about?"

"Guy," says Heather. "And Jasmine. They're both…oh, I don't know. Hey, I saw the new girl in the changing room."

Chloe's heart is skipping as she opens the glass door. Everyone's on the poolside now. Heather is talking to the thin girl with red hair. The young bloke goes over to them, with a towel around his neck.

"Here she is," Heather says and smiles at her.

"Chloe, I'm Christa." The instructor shakes her hand, then re-ties her faded ponytail. "We've got Heather, Kat, Jason, Rob, and Tim."

Chloe smiles round, sure they can see the juddering in her stomach, the trembling in her legs. The pool is empty. Turquoise and glassy. Depth is deceptive. It looks both shallow and deep.

"I'm coming in with you, Chloe." Christa peels off her tracksuit bottoms. "Well done, you three, see you all next week."

That's what Chloe liked about Christa's advert in the local paper. Small groups, instructor in the water.

"You're from St Michael." Heather says to Chloe. "I've seen you with your little girl."

"Evie. That's why I'm here tonight. For her." Chloe stops; she doesn't know whether to say anything about Guy. *Oh, what the hell?* "I think you married my English teacher."

"You went to school in St Michael? I didn't know you'd been living there so long."

"I came back," Chloe says. She finds a long strand of hair that never made it into her swimming cap.

11

"Hurry up, ladies," Christa says, climbing down the metal ladder, and the water surface breaks again. "Chloe, you come next."

Chloe grips the handrails, and lowers one foot. It's cold, much colder than she expected from the heat on the poolside, and she catches her breath. The water slapping round her waist feels thin, less viscous than she imagined. More fragile; more untrustworthy; more treacherous.

~

It's her. It's got to be. Chloe's an unusual name. She's the right kind of age. She's got hazel eyes and freckles; there's a string of gold-brown hair trailing from her hat. Kat watches Chloe bobbing nervously in the water, right beside Christa, while Heather glides off into deeper water.

"You joining us?" Christa calls up with a grin.

"Coming." Kat immerses herself quickly, to get used to the chill.

When she comes up again, Heather's swimming a graceful width, and Chloe is gripping the handrail.

"Kat, you warm up, while I get Chloe used to the water."

Kat pushes off the side, keeps her eyes down to the floor tiles sliding beneath her.

It's got to be her. Chloe Johnstone. She hasn't changed much.

She'd never know Kat Glanville was once Kathryn Smith though. Kat's confident of that. No one does.

Chloe is frightened of putting her head underwater. Christa stands beside her in the shallow end, tells her to hold the bar with one hand, and slide the other down the length of her thigh until she can reach a sunken weight on the tiled floor. The blue rises up to meet her, covers her goggles, and suddenly she's beneath the surface, and the pool floor is clear, the water still and calm. Her breath is silent in her chest, held, suspended, for those few seconds; then, sinker in hand, her head is out, and air rushes out of her lungs.

Christa shows her how to hold the rail and kick her legs. Chloe had done this before when she was little: school lessons at the big pool in Penzance. But she doesn't remember anyone telling her about keeping her legs straight, and kicking from the hips, and certainly no one suggested dipping her head underwater. She tries it, and it's quieter down there, almost peaceful. She can hold her breath. Her legs are still up, still moving. After a moment she stands to catch her breath and look around.

"OK, Heather, Chloe," Christa says. "Kat's going to do a length now, so can you stay together at the shallow end?"

Heather plunges into the water and glides down to Chloe, then emerges next to her and tugs her goggles up onto her head.

"How's it going?" she asks.

"OK. Better than the lessons I had at school."

Chloe's shoulders grow cold. Heather has hunkered down in the water. Chloe keeps one hand on the rail, and does the same. Kat's in the deep end. Chloe wonders how deep the water is there, how far below Kat's toes the tiles are. Christa's bobbing beside Kat; Kat nods and Christa moves aside. Kat drops her head; her back arm swoops over, and she's cutting arrow-straight

13

through the water towards Chloe and Heather. Chloe feels almost nauseous with both fear and envy. She'll never be able to do that.

Yes, you will, she tells herself. Think of Evie.

The time goes so quickly. By the end of the lesson, Chloe can just judder halfway across the shallow end, gripping a neon pink float. Her legs drag down, and she splutters and stumbles, gulping blue water, and Christa explains that her head isn't deep enough, isn't straight enough, she is not kicking from the hips. At the end, for relaxation, Heather and Kat float, suspended like drifting corpses. Chloe grips the rail, and ducks her head; her legs swing up with the force of the water under her. It's extraordinary: like lying on a soft, invisible mattress. She isn't even thinking about holding her breath. She's just looking down through the water molecules to the tiles below, thinking, suddenly, how easy it would be to let go.

After the lesson, Heather's wet hair drips down her collar as she crosses the carpark. The sky is so dark. Cold air bites at her face. She breathes in, and that cold mixes with the remains of chlorine in her airway, and it feels like she's inhaled Listerine.

The car is freezing and misty inside. She turns the ignition, the engine roars, and Guy's voice jumps in her ears. She's definitely not imagining it: he is very hoarse. Jasmine has noticed it too. After everything, they must get him to see a doctor, and that is the hardest thing to ask of him.

Heather reverses out of her parking space, the heater roaring over Guy's crackly voice. She waves at Chloe who is walking across the carpark, but she can't possibly see her in the dark.

14

In the changing room cubicle Kat stands under the hot shower jet and shampoos the chlorine from her short spiky hair. She likes to have a shower straight after swimming; that way, when she arrives home, it's all done, and she can get something to eat – a salad or maybe a yoghurt, but that's all – and throw herself down on the sofa and read or watch TV or recall those few words she might have exchanged with Jason – *that was good, your arm pull's come on, nice glide* – but now there won't be any more interactions like that. Chloe has a habit of turning up in the wrong places, Kat thinks, as she towels her hair quickly.

She hears men's voices and footsteps heading for the changing room. The clang, clang of two cubicle doors slamming. Kat flaps out her jeans and wriggles into them. Then, the clack, clack, of the two cubicles opening, the slap of feet on tiles, the clink of the lockers, and the guys have gone. Kat slides on her boots, grabs her coat as it's too hot to put it on in the humid changing room, and glances round for her possessions.

As she leaves she stops at the long mirror over the row of three sinks. She's average height, slim, maybe even thin, with jagged red hair. She doesn't look anything like Kathryn Smith. OK, her eyes are the same grey-blue, and her Midlands vowels still lurk in her voice despite her hard work to kill them. She still has that birthmark on her side, but the other scars are buried deeper. She wonders how long it will take Chloe Johnstone to realise who she is – who she was.

As she passes the glass door to the pool, Kat looks in. One of the guys is doing some kind of underwater somersault in the deep end; the other is floating on his back, shouting something at his friend. Kat feels resentful as she always does when she sees

15

others in the water. Not jealousy because they are confident and can really swim and do underwater somersaults. No, a simple envy that they are in that cool-warm blue pool, inhaling the chlorine, feeling the power and kick of the water under their bodies. Doing what she has only just had the courage to try. She could so easily have never done it.

~

Seven-year-old Kathryn Smith could not swim. And everyone was about to find out. Now. Publically. Mr Hawker had told them they would be starting swimming lessons after Christmas. He needed to find out who could swim, and how far, and who couldn't swim at all.

Kathryn was on a table for four in front of the blackboard. Now they were in the juniors they had wooden lift-up desks where you could store your pencils and ruler and felt- tips and crayons. The desks must have been a lot older than the school itself because the golden wood was scratched, there were initials engraved with compass points, and there were even inkwells in the right-hand corners. Kathryn was left-handed. The desks didn't seem to accommodate the left-handed writers from past years.

Ten metres, five metres, twenty-five metres, ten metres, twenty-five metres.

Mr Hawker noted down the distances next to the names in the register. Fiona Clarke had even brought her swimsuit in to school with her, and was flashing the coloured badges sewn onto it.

16

"Kathryn?" Mr Hawker said.

Kathryn felt the heat rise up her cheeks. "I can't," she muttered.

"You can't swim?" Fiona Clarke whooped from the other side of the room.

"Quiet, Fiona." Mr Hawker hovered his pen. "You can't swim at all, Kathryn?"

"No," she said miserably. Kids were sniggering.

"Have you ever been in a pool?"

"No," she said again, and the heat in her face was burning so much that she almost wouldn't mind the cool wash of water over her skin.

"Can't swim," Mr Hawker said, as he wrote something, then turned to the boy opposite Kathryn.

She should have listened to the rest of the replies. She should have listened because there might be someone else – weedy Jamie Wallis perhaps, or stupid Marie Kennedy – who also couldn't swim, but instead Kathryn slid down behind her wooden desk, scraping her stubby fingernail through the grooves of someone else's graffiti, glancing up through her fringe to the wall clock, watching it gulp off the minutes to morning break, and the snide comments she could already anticipate.

Oh well. Just another ordinary day really.

Fiona Clarke started it. Obviously. She was in the playground, waiting for Kathryn.

"You can't swim!" she shrieked, and the other girls around her looked up from their skipping ropes and Sindy dolls.

Kathryn shrugged.

"You haven't even been in the pool," Fiona went on. "Is that true?"

"Course it's true," one of her cronies interjected. "There'd be no water in the pool if she had."

Fiona howled. "You'd go straight to the bottom."

Kathryn walked off. They were still sniggering behind her back. She stood at the railings at the edge of the playground. Across the access road was the teachers' carpark and, behind it, the dried-up school pond. The gates were only yards from her. Mrs Foster, who was on playground duty, was looking the other way. Kathryn could simply walk out and into the housing estate beyond, and ten minutes later she'd be home. She'd had this fantasy so many times – just walking away from the school, and the playground, and Fiona Clarke, and all the others, and their shrieking and their laughing. What did it actually matter, she wondered over and over, if she was fat? How did it hurt them? She was only seven but she already knew there was no answer to this.

That evening she handed the letter from school to her mother.

"Swimming," her mother said. "That'll be fun."

"It won't," Kathryn said.

"We'll go shopping over Christmas and get you a lovely swimsuit." Kathryn's mother folded the letter and slid it under a jam jar of pennies on the sideboard. "And a new towel. Lovely new things." When Kathryn didn't answer, her mother said, "It would be really good to be able to swim. If we do ever move to Cornwall, you'd be able to go in the sea with friends, on boats, that kind of thing. You'd need to be able to swim."

18

If we ever move to Cornwall. And, if we move, Kathryn wondered, would it be any different there?

Later, in bed, she lay in the grey half-dark and mapped out a new life for herself. Her father would get a job in Cornwall, they'd leave Birmingham for good, leave Fiona Clarke and her stupid swimming badges behind. They'd live by the sea, near the places they visited on holiday. Kathryn would suddenly, overnight, lose all her weight, and she'd be only the same as everyone else. And no one in Cornwall would know she had been the fat girl at her old school. And because she wasn't fat, she wouldn't care about being seen in a swimsuit, so she would learn to swim. And she wouldn't sink straight to the bottom, or slosh all the water out of the pool. So she could go to the beach and go on boats and all that with her new friends.

Kathryn turned over in bed. As if any of that would happen. Weight didn't just melt off you. She'd wished, prayed, for that often enough. Once she'd had a half-dream about being in the dining hall at school, and whisking up her dress – sized for an eleven-year-old – and showing everyone it was all just stuffing, she'd just been having a laugh, having a joke, letting them all believe she was huge. As if! She was thin. Really. Look, it's all padding.

She could hear the TV being silenced downstairs. Her parents would be coming up to bed soon. Outside, on the main road, someone was shrieking. Someone kicked something metallic. The city never truly slept. Her parents complained about the road noise in their bedroom at the front. The blue strobes of ambulances and police cars, the fights, the shouting. It wouldn't be like that in Penzance, her mother said. Maybe not, but some things would be the same for Kathryn.

On her bedroom walls her parents had pinned up giant posters of butterflies. She ran her eyes along the darkened illustrations: Large White, Green-veined White, Red Admiral, Peacock, Small Tortoiseshell, Painted Lady, Comma. She loved butterflies. She had books on them; she drew them; she had covered her chest of drawers with metallic butterfly stickers from the junk shop in Northfield shopping centre. She also liked caterpillars. She liked the way a caterpillar could work its own dark magic and be reborn, reincarnated into something beautiful and graceful. Life is easier for caterpillars, Kathryn thought, not for the first time.

~

I did it, I bloody well did it, Chloe thinks. It's hard not to have a grin on her face, even though she hates driving in the dark, and her rear window is misted up. The car smells of chlorine, but now it's not a terrifying smell, it's the smell of achievement, pride. Perhaps I was never really that scared, Chloe wonders. Perhaps I imagined it.

Guy Lovell sounds croaky on the radio tonight. Chloe taps her hand on the wheel to Dire Straits. The road swoops down a dip, and there's the garage on the left. *LANGFORD'S AUTOS – brakes – clutches – MOT* the sign shouts out, white lettering in the dark. There are a few cars on the forecourt. The house next door seems to have all the lights on, and a string of Christmas bulbs winking under the eaves. Jim and June Langford, Amy's

20

parents, still live there; Dave and Pete have moved out into their own homes though they both work at the garage. Chloe doesn't use Langford's. She goes to the garage on the other side of the village. She saw June in the pharmacy a few months ago – still a shade of the woman she'd once been. June didn't seem to recognise her.

Beyond Langford's, the road banks steeply to the left, and drops into the woods, and down to the Bends. Chloe eases off the accelerator. It's too dark to see the stream gushing down the rockface on the left and under the road. The way rises once more, and there's the sign, the black and white chevrons. Chloe glances at it, it's a reflex action that means nothing and everything. The wooden cross has long gone. No one leaves flowers there any more.

~

At home, Heather showers and throws her towel and swimsuit in the washing machine.

"Have you eaten?" she asks Jasmine.

Jas mumbles something affirmative. Yes, Heather realises there's a pasta bowl and a couple of saucepans stacked by the sink.

Jas slopes off to the living room. Heather hears the discordant sounds of her flicking through TV channels. She's about to follow her, ask if she's OK, then stops. Maybe she's fallen out with Andrew, her boyfriend of about six months, one of the students on her media course. In fact, Heather recalls, Andrew hasn't been round to their house for a few days. She hovers in the doorway.

"Is everything OK? I thought Andrew might've been round this weekend?" She turns it into a question.

"He was doing some stuff with his dad."

"Ah. OK. Right."

"How was swimming?"

"We had a new girl. She lives in St Michael. Guy taught her at school."

"Hardly a girl then," Jas grins. "That was a while ago."

"You know what I mean. She's called Chloe. She's got a little girl. I've seen her around. I think she lives down Barrow Lane."

"She any good?"

"Her first time. I think Kat's pissed off because Jason's been moved to another group. She really fancies Jason. OK, I'm going to get something to eat. Guy'll be back soon."

In the fridge she finds the other half of Jas's pasta sauce. That'll do for her. As for Guy, who knows what he'll eat? Whatever she cooks, it's never right. He leaves plates almost untouched, however soft a meal she's made. Mashed potato, fish, omelettes. She can't remember the last time he finished a meal.

A key in the lock, then the slam of the door. Guy's back. The radio studio is on the outskirts of Penzance, only fifteen minutes away. Heather shoves spaghetti for one into the pan of boiling water. If she grates a bit more cheese she can make Guy an omelette, with a piece of soft brown bread. He won't eat it, but she won't give up.

Guy is sixty-six now, with straggling hair which has not quite recovered from the chemotherapy damage. Never a big man, he's thin and hollow-looking round the cheekbones, under the ribs.

"Ready for some supper?"

"I'm not really…"

"You must have something. I'll make an omelette." Heather cracks two eggs in a bowl before he can say anything.

He drops his car keys into the chipped antique bowl on the dresser, pokes his head into the front room, waves at Jas.

"Guy," Heather starts with a cold, slimy feeling inside. "Something's wrong with your voice."

"I'm getting a cold," he says quickly, taking a bottle of Chenin Blanc out of the fridge. "Drink?"

"Only a small one. It's not a cold. I've noticed it for a few weeks. You're really husky. You've been coughing and wheezing."

"It's nothing." Guy pours two glasses of wine, gulps from one of them, and replaces the bottle in the fridge door.

"Will you see the doctor this week?"

Heather's spaghetti boils over in a fury of hot water, bubbles scudding across the hob. In the frying pan, she drops a handful of cheese into the eggs.

"You don't see the doctor for a cold," Guy snaps. "They get pissed off with you. They won't give me antibiotics or anything just for this."

"It might be an infection." Heather flicks the omelette into a crescent, and slides it onto the waiting plate. "Please get it checked."

23

"His voice?" Jas is in the doorway, eyes on her mother. "It's been terrible for ages. You should get it checked."

Guy doesn't answer, gets the bottle out again and tops up his glass.

~

Chloe parks erratically outside Millie and Matt's house behind the enormous arse of Matt's four-wheel drive. The ground-floor windows explode with flashing Christmas lights. Chloe wonders how long Millie will be happy to have Evie on a Sunday night while she goes swimming. Evie loves going round to the huge modern house overlooking the cemetery. Her cousins, Zac and Luca, six and five, don't even seem to mind having a girl there.

Chloe's younger sister, Millie, met Matt Sinclair when she was a nurse and he was a junior doctor. After working as a locum GP all over the county, a few years ago he was offered a partnership at St Michael surgery. Millie gave up nursing, and they moved back to the village where she'd grown up. Probably never imagining that Chloe would soon follow, not just to St Michael, but back to Orchid Cottage, their childhood home.

Chloe rings the bell, and Matt swings the door open. He's tall and blond, and dresses like a country vet in cords and checked shirts.

"*Little Mermaid* or *Titanic*?" Matt grins.

Chloe flushes, as she wipes her shoes on the mat. "Somewhere in between, I guess. How's Evie?"

"Fine. Great. Just watching a DVD with the boys. Evie! Mummy's back. Millie!"

24

Chloe is acutely aware that she smells of the pool, that her hair, quickly unbundled from the swimming hat, is damp and tangled. That she looks a mess. Millie comes running down the stairs. She and Matt look like a magazine couple: both fair, both clean and tidy, with dazzling teeth. Zac and Luca are like magazine kids, mini-Matts who eat butternut squash, whereas Evie usually has chocolate stains on her clothes, and felt-tip on her face.

"How did you get on?" Millie asks.

"Good. Much better than I thought it'd be."

"I can't believe you can't swim," Matt says – for perhaps the millionth time. "Living in Cornwall and not being able to swim." Matt grew up in London, but can swim like a bloody fish, and has already taught Zac and Luca.

Why is it so shameful to not swim? Chloe wonders – for perhaps the millionth time – as she follows Millie into the living room. People appear to take pride in not being able to cook or understand maths, but not being able to swim is an acute social embarrassment.

"Mummy!" Evie cries.

"Here I am." Chloe squats down, and Evie rushes into her arms.

"You smell all funny."

"I'll have a shower when we get home. You can come in with me. Now, don't forget Ears."

Evie snatches her greying white rabbit. "Can I come swimming?" she asks. "Zac and Luca do lots of swimming."

"Yes, one day," Chloe says, trying to get Evie's coat on her while she's still clutching Ears.

"With you, Mummy?"

"With me," Chloe says.

That's why she's doing it.

~

When Guy became ill with oesophageal cancer, he moved into the spare bedroom and he hasn't moved back in with Heather. Gradually, his clothes and books and notepads have all migrated across the landing, and Heather's nail varnishes and earrings and sudoku books have spread across the gaps where Guy's things were. From where she lies in bed, with the door ajar, she can see a slice of landing, and recalls the nights, so many nights, when she'd lie like this, eyes open, hear the squeak of Guy's door opening, and see his dark shape cross her vision, wired from his nose to the pump in his hand. At night he never shut the bathroom door properly, and Heather waited for the thump of him setting down the pump, the curses as he struggled to manage undoing buttons, pissing, washing, without tugging the fragile line from his nose.

Now she lies in the same position, tight, taut. Guy's downstairs, though it's nearly three. He coughs, and Heather jumps under the quilt. Jas has heard the difference in his voice, in his breathing. Everyone who listened to him on the radio last night must have heard it too. They may be wondering as she and Jas are: *has it come back?*

From the day of Guy's endoscopy, from the moment when the consultant approached him and Heather with a stony face and the diagnosis of oesophageal cancer, he faded day by day.

26

Soon, he wasn't able to broadcast at all, spending all day in bed, while the chemo and radiotherapy ravaged his tissues. Listeners sent cards and letters to the radio station; the Facebook page swelled with good wishes. Heather saw a shiny tear in Guy's eye as he scrolled down his laptop screen. He was missed. People wanted him back. People wanted him well.

During the long, empty hours on the day of his surgery, Heather and Jas stayed tuned to Ocean FM. There was an Elvis hour in Guy's honour.

"What's the point?" Jas asked with a wry smile. "He won't hear it."

"They might have the radio on in theatre. They did when I had my hernia done."

"You were awake. He's not."

And they waited all day for the call to say Guy was awake again, that the oesophagectomy had been successful, he had survived the deflation of a lung, the massive wound incision, the redesigning of a human being.

And now? He's not well. He ate half the omelette, didn't touch the bread. He drank most of the bottle of white. He's probably on the whisky right now.

Heather swings her legs out of bed, about to go down, thinks better of it.

~

On Monday morning Chloe wakes unusually early, as the winter sky is lightening. Evie's curled into an apostrophe against her back, warm and snuffly; when Chloe reaches down, Evie's nappy is damp and squashy.

She should have her own bed, Millie says over and over. *She should be at nursery by now.* Perhaps that last one is true. Evie will be starting school in eighteen months' time. Chloe has kept her by her side, the two of them together. It's only ever been the two of them. Chloe never told Evie's father, a married man with children of his own, that she was pregnant. As soon as she knew for sure, she ended the affair. There was nothing else she could have done. Her parents left her in tears with their kindness, and suggested she should move back in with them.

Her mother, Elaine, still owned Orchid Cottage, the two bedroomed bungalow Chloe grew up in. When the tenants handed in their notice Elaine asked Chloe if she'd like to return to St Michael. Millie and Matt were already there, and Chloe still felt the nostalgic tug of her home, even after everything that had happened.

Chloe slides out of bed, leaving Evie and Ears wrapped in the duvet, and pads down the corridor. There's a basket of laundry to sort out in the kitchen.

Her swimsuit is lying on top. She picks it up. It's cool and slippery, still damp from last night's wash. It smells faintly of chlorine. It wasn't a fantasy then, nor a dream. She really did do it.

~

Heather calls the surgery at eight thirty, and gets an emergency appointment for Guy at eleven fifteen.

"I couldn't get Dr Fieldhouse," she tells Jas, who's making tea, half-asleep.

Dr Fieldhouse saw Guy through his cancer, with home visits, and negotiations with the oncologists, but he's past retirement age now, and only doing a few clinics.

"Who did you get?" Jas opens the wall cupboard, gazes at biscuits, crackers, chocolate, rice, spaghetti.

"Dr Sinclair."

"He's hot," Jas says, closing the cupboard empty-handed. "I saw him for that eye infection."

"Do you want some toast?"

"No."

"Are you OK?" Heather asks.

Jas isn't herself either. She isn't eating properly. Maybe it's some weird infection both Guy and Jas have picked up, making them lose their appetites. Heather feels a surge of hope, but only for a second. There's nothing wrong with Jas's voice.

"I'm fine." Jas throws away her tea. "I'm going back to bed. Are you going with Dad?"

"Yes, I'll close the gallery for an hour."

Heather scoops up a handful of Christmas cards from the dresser and dumps them in a pile on the worktop. She'll take down all the cards, she decides, before she goes up to tell Guy she has booked him an appointment. He won't be pleased.

~

Kat's flat is in the attic of a house on the seafront of Penzance. It's only small – but it's hers.

She looks out of her kitchen window to a pewter sky. It looks cold. It looks like rain. She really doesn't want to go to work today, and knows she won't sell much. Some days the walk to *Imago* feels insurmountable; today is one of those days.

Kat winds a green velvet scarf round her throat, and unhooks her keys. Kathryn Smith would never have believed she could have her own shop, her own flat, that she could take charge of her body. There was a lot Kathryn Smith would never have believed.

~

Heather often heard people say cancer creeps up on you. But, she asked herself, aren't the signs there for you to read if you only notice them? Guy stopped clearing his plate. He left the crusts of toast, the tougher pieces of meat. His gullet burnt with reflux. He lost weight. When he was referred to Gastroenterology the consultant said there was a small chance it was something malignant, but most likely it'd be a hiatus hernia.

While Guy was in the endoscopy theatre, Heather sat in the waiting room, with a paperback on her knee that she wasn't reading. She watched the waxy-faced patients being called in for their procedures; smelt the fear, like iron, in the room. The consultant came out and called *Mrs Lovell*, and it took her a second to realise he meant her because she never used Guy's surname. She shoved her book into her patchwork cloth bag and, standing up, saw the consultant's face and knew.

And when she saw Guy, sitting rigid in a chair in a cubicle, behind a stained curtain, she could tell in an instant that he already knew.

"I've taken some biopsies," the consultant explained. "But it was bleeding quite badly."

"What happens now?" Heather asked.

"It depends on the staging of the tumour. Once we know that, we'll know how to move forward. I'll be writing to the oncologists, and Guy will see them very soon. He also needs a CT scan. I'm guessing he'll need some radiotherapy or chemotherapy, or even both. If the tumour hasn't spread elsewhere we should be looking at an oesophagectomy. If it has spread…"

"There's nothing," Guy said.

"A lot can be achieved with radio and chemo these days. Please don't lose hope. We're still finding out what we're dealing with. I'll hand you over to oncology, and then to the surgeons. There will be a plan. There will be a way forward."

And what a way forward it was. Daily radiotherapy, then chemotherapy. Guy's hair drifted out in straggles. He couldn't get out of bed. He could no longer swallow anything more than half-melted ice-cubes, and had a feeding tube inserted. Pale beige liquid kept him alive until the surgery.

~

"You might enjoy it. You really might." Kathryn's mother folded a bright red towel and slid it into the new swimming bag.

It was rainbow-striped and made of some funny material, almost shiny, to stop it staying wet. Kathryn was wearing her

31

swimsuit under her clothes, so she wouldn't have to expose any flesh while getting changed. It was turquoise, with a frill round the bottom. Again, the material was strange. It hugged her skin, felt both warm and cool at the same time. It made her skin tingle.

Kathryn sat at the table for four, the shiny material of her swimsuit reminding her what was to come, and Mr Hawker wrote numbers on the blackboard with dusty white chalk. Kathryn gazed round the classroom. Behind Mr Hawker's desk was the row of coat pegs, the load doubly thick today with the bulging swimming bags hanging there. A few of the bags had those hateful swimming badges sewn onto them. Kathryn's rainbow bag, near the end, was half-draped with her blue duffle coat. Her mother had forgotten to cut the label out of the coat, and skinny Jamie Wallis shrieked when he saw it and noticed that it was sized for a much older girl.

~

Imago is a tiny double-fronted premises in Adelaide Street, only a stone's throw from the old Edwardian house Kat once lived in. Back then, it was a charity shop, then a joke shop, and then a second-hand bookshop. It's been empty for periods too: the window panes smeared, a patchwork of gaudy junk mail visible through the glass door. And now, it's Kat's.

As she unlocks the door, she smiles at the flurry of coloured butterflies painted on the left-hand window, and the miniature chimes jangle over her head. Everyone wants butterflies: on mugs, on T-shirts, shower curtains, coasters. They want butter-fly teapots, and lever-arch files. Girls want metallic stickers, like hers so many years ago, and sequinned butterfly wallets. The im-agery appeals to many people, Kat has discovered. She has her own butterfly with her always: the Blue Morpho tattooed on her deltoid.

~

Evie's watching CBeebies in the living room. Chloe stands in front of the open fridge, half-listening to the tinkly tune on the telly, looking at what they need. Milk, bread, some sort of fruit, chocolate. Maybe some cold meat. She'd better write a list. They really should walk up into the village, but Evie finds it a long haul there and back, and Chloe can't hold her hand tight enough if she's carrying shopping. Taking the buggy is a hazard in its own right with the dog shit and the bumpy pavements. And if Chloe hooks bags onto the handles they bump against her knees all the time as she's pushing and Evie's wriggling out of her straps.

Chloe scoops up her car keys, calls out to Evie, "Have you got socks on? We're going shopping."

"I'm watching CBeeebies."

"You can watch it later. Come on, we have to get some food."

"Can I have an ice cream?"

Hot toddy would be more the thing, Chloe thinks, shoving Evie's reluctant feet into furry pink boots, and retrieving her parka from behind the sofa – an ant put it there, according to a guilty-looking Evie.

Outside, the air bites their skin with cold. Chloe straps Evie into the back of the Golf, and they grind up Barrow Lane, and turn right for the village centre, Ocean FM on the stereo.

Past the house where Guy Lovell used to live when he was a teacher, past the village hall, and the red phone box outside it. The turning to the surgery on the right. A dark Audi swerves across in front of Chloe and parks on the empty forecourt of Heather Read's gallery. Chloe just catches a glimpse of Guy at the wheel.

~

Heather spins the notice on the door to *Closed* and runs out to Guy. The wind slaps his jacket to his frame as he locks the car. He's so thin and gaunt; the age difference between them seems so noticeable now.

"You don't have to," he says, but it's half-hearted, and he lets her squeeze his arm as they cross the road and go into the surgery.

Guy sits down and Heather signs him in at the desk. In the corner a kid whizzes coloured wooden beads along a table maze. His mother looks up from her phone every few moments to *sssh* him, then flicks her eyes back to the screen. An elderly couple in winter overcoats and a tattooed young bloke sit opposite Guy and Heather. The radio speakers pump out Ocean FM's rival station.

The kid and his mother go in to see the nurse, then a sandy-blond doctor calls for Guy.

"I'm Matt Sinclair," he says, and ushers them down the corridor to his room.

"It's his voice," Heather says, as soon as the door closes.

Dr Sinclair glances at the computer screen in front of him. Heather knows what he's seeing: *previous oesophageal cancer.*

~

Chloe parks in the village carpark by the cemetery gate. As she and Evie walk hand-in-hand towards the shops she imagines the news has got out: Chloe Johnstone was in the swimming pool last night.

An elderly lady coming the other way says hello, smiles at Evie. She doesn't say anything about it. Neither does the guy from the top end of Barrow Lane who's in the Spar. Nor the crimson-haired girl on the till.

Evie chooses a tiny expensive tub of strawberry ice-cream, and places it carefully in her own glittery pink bag.

Returning to the car, Chloe drifts back to last night. Swimming is a total immersion for all the senses; colour, echoes, splashes, scent, the taste of the water she swallowed, the cool fluid under her hands. A whole body experience.

"Can we have a run?" Evie scampers up to the heavy wooden gate that separates the carpark from the cemetery.

"Let's put the shopping away first."

Chloe unlocks the Golf, and puts the food on the back seat. Evie reluctantly hands over her sparkly bag with its precious load.

"Only a few minutes," Chloe says, "or the ice-cream will melt."

Evie rushes off along the gravel track through the first field of graves. These are the older burials, from long before Chloe's time. Evie loves the further field, half full of granite and marble stones, half still a meadow. They are alone in the cemetery. Evie runs across the muddy grass to the hedge. Just over the spindly branches is Millie's house, the bright red of the boys' swings in the back garden, the green-painted garden shed. Chloe waits, watches Evie scampering, pink boots kicking up clods of mud. A spray of holly lies on the path by Chloe's feet; a Christmas bauble on the grass. The graves in St Michael are well-tended: there are the remains of flowers, tiny Christmas trees, and mistletoe. Chloe walks along a row of headstones.

It's a dark stone, with pale lettering. A spray of yellow roses, fresh, the petals still bright in the silver vase. To the side the ever-present ceramic angel, whose face has blunted and stained after so many years in all weathers.

"Come on," Chloe calls to Evie. "Home now. Home and ice-cream."

Evie bounds over to her, fair hair tangled, cheeks luminous.

"Love you, Mummy." She throws her arms round Chloe's legs, and Chloe staggers.

"Love you, sweetheart."

Evie slides her frozen little hand into Chloe's and they start back for the car.

I'm so lucky, Chloe thinks, looking down at Evie. So lucky to have this overwhelming love in my life. Some people never get that chance.

Chloe hates that angel on Amy Langford's grave. It looks sinister, distorted by time.

~

"Are you OK to work tonight?" Heather asks Guy.

They have not spoken on the three-minute walk from the surgery to the gallery where his car is waiting.

"Of course."

"But—"

"More music, less talking. No one'll complain."

"He seemed OK, didn't he?" Heather ventures. "I mean, he took you seriously."

"Yup," Guy says, and Heather can read the subscript: *too seriously*.

Dr Sinclair listened to Guy's voice, and to his chest. He looked in Guy's mouth with a light.

"The chest sounds OK," he'd said. "I'm sure I'm being overcautious, but, because of your history, I'd like you to see someone in ENT as soon as possible."

Because of your history. The tag, the branding, that never leaves a cancer survivor. Because a cancer survivor is only a survivor in the present tense; the future may be a different story.

~

Thursday evening, just before Guy leaves for the radio station, Heather catches him in the kitchen grasping the worktop, his whole body convulsing. Through his shirt she sees his ribs moving with each breath. She takes his arm, guides him into a chair, gives him water, doesn't know what to do.

"We know what it is," Guy says, when at last he can speak.

"No, we don't." Heather takes his hand. It feels so frail. He looks so frail. He looks grey, papery. He looks like a man with cancer.

"Not in the same place."

"What?"

"It won't be in the same place." Guy indicates his sternum. "Somewhere else." He spreads his fingers on his chest.

Lungs, Heather thinks. He means his lungs.

Guy gave up smoking ten years ago. But it was too late for his oesophagus. And now, have some rogue cells escaped drugs and radiation and surgery, burrowing into spongy lung tissue, multiplying into gross blooms?

"You can't work tonight."

"I can."

He's still broadcasting five evenings a week. Heather and Jas have stopped listening to the sound of his rattling breath on the airwaves.

~

Kat flicks channels on the TV. Do up your house, nightmare dating stories, a shitty American comedy, Rick Stein sizzling some prawns in a wok, a fat woman talking about bariatric surgery.

Kat snaps off the telly, and turns on the radio instead. It's Guy, sounding pretty wheezy. She only started listening to Guy after meeting Heather at swimming. She'd heard his name, knew he was an ex-English teacher from St Michael, but Kat had grown up on Madonna and Michael Jackson rather than Guy's oldies like Roy Orbison, Fleetwood Mac, Elvis, and Motown.

Kat picks up her phone, wonders if she could call Christa and ask to move into the earlier group with Jason and the other guys. *Don't be stupid.* She chucks down the phone. Firstly, Jason Hosking probably doesn't care one way or the other if she's in his group or not; secondly, Christa won't want one group of four, and one group of two; thirdly, Kat likes swimming with Heather; fourthly, she's not scared of Chloe Johnstone.

~

They walked to the swimming pool from school. Birmingham was cold in winter. Trodden-down leaves, piles of grey slush in the gutters. They walked in a crocodile, two by two. Kathryn walked with Debbie Green, who could swim a bit. Debbie was going on about babies coming out of their mummies' tummies. Kathryn imagined trying to cough up a baby. It would be worse than being sick. She would never have a baby if you had to do that.

Behind them, Fiona Clarke was saying how she was going to have a swimming party for her birthday, but only the good swimmers – this said deliberately loudly – would be invited.

The pool was by the church the school used for carol services, for Easter services, for the Harvest Festival. Kathryn wishes they were going in there instead, to sit quietly on the plain pews, and she could stare at the long dark crack running down from the roof above the altar, as if God Himself were about to rip the plaster apart and peer down at the rows of bored kids below.

A strange smell hit her as soon as they arrived inside the pool building. It was so hot. So hot and damp. They were shepherded to left and right. Girls to the left with two of the mothers who had come along at the back of the crocodile; boys to the right with Mr Hawker.

Kathryn was boiling in her thick coat. Even the air she breathed was hot and viscous. Suddenly there was the pool: huge and blue and still, stretching away to the far end and a red *Deep Water* notice. There was a row of changing rooms along each side of the pool. Half walls to hide behind, tiles wet and slippery. The girls were shoved into the changing rooms in their pairs. Inside theirs, Kathryn and Debbie found a narrow wet bench, and some graffiti on the wall. Debbie knew all about the place already because she had come with her parents before. Kathryn struggled out of her coat, without banging Debbie in the eye. She could hear the chatter of the girls in the neighbouring cubicle, the hoots from the boys across the water. She peeled off her clothes and stood, hot but shivery, in her turquoise swimsuit. The mothers stuck their heads into the cubicles, chivvied the girls out to the poolside. One of them, Jonathan Roberts' mother, was stripped down to a sleek black swimsuit.

Kathryn shambled miserably onto the poolside, gripping the tiles firmly with her toes so she didn't slip. Her changing room was not even halfway along the pool, but the water, just there to her left, looked so deep and dark, so blue and silent, like it could suck her right down.

"Oh look!" Jamie Wallis shrieked from the other side. "It's a blue whale."

~

Kat remembers her first time at the pool. Every bit of it. She remembers Jamie Wallis and the blue whale comment. She remembers how Jonathan Roberts' mother had to quickly stifle a smirk.

~

Sunday evening again. Chloe drops Evie at Millie's. Evie scrambles out of the Golf, clutching Ears and her glittery bag containing a pebble, a folded up piece of paper – "my list" – and a broken plastic fork.

"How are you feeling?" Millie asks Chloe on the doorstep.

"Scared." It's true. Now there's only half an hour to go Chloe's heart-rate has soared.

"You'll be fine. You were fine last time."

"OK. Scared and a bit excited." Chloe watches Evie throw her coat in the general direction of the hall table and disappear into the kitchen to look for Matt and the boys.

"You're brave," Millie says.

"Or stupid. What if I drown? You'll look after Evie, won't you?"

"Now you are being stupid. The teacher's in the water. What could possibly happen?" Millie glances towards the kitchen. "And don't say things like that. Evie might hear."

"Yes, I know, sorry."

"You don't want to pass this fear on to her, do you?"

~

What fear, Chloe demands of herself as she parks outside the hotel. *The only thing to fear is fear itself. Jump for the moon*, and all that.

It's a cold winter's night but there are several cars outside, and lights on in the hotel. Chloe walks towards the sports club and glances into a ground-floor room where two guys are playing pool. She taps in the entry code to the spa, and is hit straight away by the warmth and the damp, the smell, and that blue painting on the stairwell.

She steps into the foyer and, through the floor-length panes, she sees the water: jagged and choppy. Christa's in the pool with the three men, down in the deep end. The younger one, Jason, pushes off from the wall, slicing through the water, Christa bobbing along beside him. There are two women also in the pool, half-heartedly swimming up and down the near side, and a young couple cosied up in the hot tub.

~

Heather drives to the hotel. No radio, no Guy. No CD. Just the rumble of the wheels on the tarmac and the whoosh of the heater. It makes her feel even more enclosed in her car, in the dark night, in the quiet that is not quiet. She hasn't turned the radio off, just turned the volume down; the tiny red lights show her Guy is still there, in the ether. Nothing works out quite how you imagine it will. Guy's beautiful voice, the voice that she fell in love with, is damaged, broken.

As she swings into the Headland carpark, she twists the volume dial. The Hollies: *The Air That I Breathe*. Heather kills the sound again.

~

"Chloe, come to the deep end."

Chloe lifts her goggles, rubs her eyes. The deep end.

"It's not that deep," Heather says. "I can just touch the bottom."

Heather's taller than Chloe.

"We won't do anything," Christa says. "Just hold the side and come down. I want you to see what it's like."

Christa swims to the deep end, a relaxed breaststroke. The couple in the hot tub clamber out and turn off the loud gurgling. The two women who were swimming have gone.

Chloe holds the rail and works her way along, hand over hand. The floor slopes alarmingly under her feet; the blue water rises suddenly to her chest, her shoulders, her chin.

"And here you are," Christa smiles at her. "Can you stand?"

Chloe shakes her head stiffly. Her goggles are digging in, but she can't loosen her hands to adjust them. There's a big window above the deep end. Nothing but black sky beyond.

"You could swim across with your float here," Christa says. "It's just the same as the shallow end. Do you want to try?"

"No," Chloe yelps.

The water laps round her mouth. It looks even bluer here. There's no way she'd be able to glide across with her float. She'd sink, inhale water, thrash around. Sink deeper, out there, right in the middle of the deep end with no edge to grasp and no floor to stand on. She would drown.

"OK. Just hold on, have a float. It's much easier in the deeper water. Put your head in, let your legs come up."

Chloe grips tightly, gasps a breath in, puts her head under. The kick of the water is powerful; her legs swing up. She gazes down through a fathom of water to a submerged hairband on the pool floor.

When she comes up for air, Christa says, "I want you to do that again in the shallow end, and I want you to let go."

Chloe walks her hands along the rail again, back the other way. Heather's swimming fast widths, over and back, over and back, her arms curving high and triangular above her head. Kat is floating in some strange way, suspended like a ball in the water, only the curve of her bony spine showing. How can they do these things, Chloe wonders.

"Do it here."

Chloe holds the side again, lets the water lift her. She hears Christa tell her to take her hands off the side. Her voice, through the water, is mesmerising. Chloe finds her fingers uncurling and stretching and, just for a second, she's suspended in something that can't possibly support her because she could slice a hand through it; she gulps and flails, snatching for the edge. She must have drifted a few inches because her fingers flutter in thin, sly water, and she's going down, down.

"I'm here." Christa rights her.

Water pours off her; she gasps, and her breathing subsides.

The glass doors open. Three guys stride in, make straight for the deep end, and jump in with three giant splashes. The water shudders and surges.

"OK, everyone," Christa says. "We'll call it a night."

~

Heather wakes with her alarm. She's about to snuggle the quilt round her for another few moments when she hears a noise. The noise.

"Guy!" She slides out of bed and crashes into his room.

He's half-sitting, half-lying on the bed, with streaming eyes, and it's the noise, the noise, that gasping, rasping. The gulping noise of a drowning man. She snatches Guy's bedside water glass and shoves it at him.

"What's happening?" Jas is in the bedroom doorway, dark hair tousled down her back, mobile in her hand. "Shall I call 999?" Her fingers dither over the numbers.

"No," Guy gasps at last. "It's OK. It's OK."

He's sweating, shivering, trembling. His whole body shakes with the effort of breathing. Heather turns back to Jas, and their eyes meet.

"We're going back to the doctor," Heather says. "This morning. I don't care who we see."

Jas creeps into the room and sits on the edge of the bed, reaches for Heather's hand. Heather's heartbeat is dancing. This isn't a cold. Or the flu. Or an allergy. It's back. Back in the fucking house with them.

"You can't work tonight, Dad."

"Ah, well—"

"No," Heather and Jas interrupt him.

"Listen." His voice is calmer now, his breathing ragged but steady. "Rick was there when I got in last night. He told me to take a break. I'm not working tonight."

Rick, the station manager, has told Guy not to broadcast. Because he knows too.

"I'll get you a tea," Heather says. "Then I'll ring the surgery."

Guy nods, eyes closed.

Heather and Jas go downstairs together. Heather leans her elbows on the kitchen worktop and buries her face in her hands. Behind her the kettle hisses and clicks off. She ignores it.

"I can't do it all again," she whispers.

"You can. We can. He can."

Heather looks up. Jas has slung a chunky cardigan on over her pyjamas. She doesn't look so well either.

"Are you all right?" Heather asks.

"I'm fine. No, no. I'm frightened."

"I can't do it all again," Heather says again. "The chemo, the radio, the tube, that fucking tube."

"It's back, isn't it?"

"I think so."

"He thinks so too, doesn't he?"

"Yes."

46

Heather opens the cupboard and lines up three mugs on the worktop.

"D'you want anything to eat?"

"No, thanks."

"You sure you're alright?"

Jas hesitates, and that second is all it takes.

"You're not?" Heather asks. "Jas, you're not...pregnant?"

Jas bites her lip, slides her eyes to the kitchen window, the grey autumn dawn, the scraggy bushes.

"I wanted to tell you. I just couldn't. Not with Dad."

The kettle boils again and Heather sloshes water into the mugs. *Jas is pregnant. Jas is only twenty. She's at college. Jesus. Fuck.*

"Mum?" Jas starts. "Say something."

"I just...I don't know...When? What are you going to do?"

"July, I think."

"Are you going to keep it?" And suddenly Heather's suspended, her whole life dependent on what Jas says. Because she knows in that instant that she wants Jas to have this baby. The thought of her daughter killing her grandchild is too appalling. She finds tears in her eyes.

"Yes."

"Oh Jas, my darling girl."

"But I'm scared."

"Of course you are. You must see a doctor too."

"I know. I know. I wasn't sure if I was pleased or not. I wasn't planning this. I don't know what to do about my course."

"What about Andrew?"

"We didn't plan it."

"Does he know?"

47

"He knows. He's kind of shell-shocked, I think."

"Is he trying to bully you into anything?"

"He hasn't said anything, to be honest. I told him I was keeping it."

"Whatever happens, you don't need him." Heather wipes damp from her eyes. She doesn't know if she's crying for Jas or for Guy or both of them, or for the tiny clump of cells, strengthening each day into a person.

"I don't expect him to give up the course or anything. Oh, I don't know."

"I must take this tea up."

"Don't say anything."

"I won't. Not today. But he must know. And you must see someone."

"Let's get Dad sorted out first."

"Of course. I'll get him an appointment. But you too."

Heather puts Guy's tea down again and hugs Jas.

"Sure you don't want any breakfast?"

"I'm OK. I'd better get ready…unless you want me to stay with Dad."

It's Jas's first day back after the holidays. Does she want an excuse not to go in, not to see Andrew? Delaying it won't help.

"No, you go in. I'll call you with any news."

Heather hesitates at the door, turns round. Jas is still at the window. She looks suddenly more relaxed, like a tight thread has been cut. Her hand creeps round to her pelvis.

~

48

Sometimes Chloe is overwhelmed by Evie. She finds it almost impossible to believe Evie is hers, hers alone really. She doesn't even think about Evie's father. She's never set eyes on him since they parted; she doesn't want to. She is aware that, once Evie starts mixing with other kids, they will ask about her father and where he is, and why she doesn't see him or know his name. Perhaps this is one of the reasons why Chloe has kept Evie close beside her, not abandoned her to groups and nurseries.

Chloe untangles Evie's pale gold curls with a purple metallic brush. Evie squirms as always, tries to tug away. The last two years Chloe has been happier than she's ever been, thanks to Evie. She loves bringing up Evie in her childhood home. Although it has been redecorated many times, the familiar features remain: the slate mantelpiece in the living room, the crumbling garden wall, the blue tits' nesting box outside the kitchen window.

Evie started on a New Year's Eve. She wasn't due for ten days, but Chloe's mother had nagged her into packing her hospital bag. Chloe can't remember much of those few hours other than the sudden realisation that the pains were hard and fast, Rod driving her through the sleety rain, even though it was New Year's Eve and he was already over the limit, her mother in the back seat beside her. The Christmas tree outside the maternity wing, its red and gold bulbs starry in the wet, then the bright fluorescents inside, and, all the time, the squeezing; then, as New Year's Day dawned grey and cold, a tiny, screwed-up, crinkly-faced Evie was placed in Chloe's arms.

Elaine crying, Rod snapping pictures on his phone, overcome when Chloe called Evie his granddaughter.

All very different from when Millie had the boys. Millie and Matt had been to the couples' antenatal classes. Zac was born in a birth pool, and Matt cut the cord. Of course. Millie planned a home birth for Luca, but he too came early, and Matt delivered him on the kitchen floor with only a bread-knife and a cappuccino machine to help. Or something like that. Whatever.

It's not that Chloe really dislikes Millie and Matt, of course she doesn't. She envies them their relationship, while knowing that it would drive her crazy. The boys have both of their shiny magazine parents, and their shiny magazine house, and their parents' shiny magazine Land Rover. What does Evie have? A mother who drifted from crappy job to crappy job, and now has nothing. Indeed, what sort of job could she even find in St Michael? Once Evie goes to school she'll have to sort out something. Re-train or whatever. She doesn't want to be a nobody for ever. She doesn't want Evie to have a nobody for a mother.

She is already making tiny steps. She's learning to swim. Chloe suspects that no one really knows what that means for her, what a giant leap of faith she's made. Except perhaps for the other people in the group. All adults who, for whatever reason, did not – or could not – learn to swim as children. They've all made huge leaps of faith. They're all incredible.

"Stop it," Evie grumbles, and Chloe stops brushing.

Evie's hair gleams. She scampers off to talk to the goats who live behind the sofa.

~

The only appointment Heather could get for Guy was with a locum. Dr Fieldhouse was away; Dr Sinclair had no vacancies. The locum was a weedy blonde girl, who listened to Guy's chest, printed a prescription for antibiotics, and told him to come back if there was no improvement, but added it was essential he went to ENT as soon as they offered him an appointment. Heather wasn't convinced the locum had any idea about what was wrong with him.

"I'll go to the chemist," Guy says, flapping the flimsy green prescription sheet.

"I can come with you now if you like?" Heather offers.

"No, really. I'm OK."

Heather watches him drive off the gallery forecourt and round the corner into the village. She's not happy. Not happy at all. She's pretty sure the locum had found no evidence of infection in Guy's chest; she just thought a course of antibiotics would shut him up. Heather unlocks the gallery, flicks the sign to *Open*. It's lunchtime; she'll ring Jas at college and tell her how they got on. Jas. Bloody hell. She had temporarily forgotten. How could she forget – even temporarily – that she's about to become a grandmother?

~

"Everybody strapped in?" Chloe asks, and glances in the rear-view mirror.

Evie, sitting in the back, shakes Ears hard by one leg. In the passenger seat, Elaine taps down the visor to check her make-up

51

– perfect, of course, as usual. Chloe jolts the Golf up Barrow Lane.

There are a couple of cars parked outside Heather's art gallery. It must be so hard making a living from a gallery in winter, Chloe thinks. So hard making a living in St Michael. She hasn't had any more thoughts about what she might do. Past the chip shop, the Archangel pub. The path to the cemetery. Chloe speeds out of the village, then drops down the gears for the Bends. There's mud on the road, mud and water, and a sodden cardboard box in the middle of the carriageway.

"Do you ever see any of them?" Elaine asks suddenly as they approach the Langfords' garage. Chloe almost veers across the road into the forecourt, where Pete's carrying a white car door out of the workshop. Elaine's never asked that before.

"Well, there's Pete right there," Chloe says. "I saw June a while back. Not to speak to."

"A long time ago," Elaine says.

"Yes," Chloe says tightly, feeling her heart rate rise, her skin prickle with heat.

"Ears! I've dropped Ears!" Evie wails from the back. "Mummy, stop, I've dropped Ears on the floor. There he is," she says, pointing at the rabbit lying just out of reach under the footwell. "There!"

"I can't stop, sweetheart. I've got a van behind me. We'll get him when we stop."

When they arrive in Penzance, wind from the sea rattles the rigging of the boats. A strange white noise like tapping bones. Chloe retrieves Ears for Evie, and unfolds her buggy. Evie fusses with Ears, and her mittens.

As they walk away and head into town, Elaine asks "How's your swimming going?"

"Not bad," Chloe says. "I look at the other people there and I think I'll never be able to do what they're doing, but it's only been a couple of weeks. Heather Read's in my group, did I tell you?"

"Guy was a good sort," Elaine says. "When he heard we were moving to Rod's he said he was very sorry to see you leave, and to lose Millie."

Again that tap of guilt. Because of Chloe, Millie had to change schools. Millie was dragged away from her friends and classes in St Michael and dragged up to Truro, where she knew no one, and didn't do as well in her GCSEs as she'd hoped to.

~

Kat's had a busy morning so far. Busy for *Imago* anyway. Not busy like the clothes shops in Market Jew Street will be, with the January sales crowds dismally clacking coat hangers along rails, discarding the size eights, the size twenty-fours, the skimpy sequinned postage stamps, the dresses made of weird material, the trousers with handwritten tags attached saying *broken zip*, or *tear to hem*.

In a quiet moment, she straightens the books on the shelf: butterfly and moth reference books, colouring books for kids, colouring books for adults, sticker books, books on how to plant a butterfly garden. As well as all the glittery stuff – the T-shirts, the notebooks, the fridge magnets – Kat is still trying to promote real interest in lepidoptera. The rolled-up posters in a wicker bin remind her of the ones she had on her bedroom wall in Birmingham; how, in the half light, she'd walk her eyes along the rows of butterflies, rather than count sheep. When she unwrapped the posters in Penzance, after the move, she saw they'd got squashed and torn in transit and, because she wanted to reinvent herself, she quietly and sadly threw them away. She didn't manage to reinvent herself then, but she never threw away her belief in metamorphosis.

The door opens with a tinny chime. A little girl's voice. Kat slots in the last book, and turns round. It's Chloe Johnstone, with what must be her daughter in a buggy – pink-cheeked, blonde, and giggly – and an older woman in a smart coat.

"Hi Kat," Chloe says. "Heather told me about your shop. We wanted to come and look. This is my little girl, Evie, and my mum."

"Hello Evie," Kat says. "Do you like butterflies?"

"I like butterflies and all mini-beasts," Evie announces. "I like butterflies, bees, spiders, moths, slugs…"

"Not slugs, you don't," Chloe says, unhooking a child's T-shirt with a giant swallowtail on it.

"Slugs, snails, beetles."

"Do you like that T-shirt Mummy's found?" Chloe's mother nudges the buggy round.

"Worms."

Kat slides back round the desk, straightens a pile of Red Admiral notebooks beside the till. Really, Chloe hasn't changed much at all. Her hair is the same kind of colour – a golden brown, though it may be highlighted now – and hangs loose down her back in waves. She has those startling freckles across the nose, the freckles she always had.

"Which one would you like?" Chloe holds up two T-shirts in front of Evie.

"Would you like me to get you some stickers, Evie?" asks Chloe's mother.

"Stickers!"

Kat sees a lot of kids, mostly girls, in *Imago*. They love their stickers, their pencil tins, their hairslides. Kat watches them walk out hand-in-hand with their mothers, and she feels the pain like a clenching fist. She's spent all her adult life living a lie, saying she doesn't want children, but she does, she really does. But she can never tell anyone why she's afraid to have any.

Chloe puts the swallowtail T-shirt down on the counter, and digs out her wallet. Kat folds the top into a paper bag. Chloe takes her debit card out of the machine and leaves it on the bag, while she fiddles with the zip of her wallet. Kat glances down: *Chloe Johnstone* embossed in silver. Not that she needed the proof.

~

The same streets, the same pavements: to the pool, to the church, to Bournville Green. And one day, they traced that same path but went somewhere new: Cadbury's.

Kathryn was walking with Debbie again. Behind them Jamie Wallis and one of the other boys. Jamie was going on about Cadbury's, and how he knew all about it because his dad was on the Wispa line.

They were doing a project at school about old Bournville. They'd looked at facsimiles of old maps. They'd been shown how the old tree lines remained, how the oaks on the far side of the playing field marked an old track from the days before the industrial sprawl of the city. Kathryn loved that old tree line. When they were allowed to play on the field after lunch in the summer, she searched there for butterflies, for caterpillars and flowers. At the edge of the field, the ground dipped into a sunken gulley – the old way? – shaded by the oaks, majestic trees, gnarled and stained, home to so many insects and birds.

Some old dear had come in to talk to the class about Bournville during the war: the air raids, the firewatching. She'd talked about the Meeting House, the Carillon, and Cadbury's. And so the trip to Cadbury's, where first of all they were shepherded into some kind of waiting room, while everyone – children, teachers, and the accompanying mothers – were handed white coats and hairnets before being taken into the chocolate factory.

"You'd better get an adult size coat for Kathryn," said Jonathan Roberts' mother.

~

Jonathan Roberts' mother was such a bitch, Kathryn thought to herself. His father was a doctor, a GP at a practice in a neighbouring suburb. His mother didn't work so she came to the school to "help out" a couple of afternoons a week. She must have said she was a good swimmer or something because, not only did she walk them to the pool each week, she got in with them. But she never did any teaching, Kathryn noted. She just floated about, making sure her stylish blonde bob didn't get too wet.

Kathryn wasn't the only useless swimmer, though she was the only one wearing neon armbands. And the only fat one. Down in the shallow end there were about eight of them, including revolting Jamie Wallis. Mr Hawker in a burgundy tracksuit on the poolside. Everyone with a white polystyrene float, crumbling around the edges like cheese. Kathryn gripped the float with both hands, and leaned forwards, legs kicking, splashing water up behind her. Her neck ached from keeping her head above water. The thing was this: it was actually quite fun, kicking along behind the float. She could get across the pool – sometimes stopping a couple of times if she ran out of steam, if she found she was kicking and kicking and getting nowhere.

"Kathryn," called Mr Hawker from the side. "Why not try taking off the armbands?"

Kathryn glanced down at the huge orange fins. "No," she said miserably. She would never be able to ditch them, never be able to ditch the float.

Someone beside her in the water. Jonathan Roberts' mother bobbing elegantly up and down in her shiny black swimsuit.

"You know, you float a lot better than someone half your size."

Kathryn thrust the float forwards again and started kicking. It was only the chlorine making her eyes smart. Not tears.

~

"No Heather?" Chloe asks as she lowers herself carefully down the metal ladder to join Kat and Christa in the shallow end.

"Ah, no, she texted me," Christa says. "She can't come tonight."

Chloe starts by holding the rail, and dropping her head under the blue waterline. She blows bubbles out through her nose, remembers not to inhale.

"I'm going to get you started on your arms tonight, Chloe."

"But I need my float."

"Just one arm," Christa grins. "Kat, I've got a drill you might find helpful for your breathing. Watch me."

Chloe watches too. Christa glides across the pool on her side, her head bobbing just above the water. It looks both effortless and incredibly uncomfortable at the same time.

"Let me try." Kat faces the deep end, stretches out her right arm, kicks off the wall.

"Legs, legs," Christa says. "Kick, kick, head down."

Halfway across, Kat sinks, her bright head disappearing. She bounces up, coughing, but unruffled, calm.

I'd have had a heart attack, Chloe thinks.

~

Heather glances at the kitchen clock enviously. Kat and Chloe will be in the pool, the cool blue water lapping round their shoulders. Heather is always miserable if she has to miss swimming. She's home tonight because Guy has had an awful day. His breath wheezes and rattles all the time, getting worse by the day. Heather is going to make urgent enquiries about a private

ENT appointment, as nothing has come from the hospital yet, and the antibiotics aren't doing a thing.

Jas is out in Penzance. Her friend Kelly picked her up and will bring her home later. Andrew will be there. The baby's father. Heather feels a flick of resentment that this baby has to have a father at all, and that it should be someone like lanky, dozy Andrew, who clearly isn't supporting Jas or helping her. He's just stuck his head in the sand. Well, babies don't just disappear, mate, Heather tells him in her head. Sooner or later you have to acknowledge them.

She didn't want to leave Guy alone, so she texted Christa and told her she couldn't make it. She didn't say why.

Guy's lying on the sofa watching *Countryfile*. He told her to go swimming, he'd be fine on his own, but Heather couldn't leave him.

She is surprised to hear a key in the front door. Jas comes in, unwinds her scarf and chucks it over a hook. She's wearing big jangly earrings; one is caught in her hair. She looks very young and lost.

"I thought you were swimming," she says. "Is Dad OK?"

Heather glances towards the closed door. The telly's still on.

"He's not well," she says at last. "I stayed at home. I didn't want him alone. Anyway, why are you back so early?"

"Got there, changed my mind, got a taxi."

"Was Andrew there?"

"Yeah. Course."

"You didn't want to stay on with him?"

"He didn't want me there."

The living room door opens. Guy comes out, wine glass in hand.

"I thought I heard you. I wasn't expecting you for hours."

"Is it because..." Heather starts. Fuck. Guy doesn't know about the baby.

Jas scowls. "I'm getting out of all this shit."

She unhooks her earrings as she stalks by. Heather tries to catch her eye, but Jas ignores her. She doesn't look like she's been crying, Heather thinks. She looks tense, wired, coiled up, angry more than sad.

"She's fallen out with Andrew," Guy says.

On the floor above Jas's feet pad from landing to bathroom to bedroom. A bang. Her wardrobe door? Guy goes back into the living room. He must feel disorientated being at home at this time in the evening when he's usually broadcasting. Heather waits a moment longer in the hall, then runs upstairs. The light is on in Jas's room. Jas is sitting on the bed, in pink checked pyjamas. She has an open tub of Nivea on the quilt, and a blackened cotton-wool ball in her hand.

"You all right?" Heather asks, leaning in the doorway.

Jas tugs the cotton wool over her eyes and dark streaks smudge on her face. She shrugs.

"What's he done? What's he said?"

"Who?"

"Andrew."

"Oh. Well. I don't know. He was all over this other chick. He's still going to be free and single, not tied up with me and a kid."

Heather comes into the room and sits on the other side of the bed.

"I'm sorry. I hoped he'd stand by you."

"Maybe he thought I was lying. Now he realises it's true. He doesn't want to be a father. I guess he might be happier if I told him I'd get rid of it."

Heather's heart jumps. "You wouldn't?"

"Of course not." Jas trails her hand over her stomach. Nothing shows yet.

"We'll deal with this. You, me, and Dad. We're here with you. I told you before: you don't need Andrew. If he doesn't want this, that's his loss."

"His loss," Jas repeats.

Heather wonders when the tears will come. Jas is so flinty and cool. If she and Andrew have broken up, what will happen? What will happen at college? Jas hasn't even seen a midwife yet. What if something is wrong?

"You must see the doctor," Heather says. "Please get an appointment tomorrow. I'll come with you if you like."

"I'll sort it out."

"Please. Come down, have some dinner. I've got to find something Guy will eat." Heather stands up, adjusts the quilt, makes for the door.

"Will you come with me?" Jas asks quietly.

"Of course. I'd love to. See if you can get Dr Sinclair."

She goes out onto the landing. Guy's halfway up the stairs. She never heard him coming, not even his harsh breathing.

"Does she need a doctor?"

"Oh," Heather starts. She senses Jas at her shoulder.

61

"Jas. Are you ill? Or just upset?"

"I'm not upset."

Heather glances at her daughter – tall, angular, drifts of dark hair – and then down at Guy, still waiting on the stairs. His skin is waxy, and his hair threadbare.

"Guy," she says.

Jas inhales sharply.

"Please," Heather says, turning to Jas.

"What the fuck's going on?" Guy strides up the stairs, gasps on the landing. "What's the matter?" he asks Jas.

"Tell him," Heather says. "Please."

"You're scaring me," Guy says.

"It's nothing to be scared of. It's lovely. Jas. Tell him."

Heather leans against the wall, and watches Jas's lips form the words, watches Guy's eyes narrow, and widen, his sigh, his smile. Suddenly, out of nowhere, Guy and Jas hug awkwardly on the landing, jammed between the door-frame and the overflowing bookcase. She wonders: will Guy live to see this baby?

~

When Elaine came down to see Chloe and Evie she'd brought some boxes of Chloe's things from the attic in Truro. They've been sitting in the hall now for several days, and Evie has already tottered into them and hurt her foot. Chloe settles Evie in front of CBeebies, and drags the first box into the living room.

"What are you doing?" Evie asks.

"Just looking at the stuff Granny brought for me."

"What's in there?"

"I don't know."

"Can I help?"

"You can watch telly," Chloe says, already realising she should have done this in the hall, away from Evie's eyes. Evie has already lost interest in Mr Tumble.

Chloe opens up the cardboard box, and a dusty waft escapes.

"Let me see."

"No, let me do it, sweetheart," Chloe says.

It's a lot of her old school stuff. Books and folders she hasn't seen for twenty-odd years. She recognises the Aztec patterns of her geography folder, the pink stripy one for RE, the massive ringbinder for French, split up so carefully into sections with coloured dividers: *food and drink, going on holiday, hobbies, travel.*

Evie reaches in, starts tugging at the bright folders.

"Pretty. I want this."

"No, they're mine."

This was a mistake, Chloe thinks ruefully. I should have done it when she's in bed. Chloe prises an exercise book out of Evie's hands, and shoves it back into the box. That's what she'll do: look at them later.

"Come on, Evie, if you're not watching that, let's go for a walk. It's a lovely afternoon."

Cold, grey, but not wet and not windy. A walk usually tires Evie out. Chloe nudges the big cardboard box against the wall with her knee, and looks around for Evie's trainers.

~

Kat doesn't open the shop on Wednesdays because she works Saturdays. She still sets the alarm for stupid o'clock, just so she can have the pleasure of reaching out and snapping it off, snuggling back under the duvet. Today, she can't drift off to sleep again. The seagulls are shouting outside the window; there's a car alarm going off in one of the backstreets. Kat lies there on her back and realises, as she does increasingly these days, that she's lonely. She has no life, so social life at all, other than swimming on Sunday nights. She hasn't been on a date in over twelve months. She hasn't even had a proper boyfriend since coming back to Penzance a few years ago.

At twenty Kat left Cornwall, and another package of painful memories. It was the only way to reinvent herself: to leave. She surprised herself, shocked herself even, at her capabilities. Downtrodden, fat, unattractive, unworthy, scared Kathryn Smith left Cornwall and moved to Plymouth, then Exeter, then Bath, and even for a short time to the wilds of Somerset. These years were her chrysalis. She stopped eating carbs, exercised, cut and coloured her hair, went on courses and studied, found work, grew confident, took lovers and left them. And gradually the green flesh of the chrysalis split, and Kat Glanville slid out, stunned by the changes in herself. Only then could she return to the far west.

Kat chucks back the quilt – a swarm of purple and blue butterflies – and goes into the bathroom for her morning weigh-in. She's gained a kilo. Shit. Not that anyone would know. Not that her clothes will be any tighter. But a kilo is a kilo. A kilo quickly becomes two, three, five, ten. Nothing terrifies Kat more than the thought of getting fat again.

64

She looks at her body. She may be thin, but she knows there is baggy skin under her bottom, on her upper arms. She has stretch marks on her stomach, thighs, sides, bottom. They're faded now to a spiderweb of the palest white-silver, but they'll always be there, tattoos of her caterpillar life.

~

Kathryn waddled out of the changing room she shared with Debbie Green. She remembered to keep her eyes down, just watch her pale feet on the tiles, ignore the whispers and the nudges.

This year Kathryn's teacher was Mrs Anderson who, like Mr Hawker before her, strode along the edge of the pool in a track-suit with a whistle round her neck. Kathryn felt Mrs Anderson's eyes on her, taking in the bright turquoise swimsuit stretching over her huge stomach. Debbie was now in the "middle group": people who could swim without floats, and went into deeper water. There were only a few left in the shallow end with Kathryn now.

"Here are your armbands," said Jonathan Roberts' mother, holding out two neon water-wings.

By the time Kathryn had squeezed them on to her upper arms, everyone else was in the pool. She backed down the ladder miserably. The water was cold, the acoustics painfully magnifying Fiona Clarke shrieking in the deep end.

Kathryn snatched a float. At the other side of the pool there was some kind of altercation between Jonathan Roberts of the middle group, and Jamie Wallis, whose father was on the Wispa line at Cadbury's.

"My dad's a doctor. He makes people well," said Jonathan Roberts.

Kathryn didn't catch Jamie's reply.

"Your dad just makes people fat," Jonathan Roberts sneered, and pointed at Kathryn. "People like her. Your dad helps make her fat."

"No, he doesn't," said Jamie Wallis. "She makes herself fat."

~

And now I have made myself thin, Kat thinks. But what a journey it's been. I'm halfway through my life, and I'm only just becoming the person I want to be. All those years of pain, of degradation, of worthlessness.

Kat's not on Facebook. Well, she probably is, or rather, Kathryn Smith will be. In school photos on other people's profiles, the hunched lump in the back row, hair over eyes. People will be tagged in the pictures, and underneath there will be comments: *Those were the days, remember when…?, who's that girl in the back row? Oh yes, Kathryn Smith, what happened to her? Probably dropped dead of a heart attack.*

She doesn't want to see those pictures, see those words, relive those days.

She wants Kathryn Smith to simply not exist.

She picks up her phone and scrolls through her contacts, hits green.

"Hi, Christa, it's Kat."

"Hey, how's it going?"

"Fine, yes, my day off today. I was wondering…" Kat's heart rate always skips a bit when she's bullshitting. "I was wondering if next Sunday I could possibly come to the earlier group. The one with the guys."

"What, just for the one week?"

"Yes, you see, I'll be driving home past the hotel about that time. It'd be much easier if I could, please."

"Yeah, that's fine. That group's down to two next week."

Oh shit, Kat thinks. Supposing it's Jason who's not coming? And she's wasted this chance.

"Tim's going up country for a few days."

Kat exhales. "Thanks, Christa. I'll see you then."

~

Heather and Jas have just been to see Dr Sinclair. He asked Jas for a urine sample, went through some dates with her, didn't ask anything about the father. Told her the midwife would call to arrange an appointment.

"And congratulations," he said, as Jas rolled down her sleeve after having her blood pressure measured. "Don't look so scared."

"I am scared," Jas said.

"I'm sure you'll feel much better once you've seen Diana, and got your scans all sorted." Dr Sinclair turned to Heather. "How's Guy getting on?"

"No better," Heather said. "We saw a locum who gave him antibiotics. They're not helping."

"His breathing is terrible," Jas said.

"No word from ENT?"

"Not a thing."

"OK, leave it with me. I'll chase it up."

Now Heather and Jas are standing on the asphalt outside the gallery. Heather fingers the key in her pocket: cold metal in cold fingers.

"If he's going to chase it up, that means he thinks it's serious, doesn't it?" Jas says, voicing Heather's thoughts.

"Let's just hope he makes them get on with it," Heather says. "Are you coming in?"

"I'll go home. See how Dad is. He was still in bed when I came out."

"Are you going to college this afternoon?"

"Yes. I want to talk to Andrew."

"Don't rush into saying anything."

"I'm not rushing. I'm going to tell him I want some space. It's not working. You know that. I kind of wish I could be having this baby without it being anything to do with him."

"Don't say anything just yet. Did he know you were going to the doctor this morning?"

"I didn't tell him," Jas says. "He might suddenly have wanted to come, so he looks *involved*. He's not interested, you know that too. I dunno. I thought I'd be more sad than I am. Perhaps it'll hit me later. OK, I'm off home."

"Look, it's Chloe from my swimming group." Heather gestures to the two figures walking towards them. "And her little girl, Evie."

She senses Jas hesitating beside her, wanting to go.

"This is my daughter, Jasmine," Heather says.

Jas is gazing down at Evie, at the curls tumbling from under her pink and white woolly hat, at her gloved hand held tightly in Chloe's, her wide eyes, her muddy trainers. Evie grins a toothy grin. Jas smiles back.

~

Evie's asleep at last, spread like a starfish in the middle of Chloe's bed. Her pyjama top has slid up, and Chloe strokes her soft, white tummy. Evie snuffles and twitches. Chloe folds the duvet over her; Evie kicks out. Chloe watches her sleeping, as she always does: the slow rise and fall of her chest, the flare of goosebumps on her middle, where the cover has gone again, the round curve of her cheek, and the flick of lashes, so much darker than her hair. In everyday life when Chloe's trying to force tomatoes into Evie's reluctant mouth, or searching for trainers and socks that have been hidden by ants or goats or moles, or when she's struggling to get Evie out the front door and into the car, she takes her daughter for granted. Sometimes she's short-tempered with her, sometimes she nags. But, at night, when Evie curls on her side like a comma, her fair hair spilling across the pillow, in the pale light from the bedside lamp, Chloe marvels at her. At how she, Chloe Johnstone, could have nurtured this little person inside her for nine months, how she could have pushed her out into that grey January dawn, how she has watched over her from breast to mashed banana to Pom-Bears; from pumping legs in a Moses basket to rolling on a mat, to crawling, to running; from whimpers to babbling to sentences.

Chloe has excised Tony Connolly from her mind, her memory. Without him she wouldn't have Evie, so in some perverse way she has to thank him for this gift. But he wouldn't have seen Evie as a gift; she'd have been an embarrassment, a terrible accident, a *how-the-fuck-did-it-happen*. He would never have acknowledged Evie. So Chloe no longer acknowledges him. One day, she'll have to tell Evie about Tony, but that is for another time.

Chloe drapes the quilt over Evie once more, kisses her warm cheek.

She drags the box in the hall back into the living room. The TV is on, volume low, *Top of the Pops* from the 80s. The soundtrack of her youth. Chloe takes out the folders and books. They haven't been stored in any kind of order. She opens an exercise book covered in floral wrapping paper. Home Economics from the third year. Her childish handwriting. *Grains of the world: wheat, rice, oats, barley, rye.* A few blank pages. Something drops out of the back of the book. A twist of knotted threads. Chloe snatches it off her knee. It's a friendship bracelet; diagonal rows of pink, yellow, and lavender, like a knobbly stick of rock. Amy Langford made it for her. They made so many of them when they were twelve, thirteen, their arms knotty rainbows. Chloe hasn't thought about them in decades, and here's one in the palm of her hand, one made by Amy. She got one of the knots wrong; there's a dot of pink showing in the yellow band. Chloe remembers how the bracelets got wet when she washed her hands, how the embroidery threads stayed clammy, made her wrist sore and chapped. She sniffs the bracelet for any lingering smell of damp or sweat or Amy, but there's nothing.

Home Economics in that huge echoey classroom with the black and white chequered floor, the kitchens off to one side. Chloe and Amy in the second row by the windows overlooking the netball courts, and the boys' football field below. A memory of her and Amy cooking a giant pan of pasta in their kitchen with two or three of the boys, and the boys already noticing Amy: her pale hair, her long legs, her changing figure.

How old were we? Fourteen? And Amy almost at the end of her life.

~

When Kat arrives at the pool on Sunday Christa is swimming fast lengths of front crawl. She's alone in the water. Kat pauses by the glass doors watching Christa: the easy roll of her shoulders, the twist of her hips as she takes a breath, the decisive cut of her hand through the blue. Christa sees Kat, stops at the shallow end and waves. Kat waves back and starts for the changing rooms. The tiles are wet from the feet of earlier swimmers. The air is tropical in the cubicles. She peels off her clothes quickly, fixes her goggles over her head. Footsteps come into the changing area, the clang of a cubicle door shutting. Kat waits, her clothes folded in her bag, her towel over her arm. Scuffles and a thump from the neighbouring cubicle, a muttered curse. It's Jason.

At last she opens her door and walks to the lockers, her flip-flops slapping on the wet tiles. As she takes the key from the locker, Jason comes out of his cubicle.

"Hey," he says, almost dropping his towel, as he jams a pound coin into a locker. "Wasn't expecting you. How's it going?"

"I'm with you tonight," Kat says.

"Cool. I think Tim's away."

"You ready? Shall we go?"

As they pass the row of sinks Kat glances in the mirror at their reflections. Her choppy red hair and jutting clavicles; Jason's chaotic auburn mop, strong freckled shoulders.

"How are the kids?" Kat asks.

"Driving me nuts on a daily basis." He grins at her as he opens the glass door. "But I wouldn't be without them. It's hard, hard work, but they're everything."

Kat knows they are. Jason's a single father. She's not sure how old he is, early thirties maybe, a bit younger than she is. He and his children live with his mother in Marazion. He has the kids' names tattooed on his arm, Thomas and Flora in interwoven script.

"Just you two tonight," Christa calls to them. "Rob's wife's not well." She looks from Kat to Jason. "You can have a race at the end."

Jason goes down the steps, slides his goggles over his eyes, and glides across the pool. When he surfaces his hair is dark and plastered to his head. Water droplets shimmer on the names of his children. Kat steps down into the water. It's cold. Sometimes it feels so cold when she first gets in. Jason's gliding back towards her. She leans forward, spreads her arms and lets the water lift her into a float. She never stays completely still; the tiny tiles shift under her. It's a beautiful sensation, being held by all those molecules.

"Go. Go. We'll be fine," Jas whispers to Heather.

Still Heather hesitates, her coat on, car keys in her hand. "I could stay."

"You missed one the other day. You won't be long. He'll probably still be asleep when you get back. I won't wake him."

"Don't be afraid to call 999 if you need to."

"I know. Go on."

The rear windscreen is misted in the dark; grey swirls obscure Heather's vision as she reverses out of the drive. She turns the radio right off, so there are no coloured lights marking where Guy's voice used to be. She drives to the Headland on autopilot. It's been so long since Guy was well, since he ate a proper meal, since he laughed. Jagged images judder through her memory: Guy hooked up to chemo, the soft bag of poison shrouded from the light under its executioner's hood; Guy spitting blood into a bowl after radiotherapy; Guy choking on a tiny shard of ice; the massive slash of the oesophagectomy, puffy and red when the dressings came off.

~

"What do you say then?" Christa asks. "A race?"

Kat looks at Jason. He grins and shrugs.

"Come on," she says. "You'll win anyway. You're much better than me."

"I'm not," Jason says.

73

Jason joined Christa's lessons after Kat, about the time she was just starting to jerk across a width without a float. He said he'd never been taught at school, but wanted to swim with his children. A few weeks later Heather asked him something about his partner, and he said he was bringing up the children alone.

Kat's next to Jason at the deep end, two feet on the wall, one hand in front, one holding on.

"Go," says Christa, and Kat gulps a huge lungful of air, drops her head into the water.

It's all wrong. Her legs are kicking hard, splashing, but she doesn't seem to be moving, and the water beneath her chest is as deep as it was when she began. She snaps her legs closer together, drags her arm overhead, but she's losing it, she's going down, and she needs air.

Her feet touch the bottom in the middle of the pool. She coughs on the peppery water. Ahead of her Jason's still going, then suddenly he too stumbles, and staggers up spluttering.

"No score draw, I think," Christa laughs. "Look, Heather's arriving, let's have a quick float to relax."

Kat floats on her front, staring through blue. She wants to stay in the water all evening, but her time has run out.

She hauls herself up the ladder, the water slides off her, she feels heavy again. Chloe is hurrying through the lobby to the changing room. Jason and Christa are still in the water. The doors open, Heather pads in, and says "Hey, you've finished?"

"I had to come earlier today." Kat towels her hair roughly so the spikes stand up.

The kids' mother must have died, Kat thinks to herself, as she heads back to the changing room. That's why Jason's a single father. Women don't run off and abandon their children. Kat wants to know who she was, when she died, how she died, but it's not something she can ask. No one knows any details of Jason's life, except that he and the children live with his mother. But that only makes him the same as her. No one here knows about her previous caterpillar existence. They can't know the real reason she never learnt to swim: because she could no longer take the bitching and the nastiness every time she stepped out in a swimsuit.

Clang, clang, go the two doors. Whoosh, whoosh go the two showers. Kat peels her swimsuit down over her body, and steps out of it in the warm haze. Her fingertips and toes have puckered from the water. She unzips her sponge bag, takes out her soap and shampoo. Jason's on the other side of that wall, standing naked under running water. Kat imagines him with his face turned to the jet, rivulets cascading over his freckled shoulders and chest. She soaps her body, feels the ridges of her ribs and hips. She adds shampoo to her hair, and massages it in. The neighbouring shower snaps off.

"What's this shop of yours, Kat?" Jason calls.

"*Imago*. Butterfly stuff. Gifts, you know, pretty stuff, fun stuff, and some serious stuff too. Books, guides."

"Next time we're in town we'll have a look. I reckon Flora'd like it."

"Yes, do bring her in." Kat turns off her own shower, rubs herself roughly. "How old is she?"

"Seven; Thomas is nine."

Now. Now would be the time to ask him. Through the tiled walls of the shower, through the scented clouds of steam. But she can't. She knows what it's like to hold a secret close to the heart.

She shoves her arms in her jumper and tugs on her jeans, throws her cosmetics into the bag. Beside her Jason opens his door. She hasn't got her boots on yet, but she opens her door too, almost slips over in a puddle. Wet socks. Yuck.

"You got a picture of them?" she asks, zipping up a boot. The wet sock squishes under her foot. How she hates wet socks.

"You'd like to see them?" He sounds surprised, but he's taking his phone out of his jacket pocket. "Here they are."

Thomas and Flora side by side on a garden bench. Thomas has the same dark auburn springy hair as Jason; Flora is a tiny strawberry blonde.

"They look like you," Kat says.

"Hope so."

He swipes a few more pictures: Thomas ripping open a present, Flora dancing under a tree, amber and gold autumn leaves at her feet, the colours of her hair.

"Your mum has them while you're swimming?"

"Yes. Speaking of which, I must go and relieve her."

Jason puts the phone away, runs a hand through his unruly hair.

"You're lucky," Kat says without thinking.

"What? Oh. Well, we all live together so it's no big deal really."

"I meant lucky to have them."

"Yes. I know."

~

76

"Think of Evie," Christa says. "Imagine Evie on the other side, and you're swimming to her."

Chloe stares across the width of the shallow end. She can do this. Of course she can. She's about to launch across the pool, just herself and the water.

She stretches out her pointed hands. Like a pencil, an arrow, a torpedo. Evie, think of Evie, she tells herself, and kicks back at the wall. The water lifts her, takes her, and the tiles are whizzing beneath her, and her hands bump the opposite rail, reaching for Evie's phantom fingers.

"Now you, Heather. Are you going to try a length?"

Heather hesitates. "OK," she says.

Chloe's been gliding back and forth across the shallow end, coming up laughing. Heather remembers that ecstatic feeling when she realised she was moving through water all by herself.

"I'll start this end." Heather gestures to the shallow end.

"It'll all be over in moments. You'll be wondering what you were scared of."

Heather inhales, fills her lungs with air to keep her afloat, ducks her head down between her outstretched arms, launches off. Over the cracked part of the mosaic floor, legs, legs, keep them straight, blow bubbles, arm pull, left, right, now turn and breathe, roll those shoulders, remember to exhale again. She sees the floor of the pool falling away beneath her. She didn't get that last breath, her lungs feel hot, and in front of her she sees Christa's legs underwater, pale, blue-washed, moving aside for her, and she can just hear Christa saying *keep going, keep going*. She's in six feet of blue water now, and there's the line of black tiles. As her fingers grasp the end rail, she spurts out of the pool, gulping and laughing.

In the shallow end, Chloe's clapping. Heather gazes back down the length of blue water she has travelled all by herself. And suddenly, she forms an image of herself holding up a tiny, wriggling baby in a bright swimsuit, gurgling and chuckling at the bubbles tickling its skin and nose. I'm going to be a grand-mother, Heather thinks, and I've just swum a length. She isn't sure which is more remarkable.

~

Chloe still has one box to sort through. When Evie's asleep – which took longer than usual because she wanted to tell Chloe over and over about the game she'd been playing with Matt and Zac and Luca – Chloe rips open the parcel tape on the top. More school stuff. Maths books of squared paper and cramped figures, an old furry pencil case with a chipped set-square inside, a large brown envelope. A memory somewhere: she knows what's in it, but can't quite remember. She opens it.

A single large photograph, framed in navy cardboard. Two sixteen-year-old girls: Chloe and Amy at the school leavers' Prom. Chloe in the dusky pink dress she never wore again, her hair curled strand by strand with Elaine's tongs. Amy, beside her, long pale hair loose, dishevelled and perfect, cascading over her bare shoulders and onto her black dress. Grey eyes holding Chloe's gaze now.

I didn't kill her.

~

Once again Kat recalls that Hallowe'en so many years ago. The night Amy Langford died in a flash flood, swept off the road in her car. Kat was a different girl then. She was Kathryn Smith: fat, ugly, derided. If only when Kat lost her weight she could have excised all those memories from her brain. They're still there, through a foggy glass, yes, but still there and, even now, she can remember the coldness of the rain that night, dripping through her long, lank hair, the brutal howl of the wind coming off the sea, the moment when a choice was made.

I didn't kill her.

~

Kathryn's mother woke her early. It was the first day at her new secondary school in Penzance. They'd moved down over the summer into a tall narrow house above the railway station, close enough to the District Council offices where her father had been working for the last few weeks. The house was still chaotic in September: boxes stacked in corners, piles of things not properly packed away, a jumble of unsorted shoes by the back door. Somewhere, a box of rolled-up butterfly posters.

Kathryn's mother was anxious she should start school on the first day of the autumn term, with everyone else. Kathryn knew arrangements to get her into the comprehensive school had been going on over the summer, ever since her father got offered the job in May, but she didn't listen, didn't talk about it. It was another school, with other kids and, no doubt, other ways to torment her. She wasn't bothered about leaving Birmingham. They had no close family in the city now; she had no close friends. Debbie Green said she'd write, and Kathryn's mother said when the girls were older perhaps Debbie could catch the train to Penzance and stay for a few days. At this point Kathryn drifted off into fantasy: she was now thin and toned, she had exciting friends at school, she'd take Debbie down to the beach where they'd lie on towels in bikinis and watch the surfers. Perhaps they'd run into the shallows and swim in the foam, because, in this fantasy, Kathryn could swim, lean and lithe as a fish.

Yeah right. She didn't even want Debbie Green to come and visit. She wanted no reminders of before. No people who knew her then.

"You look lovely," Kathryn's mother said.

Kathryn could hardly drag her eyes to the mirror. They'd bought her school uniform from a women's catalogue to get big enough sizes. She wore a navy pleated skirt with an elasticated waist; because it was for an adult it was too long, and scuffed the tops of her knee socks. Her shirt was made of some weird shiny material that reminded her too much of a swimsuit. She would sweat in it. She had two small squishy breasts and a solid slab for a stomach. Loose hair, a pale biscuit colour, with a lank fringe.

Lovely, she was not.

~

Heather's standing on the top platform of a stepladder, reaching for a canvas. It's an acrylic of the moorlands around Zennor:

angry red undergrowth, black granite outcrops, a shaft of white light. She wants to take it off the top shelf and put it in the window. She's stretching for the canvas, as though she's taking a breath in front crawl, she thinks absurdly, when there's a buzzing and a jingle in the pocket of her jeans. She wobbles, picture hanging in one hand; with the other she grabs her mobile. *Home*, it says.

"Guy?"

"Can you come home?" He gasps between each word. "I wouldn't ask but—"

"I'm coming."

Heather props the picture back where it was. Her legs are shaking as she backs down the ladder. Quick, turn off lights, heater. She snatches her bag and coat and dashes out, locking the door but forgetting to flick the sign to *Closed*.

Some days she walks to the gallery, some days she drives. Today she has the car. Guy wouldn't ask her to come home unless he was very ill or afraid. She engages the gear, then remembers to put on her driving glasses. Her foot judders on the clutch and she stalls.

Calm down, Read. Just get home.

She drives through the village. The postman waves cheerfully at her; she hardly acknowledges him. Her house looks ominous and empty from the outside. Guy's car is there. He's in. Of course he's in.

She unlocks the front door, and it pushes against a pile of letters. She kicks them aside.

"Guy, where are you?"

But she doesn't need to call out, because she can hear gasping and whistling coming from the kitchen. She drops her bag and runs to him.

"What happened? Sit down, let me get you a drink. Guy, have a drink."

She splashes water into a tea mug that's drying on the drainer. Should he be drinking? Will it help? He doesn't sit down; he grasps the worktop, and his whole body shudders with the effort of getting air in.

"We're going back to the surgery this afternoon," Heather says. "I'll call them."

"Yes," Guy manages, and takes a tiny sip of the tepid water.

His eyes are streaming; there are sweat patches on his shirt. Heather puts her arms round him; the tension in his muscles almost knocks her back. His body is coiled, wound. She wets a cloth and presses it to his forehead.

Perhaps whatever attack it is passes, or perhaps it's because he's not alone any more, but his breath evens out, and he lowers himself carefully into a chair, takes another mouthful of water. Heather's sweating too. She takes off her coat, goes to hang it in the hall, and scoops up the pile of letters. Catalogues, junk, and an NHS envelope for Guy.

"Heather."

She puts the mail on the table, sits by him, takes his hand, and he doesn't pull away.

"What?"

"It's back."

She doesn't answer, just hands him the letter. He glances down, shoves it back to her.

"You do it." His voice breaks again between words, and he splutters.

Heather rips the paper, glances down the printed pro forma, snorts.

"Great. You've got an ENT appointment in March."

"Groovy."

Heather smiles. *Groovy.* Guy's joke with Jas about his taste in music.

"I'll ring the surgery," she says.

~

Heather feels faint. Faint with fear, faint with relief that they are now sitting in Dr Sinclair's consulting room, faint because she hasn't eaten and her blood sugar has probably fallen through her boots.

"No, March is no good," Dr Sinclair says. He picks up the phone on his desk. "I'm going to speak to whoever's on call for ENT and see if we can get you admitted today."

Heather's hand finds Guy's. He is staring rigidly out of the window at the white winter sky, the bony hedge.

"Hello, this is Dr Sinclair from St Michael Surgery. Could I speak to the ENT SHO please?"

Guy's breathing is harsh but he, too, seems to be calmer now he's here in the surgery, now that something is happening.

Heather listens to the rasp of his airway, and Dr Sinclair on the phone.

"Previous oesophageal cancer, had an Ivor Lewis…yes, all seemed OK. Yes, tried antibiotics…he's got an outpatient appointment for March…really needs to be seen…upper airway…yes, today. Thanks, thank you."

Dr Sinclair drops the phone down again, swivels in his chair.

"Go to A&E, and ask for the ENT SHO. They're expecting you. Let's see what's going on in there. Pack an overnight bag. By the time you get there they'll keep you in, no doubt."

"Thank you," Heather whispers.

They don't speak as they walk back through the waiting room, where two kids are shrieking, where a woman, bent as a hook, is leaning on the counter shouting at the receptionist through the window. They don't speak crossing the carpark. Heather's car opens with a beep. They get in and still they don't speak.

Heather reverses out of the parking space and turns into the road.

"I'll text Jas when we get home," she says at last. "She should know."

In her peripheral vision she sees Guy nod.

"Jas has enough going on," he says.

"I think she and Andrew are going their separate ways. I should be angry and say he should stick by her, but actually I'm glad." Heather takes her hand off the gearstick to squeeze Guy's knee. It's so bony through his jeans. "Grandad," she says.

"I won't make it, I won't see it."

Air whistles through Guy's windpipe. Heather feels hot tears, and roars right up to the back of a silver hatchback creeping past the Archangel.

Kat's watching the evening news, cross-legged on her sofa with a plate on her knee. Cubes of cheese and chopped salad. She savours each small mouthful: the sharpness of the cheese, salt crystals on the cherry tomato halves. She's learnt that, if she takes time with food, it fills her more, satisfies her more, occupies her for longer.

The newsreader looks up at his autocue. A fourteen-year-old girl in Hampshire has killed herself because she was being bullied at school. An overdose of painkillers and alcohol. Kat puts down her fork, studies the picture of the girl on the screen. Just an ordinary looking teenager, with ordinary dark hair. The news report doesn't say what she'd been bullied about. She doesn't look fat, or thin, she isn't wearing ugly glasses, she doesn't have a strawberry mark on her face. Perhaps she was extremely bright or extremely stupid, excellent at sport or terrible. Maybe she had a boyfriend and the other girls were jealous. Maybe it was nothing.

There's a hierarchy to being bullied. In Birmingham, if fat Kathryn Smith didn't exist, it would probably have been the boy in the year above who had eczema all over his body. If she hadn't moved schools to Penzance, it would have been the skinny boy who walked with a limp, or the girl with a burnt hand, or someone with spots or something. But no, there was a fat person there and available, and fat people are the best to bully. Fat people don't deserve respect, fat people's feelings don't matter. If fat people kill themselves because of remarks made to them, no one cares.

Kat often wondered: what if she had died in the Hallowe'en storm instead of Amy? Her podgy, blank face on the front page of the local paper, instead of willowy, blonde Amy, photographed on a sunny beach. She wouldn't have been the tragedy that Amy was because she wasn't slim and beautiful and popular.

Kat snaps at a slice of cucumber. She's so angry. Angry about the dead girl, angry about the countless girls and boys being hurt and taunted and mocked and degraded every single day. Angry about how everyone responded to Amy's death, when she knows, fucking hell, she knows, it would never have been like that for her. Angry that she was ever part of it that Hallowe'en.

~

Heather has put her phone onto charge while she helps Guy pack an overnight bag. Guy sits on his bed, head in hands, while Heather throws a couple of pairs of socks, his glasses case, his wallet, into a holdall.

Downstairs, the key in the lock.

"Jas," Heather calls. "Can you come up here a sec? Did you get my text?"

Jas comes up the stairs, stops in the doorway.

"Sorry, I didn't see a text. What's going on?"

"We went back to the doctor. He's getting Guy admitted tonight."

"To the hospital?"

"Yes. It's been arranged." Heather zips up the bag. "OK, Guy, get your coat, let's go." She glances over at Jas. "I'm sorry, love, how are you?"

86

Jas looks like she wants to speak, thinks better of it.

"Fine. D'you want me to come too?"

"No," Guy croaks. "We could be ages."

"You stay here." Heather gives her a quick hug. Poor Jas. She should be talking to her, about the baby, about Andrew. Jas is seeing the midwife in the morning.

Heather runs down the stairs, the holdall bumping on the bannisters. Guy follows more slowly, Jas behind him. Heather unplugs her phone, without looking at it, and shoves it in her pocket.

"I'll call you," she promises Jas, as Guy opens the front door. The cold evening air makes him choke.

~

Kat turns the TV over to another channel. Buying a holiday house in Italy. Much safer. The presenter in a floaty maxi dress and sunhat. Blue sea. People swimming. Kat reaches for her mobile and texts Heather.

Hi, how are you? Guy any better? Will you be swimming on Sunday?

A ramshackle stone building, half fallen down, with a dirt track and an olive grove. The couple looking for a house, hands surgically attached to each other, gaze at the crumbling upper floor. Kat can't concentrate. Sometimes her memories overwhelm her. That girl's death has hurt her as though they had been friends.

Just because people from school in Penzance don't recognise Kat it doesn't mean she doesn't recognise them. She sees quite a few of them, even now. She sees the girl working in Boots who was once thin, but is now stout with grey roots; she's seen another girl from her year dragging four kids round town, cigarette clamped in burgundy mouth; she almost sat next to a guy in the dentist's waiting room, and then realised he'd shoved her against the school wall and spat at her in another life.

And then Chloe Johnstone turned up at swimming. Where Kat thought she was safe. Safe from her past, safe from her failures. Though, back then, she and Chloe hardly crossed paths. Chloe was never rude to her. Chloe Johnstone with her little girl Evie.

That's the one thing about those people from school that does really hurt Kat now: so many of them have families. She doesn't believe she will ever have a child of her own. She's getting older; she's alone; most of all, she is terrified – beyond terrified – of growing huge again.

She wonders what Jason is doing with his children tonight. Does he think often of his dead wife? Are there photographs of her in his bedroom? Do Thomas and Flora have memory boxes? Do they take flowers to a grave? Who was she?

~

The doors hiss open and Heather inhales sharply. It's all the same. Zombie-eyed people in outdoor coats slumped in plastic chairs. A child wailing. A guy hobbling out of the gents with a stick. A girl with a bloodstained bandage wrapped around her hand. Two lads at the vending machine. It's just like before, when Guy coughed up his NG tube – she still feels ill recalling that – when the tube got blocked, when Guy picked up an infection during chemo. The huge TV on the wall. Some soap or drama. No sound, just subtitles. A row of patients staring up at the screen as though a solar eclipse were happening above them. Noise. Smells.

Heather settles Guy in a chair, and goes to the desk to sign in. She tells the gormless youth tapping on the computer that Dr Sinclair has arranged this admission with ENT. The youth rubs his spotty chin, and says he'll have to ask someone.

The seat beside Guy has a dark stain on it. Probably coffee or tea, could be worse. Heather will wash these jeans after this. Guy's breathing is hard and noisy again. The stress of the journey? The cold outside? The thick hot air here? Heather smiles at him; he shrugs.

Overhead the silent drama continues on the TV. A slutty blonde slams out of a car, silently shouting back at the driver. *How-could-you? I-hate-you*: staccato typing on the screen.

Heather takes out her phone to text Jas. One new message. It's from Kat. *Guy any better?* Heather doesn't reply immediately. Instead she texts Jas to say they have arrived and signed in.

"Guy Lovell."

Heather jumps, stuffs the phone away, and grabs Guy's bag from the floor. A couple of heads swivel as they tramp through the horde. Do any of these people know Guy's name? Do they listen to him on Ocean FM? Have they heard his voice worsening?

The nurse looks barely out of training: short russet ponytail, electric blue eyeliner. She takes them into a side room.

"Dr Sinclair from St Michael spoke to someone in ENT earlier," Heather says. "They're coming down to see Guy if someone pages them. I told them at reception…"

The nurse takes Guy's blood pressure. It's high. She listens to his breathing. Heather holds her own breath.

"I haven't seen anyone from ENT down here," the nurse says. "Let me go and find out what's happening. Are you alright there, Guy? Do you have any pain?"

"No pain," Guy says.

The nurse opens a second door which leads into the bowels of A&E. A man in blues is walking by. The nurse taps his arm, speaks to him a moment.

"That was the orthopaedic SHO," she says to Heather, when she comes back in. "He hasn't seen anyone from ENT either. I'll page them now. It might be a while, they might be in the middle of something."

No doubt, Heather thinks.

The nurse turns to her. "If his breathing gets any worse, come and knock on my door."

That jolts Heather too. The triage nurse thinks Guy's breathing is bad. When he hacked up his feeding tube he was left on a trolley for hours. No one was bothered. They'd insert a new tube when they got round to it. Until then he'd have no food. But this time, the nurse is telling Heather to come back to her if he gets worse.

The chairs they were sitting in before have been taken by two girls, both in miniskirts and heels, both texting on sleek silver mobiles.

Heather tugs Guy into a seat by a young couple with a baby in a car-chair. The baby is sleeping quietly, tiny fingers resting on a blanket. Heather gazes at its translucent skin, the curl of its ear, thinks *we must get a car-chair.* There's a brightly coloured fluffy duck attached to the chair's handle. Heather hopes it's not the baby who is ill.

Guy slouches in his chair, eyes shut, breath rattling. Heather gets out her phone. One bar of signal. She is about to call Jas when the phone beeps and the signal disappears. She doesn't want to go outside to get a signal; she doesn't want to leave Guy.

Just seen the nurse, she texts instead. *Waiting for ENT.*

Another nurse, a fat one in a too-tight dress, comes out of another door and calls the baby's family in. The baby's father scoops up the chair; the baby fidgets and settles.

I wonder if Jas will breastfeed or bottle-feed?

The TV programme has changed to something dark and jumpy. Guys in a darkened car. *Six-murders-a-day-connected-to-cocaine-trafficking,* click out the subtitles. Heather sighs and looks away. A gang of boys in baggy jeans and baseball caps shamble into A&E. Two are holding cans of beer.

God, I hate this fucking place.

The russet-haired nurse they saw comes out for a woman on crutches. *Tap tap tap* she goes across the dirty linoleum.

Heather's jigging her knee, nibbling her nail.

Come on, come on.

She knows that tonight, in moments or – more likely – hours, their lives will change.

91

Chloe's wasting time on the internet. Evie has just watched some CBeebies on iPlayer, and has now fallen asleep in the middle of the bed. Chloe's sitting beside her with the laptop on her knee. She clicks onto Facebook. A few boring notifications. Someone's birthday she used to work with in Truro years ago. She looks at the friend suggestions. Peter Langford. Twelve mutual friends, it says. People from school, people from the village. Amy once told her Pete fancied her, freckled sandy-haired Pete. Chloe went hot because she hadn't ever considered Pete like that but, once Amy had said it, she could not un-think it, and Pete had left school, and had a motorbike, and was probably pretty cool. Dave Langford comes up too as a friend suggestion. They always do. She must come up on their pages too. *Chloe Johnstone*, and the thumbnail photo of her and Evie taken by Rod when Evie was about one, and her curls were starting to grow.

Chloe types *Heather Read* into the search. There she is. Chloe hesitates a moment, then hits *add friend*. She runs through Heather's friends, finds Guy and Jasmine, also Christa. Chloe thinks Jason Hosking might be the Jason from swimming, but his photo is of two kids so she can't be sure. Chloe adds Christa too. She can't find a picture of Kat amongst Heather's friends, but she's not sure she would add Kat if she were there. She has a feeling Kat wouldn't accept her offer.

~

"OK, Guy, we're just going to put this very thin scope up your nose, and down into your throat. It doesn't hurt, just a bit un-comfortable."

Heather tries to smile at Guy, who is lying on the bed, but she thinks she must look manic. Her own heart is thumping. It's hot in the examination room. She's perched on a tiny stool at the foot of the bed. There are two ENT doctors bent over Guy. Someone thumps on the door and shoves it open.

"Excuse me, just need this." A male nurse clanks a trolley out and slams the door closed.

He interrupted a moment, Heather thinks. He won't ever know it, but his arrival delayed Guy's procedure a minute or two, stretched out the time of not knowing just a little longer.

The registrar is a tall, skinny woman in a droopy skirt. Heather can just see her sliding the tube into Guy. There is a TV screen angled away from Heather. The younger doctor, a bloke with spiky hair and glasses, is watching the screen. The registrar murmurs something to him; Guy wheezes; Heather feels her bowel sliding. From beyond the door, the sounds of wheels, shoes, voices. The registrar asks Guy to make sounds. His voice breaks each time.

"OK, well done." The registrar extracts the tube, hands Guy a box of tissues. He coughs, hacks. His eyes stream, and meet Heather's.

"What is it?" Heather says.

"There's a mass on the right," the registrar starts. "I think it may be cancer."

Guy snorts or laughs, wheezes. "I knew it. I knew it."

"The only way to be sure will be to do some scans and a biopsy," the registrar goes on.

Cancer, cancer, cancer. Like we didn't know. Radiotherapy, chemotherapy, feeding tubes, surgery. Here we go again.

"Where? Where is the cancer?" Heather demands.

"The larynx. That's the voice box."

"What happens after the scans?" Heather searches the doctors' eyes for a clue, for anything.

"It's impossible to plan how to deal with it until we know exactly what's happening. There is a chance it's not malignant."

"It is," Guy interrupts.

"It probably is, yes. But the airway is clear. You can get air into your lungs. Remember that."

"When will the scan be?"

"We'll speak to our consultant tomorrow and get it arranged for early next week."

Early next week. Shit. It must be bad.

"Are you going to admit him?"

"I don't think there's any point. You won't get the scan done any quicker. Someone will be in touch in the next couple of days." The registrar squeezes Guy's arm. "I am very sorry. I see you've already been through all this before."

"I knew it would come back," Guy says. "This time it'll get me."

~

The huge glass doors hiss open, and Heather and Guy step outside. In a heartbeat the stuffy, sweaty heat from A&E becomes the icy breath of a winter's night. The doors wheeze shut again. Guy stops, gazes up at the stars. Despite the sodium lamps, they're there, always there. Heather too looks up. Her eyes flick from one lit hospital window to another: a row of cards on a sill, a spindly pot plant, a figure tugging down a blind. All the stories of the hospital at night.

"I'm so sorry," Heather says. Inadequate words. There are no words.

Guy starts walking towards the car. "Nothing we didn't know."

"I should ring Jas. Tell her we're on the way." Heather takes out her phone. Signal flares; she dials home. "Jas, it's me. We're just leaving."

"Isn't he staying in?"

"No, they said there wasn't any point at the moment."

"Is it cancer?"

Heather hesitates. Guy's walking on ahead, slow steps, tired steps.

"Probably."

"Why aren't they keeping him in then? What are they going to do?"

"We'll talk later."

Heather runs after Guy, the holdall awkward in her hand. He's waiting by the car. She unlocks the doors, goes round to the boot to dump the bag. Guy gets into the passenger seat. An ambulance grinds towards A&E, blue lights spinning, no siren. A burst of laughter from the main road. Heather slams down the boot, walks through the parked cars and the shadows to the ticket machine. It's in a glass shelter, with a sickly lightbulb. A young bloke is shoving coins into the slot. One falls down, rejected, with a clang. He tries again, it falls again. Get the fuck on with it, Heather thinks, though she knows it's not his fault. Right now, the drive home feels impossible. She sees the young bloke's shaved head in the gloom, hears the traffic and the clatter of coins, feels the cold, cold night, and knows she'll remember all these for the rest of her life.

Jas is waiting for them; she must have heard Heather pull up, or seen the headlights, because she has the door open.

"Dad, Dad," she says, hugging Guy, hiding her face in his chest.

"Hey, it's OK," he croaks. "We've been here before."

"We've seen it off before, we'll see it off again," Heather mutters, but she's glad Guy's at least trying to sound upbeat for Jas. She wonders if Jas believes him, because she doesn't.

Guy goes straight to the kitchen, slides a bottle of red out of the wine rack.

Heather's about to say something, stops herself.

"Drink?" Guy waves the bottle at them.

"Just a small one," Heather says.

"I can't." Jas indicates her flat stomach.

"A toast to the future." Guy's voice breaks on the word *future*, he drinks, and tops up his glass immediately.

Heather takes a sip. It's rough and bitter. She only accepted a glass to stop Guy finishing the whole bottle.

When Guy's drunk all but Heather's one glass he goes up to bed. Heather reaches out to him as he passes her, but he shrugs her off.

"I guess he wants to be alone," Heather says to Jas, because it's so unlike him to go up first.

"What did they say? Really?"

Guy hadn't let them talk about the hospital, other than Heather telling Jas the barest facts.

"I think they were shocked at what they saw. They said he needs a scan first."

"And that's next week?"

"They said so."

"But why didn't they keep him in?"

"They said nothing would happen if he stayed in."

"They might forget about him."

"Well, they won't," Heather says, rinsing the two glasses in cold water. "Because I'll get onto them." She dries her hands on a tea towel and turns to Jas. "You must get to bed. Midwife in the morning. Would you still like me to come?"

"Won't you want to be with Dad?"

"I don't expect he'll want me around."

"Come with me then, please."

~

Evie takes forever to eat breakfast. She doesn't like breakfast. Chloe's tried all sorts – toast, cereal, yoghurt, fruit – but it's always the same. Evie might pick up a finger of toast and delicately lick off the butter, chattering about Ears, about Zac and Luca, about CBeebies, waving the dry toast about, then put it down again. Or she might slide tiny fragments of strawberries into her mouth and keep them there as a red pulp until they dribble out of her lips.

Now it's almost lunchtime. Chloe chooses to ignore Evie fiddling, to not say as she usually does *please Evie, come on, just a bit of toast, here's a crunchy bit, please, please eat up*; instead she taps her phone onto Facebook to see if Heather and Christa have accepted her friend requests. They have, and someone has requested her as a friend.

"Mummy, I need to tell you something. Toast is…"

Chloe's not listening.

"Mummy. I need to tell you."

"Hang on, sweetie."

After all these years, Olly Bradshaw has added her on Facebook.

~

They would have stared at her anyway, Kathryn thought. She was the new girl. She didn't know anyone. She hadn't been to primary school in Penzance; she hadn't played on the beach over the summer. Even if she were thin, people would be staring.

"This is Kathryn Smith. She's new to Penzance." A frazzled woman, the music teacher, handed her over to her group tutor in the school hall.

There was a gaggle of kids around him, all talking together, all knowing each other.

"Hello Kathryn, I'm Mr Underwood. I'm your group tutor. Where have you moved from?"

"Birmingham," Kathryn whispered, conscious of her Midlands vowels, and wishing she had said somewhere more exciting: the Lake District, the New Forest, Pembrokeshire.

Mr Underwood introduced her quickly to some of the girls. They all eyed her up, a couple smiled, one smirked and turned back to the lanky boy she was talking to. Moments later. Mr

Underwood led them all out of the hall, and down a glass-sided corridor to their room in the maths department.

In the classroom there were two long tables; she sat next to one of the girls who'd smiled at her. Mr Underwood asked everyone to introduce themselves, say a few lines.

"I'm Kathryn. We moved here in the summer. We've been coming to Cornwall all my life," Kathryn said.

"I'm sure everyone will do their best to make you feel at home," Mr Underwood said.

Farther down the table, on the opposite side, two boys sniggered. Kathryn felt her face heat up, and sweat prickle her neck under the shiny shirt. They were laughing at her. People always were. It wasn't a question of guessing; it was simply knowing.

~

Chloe chucks down her phone and flicks open her laptop. She needs a proper screen for this. Evie tries to prod the keyboard with her buttery fingers.

"Go and wipe your hands if you've finished," Chloe says automatically.

Evie tugs at the packet of Huggies Chloe keeps on the table.

"What are you doing?"

"Just looking at something. I won't be long."

Chloe should delete Olly Bradshaw. Forget about him. Of course, she has looked for him on Facebook before, seen the profile picture of him holding a glass of beer somewhere outdoors in the sunshine – a pub garden maybe, or at a party. His tawny hair is severely cut in the picture; he doesn't much look like the tousled eighteen-year-old from so long ago. Many times Chloe has looked at that photograph and wondered for a crazy second if she should add him. Then she's clicked away to another page. But she's always known he's been there.

Evie drops her almost-empty beaker on the kitchen floor.

"Mummy, Mummy, orange juice!"

"I'll sort it out in a moment."

Chloe's finger hovers a moment on the mousepad, then she clicks down. She has accepted Olly Bradshaw. Now she can look at his profile. He lives in London; he works in a bank. He has lots of photos: him with girls, him with guys, cars, stupid things like a banana shoved into the top of a road cone. His profile says he is single. Chloe scrolls through his photos, the posts on his wall, his likes. She's forgotten about the sticky puddle of orange juice on the floor.

~

"We'll talk later, I promise." Heather says to Jas as they leave the surgery.

Heather feels like she never leaves the place.

"Talk about what?"

"About you, the baby, Andrew."

"There is no Andrew. It doesn't matter. He's not interested. He'd prefer me to have got rid of it."

The appointment with the midwife went well. Jas's blood-pressure and urine are fine. The midwife has calculated a due date in July. She says Jas will have an ultrasound soon.

Heather is confused. She thought Jas was really into Andrew. Perhaps she's in denial, or just giving him space or something. Not that Heather's sorry. She sighs. She's neglected Jas lately because of Guy. Even at the appointment with the midwife Heather was thinking about Guy, alone at home, knowing now there is another alien growth inside him.

"I was thinking," Jas says, as they cross the road to the gallery.

"Mmm?"

"I think I'm going to give up my course now."

"You won't have to yet."

Heather unlocks the gallery, turns the sign to *Open*.

"Just listen. I'll have to stop before the end of the year. And with Dad poorly again. You know what it was like before. You'll need me."

"Don't rush into anything. You don't have to decide right now. Let's get you both scanned, see what's happening. What the outlook is for Guy. Make sure your baby is OK."

When Guy was ill before with oesophageal cancer Heather almost lost her business. A friend in the village opened up for her sometimes for short days when she couldn't leave Guy, or when she was taking him to his daily radiotherapy. Other days Guy would get a lift to the hospital with a friend of his, and Heather would find herself too stressed, too sad, too utterly exhausted, to open the gallery. A couple of artists withdrew their work. The gallery could not survive this again.

~

Kat's unloading a new order of butterfly pendants and earrings when her phone beeps.

Hi Kat, sorry was in A&E last night with Guy. Cancer again. Scans next week. Terrified.

Shit, Kat thinks, reads it again.

I'm so so sorry. If there's anything I can do let me know.

~

"Earth tremors," the boy hissed as he edged past Kathryn in the corridor.

She didn't know who he was. He was older, by a year or two. When he passed her in the corridor he'd say *earth tremors*. Sometimes he shouted it, and his mates would erupt into laughter; sometimes he hissed it like a dirty secret for her ears alone.

Kathryn trudged on, in the slipstream of the rest of her form, moving from maths to English. The novelty of being the new girl had worn off. The girls Mr Underwood introduced her to on the first day smirked at each other in the long, tiled tunnel of the changing room showers.

The showers. Kathryn didn't know about that horror until the end of her first day at secondary school when they'd been told to bring towels for games the next day. They played netball with the girls from another first-year tutor group. Somehow the ball ended up in Kathryn's hand at an apparently crucial moment. *Over here, Fatty*, someone shouted. A few laughs. Not a word from the games teacher, who was no doubt thinking the same.

And then the showers. The stink of feet and sweat and decades of girls in the changing rooms. The eyeing up of others' bodies as they peeled off their sexy little games skirts – Kathryn wore baggy shorts. The girls were sent into the showers in groups of four or five; the games teacher stood at the far end with the towels over her arm. Kathryn huddled into the wall, facing the tiles, as tepid water sluiced her hair. She kept her arms crossed over her torso. Next to her, one of the other girls, back to the wall, water streaming over two perfect tiny breasts, silently inviting everyone to look at her body.

Kathryn hunched over and sloshed through the wet to the end.

"Is it this one?" The games teacher held up someone else's towel. Deliberately, Kathryn knew, so she stood there, a fat pale lump, in front of everyone.

Almost snatching her towel from the woman, she threw it round herself. Oblivious even to the horrible wet muddy floor under her bare feet.

Cool girls were spraying deodorant under their arms, fixing cute little bras, combing their hair. Kathryn tugged her clothes on; they stuck on her damp skin. Her wet hair dripped down the collar of her shiny blouse.

The scream of the bell for lunch break. Kathryn gathered up her stuff, wet towel trailing from her arms, and ran from the changing room.

Her locker was on the other side of the school. She thought she could remember the way, and set off across the courtyard. She was sharing the locker with someone else. An older girl. She didn't know her name. When she opened the locker to dump her towel there was a pile of lever-arch folders and a can of hairspray on the top shelf, a coat on a hook, a hockey stick. Kathryn rubbed miserably at her hair again and reached for her packed lunch – crispbreads, apple, and a two-finger Kit Kat. Some boys appeared. One threw a sports bag on top of the row of lockers. Another kicked the lockers, a deep clanging sound. Kathryn didn't pay attention to what they were saying; she locked up and started walking to the corridor.

"Earth tremors," one of the boys shouted, and the others whooped and cackled. "The ground's breaking. Earth tremors."

~

He was in the year above, Kathryn found out later. She'd become kind of friendly with some twins in her tutor group. Jenny and Judith didn't even look like twins. Jenny was tall with black hair; Judith small with brown hair and freckles. They were quiet, kept themselves to themselves, and they had a brother in the fourth year, so they knew some of the older kids.

"Who's he?" Kathryn asked.

She and the twins were crossing the courtyard. The earth tremors boy and a couple of cronies were on the higher decking, walking the other way. He was in the middle, flicking through a magazine, showing the others something.

"Who?" Jenny asked.

"The one with the magazine. He's always rude to me."

"Oh, him," Jenny said. Judith didn't speak much. "That's Oliver Bradshaw."

Now Kathryn knew his name.

~

Well hello. And how are you? It's been a long time since you disappeared out of my life. I have thought of you often. O xx

~

Low lights on the ward. Curtains pulled around other beds. The porter stops the wheelchair at the nurses' station.

"This is Mr Lovell, come up from A&E," the porter says to the nurse.

Heather gazes round the ward. A whiteboard with rows of extension numbers written in coloured markers. Cards pinned up on cork: flowers, cartoons, cute bunnies, arty photographs, a Terry Frost. That ward smell Heather would know if she were blindfolded. Institutional food, sweat, wounds. She's so tired. The clock over the nurses' station says it's almost two in the morning. Beside her Jas is wilting, with old make-up crusting around her eyes.

The nurse thanks the porters and spins the wheelchair round, leads them to an empty bed. Snores from behind the other curtains in the bay. The nurse turns the lamp on, sending a sickly beam onto the thin blanket.

"My wife, Heather, my daughter, Jasmine." Guy hauls himself out of the wheelchair and onto the bed.

Heather fusses with his overnight bag, opening it, looking for his mobile, his book, his washbag. The nurse says she will fetch Guy a cup of tea while he settles in.

Jas perches on the end of the bed, tears at her fingernails. Heather straightens up from the bedside locker.

"You two get off," Guy wheezes. "It's so late."

The nurse comes back with a cup of tea and puts it on the bedside table.

Only two nights ago Heather was in A&E with Guy, feeling the drive home was impossible. Here she is again. She's glad Jas is with her this time. She'll need someone to talk to on the way home to keep her awake.

Earlier Heather shut up the gallery and went home. Guy's body shook and lurched with the effort of breathing, his face a death rictus. Heather called the surgery, gabbled in panic at the receptionist, who said she would find a doctor. A few moments later Dr Sinclair picked up. When Heather told him they'd been to hospital two nights ago, and that there was a tumour in Guy's throat, he caught his breath.

"And they sent him home?" Incredulous.

"Yes," Heather said, watching Guy grasping the kitchen worktop, as he tried to inhale.

"They shouldn't have done that," Dr Sinclair said. "I'll get onto ENT again, get him admitted properly this time. With his breathing he should be in hospital. They can give him steroids, a nebuliser. I'll call you back very soon."

Heather hung up, went to hug Guy. The kitchen clock bit off moments of the darkening afternoon. How long till she rang the surgery again? They closed at six. She'd have to call back before then. What if Dr Sinclair was too busy to ring ENT?

"Shall I just call 999?" she asked Guy.

The phone shrieked; Heather pounced.

106

"Heather, it's Matt Sinclair. I've spoken to ENT. They're going to find a bed for him tonight."

"Thank you," Heather whispered.

By the time she had packed for Guy, Jas was home and wanted to come too. They waited for long hours in A&E, with Guy on a trolley, drifting into uneasy dozes, gasping awake. The russet-haired nurse was not there; they were seen by a skinny angry one. The ENT doctor was different too: an Indian guy with a northern accent.

"Go on," Guy says now. "You're both done in. Jas needs to rest."

"All right." Heather stoops to kiss him. His forehead is cold and sweaty, his hair stuck to the skin. He looks ghoulish in the strange light.

Jas leans down to kiss him too; Heather fumbles in her pocket for the car keys. Someone groans from behind another curtain. At the end of the ward there's a wide window. Through the glass, the perimeter lamps of the hospital complex sparkle amber and white.

"We'll see you tomorrow," Heather says as they leave the bay.

"Love you," Jas mutters.

The nurses are talking at their station. Someone somewhere is making toast. Heather's throat gags. Another smell of hospital.

The corridor is deserted. Their reflections swoop at them from darkened glass doors. Just the tap of their feet going down the empty stairs. Heather shivers, sensing the unseen companions of the hospital at night. There must be many ghosts here, trapped on the corridors, the stairs, the lift shafts. If she listens hard enough, if she can find the right frequency, could she hear their broadcasts?

~

Chloe hasn't responded to Olly's Facebook message. She doesn't know what to write. She wishes there were someone she could ask. She can't say anything to Millie or Elaine. They would say she should never have accepted his request. And it would bring everything back. How Chloe, Millie, and Elaine had to move so quickly to Rod's. Rod was always kind to her about it. He spent hours with her, just talking about what had happened. Not blaming her for uprooting everyone as Millie had; not embarrassed and shocked like Elaine.

Chloe opens up her laptop, thinks about Rod. He'd be disappointed, she thinks.

Hi Olly, how are you? What are you doing these days? I'm living in St Michael again, with my little girl, Evie. She's three. Have you got any kids? Chloe

One of the most powerful memories Chloe has of Olly was from the swimming pool. Or rather, the public gallery above. The minty-blue of the water far below, the shatterproof glass with red wooden frames. If she were painting the memory it would be blue – that blue that smells of chlorine – with a scarlet border, and then the tiny black check lines of the thick glass.

Into the memory comes the stamping of feet. That fat girl, Kathryn Smith, coming up the steps. The look on her face.

Earth tremors, earth tremors. Kathryn wished she had the courage to spit the words in Oliver Bradshaw's smirking face before he could get them out. He was in the year above; his tutor room was one of the science labs just along from Kathryn's room, so he got her on the corridor there. He got her at the lockers. Other kids heard and laughed. No one ever stuck up for Kathryn, no one ever told him to shut up.

The games teacher, having flexed her muscles with the show-ers, soon could not be bothered to stand around holding towels. The girls tramped in from hockey and netball, and got dressed again, still sweaty and muddy. There were always comments then, sometimes snide behind hands, sometimes to her face. They laughed at her old woman's school uniform. They laughed when they had to run round the perimeter of the hockey field, and Kathryn was always last. One of the girls from her form told her the games teacher had said *we'll be waiting all day for Kathryn*. Probably it was true: the woman was a cow.

Next to the comprehensive was the sixth-form college and, next to that, the sports centre and swimming pool. Kathryn knew it was there, sensed its blue pull through her first term in Penzance. One thing she had decided: no one was ever going to see her in a swimsuit again. Not the sleek, slim, girls, not the floppy-haired surfer boys. No one ever would.

The day of their first swimming lesson in the New Year her mother wrote a note saying she had an ear infection. The games teacher – hand outstretched for the note before Kathryn even

109

said she had it – hardly glanced at the writing, just sighed, and turned away.

"Go and watch from the gallery upstairs."

There were three people not swimming that day. She didn't know the other two well; they were from parallel forms. A girl with her wrist in a plaster cast, and a skinny boy with thick glasses. When the rest of the year filtered like driven sheep into the changing rooms, Kathryn and the other two padded along a softly-carpeted corridor to a flight of steps. The girl with the plaster cast knew where to go; the others followed her. Up the stairs, carpeted in a beige-grey colour, to an open space above. There were a few tables and chairs, a couple of vending machines, one for fizzy drinks, the other for chocolate and crisps. On the left was a large square window. Aggressive thumps. A shout. Kathryn looked down into a squash court, and two frazzled men chasing a black dot around red lines.

On the other side of the gallery was a huge plate-glass window set in a red painted frame. Kathryn stood right in front of it, one hand on the pane to steady herself from vertigo. Far below was the pool, a pale turquoise blue. If Kathryn fell straight through the glass, how deep would the water be below her?

The skinny boy flicked back the ring pull on a can of Coke, threw himself into one of the chairs. The other girl was at the vending machine. A beep and a clank, something falling. Kathryn turned round, heard her cursing, trying to open a packet of crisps with one hand in plaster of Paris. Kathryn would love to buy some chocolate from the machine, but she hadn't any money on her. The girl and the boy sat together, crunching and slurping. Kathryn watched the kids from school spill out of the changing rooms and onto the poolside. Boys and girls eyeing up bodies. One of the bitches arching her back, sticking out her tits, to adjust her ponytail. A scuffle with some of the boys. Then someone blew a whistle, and kids jumped in, slid in off the side, climbed down the steps. The water seethed and boiled.

Over the rest of the term, there were usually a couple of other kids up in the viewing gallery with Kathryn. The girl with the plaster cast was there for several weeks but, one day, towards the end of the swimming term, Kathryn was the only person up there. Alone, she took out her money that she kept in case this chance arose, and shoved it into the vending machine. Chocolate bars danced out from the compartments and landed with a hefty, sugary thump in the tray below. Kathryn carried her treasures to the window and unwrapped a Mars. The kids below thrashed the water into white-blue bubbles. One of the boys glanced up mid-stroke; Kathryn clenched her fist around the remains of the bar in case he'd seen what she held.

She moved back from the glass. Still she was alone. She padded down the beige-grey stairs to the reception area. Another vending machine, this one selling squash balls in little boxes, chlorine shampoo, bottles of Lucozade and mineral water. Sporty things. Next to it, a public phone. The reception desk. A blond man – tall, good-looking – in sportswear, behind the desk, writing something down. Kathryn hesitated. She had been about to walk out past the desk, into the spring sunshine, and just keep on walking. But then she saw herself as the young man would see her if he looked over: a fat, ugly schoolgirl wearing an old woman's skirt, clutching a chocolate bar. Before the guy could look up from his pad, she stumbled back up the stairs to her lonely vigil. When the kids scrambled out of the pool and ran, shouting, back to the changing rooms, she wondered if she could just stay where she was. Would anyone notice her absence?

But she walked down eventually and tagged onto the wet-haired, chlorine-scented mob of classmates in the lobby. She hadn't the courage to leave; she hadn't the courage to stay and hide.

~

Saturday afternoon, and Heather and Jas are back on the ward. Guy's lying on top of the bedcovers in his old jeans and the shirt he came in wearing. He has a nebuliser mask over his face.

"It helps a bit," he says, moving it aside. "I've got steroids too."

Heather gazes helplessly at him. Maybe it's the hard light of the ward, but he seems to have shrunk, his face bony, his skin greyer.

A nurse comes over to take his obs.

"Has Guy told you about the scan?" she asks, fixing the blood pressure cuff round his arm.

"No," says Heather.

"What scan?" asks Jas.

Guy removes the mask. "It's a PET scan," he whispers. "On Monday."

A PET scan. Of course. The words and phrases come flooding back. Guy had a PET scan for the oesophageal tumour. Heather wonders why she has forgotten the drill, why her mind

112

jumps all over the place. Sometimes she feels she wouldn't even be able to describe Guy's medical history to anyone.

"I've got a scan soon too," Jas says, awkwardly.

Heather feels her embarrassment, takes her arm. The scans are poles apart: one shows the blossoming of a new life, the other the last flickerings of a ravaged body.

~

Even the actions of hunters above the frozen Arctic Circle ricocheted down the lines of longitude to torment Kathryn. In an English class they were shown a video about whaling, so they could write emotional poetry and angry articles afterwards.

Kathryn thought she'd probably like whales, with their lovely tails, if the word *whale* didn't remind her of Jamie Wallis shrieking it at her in her swimsuit, and Jonathan Roberts' mother sniggering. Why are we supposed to care if whales get brutally butchered, she wondered, if they are fat, gross creatures to be despised? She couldn't despise them though, with their serenity and gravity, the way they glide through the cold blue sea.

She stared at the TV screen: the red-purple blood spilling from the ship's deck into the ocean, the hauling ropes, the massive black carcasses.

Whispers behind her. Her name: *Kathryn*.

The TV narrator said something about blubber.

"Hey, Blubber." A finger in her spine.

Kathryn wished for a flensing knife of her own. She could slice strips of her hated blubber from her frame, throw them down on the bloody floor.

The smell calms Heather as soon as the door-catch releases. The fresh smell of chlorine.

She looks through the window as she passes. The water is angry and jagged. Tim and Rob are halfway down the pool with Christa. Jason is trying to tread water in the deep end; his head submerges and he springs up and grabs the rail. Two older women, nothing to do with the class, are swimming side by side, laborious breaststroke, their heads jutting above the water. Like strange creatures, Loch Ness monsters.

Slapping on the tiled corridor. Kat coming towards her in her swimsuit and flip-flops.

"Heather, how are things? How's Guy? I would have texted but I thought you'd want some space."

"He's on the ward now," Heather says. "We had to go back again. He couldn't breathe at all. He's got a scan tomorrow morning."

"It's definitely cancer, then?"

"Definitely. Again." Heather feels like she might crumple there on the damp floor. "And Jas is pregnant, did I tell you?"

"No, no, you didn't. When's it due? Is she happy?"

"In July. Yes, she's happy about the baby. Not about the father much. Oh, I don't know. I haven't given her the time she needs right now. But it's lovely. Guy's pleased. So am I. Something nice, you know."

Behind her the door opens and Chloe comes in.

"A baby's always wonderful," Kat says.

In the wet heat of the pool room, Kat chucks down her towel and slides off her shoes. Jason waves at her from the deep end, and she waves back. The two women swimmers haul out of the pool and fuss round a pile of towels, robes, and bags.

Christa calls the three men together for their relaxation at the end. Tim and Rob float on their backs; Jason falls forward holding his knees, rocks a moment in the water, and all Kat can see of him is the freckled curve of his back.

Strange she should remember that whaling video earlier. Perhaps she is a whale after all. They're fantastic swimmers.

Kat imagines a school reunion, and she could turn up and no one would even recognise her. They wouldn't know who she was, and then someone would hear her Midlands voice, and then it would come like a tsunami: *Haven't you lost weight? You look wonderful! You're amazing.* And they'd pretend they were her friends, they'd always been her friends. Anything that happened was just a silly little misunderstanding. Or a joke. The ball on the back of the skull, the whale photograph taped to her locker, the whispers, the cackles. Jokes.

~

Heather can't swim tonight. All she can think about is her airway, that narrow tube keeping her lungs alive with oxygen. She puts her head underwater, and inhales through her nose, stumbles up, choking. She smacks her palm down on the water surface in anger, rips off her goggles. She's going to cry.

Kat's beside her. "It's OK, it's OK. It'll come back. Don't be so angry with yourself."

"Yes, I know." Heather rubs her eyes and they sting with chlorine and tears.

Christa and Chloe wade across to her.

"I'm sorry, everyone." Heather plays with her goggles. "It's Guy," she says, and trails her hand through the water. Her upper body is getting cold. "The cancer's back."

~

Five minutes before the end of the lesson a man comes into the pool. Kat stands in waist-deep water and stares. With a huge powerful glide, he kicks both legs together like a whale tail, to surge him forwards. Water pours off his shoulders. A flash of his blanked-out goggled eyes as he sucks a breath over his shoulder, and he's already at the deep end, then he's off again, past Christa and Heather and Chloe. Kat is mesmerised by the strength and fluidity of his stroke.

~

"Please give Guy my love," Chloe says to Heather as they walk back to the changing room.

"Thanks. I will."

"Sounds like you're lucky with your GP," Kat says.

"Yes, Dr Sinclair. He's been great."

"Matt Sinclair's my brother-in-law." Chloe tugs at her swimming hat, and it comes away with a snap. "My sister Millie's married to him. They have Evie while I'm swimming."

"He's been so kind," Heather says. "I never knew he was related to you. And Guy being your teacher. Small world, isn't it?"

"Sure is," Kat says, as she clangs into a shower cubicle.

Under the hot water, Kat thinks about Chloe. She's not even sure why she feels so hostile to her. Chloe never did anything. Not to her. She should find it refreshing that Chloe didn't even find her interesting enough to prod; that she chose to hurt someone else instead.

Over the rush of the water, she can hear Chloe and Heather talking behind their doors. Odd words – *breathless, steroids, so frightened, PET scan* – drift into her cubicle. Kat showers quickly, turns off the water, and wraps herself in her towel. The voices are louder now.

Heather says, "Chloe, I must tell you something nice too. Jasmine's having a baby in the summer."

"That's lovely," Chloe cries. "You deserve something happy."

Kat rubs her scalp viciously. She's almost forty, on her own. What chance has she got of having a baby? And could she even bring herself to do it? The thought of growing huge and bulky fills her with terror. She's read so many tales of women who couldn't lose their baby weight, how eating the remains of children's dinners adds a stone a year to your body or something.

Chloe's a mother. She's not huge. She just looks average. But she's only ever been average. Kat always feels her new thin body is just something on loan, she'll have to return it to whoever lent it to her, and clamber back inside her blubber once more. She still dreams she's fat; she wakes sometimes and has to walk her hands down her stomach and legs to discover that she isn't still the girl who wanted to slice strips off her body with a flensing knife.

~

Driving home, Chloe listens to Ocean FM, and some other presenter broadcasting Guy's programme of Sixties and Seventies classics. Will Guy ever go back to the radio? Will he live? She's given Heather her number, and asked her to let her know about the scan results if she possibly has time. She's driving behind Heather, eyes on her rear lights. She's behind Heather past Langford's, through the Bends, and into the village. Heather must know it's Chloe behind; she hoots as she turns into her road, and Chloe drives on to Matt and Millie's.

Kat. There's something about Kat. Chloe knows Kat. She just can't think where from. Kat lives in Penzance now. Did she once live in St Michael and go to school there? Or was she from Penzance sixth form? Or could it even have been from Truro? People move. Chloe moved. Had to move.

Chloe runs through all the girls who might now be called Kat. Katherine Hewson, from her year at St Michael? No, she was dark. Catherine Isles in her A-level English group in Penzance? No, she was very tall. There was a Kathy, and a Catrina, in Truro, but she's friends with them both on Facebook and knows exactly what they're up to.

She parks and gets out. There's a glittery crust forming on Matt's 4x4. Lights on in the house. It looks homely and perfect. As she walks up to the front door she finds herself thinking about someone else from the past: Olly Bradshaw. And the memory tumbles back of her and Olly in the viewing gallery at the sports centre, and that fat Kathryn Smith stomping up the stairs. Kathryn Smith? No, not her. She was huge.

~

By the time Kathryn was fourteen, and the tutor groups were mixing for lessons, she'd found, if not friends, other outsiders pulled together like iron filings by the magnet of weirdness. Davy, the skinny boy from the swimming pool gallery, who was short-sighted and weedy; Lorna, a spotty ginger girl whose father had shot himself, and who doodled gravestones on the covers of her exercise books and inside her ring-binders; Sharon, who was just weird.

But Kathryn wasn't with them all the time. And she knew they only tolerated her because if it weren't for her, the fat one, they might be the victims instead. They owed her a pathetic gratitude. She was lonely in her own tutor group. She had Oliver Bradshaw hissing abuse at her in the corridor. And it wasn't as if the rest of her band were supportive to her about him and the others. Davy and Lorna were just as likely to snigger if they thought she wasn't looking, and Kathryn never really knew what went on behind Sharon's glassy gaze.

One day in chemistry they were watching a video about the periodic table. The blinds were down, the lights off. Beside her Lorna was sketching an elaborate gravestone with an angel etched on it, and flowers growing around its base. Kathryn turned to a clean page in her notebook and made a list of all the names she could think of she'd been called: *earth tremors, blue whale, fatty, fatsmith, fatso, blubber, scales, womble, fat arse.* They were just words, stupid words, just certain letters in a certain order. She turned to another page, and started listing butterflies. As the credits rolled at the end of the video, and the teacher snapped on the fluorescents, she wrote *Glanville Fritillary.* A most rare butterfly, hardly seen.

~

Yes, I see her in the picture. But you don't say anything about her dad. Does that mean you're single? You look amazing, by the way. O xx

~

Heather's eyes smart from the blue-white glare of the screen in her darkened bedroom. She'll stop now. She's been emailing a few people, typing over and over the same dreadful words. She's told her parents in Norfolk; she's told Guy's brother Robin in Melbourne. Guy's parents are both long-dead, not that she knew them well. She has no brothers or sisters. She's emailed some friends, people from Ocean FM, one of the men Guy met last time round when they were both in for oesophagectomies.

At lunchtime Guy had called her on his mobile. Poor signal cracked his voice even more. The scan a couple of days ago had shown a massive tumour. He needed urgent surgery. He would lose his larynx. He would lose his voice for ever.

The screen dies on Heather's knee. The room is dark. No sound from Jas over the landing. Heather simply sits there, her breath going in and out, in and out.

When she went to see Guy that evening, he was so tired. He hardly woke up to talk to her. She asked to speak to a doctor; eventually a junior appeared at the bedside, all Colgate teeth and striped shirt. He took her out of the bay, to a recess where the crash trolley was stored, starkly told her the facts. Guy needed a total laryngectomy. He would lose his thyroid as well, possibly other structures in the neck. A permanent tracheostomy would be created. This, the doctor explained to her, could be done before the surgery if necessary, if his breathing became too compromised. He would always breathe through his neck. He would have to learn to speak again with an internal valve or an electronic device. *Too much, too much*, Heather wanted to shout. *Too much, too soon.*

Instead, she said, "When will the surgery be done?"

"Within a couple of weeks, I would hope."

"But his breathing. It gets worse by the day."

"That's why we might have to put the tracheostomy in sooner."

And then, "What about the future? What are his chances?"

"It's too early to say." The junior doctor's pager beeped on his belt. He unhooked it, glanced at the display, a reflex arc saying: *Look, I am important. I have a pager. People need me.*

Heather stood alone at the crash trolley, absorbing everything. The whiteboard, the thank-you cards. The ward clerk on the nurses' station reaching for something in a drawer behind her. Two nurses having a joke together. A carer walking into another bay holding a urine bottle. The noises: beeping, telephones, the tapping of a patient walking out of the bathroom on sticks. The hot dry air of the ward, the smell, always that smell.

Heather turned round to Guy's bay, saw him awake, watching her. She smiled, swallowed her tears, the rawness in her own throat, and went back to him.

~

The whole school was packed into the hall for the leavers' assembly. Kathryn was squashed between Lorna and Sharon. Kathryn hated sitting on the floor. She imagined an aerial view of the school hall, and the parquet flooring, and each person was allocated a certain amount of floor, a certain number of parquet squares, and pictured herself spilling over her ration into someone else's space.

But today was a good day. They were here, on this stifling afternoon, watching the kids from the year above file out, past the beaming headmaster. The leavers. Kathryn wondered if Oliver Bradshaw would turn round and mouth *earth tremors* at her one last time, but he just swaggered across the front of the hall behind one of his cronies. Kathryn watched him, watched the darkness of the corridor swallow him. Gone for ever.

"I know you don't like Olly," Lorna whispered to her, "but don't you think he's gorgeous?"

"What?" Kathryn spat, incredulous. Even her so-called friend was disloyal.

She thought about Oliver Bradshaw, striding through the hall, raking a hand through his thick tawny hair, and thought that, in another life, another universe, maybe Lorna was right.

~

Thursday morning and it's quiet in *Imago*. Kat's been reading a paperback behind the desk. She hasn't made a sale all morning. She gets up to make another tea. Tea – without milk or sugar – keeps her going. It warms the cold hollow empty places that are screaming for chocolate or biscuits.

While the kettle boils she flicks open her notebook to make a list. Things she knows about Jason Hosking.

Has two kids, Thomas and Flora
Wife/partner dead? Of what? When?
Lives with mother in Marazion
Works as gardener
Age – 30s?

It's a pretty short list. She doesn't know much about him at all.

But he doesn't know much about her either.

~

"Lovely," Guy whispers and gives Jas a thumbs-up. He hands the photo back to her: a curl of shiny paper, a tiny blur floating in the dark space of her womb. "It won't know my voice."

Heather stares at the scrap in Jas's hand. "It'll know a different voice. You will be able to speak again. Just differently."

Guy barks – is it a laugh? – and splutters.

I loved his voice from the beginning, Heather thinks. When we met on the street in St Michael.

"I'm leaving college," Jas tells Guy. "I can't stay on next year with the baby, and I want to be here to help look after you."

"No, no," Guy starts.

"Come on," Jas says gently. "You know what it was like before. You'll need us both." She glances at Heather.

"Jas would have to leave before the end of summer. And she's not going to dump the baby on a childminder."

"I'd like a bit of space from Andrew too," Jas says.

"I thought better of him," Guy says. "He should have stuck around for you."

"I don't want him to. I wish this baby was mine alone."

"It can be," Heather says.

"No, he's the father. He has a right to see it."

"I don't think he'll want to, Dad."

"Jas hasn't made up her mind for sure," Heather interjects. Guy looks tired; they should be off soon.

"Don't rush into anything," says Guy. Half the time it's more like he's mouthing words than speaking them.

"I haven't. I just told them I'd be taking a break."

~

Kat knows how different her childhood would have been if she'd been thin. Sometimes when she was very young, she wished she was Debbie Green, living in her little shoebox house, with a front door that opened straight into the living room. With Debbie Green's older brother, and Debbie Green's parents. Not because she wanted that tiny house or that family, just because she'd be thin then. She'd have traded in her whole life and family to be thin, to be someone else.

And then, when she moved to Cornwall, she had the chance of a fresh start with new people, but she'd brought her old fat body with her, so it was never truly a fresh start. If she had been thin, she knows all the things that would have been different.

She'd have had proper friends, not just the other runts of the year. Real friends, girls she could have talked to about school and boys, make-up and clothes, *EastEnders* and music. Instead she pretended she wasn't interested in any of those things. She was above all that. She was interested in nature and books and art. Because a fat person couldn't be interested in the everyday, trifling things. Because to try on clothes, to experiment with make-up, to talk to boys and dream of romance, you had to be pretty.

If she'd been thin and pretty, at the weekend she would have been at these girls' houses, not lying on her bed in a neon-pink shell-suit, or watching *Blind Date* with a bowl of ice cream.

She looks back on her years at secondary school, and it's like they were wasted. She never had the fun or the friends. She was disliked at best, despised at worst. Her whole life could have been different if she'd been one of the gang but, to be one of the gang, she'd have had to be thin. And would she really want to be part of a gang that judged people like that?

Grown up now, Kat knows the answer is *no*. But then, the answer was *yes*.

~

Saturday morning, and there's been a constant trickle of customers in *Imago*. Kat's wrapping up a pair of china mugs for a customer – one with a Red Admiral, the other with a Comma – when the door-chimes ring again. As she glances up to see the new arrival, her hands freeze on the mauve tissue paper. It's Jason Hosking and his two children.

They're not looking at her; they're looking at the T-shirts, the pencil cases, the posters. Thomas says something about slugs being better than butterflies, and Flora shrieks. Kat tapes down the last flap of tissue, and puts the mugs into a bag as the woman slides her debit card into the machine.

"Thomas, put that down," Jason says. "No, now."

Kat hands the woman her receipt.

"That's Kat, sweetheart," Jason says to Flora. "She's my friend from swimming."

My friend.

The woman with the mugs leaves the shop. Jason grins at Kat, comes over to the counter.

"Hi. I said we'd come in. Guys, come and say hello to Kat."

"Hello," Flora smiles at her. She's holding a sparkly butterfly hair accessory. "Can I have this, Daddy?"

Jason pulls a face at Kat. "If I'm up to putting it in your hair."

"Have you got anything with slugs on?" Thomas asks.

"No slugs, but I can do caterpillars."

"Hmm. Caterpillars. Caterpillars are kind of cool."

"I think so too," Kat agrees.

"I don't," says Jason. "Slugs, caterpillars, snails. They all eat plants."

Flora has shoved the pink butterfly clip into her amber hair, and is sifting methodically through a basket of pencil cases. Kat watches her, thinks how pretty she is, how perfect, with those bright curls, and heart-shaped face. She wouldn't have a childhood like Kat did. She'd be popular, happy, wanted.

"I think Flora will be bringing me in here again," Jason says.

"That's good." Kat's flustered.

She hardly – it sounds dreadful to even word it in her head – recognises Jason in his jeans and parka, hair windblown. She thinks of the freckles on his back, below the coat and the jumper underneath. The children's names tattooed on his arm. Out of nowhere it hits her that he doesn't have his dead wife's name inked on his body. She knows his body well.

"…works out better for me, really. I can get back to eat with the kids and get them off to bed."

"Yes, of course." She doesn't know what he was saying; she was still thinking of his pale shoulders, speckled with water droplets, the way his auburn hair darkens like seaweed underwater.

"But I miss you and Heather. Tim and Rob are so competitive. They're both better than me."

"You're a great swimmer," Kat says.

"Well, thanks, but…I just want to be able to do it with them, you know. Thomas can swim already. Flora's having lessons at school."

"I hate swimming," Flora interrupts. "I'd like this too, Daddy. This pencil case."

"That's one of my favourites," Kat tells her. It's a shiny pouch covered with a swarm of tropical butterflies, red, gold, and green wings, iridescent and vibrant. "Are you going to take it to school?"

"No," Flora says violently as Jason hands over a twenty. "No, it's too nice. I'd…lose it."

"You mean they'd nick it." Thomas digs Flora in the ribs. "They took her woolly hat, and they took her felt-tips and they took her towel after swimming—"

"Stop it," cries Flora.

"Thomas, shut up. Flora's upset." Jason turns to Kat. "There are some not very nice kids at their school."

"I'm so sorry. There were some not very nice kids at my school too. Both my schools." Kat stops short, hands Jason his change. She's never done that before, spoken about her past, shown her vulnerability.

"It's not true, what they say." Flora jabs the butterfly back into her curls. It's lopsided. Kat aches to reach over and straighten it. "They say Mummy doesn't love me anymore. But she's not well, is she, Daddy?"

Jason colours. "I told you, sweetheart, don't believe a word they say. They're only trying to hurt you." He glances to the front door where a squall of rain hits the glass.

Prodding her for her weak spots. Her Achilles heel. It's not her looks. She's thin and pretty with strawberry hair and blue eyes. They couldn't find anything superficial like her looks. They had to dig deeper still. Kat feels sick.

"Come on, then." Jason zips up his parka. "Let's put that safe for now, as you'll need your hood on." Gently he takes out the hair decoration and puts it in his rucksack. "Good to see your place, Kat."

The kids run to the door. Thomas tugs it open; the chimes jangle, and cold rainy air blasts in. "I'll see you Sunday," Jason says.

128

Hey, aren't you talking to me? Is it because I said you look amazing? You do. You always did xxx

~

Evie's colouring on the mat. She hasn't yet got the idea of staying within the lines. Unruly red streaks bleed out from a rabbit's face in her colouring book. Chloe takes her eyes off the laptop for a moment to watch Evie select a blue wax crayon and press down too hard. The crayon snaps; Evie wails.

"It doesn't matter. You've got two now."

~

Of course I'm talking to you. I've just been busy. Anyway, you haven't answered my question. X

The kiss doesn't mean anything; it's what people do on the internet.

"Come on, sweetie. What are you taking to Millie's tonight?"

"When can I come swimming with you?"

Chloe shuts the laptop, yanks the plug out and replaces the socket cover so Evie can't fry her fingers.

"I don't know," she says. "I can't swim properly yet."

"You've been swimming for aaaaages."

"Only a few weeks."

"So when can I come?"

"As soon as I can do it, you'll be the very first person I swim with. Now, where's Ears?"

~

Heather drives to swimming with the radio off. She'll never hear Guy on the airwaves again. Even if he does learn to speak once more, he'll never broadcast. The last couple of days she's had emails and phone calls from Guy's friends at Ocean FM. No one's asked her if he'd want to come back. They know the answer, as she does.

Headlights in the rear view mirror. Heather wonders if it's Chloe. The car has been behind her since just outside St Michael.

She and Jas had only just got back from the hospital in time for her to throw her swimming things together and set off again. Part of her didn't want to go; she just wanted to curl up on the sofa.

She's almost at the hotel. The bay opens up, huge and dark, before her. The white light of a ship on the horizon.

Heather wonders once more: did Jas get pregnant intentionally? Whatever she says about needing a break from Andrew, she doesn't seem that upset. Has Andrew done what she needed of him? Or is Jas just so upset about Guy that the Andrew thing hasn't fully hit her? Heather couldn't blame Jas if she set out to have a baby. Something beautiful and hopeful and life-affirming after the time they've had. The time they're still having.

Heather parks; the car is still behind her and pulls in beside her. It's Chloe.

The floor between the changing room and the pool is wet. There must have been a lot of swimmers recently. Kat slaps through the puddles in her flip-flops and opens the door to the pool. Christa's on the side; the three men are in the deep end. Kat dumps her towel, kicks off her shoes, and watches, waiting for Jason to look over. He's holding on with one arm; the water's trying to prise him off the edge.

"OK, Jason, you go first," Christa says.

Jason adjusts his position. He sees Kat and waves with his free arm. Kat waves back. Will he say anything to her about his visit to *Imago*? About what Flora said?

He launches off the back wall. Everyone watches him: Kat, Christa, Tim, and Rob. Foam splutters round his legs. He's kicking too hard. Halfway down the pool he stumbles to his feet, coughs up water.

"What happened there?" Christa calls.

"I don't know."

He drops his head and glides, straight and lean as an arrow, to the steps in the corner. Behind him, Rob has started swimming, but Kat's not interested in Rob. Jason hauls himself up the steps.

"Hi," he says.

"Hi."

"I screwed that one up." He tugs off his goggles, doesn't reach for his towel. He stands there before Kat, wet hair tufted, shoulders dappled with water droplets. The tattoo on his arm. His children's names.

"When did you get that done?" Kat asks.

He glances down at his arm. "Oh, couple of years ago. Hurt like hell."

Kat smiles. Her Morpho hurt too, but not as much as words.

"Kat, about what Flora said...about her mother."

"Excellent, Rob, well done," Christa calls. "Now Tim, off you go."

"You don't have to..."

"Yes, look, the kids at school are saying their mother doesn't love them and that's why she left us."

She left? Not dead? She left? She walked out on gorgeous Jason Hosking and those two pixie children?

"Their mother...Dawn...she was...not well. I mean, she had habits. Drugs. She took Thomas and Flora with her for a bit. They were so unhappy. They wanted to come back to me. She didn't really want them, just wanted to stop me having them, but she couldn't cope, and there were men turning up and all sorts." Jason runs out of air as though he's swum a length underwater. "Sorry, you don't want to hear all that."

"I'm sorry," Kat says. "That must have been awful. For the kids. And you."

"Yes. But they're much happier now. Mum's around for them too. It's just that some of the kids at school, their mothers know about Dawn and must have said things. I told Flora her mum wasn't well and needed some time so she could get better and come back to us, and I shouldn't have said that. I thought she understood now that Dawn's gone, but then these kids..."

"They're not worth anything."

"Easy to say but—"

Splashing. Tim and Rob hauling themselves up the steps one after the other. The blue water surging, then settling. Christa walking over in her tracksuit. Heather and Chloe going past the glass windows to the changing room. Kat doesn't have long.

"I had the most awful time at school."

"You?" Jason picks up his towel at last and throws it round his shoulders. "What happened to you?"

Kat stares down the pool. The waves have become ripples. The lines of the tiles are re-forming under the surface.

"They said all the things that would hurt me the most. Like what they're doing to Flora. So I know how she's feeling."

~

Chloe screws her hair into a knot and eases on her swimming hat. She shivers, despite the heat in the changing room, because she always has a cold kernel of fear inside when she comes swimming. Heather's been talking about Guy. The surgery sounds even worse than the oesophagectomy he had before. There will hardly be anything left of Guy inside.

Chloe wonders if Guy still thinks of the night Amy died. Chloe wasn't in St Michael but she knows what happened. What happened to Amy in the phone box, what Amy's friends told Guy, how Guy suggested Dave and Pete should chase after her. What they found.

~

Kat hangs suspended in a ball, her hands around her bent legs. Like a foetus. She can't hold this float motionless; her body

133

slowly rotates, and the tiles move under her. She can hear the muffled noises of Christa greeting Heather and Chloe, of Tim and Rob talking on the poolside. Jason's already gone to get dressed. He never loiters after swimming; he always rushes back to his children.

Kat finds it surprisingly easy to hold her breath in this position. By not breathing she's keeping everything in stasis, held, for these moments, between the worlds of water and air. At last she drops her feet to the tiles and stands. Christa's peeling off her tracksuit to get into the water. The men are leaving. Chloe's fiddling with her hat, and Heather's standing there on the edge of the pool, looking as if she's forgotten how to climb down the ladder.

"How are things?" Kat asks.

Heather shakes her head. "Awful," she says. "Awful."

"Use this time as your time," Christa says. "You can't do anything for Guy in the next half hour, so relax and enjoy the water."

Heather nods, slowly descends into the water. Kat wades over to hug her.

Chloe glides across the pool, holding her neon pink float in front. It's pointed like an arrowhead, cuts a swathe through the water, pulling her behind it. She's across in seconds.

"OK, now try without the float," Christa says. "I'm here beside you. You know you can do it. Come into the deeper water."

Christa swims a few lazy breaststrokes towards the deep end. Chloe follows her, one hand on the side. Under her feet, the floor dips sharply. She curls her toes onto the tiles to grip. The water's suddenly round her chest.

134

Chloe's feet shudder on the slope. Already the water threatens to kick her up. She inhales, puts her face in, and pushes awkwardly off the wall. She's away, but her legs are sinking, and she knows they're not together like a mermaid's tail, but spread like a starfish, and she's taking in water, liquid fire, and she's going down, down, and it feels like the water's closing over her head, but there's Christa's firm grasp, and Chloe's standing, shaking, coughing.

Heather's swimming widths in the deep end with Kat. She's not enjoying the water. She's convinced something terrible is about to happen. She's convinced Guy is going to die.

"I'm so frightened I'm going to lose him," she says to Kat as they stop for a breather.

Heather can just touch the bottom of the pool with her toes outstretched like a ballerina. Kat holds the side with one hand, half-treading water.

"Look how well he did last time," Kat says. "He's a fighter. I know people say that all the time, but he really is."

"How long can he fight?"

Chloe pulls herself to the deep end with her left hand. In her right is the pink float. Her lifeline. Like the piece of wood Kate Winslet hung on to at the end of *Titanic*. Christa asks Heather and Kat to move aside. Chloe's going to try a length with her float. She's far too frightened to push off into a fathom of water without the float; in fact, after her stumble, she's too frightened to even try it with the float, but she's doing it for Evie. Always for Evie. So they can swim together one day. Right now, as she clutches the back rail with one hand, and her float with the other, she could almost laugh aloud at the idea.

135

Movement to the left, behind Heather's head. A couple walking past the glass windows, holding towels, heading for the changing room.

Do it now, Chloe thinks. Just fucking do it.

She wishes Kat weren't there, with her goggles on her head, watching her. Chloe knows she and Kat have met before, somehow, somewhere. And Kat didn't like her.

The shallow end, and the metal steps are so far away. I'll never be able to do it, she thinks. Where does the floor start to slope upwards? Chloe drops her head underwater to look. The black edging tiles stretch away into blurry blue. The water is so deceptive. It doesn't even look that deep below the surface. She can see Christa's legs ahead of her, calmly treading water, kick, kick, kick, kick. To the left, two more pairs of legs: Heather's and Kat's. Chloe comes up for air. The shallow end is still far, far away. Everyone's watching her. She places both feet on the wall and launches off. Her head's too high, she's kicking too roughly, she can hear the splashing, she can feel herself stalling, and her breath running out. When at last she staggers to her feet, she's drifted further than she thought. She can stand on the floor, on the slope, right in the middle of the pool. Water all around.

~

"Mum," Jas calls, and runs into the hall before Heather can shut the front door.

"What?" A cold, icy, slidy feeling inside. Guy. The baby.

"It's OK. One of the nurses rang."

"Is he all right?"

"She said he was OK, but couldn't talk because of his breathing. She says the consultant came to see him."

"On a Sunday night? We must have just missed him."

Jas shrugs. "He came in specially. And he wants to meet us all tomorrow evening. On the ward. To talk about the operation."

Heather slides down onto the hall chair. There's a coat on it, and something hard beneath the coat, but her legs need support. She rummages under her for the long hard lump, brings out a Maglite.

"If I'd known the consultant was coming I would have missed swimming."

"It doesn't matter. The nurse says tomorrow is fine. I said we'd be there about six. I hope that's OK."

"Yes. Yes, of course."

Jas smiles. "This nurse, her name's Cassie – do we know her? – we were just talking about Dad, and how she didn't realise who he was to start with, and she said she took him for his PET scan the other day, and how she was so cold down there while they were waiting, he gave her one of his blankets. Did you know that?"

Heather smiles too. One of those smiles that tip off-balance into tears. "No, I didn't. But he would do that. I think Cassie's the little blonde one with glasses."

"Oh, yes, she might be. She says she's on overnight if you want to call her back."

Heather stands up slowly. It's good news, surely, that the consultant wants to get going with the surgery. It frustrated them all so much when Guy had oesophageal cancer and he had to have weeks of radio and chemotherapy before anyone would even give him a date for surgery. Then he had to wait for the effects of radiotherapy to calm down, the burns and the scarring, and only then was he told the oesophagectomy could go ahead. This time it's different. They're moving swiftly. That's good. Or is it worse?

~

Chloe parks outside Millie's, and quickly checks her Facebook for messages. Nothing. Guiltily she shoves her phone in her pocket, and wonders how long it will be before Millie notices she has become Facebook friends with Olly.

~

Heather rings the ward just after ten. Cassie picks up.

"I just wondered how he is," Heather says. "Jas says you called earlier."

Cassie hesitates. "His breathing hasn't been so good. He's been using the nebuliser a lot. He was asleep when I looked in on him a few moments ago. I'll keep an eye on him. I've told him I will. You can call any time, you know."

"Thanks."

Heather hangs up. The nurses seem to be pretty nice on Guy's ward. She can bring Cassie to mind: short, round, fair hair in a loose bun, glasses. Heather imagines Guy offering her his blanket in the cold radiology department.

~

On Monday morning Jas goes into college to confirm she is leaving. Nothing Heather or Guy or anyone could say would change her mind. Heather's glad. She wants Jas around now. The coming months are going to be so very hard. Perhaps, Heather thinks, when Jas has gone, Andrew might forget she was ever carrying his baby.

Heather has opened up the gallery and has sold two pieces of stained glass to a man from Penzance who's been in before, who she half-knows. He asked after Guy. Heather said he was in hospital and the man didn't pry. Just said to send his best wishes.

The gallery's quiet. Heather dials.

"Langford's Autos. Dave speaking."

"Dave, hello. It's Heather Read. I was hoping I could book an MOT for Guy's car…the Audi."

"We've had a cancellation tomorrow afternoon. Can he drop it in some time before twelve?"

"Thanks, that's great."

Jas will have to drive Guy's car and Heather can follow her. Jas hates driving, but she is insured on Guy's Audi. Heather will have to tell the Langfords about Guy, they've known him for so long.

~

If you mean do I have any kids, then yes, I do, but my ex won't let me put pictures of them on FB. Twins – Jeremy and Isaac – twelve now. Anyway, you haven't answered my question. Are you single? xxx

139

Chloe is shocked that the question should get to her so much. She could lie, and say no, because she doesn't want Olly to think no one wants her. Or she could say, yes, she is single. And why would that matter? He lives in London. He's only asking, being friendly, catching up with someone from forever ago with the usual opening questions. In fact, why is she even sitting here in front of her laptop wondering how to phrase her reply? It's hardly important.

~

"Phil Rowan. Thank you for coming in."

Heather shakes the hand he offers. His grip is firm, fingers cool. Tyneside accent.

"I'm his wife. Guy's wife," Heather starts. "This is Jasmine, our daughter."

"Hello," Jasmine whispers. She's clutching a bottle of tropical fruit juice. Her recent craving. She looks pale and queasy now; must be the lingering stink of hospital food.

Phil Rowan was on the phone at the nurses' station when they arrived on the ward. One of the nurses gestured that they should hover and wait for him. Heather assessed the man who would cut Guy open: small and wiry with dark hair, going grey, a deep blue shirt.

"How is Guy?" Heather asks. She can see the curtains are half-closed round Guy's bed.

"I've just been to see him again. We had a talk about what I plan to do. Let's go to him."

Jas sucks her bottle as they follow the consultant to Guy's bed. Heather's heart jumps. Guy's breathing is ragged and tortured. Sweat beads his forehead and darkens his hair. A desk fan whirrs on the bedside cabinet. There's a cardboard bowl of half-melted ice. All Guy could swallow in the weeks before his oesophagectomy.

"Oh Guy." Heather bends to kiss him, and tastes the sweat.

Guy tugs at the nebuliser.

"Keep it on," Jas says.

"Guy, is it OK for me to talk to Heather and Jasmine about what we're going to do?"

Guy nods. "Somewhere else," he wheezes. "Don't want to hear it again."

Heather and Jas glance at each other.

"We'll go to the relatives' room. Put that neb on again, Guy. We've talked about this."

The relatives' room is bleak. A few plastic chairs. A box of grubby-looking toys. A single red Lego brick on the floor. A pile of magazines on a table, a box of tissues.

"You don't need me to tell you how bad this is," Mr Rowan starts. He looks from Heather to Jas, then back to Heather again. Heather notices he has startling green eyes.

"You can do something for him?" she asks. "After everything he's been through."

"I'm getting him into theatre tomorrow morning. Not for the big operation. That will need a lot more planning. I want to have a look, get some biopsies. See if I can make his breathing any better."

"Do you mean a tracheostomy?"

141

"I hope not at this stage. I'm going to bore through the tumour."

"But not take it out?" Jas sucks on her bottle again. She looks like she's swallowing nausea.

"Not tomorrow." He hesitates. "Until I have a look in there I don't know if I will be able to do anything for him. In the long term."

Heather reaches for Jas's hand. "You mean there's no hope?"

"The tumour is huge. I've seen the scans. It's been there for months. I can't promise I can cure him. But I can promise I will make his airway better tomorrow. If things have gone too far for further surgery, Guy could have radio and chemo, which would give him some time. I know he's done that before. I know you've all been through this before. I'm so sorry it's happened again."

"I'm having a baby," Jas falters. "In July. Will...will he be here for that?"

"I hope so," Rowan says evenly.

Heather inhales. This is real. An hourglass has been tipped over.

"While Guy's in theatre tomorrow, we'll put a feeding tube in. He's lost so much weight and, now his vocal cords aren't working at all, it's dangerous for him to eat. Food could go down the trachea. So we'll get him started on a food pump."

"Again," Heather whispers.

"Again." Rowan takes Heather's hand.

"He'll love that," Jas says. "What time will you operate tomorrow?"

"First thing. What I'm going to do isn't without risk. You do understand that?"

"Nothing is without risk," Heather says.

Beside her Jas is crying.

~

Kat opens the washing machine and scoops out her wet clothes. The drying rack is in front of the door to the fire escape – she's probably breaking a rule there. She starts by hooking her underwear and socks on the lower rails. Bending and stretching, bending and stretching, she snaps out wet tops and jeans. There's the bright splash of her swimming towel, the shiny swirl of her swimsuit. It's only washing but, even now, it's special to Kat. A swimsuit, still faintly scented with chlorine, size twelve skinny jeans, little lacy knickers. What so many other girls are hanging on washing racks but, to Kat, they hold a special message: she's normal. She has normal-sized clothes, she can swim. She remembers the terror she felt the first time she joined Christa's class. She knew she was thin, but she wrapped herself in a giant towel, and hunched her shoulders, curling into herself, to hide her body. An old tune her bones and muscles still danced to.

Once Kat had a nightmare about the washing machine. When she opened the door and tugged her clothes into the waiting basket, they were not her skinny jeans, not her frilly knickers; there was no swimsuit. She'd unloaded those vast elasticated skirts of her teenage years, the old-woman's blouses, the shell-suits, the oversized jumpers.

Kat's angry. She wasted her childhood and adolescence in a fat, gross body; now she catches herself wasting her adult years remembering. Remembering the clothes, the name-calling, the

143

sniggering, the embarrassment. Soon she'll have wasted her whole life on being fat.

~

Heather wakes just after five on Tuesday. It's dark; it's quiet. She lies in bed for half an hour, then flicks on her bedside lamp. A circle of light. She stumbles out of bed. It's freezing. She shoves her arms into her furry robe, and goes downstairs to make tea. A few moments later, as she huddles over the kettle, she hears footsteps above, then the flush of the lavatory.

"Are you OK?" Jas calls down.

"Yes, sorry, did I wake you?"

Jas pads down the stairs. She looks peaky: thinner, and queasy. She's wearing an old Nepalese cardigan of Heather's over her pyjamas.

"He might die," Jas says. "He might die today."

"He'll be fine." Heather pours water into two mugs. "The consultant seemed very positive. He'll make his breathing easier. Then he can get stronger for the big operation."

The next big operation.

"Are you going to ring the ward?" Jas asks.

"Yes, to wish him luck. I'll ring about seven. Can we take the car to Langford's before I open up today?"

~

They set off in a grey, misty dawn. Jas goes first, slowly, carefully. She hates driving. She only passed her driving test in the summer. Heather pulls out behind the Audi. There are people about

144

in the village: kids in school uniform, a man half-heartedly tugging a pissing dog away from the bakery steps, people in anoraks with newspapers folded under their arms. Heather's stomach judders. She's not as confident as she pretended to Jas.

She called the ward before they left, and asked them to send their love and best wishes to Guy. The nurse said someone would call Heather when Guy was back from theatre. She could not give a time at the moment; she didn't know where he was on the list. He'd had an unsettled night, she told Heather. His breathing was very bad.

Heather concentrates on Jas's rear lights in front of her. Jas brakes going into the first right-hander of the Bends. Heather flashes a glance to the left. She always does. That was where Amy Langford died. The night she first met Guy. The storm, the flash flood. There's water on the road this morning. Jas creeps through the Bends. There's a van behind Heather now, right up her arse, headlights dazzling. Up the other side of the Bends, the road flattens out, and Jas flicks on her right indicator. Heather does the same, drifts up behind her, and the van forces through on the left.

There are lights on in the workshop. Jim Langford comes out when he hears the two cars arriving. Jas shoots into a parking space beside a broken-down Honda. Heather gets out. She'll have to speak to Jim.

"Guy OK?" Jim asks, as he takes the Audi keys from Jas. "I haven't heard him on the radio lately."

"He's back in hospital," Heather says. "Cancer again."

"Oh Heather, I'm so sorry. Do give him my best, won't you?"

"Of course."

145

"We'll get this done today and give you a call."

"There's no rush, Guy won't be using it for a while."

"Is he having chemo?"

"He's having surgery today. But it's only a preliminary thing. More surgery, and probably radiotherapy again as well." Heather shivers in the cold morning air. She's described the situation, listed the events, and it's all accurate, all true, but the words do nothing to express the horror.

In the car going home, Jas turns up the heater even more.

"That Chloe from swimming," she says, as Heather approaches the Bends. "It was her, wasn't it? She went off with the Langford girl's boyfriend the night she died?"

"Well, yes, but I don't know the details. I remember the kids at the phone box, and Guy was talking to them, and I thought how lovely it was he got on with them so well even after they'd left school. Chloe and her family moved up to Truro. Her mum was a legal secretary, Guy said, and she was going out with a solicitor."

"And her sister's back too, married to Dr Mills-and-Boon."

Heather smiles. "I like Chloe. It was all unfortunate."

They rise out of the Bends, and back into the village. More people wandering about, going about their lives. Oblivious.

~

As soon as the phone goes Chloe knows it's going to be Millie, before she even looks at the flashing number on the screen. Mid-morning. Zac and Luca at school; Matt at the surgery. Millie on the internet.

"I've just been on Facebook."

"Hi Millie," Chloe says.

"I see you've become friends with him."

Chloe hesitates, about to say *friends with who?*, but decides against it.

"It's only Facebook."

"Why, for fuck's sake? After all this time? Or has something been going on?"

"Nothing's been going on."

"Amy was your best friend. We all had to leave the village."

"Well, we're back now." A bang from the front room; Chloe glances in, sees Evie has upended a pile of toys.

"You were shagging your best friend's boyfriend, and she was so upset she drove over the edge."

Chloe sits down at the kitchen table.

"She didn't drive over the edge. It was the storm, and the water."

"You weren't even there."

"That's what the inquest said. Perhaps you don't remember, Millie, how upset I was. Perhaps you were too busy whinging about us moving to Rod's to actually notice how fucking unhappy I was. How I blamed myself. But it wasn't my fault."

"Why him? Out of all the people, why him?"

"I don't want to talk about this."

"Well, I do," Millie shouts. "I had to leave school right in the middle of my GCSEs. I could have done so much better if I'd stayed at St Michael, but no, we all had to up sticks overnight because of you."

"We'd have gone anyway. Mum and Rod were going to get married. And I had to move schools in the middle of my A-levels. And I had all the…shit to deal with. It didn't work out that well for me either."

"Is he down here?" Millie asks suddenly.

"Who? Olly?"

"Yeah. Him."

"No, he's in London. He's been there years. I haven't set eyes on him since that day. You know that."

"I don't know anything. I'll tell you what I know. I know you only want men that belong to other women. First Bradshaw, then that Connolly guy. He doesn't even know about Evie, does he? And she'll never know about him. Why the hell can't you find your own man?"

"Mummy!" Evie shouts.

Chloe hangs up the landline.

"Coming."

Chloe opens the line again. Millie has gone. She'll keep it engaged for a while. Her mobile's upstairs. She won't hear it if it rings. And she won't listen to any messages from Millie, or read any texts. She really won't.

Evie's wailing about a spilled jigsaw. Chloe retrieves fragments of Iggle Piggle and the Ninky Nonk from under the sofa. Evie's chattering, but Chloe isn't listening. She's always known how Millie resented leaving the village and the school, leaving Guy Lovell's tutor group. Millie blamed her. The Langfords blamed her. Everyone blamed her. She blamed herself too. But she never ever imagined that night would end with Amy dead in a torrent of muddy water.

She never set out to be with Olly that day either. It just happened. But it was also inevitable.

~

"Hello, is that Heather?"

"Yes."

Jas is beside her, leaning in to listen. There's no one else in the gallery.

"Phil Rowan. Good news."

Heather exhales. "Tell me."

"I've stabilised Guy's airway. There was no need to put a trachy in today. He's got an NG feeding tube in, so we can get some weight on him. I've taken biopsies. They should be back in a few days."

"And will you be able to do the surgery? The big surgery?" Heather winces at her childish phrasing; she can't think straight.

"The tumour is huge. But I think I can do it. Obviously nothing will be the same again, and Guy will have a trachy then for the rest of his life. But yes, I'm feeling pretty positive about it. You've had a terrible time, but it looks like there will be light at the end of the tunnel."

"Thank you," Heather whispers.

"You'll notice a huge change in his breathing next time you see him. He's safe for now."

"When will the next surgery be done?"

"I don't know just yet. Within a couple of weeks, I hope. The thing is, I'm only here for a few more weeks, and I would like to do Guy myself."

"You're leaving?" she says, panic rising in her voice.

"I'm only working as a locum consultant," Rowan explains.

"I want you to look after Guy."

"I'll get him done before I go."

~

Chloe and Evie put on their coats and wellies to walk into the village. The air is grey and clotted with mist and rain. Chloe has put the phone back on the stand. Millie hasn't called again. Chloe leaves her mobile upstairs. They won't need it just to buy a few bits and bobs. She hopes, prays even, they won't bump into Millie.

"Why are you sad, Mummy?" Evie slips a pink-gloved hand into Chloe's as they start up Barrow Lane.

"I'm not sad."

"You are sad."

Chloe bends down and squeezes Evie till she squeaks. "I love you so much," she mutters against Evie's hair.

Evie won't miss out because she doesn't know her father. Chloe's said this to herself over and over. But she is scared of when Evie goes to school, scared of what the other kids will say, what the teachers will think.

Chloe feels alone right now. Millie was a huge part of why she came back to St Michael. The children could grow up together, she and Millie would be back together, perhaps she could bandage some of the damage from so long ago. Did she get it all wrong? Should she have stayed well away from St Michael?

There's a big shallow puddle outside Heather's gallery. Evie breaks free from Chloe and stamps up and down, shrieking gleefully. Dirty water sprays on her wellies and tights. The gallery is open. Chloe peers in, sees Heather and her daughter inside, standing close, talking. Suddenly Heather looks over to the door, sees her, waves.

"Evie. Let's go and say hello."

Chloe opens the door, gestures to the mat, and watches Evie elaborately scrape her boots free of mud.

"Hi Chloe, how are you?" Heather looks like she's been crying. "We've just had some really good news. Guy had surgery this morning and it all went well."

"That's brilliant. Is that the cancer gone then?"

"If only. This was just so he can breathe properly. He's got to have a huge operation in a week or so. Then radiotherapy again."

"The surgeon's nice," Jasmine says. "I trust him."

"That's good."

"Yeah, unfortunately we've just found out he's a locum and he's leaving soon."

"Will he be able to do Guy's operation before he goes?"

"I hope so. Anyway, how are you? You look a bit sad. Everything all right?"

"I just had a falling out with my sister. Nothing really."

Evie bounds up to them. "Aunty Millie made Mummy cry."

"Oh Chloe."

"Evie, don't worry. It's all fine."

"Aunty Millie was on the phone. Shouting. Will she let me go to her house again?" Evie wails.

"Of course darling."

151

"I'll have to come swimming with you, Mummy."

"It'll all be fine by swimming." Chloe reaches for Evie's hand. She's not sure if it will be. And if Millie won't have Evie, that'll be the end of swimming.

"I could look after Evie," Jasmine says suddenly. "I mean, if your sister can't. Hey Evie, would you like to play with me one day when Mummy's swimming?"

Evie gazes up at Jasmine.

"You'll need the practice," Heather says.

"I mean…it does depend on what happens with Dad. Obviously."

"Of course," Chloe says.

"But it's not for long. And if it might help you clear the air with your sister?"

"Thank you," Chloe says. "Why not come down to ours one day and Evie can show you round?"

~

By the evening, Chloe hasn't heard anything from Millie. She wonders whether to call her, picks up the phone, then changes her mind. It's not as though she's seeing Olly, or that she's even met up with him. It's just a few messages on Facebook. And he hasn't replied to her last message. She opens it up and reads it again.

Do your boys live near you? Yes, I'm single at the moment. Not that I'd have time for anything with Evie. X

And that is the end of the thread. He hasn't responded.

Why does it even matter?

It doesn't matter.

It does.

~

"We should have gone," Heather says. She checks the clock: she'd never get there in visiting hours.

"They said he was fine. They'd call us if anything happened." Jas swallows a mouthful of pasta. "I mean, if there was any sort of...problem."

Heather called the ward late in the afternoon. The nurse said Guy was very tired after theatre, and was resting. She suggested Heather and Jas have a night off from visiting, as everything was OK, and Guy's breathing was so much better.

Now Heather thinks she should have gone to see him. But she's so glad to have a restful night at home, knowing he is safe. Safe for now. She clatters her fork down on the remains of her spaghetti.

"Are you going to Chloe's?" she asks.

"If she'd like me to. She'll probably have sorted it all out anyway, but it'd be sad if she had to stop swimming because she had no one to look after Evie."

"I don't think she has many friends in the village," Heather says. "I guess some of them have moved away, and others remember what happened. I think she's brave moving back."

"It's not easy being a single parent," Jas says.

Heather glances up. "You'll do brilliantly. And Andrew might be there for you."

"I don't want him to. I wish he'd fuck off to Kathmandu or something."

Heather laughs. "I don't think he's the sort. But you're not alone. I'm here. And…" Heather trails off. She can't make that promise to Jas. Jas watches her, knows she can't too.

~

Chloe clicks off Facebook in irritation, and opens up her emails. There's a new message from Christa.

> *Hi everyone,*
> *Sorry, should have said there's no swimming this Sunday as it's the start of half-term. Back to normal the week after.*
> *See you all then, I hope.*
> *Christa x*

Suddenly Chloe realises. It's to all the swimmers. She looks at the names at the top of the message. Kat Glanville. It doesn't mean anything to her, yet she's sure she knows Kat. They're of an age, she reckons. It must have been at school. She could just ask Kat, but she's embarrassed. If – when – they met before, Kat didn't like her. If only Chloe could remember.

~

It's four in the morning. Chloe's been watching the red digits on her clock count down the hours till dawn. Beside her Evie's sleeping quietly. Her pyjama top has ridden up, and Chloe strokes her pale tummy. Life would have been so different without Evie, but she wouldn't have had it any other way. Without

154

Evie, what would she be doing? She'd still be working. Some crappy job somewhere. Chloe knows she's better than any of the jobs she's had, better too than the men she's hooked up with. If she hadn't been working in advertisements in the Truro paper she'd never have met Tony, whose wife didn't understand him, and whose children irritated him, and then there would be no Evie.

Chloe reaches for her mobile on the bedside table. The screen flares brightly in the dark bedroom. Facebook. Messages. Nothing.

~

A hot summer's day. Blue sky. Chloe kicked off from the gravel and the swing rose higher, as her legs stretched and bent. To her right the church tower dipped behind a tree and rose again; she watched this arc for a moment until she felt queasy and let her legs trail. With a scuffle of gravel the swing jerked to a halt.

Amy sat on the neighbouring swing, walking tiny steps to and fro with her feet, sipping at a can of Diet Coke, watching the group of boys kicking a football round the weed-choked tennis court.

"Hey, you never said, are you coming to that party?"

"Don't think so," Chloe said.

"Go on."

Chloe fingered the rusty chains of the swing and her hands came away smelling of iron. "I won't know anyone except you."

"It's not just me. Susie's coming, and Jo, Michelle...Ryan...Simon...Nina..."

Chloe wished she had a tissue to wipe her hands on. They'd just finished their exams; no more school until Penzance sixth form in the autumn. Amy had heard from her brother Pete that some kids from Penzance were having a beach party at the weekend to celebrate the end of exams. St Michael kids could come too, if they knew anyone to get an invite off. Amy knew all this because her two brothers had motorbikes, and went drinking with people in Penzance.

"I don't like beach parties," Chloe said.

The truth was embarrassing. Chloe, who'd lived all her life just a few miles from the coast, hated the sea. It was fine to look at from a distance. The colours, the blue, green and grey, the white crests, were fine. But down on the sand, the roar of the breakers, the salty spray exploding, the surging water rushing up the beach sucking at shells and shingle – that terrified her.

"You don't have to swim," Amy said, more gently.

"Well, I can't bloody swim, can I?"

"I mean no one will expect you to."

"You go."

"I will." Amy slid off her swing, stalked to the bin, and chucked in her can.

One of the boys yelled at her from the tennis court; she waved, then set off across the grass to the netting. Chloe watched her. Amy, with her sun-bleached hair, and golden tan, and denim cut-offs, was drawing away from Chloe. Amy was about to dive into something new, leaving Chloe trembling on the side. Chloe pushed off again, and the swing rocked back and forth.

Three more kids came into the park, shrieking and running towards the tennis court. Chloe felt alone suddenly, at the cusp of her life, waiting.

~

"Kathryn! Lorna for you."

Kathryn swore quietly. Downstairs her mother's voice, and Lorna's. Lorna hardly ever came to her house. Now they'd left school, Kathryn wondered if she'd ever see her again. Lorna wasn't staying on for the sixth form. Not that Kathryn was sure she was going to either; she just didn't have any other ideas. Who'd employ someone who looked like her?

She heaved off her bed, straightened her hair as best she could. The mirror showed a fat, hot-looking person in neon pink shell trousers, and a brightly patterned baggy T-shirt. Jesus. Kathryn grabbed the matching shell jacket off the back of the door and forced her arms into it. It was a boiling day but she'd rather be hotter and covered up.

Lorna was in the kitchen drinking lemonade while Kathryn's mother emptied the dishwasher.

"Hi," Kathryn said.

"Hey, I was passing, thought I'd call in. Are you going to Sennen tomorrow?"

"No," Kathryn said shortly. "Why would I be going to Sennen?"

"The party, silly!"

"What party?"

"The end-of-exams party. Didn't you know?"

157

"Nope. I guess that means I'm not invited."

"I'm sure you are." Her mother crashed two baking trays into a drawer. "I expect they just forgot to ask you."

Oh, for fuck's sake, Kathryn screamed to herself. Of course they fucking didn't.

"Whose party is it?"

"I think Nick Treloar and Emma Freeman are organising it."

Oh great. The young lovers of the fifth year.

"Are you going?" Kathryn asked Lorna.

"I might. Everyone's invited."

They talked for a few moments about the exams, about leaving school, then Lorna put her glass in the sink – Kathryn knew her mother would go ape at that – and re-tied her scrawny ginger ponytail.

"Maybe see you tomorrow then?" she said at the front door.

"No," said Kathryn.

Kathryn Smith at a beach party. No way. No fucking way.

~

Heather is nosy. She wishes she could ask Chloe about that Hallowe'en so long ago. She has no business to know, except that she was there, beside Guy as he talked to the kids at the phone box, and she was there beside Guy in the car, the next morning, the morning after her life changed, the morning that life had changed for the Langfords.

Chloe doesn't seem like the kind of girl to run off with someone else's man. She's too timid, too diffident. More like the kind of girl whose man would be stolen.

158

Guy went to Amy Langford's funeral. He told Heather about it. A cold, blue winter's day, that clouded the breath. It was on a Saturday so schoolkids and teachers could go. There was standing-room only in the parish church of St Michael. Amy's father and her brothers helped carry the coffin. June Langford pale as watered-down milk. There were so many flowers, so many young girls weeping. Girls who'd grown up in the village with Amy; girls she'd met at the sixth form.

Chloe Johnstone wasn't there, and neither was Amy's boyfriend.

~

"Chloe, oh-my-God, I have to see you. Can I come over?"

Sunday morning. Amy on the phone early. Chloe was still in the T-shirt she'd slept in. She was sticky round the neck and under the arms.

"Sure. Give me half an hour."

"Are you alone?"

"No, we're all here."

"Meet me in the village then. Outside the Arc. Pete's going to drop me off."

The party. It would be about the beach party Amy went to the day before at Sennen. The one Chloe could have gone to but she was too afraid of the waves or, rather, too afraid of someone finding out she was afraid of the waves.

She showered quickly and put on her jeans and a T-shirt. She was hot before she got to the end of Barrow Lane. The track was bumpy with long-dried-out mud. Foxgloves and poppies wilted in the dusty hedges. Butterflies, bees, an iridescent damselfly. Chloe walked on into St Michael, swallowing a dark lump of foreboding. I'm being stupid, she thought. She wished she had gone to Sennen. It was like she'd missed out on something important, a rite of passage, all because of a consuming fear.

Amy was loitering outside the pub. Her hair was in a ponytail, and she had brittle black kohl round her eyes. Chloe had tried to run an eye pencil along her inner lower lid like Amy did; her eyes spilled into tears and she was left with nothing but a few watery dots of grit. Amy's flowered dress was very short; she wore sparkly sandals Chloe had never seen, which showed scarlet toenails.

Chloe cast her eyes down her own black T-shirt and stone-washed jeans, and felt young and frumpy, and as though she had been taken out of her life and put back at some other time, a time where Amy was glamorous and sophisticated, not the girl who'd passed Chloe a stick of Wrigley's under the desk, who'd stuck up posters of rabbits inside her locker.

"The most amazing thing has happened," Amy started.

And Chloe felt again that darkness shift inside her.

"I went to Sennen yesterday. You should have come. I met this boy. This guy. He's gorgeous. He asked me out."

"OK," said Chloe, thinking: *yes, this is it.*

On Amy's neck was a soft red bruise. She'd made no effort to hide it, had even tied her hair up to show it off.

"Aren't you interested? Aren't you excited?"

"Well, yes, I guess so. What's his name? Where does he live?"

"Oliver Bradshaw. Olly. He's seventeen. He's doing A-levels at Penzance. He's got a car." Amy fingered her bruise.

"So will you as soon as you get your test."

"Yes, but he can take me out now. He's going to get Dad to check the car over for him. And don't you see? When we get to Penzance, he'll still be there in the year above us."

"So what's he like?"

They'd turned the corner by the pharmacy and the off-licence, blinds down, closed on Sunday. Chloe's throat closed up, wished somewhere was open so she could buy a bottle of water.

"He's gorgeous. Tall. Brown hair. Green eyes."

"If he's already doing A-levels, why was he at the party?"

"He knew the Penzance gang. He came with a few friends."

Chloe stole a glance at Amy beside her. Slim golden legs, glossy nails. She was different, yet she wasn't. Chloe was embarrassed to ask, but she had to.

"So, you and…Olly. Have you…you know?"

"What, had sex?" Amy asked.

"Well, yes."

"Not yet." Amy threw an arm round Chloe's shoulders. "But we will. I know it. And there's no one I'd rather do it with."

"What do your parents say?"

Amy opened the heavy wooden gate to the cemetery.

"Your parents?" Chloe asked again, closing the gate with a soft thump.

"I haven't said much," Amy said at last. "Just that I'd met a really nice boy, and he was a year older than me, and he'd be at the sixth form. And Mum went on a bit about how having a boyfriend could screw up my A-levels, and I told her I wasn't stupid, and I wouldn't let that happen. Dad thinks I'm too young. I said I'll be seventeen in September, but he just grunted like he does. Olly's going to bring his car over so he can meet them. That's a good idea, isn't it?"

"I suppose so."

They were in the first field of the cemetery, the old part. The graves here dated back a hundred years or more, lichen covered, cracked and leaning. A few bunches of bright flowers; down by the bottom hedge a man was leaning over, tending a grave. Beside the footpath were rows of marble squares marking the interred ashes. Amy's great-aunt was one of those. Amy paused a moment by the marker, then drifted on, following the track into the next field. New memorials, some without headstones, just wooden crosses. The last grave was a long hump, buried in flowers, now wilting and turning brown in the heat.

"I'm so happy," Amy said.

~

Nothing will be the same again, Chloe thought later, back home. Her mother had gone out to see Rod, her boyfriend, who was a solicitor at the firm where she was a secretary. Chloe and Millie liked Rod, were happy their mother had at last agreed to marry him. The only thing that upset Chloe about this was the thought of moving to Rod's big house in Truro, away from Amy, from drifting apart from her best friend but, that hot Sunday afternoon, she realised that had already happened.

Even if this Olly Bradshaw didn't last long, Amy had changed.

Chloe was suddenly furious with herself for not going to the party. Not that she could have stopped this guy turning up and whisking Amy off into his car or whatever, not that she could have halted the marching beat of time, but at least she could have been there, been part of it.

~

Kathryn and her mother struggled through the holiday crowds in Market Jew Street. Kathryn was boiling in her shell-suit jacket. She was glad to get into the cool interior of Boots. While her mother went searching for Elastoplast and Savlon, a support bandage and dental floss, Kathryn wandered over to the rows of cosmetics. Vivid nail varnishes, smoky eye shadows, metallic eye-liners. She glanced at her face in the narrow mirror on the Rimmel display. She had spots, in the crease by her nose, and above her eyebrows. She had no cheekbones. Just this tiny slice of her face screamed *Fat Ugly Person*. Perhaps she should get some new make-up. All she had were the bits and bobs she'd played around with, neon and glittery. She picked up a palette of eyeshadow in lilac and grey, another in moth-wing browns. She should really look at her skin, at her colouring. Look at nothing bigger than the pores and the blemishes in the mirror. Ignore the rest of her body, just concentrate on the face. Choose flattering colours, not the loudest, most vivid, she could find. No more electric blue and viridian eyeshadows, no more magenta lipstick.

"Hiya."

Kathryn swung round, a tester of shell-pink lipstick in her hand. It was Lorna. She'd had her limp sandy hair cut into a bob; she wore hoop earrings.

"Thought it was you," Lorna said.

163

Well obviously. No one else in Penzance looked like Kathryn Smith from behind. In a pink shell-suit.

"Sennen was great."

"Sennen?" Kathryn echoed. Of course. That party the other week. The beach party.

From somewhere deep and twisted came a memory: back in Birmingham her mother telling her how useful it would be to swim so when she moved to Cornwall she could go to beaches with friends, and how, later, alone, she'd fantasised about these beach parties and Debbie Green coming to stay, and how they'd just be two more slim, beautiful girls in swimsuits.

"You went then?"

"Yeah, I went with Davy. I think he fancies me. And you'll never guess who turned up out of the blue?"

"Michael Jackson."

"Oh, don't be so stupid. It was Olly Bradshaw."

Earth tremors.

"What was he doing there?" Kathryn asked, aware she was suddenly hotter than ever, despite the cooler air in the shop. She shoved the lipstick back into the display, fiddled with some nail varnishes.

"He came with some of his mates. He's got a car now. He looked so cool. I wouldn't stand a chance with him, and neither would you."

Kathryn tugged her hair over her cheek, clacked together the two bottles of nail varnish she was holding.

"He got off with this girl from St Michael. Looked like a bloody model, all long legs, blonde hair, cropped top. He only had eyes for her."

Thank God I didn't go.

Kathryn trailed home a few steps behind her mother. In her hand was a small plastic bag of make-up she'd bought in Boots, once Lorna had gone (to call on Davy to see if he wanted to go to the beach).

Lorna and Davy, together. Kathryn hadn't seen that one coming. She felt betrayed. They'd probably been laughing at her with the others. As for the others. Cool people, glamorous people, thin people. Girls in bikinis, boys in wetsuits, skin sparkling with sand crystals and sea spray. Nick and Emma, who'd organised the party, doing the moves from *Dirty Dancing*. There was beer and cider; people were smoking cigarettes and joints; Lorna hinted at other, darker, pick-ups. Girls and boys winding round each other and disappearing behind rocks. Olly Bradshaw and some hopelessly beautiful girl from St Michael.

~

Are you living in your old house? O xx
> *Yes x*
Orchid Cottage, Barrow Lane? Which isn't a cottage. Xx
> *That's it x*

That line: which isn't a cottage. Chloe sighs. The strangest, silliest things can bring tears.

Get a grip. She types Kat Glanville's name into Facebook. Nothing. She tries a few variations – Katherine, Katharine, Katrine, Kathryn – and still nothing.

The doorbell rings.

"Door, Mummy!" Evie shouts.

Chloe's not expecting anyone; she doesn't have many visitors. It'll be the postman. It won't be Millie. Chloe hasn't heard anything from her at all.

It's not the postman. It's Jasmine Lovell.

"Hi," she says.

"Hi." Chloe relaxes. "You've come to see Evie? Evie! Visitor for you! How's your dad?"

"He's a bit better since the operation." Jas heels off her muddy boots in the hall. "Is it OK to come round? I kind of want a breather. Different people. It's just me and Mum at the moment, and it's so tense. I've left college, you know, because of the baby."

"What baby?" asks Evie. "Have you got a baby?"

"Not yet, Pumpkin, but I will soon."

"Pumpkin? I'm not a Pumpkin. I'm Evie."

"Sorry. Evie. My dad called me Pumpkin when I was little."

"Would you like a drink?" Chloe asks.

"Tea would be lovely, thanks." Jas looks up and swipes a long dark twist of hair over her shoulder. "I can see Mum will be selling your work in the gallery pretty soon, Evie."

When Chloe comes back into the living room with a tray of tea and juice, Evie and Jas are laughing together, playing something loud and complicated with a shabby Iggle Piggle, Ears, some random playing cards and a kitchen-paper tube. Jas grins up at Chloe. Chloe hesitates. She's been unfair to Evie, keeping her at home, all to herself. She should be out with other people, other kids, making her own friends. She might even have lost Zac and Luca now. Chloe will have to call Millie soon and tell her there's no swimming on Sunday. It's Chloe's birthday in a few days' time. She wonders what Millie's going to do, whether or not she'll remember.

~

Heather was surprised when Jas said she would go and see Chloe so soon. Probably wants other company, she thought, someone who doesn't keep saying the dreadful words: surgery, radiotherapy, laryngectomy, tracheostomy.

Heather is sorting out some boxes of greetings cards, arranging them on the counter. What will happen to the gallery? It doesn't make much, certainly not in the winter. She and Jas can cover it between them for a while. Heather's friend, who helped out before, has got problems now with elderly parents over in Hayle. Heather knows she has a lot of difficult thinking to do about the future. Decisions she may have to make all by herself. Guy is going to need so much nursing at home after the surgery, while he learns how to speak again, how to live everyday life breathing through a hole in his throat. And then a new baby, whose ferocious shrieks will only emphasise Guy's silence.

~

Chloe shuts the door behind Jas, amazed she has been there for a couple of hours playing with Evie, meeting Ears and the other toys, admiring Evie's drawings. Jas has gone, taking a bright abstract of colour and squiggles with her, carefully folded in her jacket pocket. Chloe smiles at Evie, who's napping on the sofa under a blanket, and carries the mugs out to the kitchen to wash.

She never expected to like Jas so much. Jas is half her age, but they're not so different. They'll both be single mothers in the village. Their children will be at school together. When Evie finally said she wanted to rest, and curled up on the sofa, watching CBeebies, Chloe and Jas went into the kitchen and talked. Jas told Chloe about Guy, about what the surgery would mean for him. How, if it didn't work, there was little that could be done. About how Guy might never meet his grandchild. Jas also told Chloe about her boyfriend – or, rather, ex-boyfriend – Andrew, the baby's father. How she never really felt comfortable having a relationship with him. Not that there was anything exactly wrong with him, just that Jas didn't want that kind of commitment, but it stung knowing he's moved on so quickly. And yet, Jas would be most happy if she could bring up the child without any interference from him. And somehow, Chloe ended up telling Jas how she'd met Tony Connolly, and slept with him, knowing he was married, and how, once, when he didn't pull out in time, she didn't take the morning-after pill, as her head told her to. Instead she waited and counted the days and hoped and feared, and hoped again. And once she knew, she broke up with Tony Connolly because there was no future there for her and her child. And he still doesn't know Evie exists.

"I'd love to look after Evie while you're swimming," Jas said. "Mum could drop me off and you two could travel together. And if your sister…if there's a problem…" Jas blushed, trailed off.

"It was Tony we were rowing about," Chloe said. "And about Evie. She doesn't understand why I did what I did. But it's different for her. She married a doctor. They're well-off. It's a different life altogether."

"I know there's no swimming this week. But, after that, if you'd like me to, just give me a call."

And somehow Chloe also told Jas it was her birthday the next week, and Jas said perhaps Chloe could have a drink with her and Heather, as long as Guy was stable.

So now, as Chloe rinses the mugs under the tap, and hears Evie stirring next door with a *Muuuuuummy* she thinks that maybe, at last, things are looking up and she is making friends in the village again, making a new life.

~

Heather and Jas turn off the upper corridor into a short passage which leads to the ward. There's a metal serving trolley parked, stained with the remains of food, another trolley of bedding, and a wheelchair. Heather rolls up her sleeves to wash at the sink. It's all so familiar so quickly: the ward, the smells, the soap dispenser.

Cassie is on the nurses' station. She drops her pen and jumps up.

"Mr Rowan's on the ward," she says. "He wants to have a word with you. Nothing bad. Go on through. I'll get him."

Guy is sitting up, a paperback open on his knees. His breathing is hard but quiet. Pale gloop drips from his food pump into the NG tube. There's a bowl of crushed ice; another of blood-stained water.

"Are you spitting?" Heather asks. She remembers this from the oesophageal tumour. Sometimes Guy couldn't even swallow melting ice, had to swill it round his mouth and spit.

"Yeah. Throat isn't working. Could go down wrong way," he splutters.

"Heather, Jasmine, good evening." Phil Rowan sweeps the curtains closed around them. "I came to see Guy earlier and I was going to call you, but he said he thought you'd be coming up. The biopsies are back and they show that yes, it is malignant, which we knew all along, really. When we go to theatre, I shall have to take out the larynx, the thyroid, and the parathyroid, part of the pharynx. I'm not sure at this stage if we'll need the plastic surgeons to do reconstructive work. We might, we might not."

Heather and Jas glance at each other.

"But," Rowan pulls out a mobile phone and taps on the screen. "I have a theatre booked for Guy now. How does the 20th sound? Friday next week?"

"That's great," Jas says.

"So soon," Heather says. "I mean that's good, of course, just..."

"Just that Guy's only recently had surgery. I know. The thing is we do need to act fast on this one, particularly as I'm not here for much longer."

"I'm happy," Guy says. "Let's do it."

"It's not easy organising a procedure like this." Rowan pockets his phone again. "I have to get the theatre, the right anaesthetist, the plastics people on standby, and someone who can put

170

a J-Peg feeding tube in as well – they go straight into the stomach."

"As well as the NG?" Heather asks.

"We'll keep that one in as it's there and Guy so hates having them put back." Rowan grins at Guy. "We'll use the J-Peg once it's in. But, if there are any problems with it, we've got the NG too."

"How long will the surgery take?" asks Jas.

"Twelve, thirteen hours maybe. It does depend if we need plastics."

Later, they kiss Guy goodnight, and replace his bag of dirty washing with clean socks and shirts. When Heather's rinsing her hands once more at the sink, Jas nods to the Ladies, says, "Sorry, I need to go."

"OK, I'll wait here."

Heather hovers by a noticeboard reading the staff adverts. Offers for car-sharing, a monthly pizza night, a lottery syndicate.

"Heather."

She spins round. Phil Rowan beside her, putting on a sports jacket.

"You realise this is a very risky procedure, but it is the only way."

"Yes, I understand that."

"Afterwards, he'll need to stay in for some time – maybe up to eight weeks. And, even if all goes well, he'll need radiotherapy." Rowan hesitates. "The other day when I debulked the tumour…I knew I had to act immediately with that airway."

"Thank you," Heather whispers. She knows what his unspoken words are.

"It's going to be very hard for Guy," Rowan says. "Everyone's voice is important, of course, but for Guy, his job…We'll fit him with a valve, get him to a speech therapist and all that, but he might struggle mentally, you know, with the reality of it. I'm not sure if it's really hit him."

"I think it has," Heather says.

Jas is walking back from the ward.

"Get some rest." Rowan squeezes Heather's arm. "You too, Jasmine. I'll see you soon."

~

Chloe bites the bullet and calls Millie. She calls the house phone, not her mobile, hopes that Matt will pick up. He does.

"Hi Chloe, how are you doing?" He doesn't sound any different.

"Fine thanks." She hopes she doesn't sound manically breezy. "Is Millie around?"

"Sorry, she's just gone round to see a neighbour."

"OK, look, I just wanted to say I'm not swimming on Sunday. We don't have a class when it's school hols. So…um…Evie won't be visiting."

"I'll let her know. Swimming the next weekend?"

"Yes, we're back then, but I might not have to leave Evie with you two. A friend's offered to look after her sometimes, to give you both a break."

"It's no problem having her," Matt says.

~

Heather closes the gallery at Saturday lunchtime and dashes back to pick up Jas from home. The Langfords have done the MOT work on Guy's Audi.

As Heather pulls into the garage forecourt, and Pete Langford looks up from the raised bonnet he's hiding behind – sandy hair gone pale, athlete's body turned to fat – Jas says, "I'll drive up to Dad sometimes. I can use his car."

"Are you sure? I know you hate it."

"You can't drive up every time. We can take it in turns or something."

Heather smiles at her. "Thanks. As long as you're well enough. You have someone else to think of too."

~

The shop door bursts open with a jangle. Kat glances up from her magazine, and throws it down on the floor behind the desk. It's Flora Hosking, face flushed from the cold air, bright hair windblown.

"Hello butterfly lady," she says.

"Hello Flora," Kat says.

The door's still open, and an icy wind knifes into the shop. Windchimes clatter discordantly. Flora runs to the door.

"Come on," she shouts into the street.

Jason and Thomas come in. Jason shuts the door with a definite click.

"How are you?" he asks.

"Good, thanks," Kat says. "Shame there's no swimming tomorrow, isn't it?"

"Actually, we thought we might go for a swim this week anyway," Jason says. "I've got half-term off. Well, most of it. Just a couple of regulars on Friday."

"You're swimming at the hotel?"

"Yes – do you think I'm crazy?" Jason asks, looking uncertain. "I thought we'd be OK. Thomas is pretty good. Flora would stay in the shallow end."

"I can swim." Thomas reaches up to swish a paddle on a set of chimes. "I can swim better than Dad."

"That's true," Jason says.

"Sounds great," Kat says. "I miss it when we don't have a lesson."

"Why not come with us?" he asks.

Flora beams at Kat. "Yes, come with us."

"I could do with an extra pair of hands. I've never done this before. Taken them to a pool, I mean. That's why I took the lessons."

"When are you going?" Kat's thinking quickly. She can shut *Imago*. Whenever.

"Oh, of course, the shop. I think kids are allowed until six?"

"I'm not open on Wednesday."

"Let's go on Wednesday then." Jason smiles at Kat. "That'd be great."

"We can have cakes afterwards," Flora says. "Or chips."

"I'm sure we can." Jason flicks open his wallet and hands Kat a card. "Here's my number. Mobile reception isn't very good at home, so the landline's best."

Kat reaches out to take the card. Jason's fingers just an inch from hers.

"I'll give you my number," she says quickly, ripping a page off the desk pad. It has a tiny Monarch in the corner: orange, black, white.

"Great, thanks." Jason stuffs it in his jeans pocket. "OK, Flora, do you want that little tin?"

Kat wraps an enamel box for Flora, decorated with a flight of butterflies. Kat wonders how Flora's getting on at school, whether the other kids are still bullying her, whether she, like Kathryn Smith before her, is deliriously happy to be off for half-term.

"We'll see you Wednesday then," Jason says, as he ushers the children out.

"Wednesday," Kat repeats.

The door shuts.

Jason Hosking, Garden Maintenance, says the card. *Lawn cutting, hedge trimming, planting, pruning, fencing.*

"Wednesday," she says again, aloud.

~

On Sunday afternoon Heather stumbles into bed. She's so very tired. Jas has gone to visit Guy on her own in the Audi. Heather's seen a change in Jas lately. She's become steely, determined. She's driving. She's deleted Andrew from her Facebook, and some mutual friends. She's turning in onto herself, onto the iron core Heather always knew she had.

Sundays without swimming are strange. No watching the clock for the time to get ready, no packing of towel and goggles into her bag. No quickening of fear inside – because she still feels that flare of anxiety. Even now, when she can finally move through water by herself, it still feels as alien as if she's launched herself into the sky.

She checks the bedside clock. Jas should be there by now. She's taken a bag of clean clothes for Guy, a couple of books, some mail. Perhaps they'll talk about the baby.

There's under a week to go till surgery. I've been here before, Heather reminds herself. The long days of treatment, preparation for the oesophagectomy. Last time around, when she said *oesophageal cancer* to anyone, they'd inhale sharply, shake their heads, and seem to write Guy off. But he got through it. That endless day, listening to the radio with Jas, while he was in theatre, having his ribs opened, lung deflated, gullet excised, stomach refashioned. The next day on the ward with so many drips and drains. But he survived, and came home with a vast puckered crescent across his side and back. A warrior's tattoo.

Heather wakes over an hour later. She's sticky, and her hair's knotted. Her throat is so dry. She needs a drink. As she staggers out of bed, still dizzy from sleep, she hears the front door opening.

"I'm upstairs, hang on," she croaks.

Jas stands in the hall with a bag of Guy's washing in one hand, his car keys dangling from the other.

"How is he?"

"Not so great today," Jas says. "His breathing isn't good so he's on the nebuliser and steroids again, the tube came out overnight, they haven't put it back."

"Those fucking tubes."

"They think he ripped it out in his sleep."

"Surgery still on?"

"Surgery still on."

Heather starts down the stairs.

"I can't imagine him not having a voice," Jas says.

"He'll get speaking with the valve very soon, I'm sure. He won't want to not speak."

"He must speak," Jas says fiercely. "He must speak to my baby. It'll never know his real voice."

"His real voice went some time ago," Heather says, gently.

She can hear Guy's voice in her mind. She remembers his words the night they met. She'll never forget his voice.

"People lose their sight and their hearing and no one really thinks anything of it," Jas says. "But losing your voice? Most people don't even know that's possible." She drops the laundry bag and feels her throat. "Just this little thing here, that makes your words."

Heather feels her larynx, just below the skin. Gentle pressure makes her nauseous. She swallows and feels it rise and fall, recalls a conversation with Guy years ago, when he told her how dangerous it was to hit someone in the larynx. It can kill them, he'd said.

~

Chloe wakes early on her birthday, to the gentle rumbling of rain that's been falling for ages and isn't going to stop any time soon. She leaves Evie snuffling under the quilt and pads off to the bathroom.

177

Elaine and Rod are coming down in the afternoon; Rod's driving back, and Elaine's staying overnight. She'll look after Evie while Chloe meets Heather and Jas at the Archangel. Chloe wonders what she'll say to her mother if Millie doesn't come round or drop off a card or anything.

Just before noon the doorbell goes. Chloe looks out through the rain-spattered glass. Matt's car is parked on the lane.

"Hello, happy birthday," Matt says. He holds out a pink envelope, speckled by the rain, and a bottle of prosecco.

"Thanks. Come in."

"Can't stop." Matt looks awkward. "Millie says she's really sorry, but she won't be able to call round today. She did tell you we were going away for a few days?"

"No," Chloe says.

"Only the cottage," Matt says. "We're leaving this afternoon."

"Right. OK."

Matt's parents' cottage on the edge of Dartmoor. He and Millie and the boys stay sometimes in school holidays, but Chloe had no idea they were planning it this half-term. But surely Millie wouldn't arrange that just to avoid seeing Chloe on her birthday because she'd spoken to Olly Bradshaw on Facebook?

"Have a lovely birthday, and we'll see you soon." He kisses the air by her cheek and backs out into the rain again.

She watches the car bounce up the rutted lane. Suddenly Matt brakes, then his reversing lights come on. A van coming the other way. Matt backs into a scooped out verge, and the van trundles on slowly. It stops outside Chloe's house. And then she reads what's on the side of the van. The bell goes again and, this time, when she opens the door, there's a young woman wearing a baseball hat over lavender-washed hair, holding a giant bouquet of pink roses and lilies, tied up with a glossy pale green ribbon.

"Chloe Johnstone?"

Chloe opens her arms for the flowers. Even in the cold and the damp, the heady heartbreaking smell of lilies. Millie, Chloe thinks. No, Mum and Rod, of course.

She carries the flowers through to the kitchen. Evie gazes wide-eyed at them.

"Can I have that ribbon?"

"Of course," Chloe says absently, opening the tiny white envelope.

Happy birthday Beautiful
I remembered!
O xxx

~

Kat feels guilty that she hasn't been in touch with Heather and, because there was no swimming at the weekend, she hasn't seen her. While it's quiet in the shop she rings Heather's mobile and wanders round, phone to ear, watching the rain slicing the panes, and the purple sky outside.

"How are things?" Kat asks when Heather answers.

"He's having the surgery on Friday," Heather says. "Jas and I, we go up every day. One or both of us. I'm going up soon, and Jas is going to mind the gallery. It seems the only way to deal with it all. Oh, we're meeting Chloe tonight for a drink when I get back. It's her birthday."

Kat picks up a caterpillar-shaped pencil sharpener, twiddles it in her hand.

"Say happy birthday for me," she says at last.

"Will do."

"I'm swimming tomorrow," Kat says. "With Jason and his kids."

"Jason? From swimming?"

"Yeah, they've been in the shop a couple of times. He's taking the kids to the pool and invited me too."

"Is this like a date?" Heather asks.

"I don't know," Kat says. "I don't think so."

~

Chloe stuffs the roses and lilies into a large square vase of green glass, and stands it on the kitchen table. She reads the little card once more. A tiny pink rosebud printed in the corner. A florist's rounded writing in black biro. But Olly's words.

I remembered.

He probably didn't, Chloe thinks. He probably saw it on Facebook. She should thank him. While Evie twirls round the living room with the green ribbon on her head, Chloe opens Facebook on her phone. Lots of birthday greetings. She skims down them all. Nothing from Olly. She's in the middle of typing him a message when the doorbell goes again. Elaine and Rod.

~

How quickly this all becomes normal, Heather thinks, sliding down the car window to take the parking ticket from the machine. The red and white barbers' pole barrier rises, and she moves forward. She trundles down the rows, eventually finds a gap in a corner beside a tree.

She scoops up the *Times* and some mail for Guy off the passenger seat, and reaches for his clothes bag in the back. She can't bring him any treats because he can't eat. When she rang the ward last night the nurse told her the feeding tube had been re-sited, but Guy was waiting for an X-ray to check its position.

Inside, Heather can see another man sitting beside the bed, his back to the ward. Silver hair, tweed sports jacket. A briefcase on the floor. Guy is wearing the nebuliser over his face. Heather goes to the cubicle.

"How are you?" she asks Guy, and says "Hello Paddy" to the visitor.

"Heather, I'm so sorry to see Guy back in here," Paddy says, putting a notebook in the briefcase, and a pen in his inner pocket. He holds out a hand to Guy. "I'll see you again soon. Best of luck for Friday."

Heather watches Paddy leave.

"Did you tell him you were here?" she asks.

"I emailed him," Guy croaks, removing the nebuliser.

Paddy was another oesophagectomy patient, who had been in the bed next to Guy last time around. Another heavy drinker, another ex-smoker. He and Guy have been in touch since then. He's a solicitor from the other side of Helston.

"It wasn't just a social visit," Guy says.

181

Heather pauses unloading Guy's clothes and stashing them in the locker.

"What d'you mean?" she asks, but she thinks she already knows the answer.

"He's doing my will."

Through the radiotherapy and the chemo, through the oesophagectomy, Guy refused to make a will. Even when he despaired, said he'd never make it through, that the cancer was stronger than him, he refused to make a will.

Heather shuts the bedside locker with too loud a thump. He's only being sensible, making a will. Most men of his age have already made one.

Guy reaches for her hand.

"If anything bad happens…"

"Guy."

"On Friday." He breaks off, coughs, swallows spit, wheezes. "It won't be done in time."

"Nothing bad's going to happen on Friday." Heather fusses with the bedcover.

She glances round the ward. The curtains drawn around a corner bed; a vaguely human shape bulges through the material. Voices of other patients' visitors, suddenly too loud. The rumble of the tea trolley approaching. Guy shakes his head at the tea lady.

"Friday will be a good day." Heather perches on the side of the bed. "Get rid of this bastard tumour once and for all."

"It'll come back. It always does. That's why I knew it was time to do the will."

Heather's about to speak, but she doesn't. Guy making a will doesn't really change anything at all. The danger was there before, as it is now.

Guy's closed his eyes. His skin is sweaty, waxy. His breathing is hard again. Heather leans over for the nebuliser, pushes it into Guy's hand, lifts his hand to his face. He doesn't open his eyes. Talking to Paddy has exhausted him. Heather watches the tea lady pour drinks for patients and visitors. The curtains in the corner swish open. Cassie comes out carrying a urine bottle. She smiles at Heather, mouths a *hello* on her way to the sluice. Heather sits there, holding Guy's cold hand, watching the juddering of his airway. His hand on the nebuliser slips; he's asleep. Heather gets up gently, straightens the blanket, gathers her bags.

~

Chloe first met Oliver Bradshaw by accident. He'd been coming over to Amy's for a couple of weeks and, although Chloe and Amy had seen each other, it had never been on the days he was around.

But Chloe knew it all. About a week after they met at Sennen, Olly picked up Amy in his rusty Micra and they drove out to some remote spot in Penwith and had uncomfortable, awkward sex in the car. Chloe knew this because Amy had phoned her that night, gloating about the sex, then embarrassed because she was sore, and anxious as to whether Olly really knew what he was doing with the Durex, and whether it really was his first time as he claimed, and should she go on the Pill now, and then gushing about the romance, and the blue sky, and the moorland, and how she was in love.

One hot afternoon that summer, Chloe was loitering in the village talking to a couple of the other girls from school. They were eating ice-cream cones, and Chloe was just wondering whether to go into the shop and get one herself, when she saw Amy and Olly further along the street, looking in the gift shop window. Chloe left the girls finishing their cones and ran up the road.

"Hello stranger," she said to Amy, and wished she could gulp back the words because they sounded needy and hostile.

"Hi," said Amy. "Chloe, this is Olly. Olly, Chloe, my oldest friend."

"I've heard all about you," Chloe said.

"All good, I'm sure," Olly said, tightening his arm round Amy, squeezing her to him.

Jesus, these lines are out of a soap, Chloe thought.

"All good, silly." Amy giggled and gently punched Olly.

Amy was right about his eyes. They were a clear green. The green of moss rather than seawater. His hair was tawny with flecks of gold and auburn. He looked older than his years, more man than boy.

"I'm so happy you two have met at last," Amy said, as though it hadn't been her keeping them apart. "We were going to the park, Chloe. Come with us?"

Chloe fell into step with them. They passed the girls she'd been talking to. Amy smiled and waved at them. She's changed, Chloe thought sadly. It took so little time.

In the park they sat on the swings, Amy in the middle, holding hands with Olly as they rocked to and fro. Chloe remembered the day she sat here with Amy, when Amy asked if she would be going to Sennen. It was like Chloe knew, that day, something huge was going to happen. She pushed off the ground and swung higher; the church tower swooped, making her queasy once again. Instead she looked at the tennis court, and the tangled hedge beyond it, until she came to earth again. Amy and Olly had pulled the chains of their swings together, and were kissing. Is this for my benefit, Chloe asked silently, or would they have done it if they'd been alone? Probably, alone, they'd have done a lot more. They'd have holed up in the kids' wooden castle, which everyone knew was always littered with condoms and cigarette butts. As Chloe thought this, Amy and Olly drew apart, and Olly flicked open a packet of cigarettes to Amy. She pulled one out delicately, leaned in for him to light it.

"Chloe?" He reached round Amy and waved the box.

"No thanks," Chloe said.

She knew Amy had never smoked before she met Olly.

~

"Those are lovely," Elaine says, tweaking a rose in the flower vase. "Who are they from? Millie and Matt?"

"Mummy's swimming friends," says Evie, pulling a birthday parcel out of a carrier bag. "Can I open this for you, Mummy?"

Chloe scrunches the little card in her pocket. *Swimming friends* was the first thing that had come into her head when Evie was looking at the flowers. *They're from my swimming friends,* she'd said to Evie, knowing Elaine and Rod would ask, and having to keep her story straight with everyone.

"How about a cup of tea?" Rod nudges the kettle. "You sit down, Chloe, and get started on those presents."

"Did you know Millie and Matt are going away today?" Chloe asks.

"She texted me this morning," Elaine says. "I think it was a last minute thing."

"Can I open this?" Evie waves a parcel. She's already started tearing the paper.

"Evie and I have some secret things to do when you go out tonight." Elaine ruffles Evie's hair.

Later, when Elaine is playing with Evie, and Rod has gone home, Chloe locks herself in the bathroom with her phone to finish her message to Olly. The card is still in her pocket. She's not sure if Elaine believes her that the flowers came from her swimming friends but, if they didn't, and they didn't come from Millie, there aren't many other contenders. Chloe never goes out; she never meets people. She doesn't date men. She can't do any of these things because of Evie. She loves her constant companion but, sometimes, when she realises how isolated she has become, she feels a creeping panic. It's eighteen months till Evie starts school. Chloe's not sure she can wait that long to claw back some kind of life.

Thank you for the flowers. That was a lovely surprise. I'm going out for a birthday drink with some friends tonight, while my Mum looks after Evie. C x

You see, Olly Bradshaw. I do have a life. I am going for a birthday drink. Chloe shakes her head at herself in the bathroom mirror. What's it all about? Why is he writing to her, and sending her flowers? It's not like he lives down the road still. He's hundreds of miles away. And, even if he did live down the road, she would never get muddled up with him again.

Chloe wonders if Millie has said anything to Elaine about Olly. Luckily, Elaine isn't on Facebook; neither is Rod. They won't know he's blazed back into Chloe's life unless Millie tells them.

~

The Archangel hasn't changed. Chloe orders a gin and tonic, then takes out her phone.

They may not be the only surprise for you xx

Chloe's aware of a draught and voices, but she's gazing at that single line on the screen. What does he mean?

"Happy birthday," Heather and Jas chorus, and stoop to hug her. Heather hands her a box of Lindt truffles. "I'm sorry it's not wrapped. What with everything…"

"It's no problem. I love those. What can I get you to drink? How's Guy?"

"Sparkling water for me," Jas says, unwinding her scarf.

Chloe and Heather head back to the bar. While Heather asks the barman about the wines, Chloe slips her phone back into her pocket, and feels the now very scruffy card from Olly's flowers.

Kathryn was not looking forward to September. She was staying on at school, moving into the sixth form next door, along with many of her year group. Lorna wasn't coming; she'd signed up for a beauticians' course in Camborne. Davy would be there, doing A-levels. His romance – if that's what it was – with Lorna had fizzled out. Kathryn had heard that weird Sharon was not continuing with education, but no one knew what she'd be doing instead.

Kathryn was taking a BTEC in science. Her father was disappointed she wasn't doing A-levels, but she didn't want to go to university, so what was the point? She didn't really want to take the BTEC either; she'd have liked to find a job. Retail perhaps, or in a gallery, but no one would employ someone like her, so she didn't apply anywhere.

The sixth form meant no more school uniform, so now everyone would see her shell-suits and elasticated jeans, her vast T-shirts and shapeless jumpers. New kids would be joining from the satellite towns of St Ives, St Just, Hayle, and St Michael. New kids to shout or whisper abuse at her.

The thing was, Kathryn truly did not believe she ate that much. She was simply unable to eat anything without weight piling on and staying on. She was condemned to this life. You only live once, she thought, and I live like this. She had started to experiment with make-up, highlighting her eyes, trying to shape her cheeks, in an effort to draw attention away from her body, but she was fat. She'd always been fat. She always would be. Nothing she did would change that. Sometimes she made lists of the things she would never do because of the weight: wear a bikini, swim, run with abandon on the sand, feel sexy, find love, have children, live in the sunlight.

~

Chloe doesn't stay out long. Heather and Jas look drawn, and Evie will be staying up for her at home. When she gets back, warm in the blood, and maybe just slightly wobbly after a few G and Ts, Evie rushes to meet her.

"Mummy, Mummy, I have something for you." She's holding out a parcel, lumpily wrapped in silver paper. "I wrapped it myself. Can I open it for you? Now?"

"Let's open it together." Chloe kisses Evie, grins at Elaine over her head, and takes the parcel. There are stray blonde hairs caught in the sticky tape.

"We had a secret mission to work on," Elaine says.

"It's a necklace for you, Mummy. From me. Look." Evie tugs crossly at the jewellery box, but she can't undo it. "It's purple. Look at it, Mummy."

Chloe unclips the box, and there's a tiny amethyst on a silver chain.

"Thank you, sweetheart," she says, hugging and kissing Evie.

There's a flash as Elaine snaps a photo of them together on her phone.

Chloe remembers her own phone in her pocket and tugs it out, along with her wallet, and dumps them down on the table.

"I'll just go to the mirror and put it on."

As Chloe leaves the living room, she sees Elaine out of the corner of her eye, bending to retrieve something from the floor.

Later, when Evie has finally settled in the double bed, Chloe and Elaine go back to the kitchen. Chloe puts the kettle on for tea. She's tired. She's not used to drinking. She's not used to seeing so many other people in a day either. The spare bed is made up for Elaine, the bed that is supposed to be Evie's, but Elaine has always been a night owl, so Chloe knows they'll stay up awhile.

"You dropped this."

Chloe brings the tea to the table, and stops. Elaine has put Olly's flower card down, face up. The florist's handwriting.

Happy birthday Beautiful
I remembered!
O xxx

Chloe stands there, a mug of tea in each hand, her face burning, and no words in her throat.

"Millie said you'd got in touch with Olly Bradshaw again. Please tell me this isn't what it looks like."

Chloe thumps the teas down.

"What does it look like?" She sounds petulant, she knows it, but she's lost.

"Like you're seeing him again."

"Just because there's an O on there, you assume it's him?"

"Well, they weren't from your swimming friends, were they?"

"How did you get that?"

"It fell out of your pocket. I just picked it up, and then I saw what it was."

190

"I'm not seeing anyone, you know that."

"I don't know anything," Elaine says, wiping up a splash of tea with a tissue.

"How could I, with Evie? I don't have time or space for anything. I don't have a life of my own at all."

Too much gin. Stop it.

"It is him, isn't it?"

Chloe rubs her eyes. Why the fuck didn't she just throw the bloody card away?

"Yes, it's him."

Elaine drinks tea, says nothing.

"For Christ's sake, I haven't set eyes on him since...since then. We only spoke on Facebook. He lives in London. He's got kids of his own. I don't expect I'll ever see him again. I don't know why he sent the flowers. I wasn't expecting it. I thought they were from Millie, but no chance of that because she's in such a snot with me she's ignored my birthday and sent Matt round with a card and some tale about them going away just like that." Chloe fiddles with the tiny amethyst at her throat.

"What...happened," Elaine starts. "It had a huge effect on Millie and me too, you know. Leaving the village, Millie moving schools."

"I moved schools too. I lost my friend."

Elaine ignores her. "Moving to Rod's so quickly."

"We were going to do that anyway."

"Not quite overnight."

"Let me ask you this," Chloe shouts. "If Amy hadn't died, would you all be like this? Wouldn't it just have been *oh well, shit happens, people shag other people*? And Amy and I might have fallen out for ever, but you and Millie wouldn't fucking hate me like you do."

"Of course we don't hate you. And keep quiet, or you'll wake Evie."

Evie. Dear, soft Evie. The only person Chloe wants right now. She wants to throw herself down on the bed, still in her clothes and her flaky make-up, and cuddle Evie. Smell her hair and her sweat, trace the line under her eye where there are no purple shadows, hold her little sticky fingers, share her warm breath.

"OK, I did something wrong, and so did Olly. But it wasn't just a whim, you know. It was…inevitable. He'd gone off her. She drove off in crap weather and maybe she wasn't concentrating and that, but me and him weren't there. If you want to blame someone, blame the shit who answered the phone to her. Whoever that was. Do you know who it was?"

"Of course I don't. Someone who knew you and him and Amy."

"That's the person to blame."

~

The summer went quickly. Hot days, blue days. Chloe still saw Amy, sometimes alone, sometimes with Olly.

Chloe and Amy, and most of the kids from St Michael, were moving to the sixth form in Penzance. Chloe bought two new pairs of jeans, and some new tops. She practised and practised using a kohl pencil like Amy, drawing hard dark lines around her eyes.

192

Olly told Amy that at Penzance the upper and lower sixth forms were mixed together in tutor groups. They could be in the same group. Chloe was apprehensive. She'd hoped she would be with Amy but even if she were, if Olly was there too, she might as well not exist.

A cool early morning in September. The first breath of autumn in the dew-crystalled spiders' webs, the black slugs in the ruts of Barrow Lane. Chloe left home early for the bus, wearing her new jeans, with her new duffle bag on her shoulder. It was black, with red and green embroidery, and tiny silver mirrors, scented with the envelope of joss sticks she'd put inside. There was already a crowd at the bus stop by the Archangel, people from her year, and from the year above. The bus wheezed in. The radio was on: Abba. Chloe took a double seat halfway down. A few moments later the bus stopped opposite Langford's Autos and Amy climbed on.

When they arrived they were all sent into the hall and divided into their new tutor groups.

"You've got Mr Kendall," Amy whispered sadly to Chloe. "You're with Olly."

"Oh," Chloe said. She wasn't sure that she wanted to be with Olly.

"You'll keep an eye on him for me, won't you?" Amy asked, as she dismally followed the rest of her tutor group.

~

Kat and Jason had arranged to meet at the pool at three. It would be the first time she was in the water without Christa, and she guessed it was the same for Jason. And they'd be with two kids as well.

Kat's pretty confident in the pool where they have lessons. She probably wouldn't be so confident in Penzance pool where, so many years ago, she watched the others – little pond skaters and water boatmen – below. The deep-end there was eight feet, and there was a diving board. The lanes stretched away into a blue oblivion. But at the Headland pool, Kat is happy. She knows where the sudden slope starts, where the cracked tiles are, she knows that, even at the deepest part, the floor is only just below her outstretched toes.

~

Wednesday afternoons at the sixth form were for sport. Chloe knew that because Amy had heard it from Olly. Olly said a lot of people bunked off early if they lived nearby, or went to the library, or drifted off into town.

"We'd better look keen the first week," Amy said to Chloe on the bus, pointing to her trainers in a plastic bag.

Between the sixth-form building and the swimming pool was a vast sports hall. Basketball hoops, wall bars and ropes, coloured lines for netball and hockey and badminton. This Wednesday it was set up for badminton. Olly had dragged along one of his friends as a partner for Chloe. Dylan was ginger and bony and was, apparently, a maths genius. The four of them padded into the badminton hall, Olly and Amy draped over each other, Chloe and Dylan loitering behind. Olly fetched some racquets and shuttlecocks from the store. All the courts were full by now.

The smell of stale sweat – weeks old – and rubber, the light thumps of the racquets, the squeaks of people's trainers.

"I can get us a court." Olly strode off, dropping Amy behind.

On the farthest court a skinny guy and a very fat girl in a purple shell-suit were miserably flapping at shuttlecocks with two other girls.

"Hey, Earth Tremors," Olly shouted.

Amy gasped in shock or delight, Chloe wasn't sure.

"Clear the court please. You're not playing properly."

"We were here first," said the guy, backing away.

The fat girl turned round, ran a hand through her sticky hair. A shuttlecock whizzed over the net and smacked her on the head. Amy shrieked with laughter. Dylan snorted. Chloe wanted the floor to gulp her up.

"Oh fuck it, who cares anyway?" the thin guy said, throwing his racquet down and stomping off the court, followed by the fat girl, followed a few moments later by the other two.

"I told you I could," Olly grinned.

~

"Hey, Earth Tremors."

Unbelievable. After a year's respite, there he was again, looking tall and cool and cocky, and shouting those hateful words to the entire hall.

Beside Kathryn, Davy started protesting about them being there first, but Kathryn didn't care. She just wanted to leave. She didn't care what the other two girls did. She and Davy had only met them ten minutes ago when they arrived in the badminton hall. She couldn't even remember their names.

As she followed Davy off the court, still holding her racquet, she saw Oliver Bradshaw's friends. That ginger genius she remembered from school, an embarrassed-looking girl with long gold-brown hair. A beautiful blonde with a drifting ponytail, dark kohl round her eyes, wearing a tiny denim miniskirt. Her. The girl from St Michael.

At the door to the sports hall, Kathryn turned back. The girls she and Davy had been playing with had stopped to chat to some boys on the sidelines. On the court they'd been using, Oliver Bradshaw whacked the blonde on the bottom with his racquet.

"Chocolate?" Davy asked gloomily, and together they tramped along the path beside the sports hall leading to the pool.

The same vending machines, the same beige carpet, the same red paintwork.

Davy fumbled in his jeans pocket for change. While the vending machine clattered Kathryn stood at the huge window and watched the swimmers below, chopping through the blue.

~

Kat arrives early. It's a grey, squally day, and the waves below are jagged and metallic. She taps in the security code, and the doorlock hisses. Thumping on the wooden stairs above, and a family – parents and three boys – comes clattering down, all wet hair and towels and wafts of chlorine.

Through the inner windows the pool is heaving with bodies. Two kids in the shallow end, playing with a bright football.

There's a float drifting on a hidden current. A mother and baby in the kids' pool. A guy powering up and down the far side. Kat stops to watch his crawl: huge reaching arms, head down, his mouth hardly breaking the surface. Teenagers in the deep end splashing and shouting. A grey-haired woman, head up above the water, laboriously breaststroking up the near side.

Five minutes later Kat walks out of the changing room. For the first time in her life she's going into the water alone. Not for a lesson. She's just about to open the door to the pool when Jason, Thomas, and Flora arrive.

"Sorry we're late. Flora couldn't find her goggles."

"My pink goggles. I only like my pink goggles."

"Are you enjoying half-term?" Kat asks.

"I wish it was always half-term," Flora says sadly, and Kat swallows guilt.

"We're having cake after," Thomas says.

"We'll go over to the hotel for afternoon tea," Jason explains. "Now, come on, let's get sorted out. Kat, you go on."

"I'll try to bag us some space," Kat says, and opens the pool door.

The air is stifling. The ceiling is wet with condensation. Kat hooks up her towel, which already feels clammy, and turns to the pool. The fast-crawl guy has moved into the hot tub. The breaststroke woman is now swimming erratically on her back, almost crashing into one of the lads. The water is ragged and choppy, like the sea outside but, even so, it still looks murky, like the pool has been overused through half-term. Like the water might feel more like oil on her skin, or cream.

Tiny white suits, no bigger than handkerchiefs. Some with pink stripes. One with rosebuds. Chloe puts that to one side. It was the first thing Evie wore on New Year's Day, her first day in the world. Socks like dolls' socks. They're hardly worn. Evie tried to eat her socks, tugging them with her strong pink gums. Chloe was frightened to let her wear them in case she choked on one. A red velvet bedsuit, with tiny arms and legs. It kept Evie cosy in her Moses basket those first cold months. Chloe hesitates. These are her memories, her stories. Hers and Evie's. She folds the red bedsuit onto the rosebud one. Jas's baby is due in the heat of July. It won't need a newborn-size velvet suit.

When Chloe met Jas and Heather for a birthday drink she asked Jas if she wanted to find out the baby's sex. Jas said she wasn't sure. Chloe always hoped she'd have a girl. She was so happy when the sonographer said it looked very much like a girl and then, walking out of the darkness of the room into the bright light of the corridor, the flimsy photo in her hand, she felt a huge surge of guilt. What if it was a boy after all? What if he could read her mind? I love you whoever you are, she thought, her hand on her bump. Just be well, be healthy. I love you.

Chloe shoves some of the more neutral clothes into a Sains-bury's bag in case Jas would like them. The suits brown-stained with old milk go into the bin. The rosebud suit and the velvet one back into the hold-all they came from. They're precious.

Chloe wonders if she'll ever have another child. She doesn't think so. She's getting older, and who would she have it with? If she became pregnant by another man, no doubt Millie would make caustic remarks. It doesn't always work out perfectly, Millie. Sometimes Chloe envied Millie's security, her successful husband, her new house, her magazine-model children. And then Chloe thinks of the fun she has with Evie, splashing in puddles, making gluey messy scrapbooks, cuddling together in bed, just the two of them, and she knows the answer: she would never change that. Not for anything.

~

Kat holds Flora's hands and the little girl floats upwards on her front like a starfish. Her red-gold hair swirls in the blue water. One hand at a time, Kat lets go of Flora's fingers, stands right by her, till she stumbles up, coughing.

"That was really nice. Can we do it again?"

"Get your breath first."

Kat moves so she can keep an eye on Flora and also see what Jason and Thomas are doing. Jason's standing in the deeper water, where the pool slopes underfoot. Thomas is swimming by the tiled wall, splashing a lot, but he's moving, he's getting there.

"Daddy, I can float!" Flora shouts. "Without armbands. Look. Watch me."

Jason half turns. "When Thomas has come back to the shallow end."

Thomas thrashes past the breaststroke woman towards Kat; Jason wades over too.

"OK, Flora, let's see it."

Kat holds Flora's hands once more, until she's spread evenly on the water surface. The lads from the deep end are making a lot of noise behind her. A huge splash.

"I'll let go now," Kat says, though Flora may not hear her.

Flora drifts, suspended a moment, then one of the older boys crashes into her, and her legs go down, and her arms scrabble, and Jason swoops to grab her. Kat can see in Flora's twisted, spluttering face that the moment has gone. Jason kisses Flora's wet head. The boys have plunged back to the deep end. The breaststroke woman is hauling herself up the metal ladder.

"Have another go, sweetheart," Jason says.

"I can't."

"You can. You did. Look, let's go into the corner. Kat will get you started, and Thomas and I will stand guard round you. No one will come near you, not with all of us there."

Flora looks at Kat, lets Jason lead her to the far corner of the shallow end. There's a red plastic float on the poolside, and an abandoned pair of goggles. Flora grips Kat's fingers tightly, and Kat has a job to prise their hands apart.

~

Evie is crumbling up salt and vinegar crisps for Ears, a teddy, and a fluffy ball to eat. She has arranged her tea set on an old towel on the floor, and the three guests are sitting in front of pink and blue striped plates.

"The goats," Evie mutters, and swipes a handful of crisp chippings.

"Evie," Chloe warns.

200

Evie leans over the back of the sofa. "The goats are hungry."
Crisps flutter down onto the cushions.

"Goats don't eat crisps."

"Our goats love crisps."

"Not salt and vinegar ones."

"But—"

"Put them back on Ears' plate. He hasn't got anything to eat."
Evie reluctantly slides off the sofa. "I'll bring you some biscuits later, goats."

Chloe brushes the crisps from the cushions and sits down with her laptop on her knee. There are no messages from Olly. She looks at his photo again, wonders what he meant about flowers not being the only surprise for her. She wonders whether to write to him, but she can't think what to say. Instead she goes to Millie's page.

Off for a few days on Dartmoor! says her status. She's tagged Matt in a picture of Zac and Luca in the back seat of the Range Rover. So they really have gone. Idly Chloe turns to Matt's page, but he hasn't put anything on since Christmas. Back to Millie. Millie Sinclair. How odd. Chloe's never thought about it before, but she and Evie are the only Johnstones. Millie took Matt's name; Elaine took Rod's when she remarried. Clive Johnstone left Elaine when Millie was a baby. Chloe has few memories of him. She's not interested in him. He's out there somewhere, she supposes, unless he's dead. She knows nothing about him, but she shares his name, and so does Evie. His name will continue, carried by a girl who talks to invisible goats behind the sofa, a girl who will probably never meet him.

~

They take a window table in the hotel bar, overlooking the steely ocean. There's a tanker far out to the horizon. The ships wait offshore for a job, Thomas explains to Kat. The waitress wheels a trolley of cakes over. Kat smiles ruefully as Thomas and Flora ask her about them: chocolate fudge, coconut and cherry, coffee and walnut, lemon drizzle, Victoria sponge, eclairs, meringues, cream horns. She feels dizzy, almost nauseous with all that sugar in front of her. Pink sugar, brown sugar, white sugar. Swirls of whipped cream, chocolate flakes.

"What you having?" Jason asks her, after Thomas and Flora have chosen.

"A pot of Earl Grey please."

"What about cake?" Jason asks.

Kat hesitates, just a second. She wants to be normal, she wants to enjoy herself. Just this once.

"I'll have the lemon cake."

~

Heather pauses on the landing. It's two in the morning, and Jas's light is still on. She hasn't fallen asleep with it on, because Heather can hear her voice. Quiet, soft. A voice for the night.

"You'll never hear his voice."

Gently, Heather opens the door wider. Jas is sitting up in bed, her hand on her abdomen. She turns as Heather comes in.

"I was just talking to the baby," Jas says. "Just telling it...telling it it won't ever hear Dad's voice."

202

Heather sits on the bed. For a second it's like she's back at the hospital, perching on Guy's bed. She's tired; the images are blurring in her head.

"It will hear him," she says. "Differently. I've had a google of the artificial voice boxes you can get. And he's going to have a speech valve fitted. So, one way or another, he'll be talking."

"I've had a google too. Those artificial things, they make you sound like Stephen Hawking."

"It's still him." Heather's trying to be brave, but she's terrified too. Terrified for Friday, and terrified about what this new Guy will be like. What he will sound like. What he will be like. Will he be ruined?

"He'll never sing Elvis to this one." Jas's voice breaks.

Heather smiles sadly, remembers Guy singing *Suspicious Minds* to newborn Jas, so many years ago.

Guy's voice – what's left of it – will be gone for ever. It's intangible, ethereal, but so definitely Guy, and it will disappear into the ether as his vocal cords are cut from him. Where will that voice go? Is there a frequency somewhere it will drift to? A radio station for the lost voices?

~

Can I call you? What's your number? O xxx

~

In the immediate aftermath, Chloe waited for Olly to call her, to come round. She tried to ring him a few times, and some bloke eventually picked up and said Olly had moved back to his parents' house. Chloe rang there once; Olly's mother answered. As soon as Chloe whispered her name, Olly's mother told her not to call again, and the line buzzed. Still Chloe waited for Olly to call her. And then, as the days trickled into weeks, and the wind blew colder, and the ground hardened, and Amy was laid to rest, she understood that he was not going to, that she, as well as Amy, had vanished from his life that night.

Chloe did not return to the sixth form in Penzance. She huddled in the house, wrapped round her pain and her grief and her guilt, until the move to Rod's. A new school, Millie's sulks, Elaine scrabbling to find tenants for Orchid Cottage. Life swept on, leaving Olly behind. And leaving a fragment of Chloe behind with him.

~

Why didn't you call me after everything? I called you over and over. In the end some guy said you'd gone home again. So I rang you at home and your mother told me to leave you alone, and never ring again. And then we all moved to Truro, because everyone here hated me, and Mum couldn't wait for us to get out of St Michael. I don't think my sister has ever forgiven me for making us move.

C x

~

Guy is sitting on the side of his bed, with a towel round his shoulders. His hair seems to have grown, outwards rather than downwards, and sticks up like a fluffy halo. He looks knackered.

Heather reaches out, touches his bare arm, below the towel. He jumps.

"Sorry," she says. "You look miles away."

"I wish." His voice is bad: hard and croaky. His breathing whistles again. "I've just had a shower. I'm tired. Phil's coming to see us, yes?"

"Yes." Heather rummages in Guy's locker for a clean shirt, helps him to put it on.

His skin, damp from the shower, is cold, clammy. The plaster holding his feeding tube in place is wet and peeling off. There's a clot of dried blood in his nostril. Jas flutters around in the background, moving Guy's books into piles on his table, throwing away damp tissues.

"Can you get me some ice?" he gasps to Jas.

Jas chucks his half-melted ice down the drain, and goes over to the nurses' station, where Cassie is writing in someone's notes. Heather gazes at Jas from a distance, as Guy tugs on clean socks. She looks so tired now, and hunched. Her slim frame is changing; she looks chunky rather than pregnant.

"How is she?" Guy asks.

"She's doing all right," Heather smiles.

"Has Andrew been in touch with her?"

"Not that I know of. Anyway, she doesn't want contact for now." She doesn't need that hassle, Heather adds to herself. Not on top of this.

"Waste of space," Guy says, and dissolves into wheezing.

Jas comes back with a fresh beaker of ice. Guy reaches out for a cube, rattles it round his teeth and spits the liquid into his grey cardboard bowl. The saliva is a rust-stained colour.

Footsteps. Heather swings round. It's Phil Rowan with Guy's notes in his hand.

"Hello Guy, Heather, Jasmine." He whisks the curtains around them all. Heather flinches as the grimy fabric swishes against her back.

Rowan has had a haircut. He's wearing brown cord trousers, and a khaki shirt.

"Are you all set for tomorrow?" he asks Guy.

"I'm set," Guy says.

"Good man."

"What will I feel first? When I wake up?"

"You'll feel how much easier it is to breathe," Rowan says.

"That'll be wonderful." Heather squeezes Guy's hands. A fistful of bones.

"You won't be able to eat or drink anything for two weeks. You won't even be able to clean your teeth. None of that." Rowan gestures to the beaker of ice.

"I spit."

"Even so, tiny drops can still get down. Absolutely nothing must get down. We'll get started with the speech therapists as soon as possible. It won't happen overnight. You know that, Guy."

"I know that."

"Or there are the handheld devices. But we like to get people to use the valves if they possibly can."

"I've brought a pad, and some new pens." Heather says.

"Cassie has something for you too." Rowan sticks his head through the curtains and calls for Cassie.

A moment later, she squeezes through, and hands Guy a slim tablet and stylus.

"These are given by the support group," she explains. "It's called a Boogie Board. It's yours to keep."

"Not an excuse not to use your valve," Rowan says. "But it'll get you going straight after."

The phone rings on the nurses' station.

"That might be radiology ringing me back." Cassie dashes out through the curtains.

Guy scribbles a few words on the Boogie Board, and clears the screen.

"One last thing," Rowan says. "Can you shave off your beard tonight?"

"If I can remember how." Guy shakes hands with Phil Rowan.

Heather feels tears in her eyes. The moments are counting down again. Rowan is going home now, and the next time he arrives at the hospital it will be to split open Guy's throat. Rowan reaches for her hand too.

"Now, you look after yourself, Heather, you and Jasmine. Guy will need a lot of support."

"Will you ring us when it's done?" Heather asks.

"Of course. But it will be late. Probably not before seven. It depends on how much reconstruction work there is to do. You OK, Jasmine?" Rowan shakes hands with Jas, and turns back to Guy. "Tomorrow," he says, and then he's gone.

~

I didn't know. I did go home soon after. I didn't know you'd been ringing. Mum never said either. I was completely headfucked. I didn't know what I was doing. I should have called you. I know that now. O xxx

Chloe doesn't know if she believes him. What does it matter anyway? What's the point of going over all this anyway? Still she writes back.

Yes, you should have called me. I was upset too. I'd lost my best friend. C x

~

Cassie has given Heather a pair of scissors. She snips carefully at Guy's beard, until she's left only stubble.

"I like it," Jas says. "I've never seen you like that before."

"I only have in photos." Heather brushes a few sharp hairs off the bedcover.

"I'm really tired," Guy says. "If you don't mind..."

"Of course." Heather's stomach surges. This is it then. "I love you."

"I love you," Jas says.

The three of them hold each other a moment, not speaking. Gently Guy pushes them both away.

"I hope this is just *au revoir*," he says.

Au revoir, au revoir, the last words he'll say to me. Those two words beat a ferocious tattoo in Heather's head as they walk down the darkened corridor to the stairwell, past the shop and café with shutters down, and to the huge hissing glass doors.

Au revoir.

~

Chloe can remember Olly's voice, even though she hasn't heard it for over twenty years. She hasn't heard it since that night. He brought her home in his car, along the narrow lanes awash with mud and running water. The back road so he didn't have to drive past Amy's. If we hadn't gone that way, Chloe thinks, we might have found Amy's car upside down in the ravine, head-lamps pointing blindly into the rainy sky.

~

Kathryn trudged home from the sixth form, her rucksack bouncing heavily on her back. A group of older lads went by, shouting, cuffing each other. One stumbled into the gutter; his friend said something about there not being much room on the pavement, and they all laughed.

As she walked she thought about the stupid concept of fat jolly people. She didn't believe there was a fat, jolly person in the world. There might be fat people who were good actors, who laughed indulgently at every insult because it was better than showing weakness and hurt. But, surely, no fat person was ever truly happy with being fat, being ugly, having hideous clothes, being out of breath, being laughed at and ridiculed. Being un-popular. At sixteen, Kathryn still hadn't worked out why being fat made people dislike you, avoid you, ignore you, if they weren't being rude to you. Perhaps it was fear. Perhaps they thought fatness was like a disease, passed on by proximity, by touching the same things, by breathing the same air.

~

Heather doesn't open the gallery on Friday. At nine o'clock she rings the ward. The nurse who answers tells her Guy went to theatre an hour ago. Heather washes and dresses, and goes to wake Jas. She's fallen asleep with the bedside lamp on. A paperback novel lies on the floor, pages fanning up like a napkin in a restaurant. Heather shakes Jas on the shoulder.

Jas starts awake.

"What's happened?"

"Nothing. It's OK. I just rang the ward. He's gone to theatre."

"Oh. Oh. I thought..."

"No, I'm sorry, I didn't mean to scare you."

Heather scoops up the book and puts it on the bedside table. Jas sits up, drags her hand through her hair, swings her legs over the edge.

"You all right?" Heather asks sharply.

Jas is staring ahead, almost glazed, and then she smiles, puts her hand on her abdomen.

"It moved," she says. "I just felt it. Like a flutter."

"I remember the first time you fluttered. I was setting up a still life in the art room. It was all green things. A green jug with leaves, green peppers, a leek, a swede. I was just ruffling the cloth, and there you were. A little nudge, a little flutter."

"Nothing now. Perhaps it was just fear. I'm scared."

"So am I. But I'm sure it was real."

Heather goes to make tea downstairs. It's going to be a long, long day. She doesn't turn on Ocean FM, to hear if they have remembered Guy, to hear if they're playing Elvis for him again. Somehow she knows they won't. With no voice, Guy is nothing to them. It's like he never existed.

~

For the second day Kat glances up every time the door opens in case it's Jason and the children, and it's stupid because he said he would be working on Friday.

"Will you come swimming with us again?" Flora asked in the hotel, her lips smeared with whipped cream.

And Kat didn't know what to say, mopped up an amber splash of tea with a paper napkin, and Jason smiled at her.

"You're always welcome," he said. "We'd like you to come."

After tea, Thomas wanted to look at some glass fishing floats hung on the wall, and Flora stood at the huge wide window watching the pewter sea surging into the rocks below.

"This is why I did it," Jason said.

"Why you did what?"

"Why I learnt to swim. So I could bring them, so I could be like other dads. I'm all they've got. I have to do it all and more."

"So...Dawn doesn't ever see them?"

"No. She's made it quite clear she doesn't want any of us. That's why the kids are nasty to Flora."

"Poor Flora. I feel for her. I know what it's like."

Flora came running back to the table.

211

"So, would you like to come swimming with us another time?" Jason asked Kat.

You really are ridiculous, Kat snaps to herself, as she walks round the shop, stretching her legs. You're behaving like those stupid girls did with Oliver Bradshaw. But no. She doesn't know Jason very well, but she does know he's nothing like Oliver Bradshaw.

Kat decides to close up early. Even though it's half-term it's been a quiet afternoon. It's only when she's turning off the lights and setting the alarm that she remembers Guy is having his huge operation today. She's been so preoccupied she forgot. She completely forgot. On the pavement outside *Imago* she digs out her phone and sends a text to Heather.

Hi Heather. Hope you are bearing up OK. Any news? X

She wonders whether she could text Jason. Just a *hi-how-are-you?* kind of message. A *how-are-the-children* kind of message?

No. She'll see him on Sunday night at swimming. Only two more days to go.

~

Mr Kendall was one of the geography teachers. He was short and thin with a dark moustache. The geography room was on the top floor of the sixth form, up two flights of stairs, the last door on the left. A forgotten appendix of a room. This was Chloe's tutor room. There were the usual maps on the wall, countries painted in pink and yellow and green. There were posters about global warming, volcanoes, industry. A row of cupboards ran

212

underneath the window. The cool girls from the year above, Olly's year, sat on the cupboard tops, their backs to the windows, during registration. Chloe couldn't get near those windows. She didn't know what the view was, what the room overlooked.

One morning Mr Kendall hooked up a dartboard. Olly and his friends played with a grimy set of darts. Chloe sat at a corner table, with two boys also from St Michael. They weren't friends of hers, and they rarely spoke to her.

"Hey Chloe, have a go." Olly stood over her with a dart in his hand.

"I'm crap," Chloe said.

"Ah. Go on. You can't be as crap as Amy."

Chloe wondered fleetingly when Amy had played darts. In the Archangel maybe? Reluctantly she put aside her book – Fay Weldon, for English, boring – and let Olly lead her by the arm to the dartboard. Chloe had only thrown a dart a couple of times before. She didn't know what she was supposed to be aiming for. Olly handed her the dart. His fingers brushed hers. Something jolted inside her, something unexpected. Flustered, she threw the dart wildly; it jabbed into the wall.

"OK, you're worse than Amy," Olly said.

The bell rang for the end of registration. Chloe shoved her stuff into her bag, and rushed out of the door. Amy was on the corridor, all black kohl and Body Shop scent.

"Hello gorgeous."

Chloe spun round. Stupid girl. Olly was talking to Amy. He brushed past Chloe. She caught the faint smell of tobacco and soap that she now realised was him. He threw his rucksack on the floor and slid his arms round Amy. His friends wolf-whistled. Chloe was jammed between the classroom door and Amy and Olly, now entwined and kissing. At last one of the guys shouted for Olly; he picked up his bag, slapped Amy on the bottom, and ran down the stairs.

Smoothing her hair, Amy asked Chloe "You look a bit weird, everything OK?"

"It's nothing. See you later."

The rest of Amy's geography class was arriving. Chloe slid through the throng on the narrow passage to the stairwell, kept her face down all the way to the history department.

~

Seven o'clock. No word from the hospital. No news is good news, surely. Heather remembers the day of Guy's oesophagectomy. The surgeon called her about five. People said an oesophagectomy was the worst procedure possible, yet now it seems quick, almost easy. Each hurdle for Guy is higher than the last.

"I'm going to call the ward," Heather says.

Jas looks up from the magazine she's been flicking through.

"They'd have called us if they had anything to tell us, wouldn't they?"

"Perhaps they can ring down to theatres," Heather says, already dialling the number she knows by heart. Cassie answers. "It's Heather. Is there any news?" She knows she's being curt, rude even, but there's a hard lump somewhere in her own larynx turning the words to stone.

214

"He's not back yet." Cassie says. "We haven't heard anything."

"Could you ring down and see? Please?"

"OK," Cassie says. "But I may not be able to speak to anyone. I'm just about to go off shift, so if I don't have any luck I'll ask the night girls."

Heather thanks her and hangs up.

"Cassie's going to find out and call us back."

Heather hovers in the kitchen, the phone in her hand. She picks a grape from the bunch in the fruit bowl, black, dusty with bloom. It's sweet-sour in her mouth, and she picks another, and another, until her fingers are sticky, and the phone goes, and she knows the taste of grapes will always remind her of this moment.

"Heather, it's Cassie. I called theatre. Mr Rowan says it's almost done. It's gone very well. He'll call you himself shortly. They didn't need the plastic surgeons after all."

Sweet-sour grapes. Jas looking at her, wide-eyed.

"Heather?"

"Yes, sorry, Cassie. That's wonderful news. Thank you."

Jas grins, and throws down her magazine.

"I'm going home now," Cassie says. "I don't know if he'll come back to the ward tonight or tomorrow. Mr Rowan will be able to tell you. And you can ring any time, you know that."

It's done. Almost done. Nearly twelve hours in theatre, but Guy's still there.

"He's still there," she whispers to Jas.

"In theatre?" Jas's voice seems to come from a long way away, as if Heather is underwater. She suddenly sees the blue-green

215

water of the hotel pool. She feels she might faint, or her legs might crumple under her.

"Still there. Still here." The words are thick, coming from somewhere deep in her throat.

"He hasn't got a voice anymore," Jas whispers.

"No," Heather says, and that word, that two-letter word, suddenly swells in power because even that is a word Guy no longer has.

Words are precious, so precious, but Heather can't find the words to say this. Or the breath. Words and breath. But for her, they will return.

~

Chloe's first weeks at the sixth form tumbled past in a headache of new kids, new teachers, new rooms, new things. There was an afternoon break, which there had never been at St Michael. There were free periods when she could go into the study room to work, or the library to flick through thumbed copies of *Just Seventeen*, or to the common room, thick with its fug of teenage sweat, deodorant, and forbidden undercurrents of tobacco and weed.

Amy's seventeenth birthday was at the end of September, the coming weekend. She hadn't said anything to Chloe about what she was going to do. They always met up on their birthdays, went shopping in Penzance or out for an ice-cream. Chloe knew this year was going to be different.

"What are you doing for your birthday?" she asked Amy one lunchtime.

216

They were in the common room, which Chloe hated, but the Penzance gang hung out there so, obviously, Amy was there with Olly and his mates. The chairs were squashy, with torn fabric, innards crumbling out. There was a used apple juice carton on the floor, the straw pointing down, dripping onto the carpet. Chloe felt trapped, almost unable to breathe.

"I'm taking her away for the night," said Olly.

"Taking her away?" Chloe stammered.

"Yeah, taking her out for dinner and a night away in St Ives."

"A night away in St Ives?"

Chloe knew she sounded stupid, but she couldn't believe Amy was going away for the night with Olly on her seventeenth birthday. Her parents would go nuts. And, also, Chloe found when Olly was around – and even when he wasn't – she kept feeling again that momentary touch of his skin on hers.

"I might need your help with that," Amy said to Chloe.

"My help?"

"Yeah, I might need to say I'm staying at yours."

"Oh no, no way. What if your parents ring up?"

"They won't."

"Where are you going?" Chloe asked.

"It's no big deal." Olly sat down beside Amy, so they were both in the same chair. "My aunt and uncle have a hotel in St Ives. We're going there."

"No big deal." Amy echoed.

Chloe fiddled with her embroidered duffle bag on her knee. "If it's no big deal, just tell your parents."

"You know I can't. You know what dinosaurs they are."

"No." Chloe stood up, swung her bag onto her shoulder. "I'm not doing it."

She stalked off into the Ladies. She wasn't going to be part of this. She wasn't some pimp. She wasn't going to sit around at home, terrified the phone would go, while Amy and Olly were…

The door opened behind her. Amy.

"Please Chloe."

"We always do stuff on our birthdays."

"Is that what this is about?" Amy took out her make-up bag, found her eyeliner pencil.

"I'm not lying to your parents. They know about Olly. Just tell them."

Chloe stared at their two reflections in the grimy mirror. Amy scraped her eyeliner along her lids. The door opened behind them. A burst of noise from the common room.

"Are you jealous?" Amy asked, screwing the lid on the pencil.

A large blurry shape in the mirror. Chloe recognised the fat girl Olly had been so rude to on the badminton court a few weeks ago.

"Are you?" Amy demanded.

"Of course not."

~

She was there in front of the mirror. That beautiful blonde from St Michael. Amy Langford. Kathryn had found out her name. She was standing there with her friend beside her. They were doing their faces. They looked tense.

"Are you jealous?" Amy Langford asked her friend.

218

Kathryn clanged into a cubicle and locked the door. Perhaps they wouldn't say any more now she was in there. Or perhaps she was so unimportant because she wasn't slim and beautiful, she was fat and ugly, and couldn't be part of their world of make-up, boys, and jealousy, that they'd simply carry on talking. Kathryn wasn't sure which was the more insulting.

"Are you?"

Kathryn stood there in the cubicle, doing nothing, hardly breathing.

"Of course not," said the friend.

Chloe Johnstone. That was her name.

~

Kat surveys the plate of food on her knee. It's very pretty. If she's actually eating off a plate, not just a yoghurt or a banana, she tries to spend time on the presentation. If she makes it look attractive she'll eat it more neatly, slower, make it last. Tonight she has chopped a chicken breast and mixed it with the most colourful salad she can find: cherry tomatoes, shredded carrot, chard leaves, shards of red pepper, sweetcorn, tiny cubes of beetroot, bleeding dark juice onto the meat. Before she picks up her fork she checks her phone. Nothing further from Heather, after her *no news yet* reply.

Kat spears a piece of chicken and a rocket leaf, chews slowly. What kind of idiot is this Dawn? She doesn't even see her children occasionally. No wonder poor Flora is so fucked up. Kat is furious on Flora's behalf. Useless, selfish, vile mother. And yet, if Dawn were around, it would be her going swimming with

Flora and Thomas, her holding Flora's hands while she floats, then smiling up at Jason as they share this moment of their daughter's achievement.

~

"I'm not doing it," Chloe said again on the bus home that afternoon. "And I'll tell you why. I'm not lying to your parents because they've always been nice to me. But also, they'd never believe me. And d'you know why? Because they must know you hardly ever spend any time with me now. It's always Olly. So who will they think you're spending your birthday with? It won't be me."

She hadn't intended to sound so angry.

"You *are* jealous," Amy said. "I knew it."

Yes, Chloe thought. Jealous because Amy wanted Olly rather than her; jealous also that Amy had Olly.

Because Chloe had spent most of the afternoon thinking about Olly.

~

"Heather? Phil Rowan. How are you doing?"

"Frightened," Heather says.

"Well, don't be. It went very well. We didn't need the plastic surgeons."

"How is he now?"

"He's in Recovery still. The anaesthetist is with him. His blood pressure's a bit low, but I don't think that's anything to worry about. I think he might stay in Recovery overnight and go back to the ward in the morning."

"When can we see him?"

"I'm sure the ward staff will let you visit whenever you can tomorrow. But he'll be very tired, and depressed. Also, he'll look quite swollen around the face and neck and, of course, he won't be able to speak."

"That doesn't matter," Heather whispers. "Thank you. Thank you. I don't know what else to say."

~

On the bus on Friday morning Amy told Chloe that Olly came round the night before and talked to her parents about the birthday weekend in St Ives. He gave them the number of his aunt and uncle's hotel, and suggested they called them first.

"He was so charming to them," Amy gushed, checking her face in her compact. "Dad was a bit grim to start with, but he and Olly talked about cars and football, and they told him to look after me, and it's all fine. All lovely. I can't wait for tomorrow night."

~

Please can I ring you? I'd love to talk to you. Or would you ring me? O xxx

~

Heather and Jas run out to the car through a jabbing frenzy of hailstones. Heather called Recovery twice in the night. The first time, about nine, Guy was still ventilated. By midnight he was off it, and awake, his blood pressure stabilised. When she called Recovery a third time at eight in the morning, the nurse told her Guy had already gone back to the ward. The nurse put Heather through to the ward; she recognised the Scouse accent of the healthcare, who said they could come in whenever they wanted.

"Let's wait a moment, see if the rain stops." Heather slips the keys in the ignition. Her crystal key fob dangles brightly.

"Here it is again." Jas smiles at Heather, feeling the baby move with her hand on her stomach.

"Can I?"

Heather reaches out to Jas's stomach. "I don't think I can feel anything at this stage. You wait though, you'll be seeing little feet and knees bulging out before you know it."

"I'm not sure I'll like that."

A ringing. Heather dives her hand into the back seat, for her bag, her phone.

"It's mine," Jas says, pulling her mobile out of her pocket. Her face freezes a moment.

"The hospital?"

"No." Jas jabs at the phone. "Hello?"

Heather watches the hailstones pinging onto the windscreen and bonnet.

"Hi Andrew," Jas says. "Sorry, I didn't realise it was you. I deleted your number."

Delete him as well as his number, Heather thinks.

"I can't talk right now. A lot's been going on...One hell of a lot. I'll email you. I have to go now."

"What did he want?" Heather starts the ignition, turns on the wipers. The sky is lightening.

"To talk. But I don't want to see him again."

"Then don't."

~

Hi Chloe. Back now. Lovely few days away. Boys had great fun. Have you seen the FB photos? See you soon.
   Millie x

Chloe has seen the Facebook photos. Zac and Luca covered in mud, feeding goats at a farm. Matt looking weary in a wood-panelled pub, holding a glass of cider. Millie carrying a huge roast chicken on a platter of roast potatoes, with the caption *Feeding the troops!!*

"What are you looking at, Mummy?" Evie slides onto Chloe's knee.

"Nothing, sweetheart." Chloe puts her phone down, and nuzzles Evie's neck. "How are those goats of yours?"

"They still want their crisps."

"Do you remember Jas?" Chloe changes the subject. "Jasmine?"

"She's got black hair."

"Yes, her. Would you like her to look after you when I go swimming tomorrow? If she can."

"Yes."

"You sure? I could ask Aunty Millie if you'd prefer."

223

"No. Jas-meen."

Evie bounces to the ground, and runs into the living room. There's a crash, and a skittering noise.

"Mummy," Evie wails.

Chloe crawls round on her hands and knees picking up spilt crayons and jigsaw pieces. Then she sets Evie up with paper to draw a picture for Jas.

"Jas has been very worried," she says. "Her Daddy isn't very well."

Evie stops drawing, and discards the purple crayon she's been using for Jas's hair.

"My Daddy isn't very well."

"I'm sure your Daddy is fine."

"Where is my Daddy?"

"I don't know," Chloe says. "He doesn't live with us. Jas is having a baby too. The baby's daddy doesn't live with Jas. My daddy didn't live with me and Aunty Millie when we were little."

"That's Grandad Rod."

Oh shit, this is complicated.

"Grandad Rod isn't my daddy," Chloe explains, thinking how Rod has been more of a father to her than Clive Johnstone ever was.

"Is he Jas's daddy?"

"No."

"Oh. OK." Evie picks a red crayon. "Big smiley mouth."

~

"I feel sick," Jas says, as they walk along the upper corridor to the ward.

There's no official visiting on Saturday morning, and no regular clinics, so there are only a few people wandering about: two guys in theatre blues, a porter with a crackling radio, a healthcare assistant pushing an elderly man in a wheelchair, a girl in baggy pyjamas, her arm attached to a mobile drip.

"So do I," Heather admits. "But we could be feeling much sicker."

When they get to the ward there's a laundry trolley half-blocking the door. They wash quickly at the sink, dry their hands on rough paper towels, and go in. One of the nurses is writing on the whiteboard with a red marker. He turns as they approach. Heather looks past him, through the open doors to Guy's bay, but the curtain is drawn around Guy's bed.

"Hello ladies," the nurse greets them.

"Hi." Heather peers at his name badge. "Kevin."

"He's quite sleepy," Kevin says. "Go on through."

Heather swishes the curtain aside gently. Guy's asleep. His throat is swollen. There's gingery stubble on his chin. IV lines. Tubes and mask covering what must be the tracheostomy. His hospital gown has slipped off his shoulders. Heather strokes the bare skin there. The familiar freckles, the one brown mole. His skin is icy.

"He's so cold," she says to Jas.

Jas reaches out, touches Guy's shoulder. "Let's get him warm." She drags up the flimsy green blanket, but the tubes get in the way.

"Careful. We don't want to knock anything out. Guy, Guy. We're here. Can you hear us?"

Guy shivers, throws out one hand. Jas goes round the other side of the bed.

"Dad. It's all done. You're going to be OK," she says. "I like the designer stubble." Her voice breaks. "Can he hear us?"

"I'm sure he can."

Together they carefully arrange Guy's gown to cover his freezing shoulders.

"I'll ask for a blanket," Jas says, as Kevin ambles past the door to the bay.

"Mr Rowan's really pleased with you," Heather says. "I'm sure he's told you – you probably won't remember – but here you are. All done." She glances up as Jas returns with a blanket.

As they arrange it around Guy he opens his eyes. Two narrow slits.

"You're awake," Jas cries. "Well done! We're just getting you warmer."

Guy opens his mouth as if to speak, closes it, and closes his eyes once more.

~

The park has changed since Chloe was a teenager. The row of eight swings, each higher than its neighbour, all a different colour, is long gone, replaced by four black plastic ones. Where there was once a tall witch's hat roundabout there's now a tiny round one with green handrails. Chloe still remembers the rusting climbing frame, ancient in her day, with the hollowed out

226

sand-bed under it. Its replacement is red and yellow and blue, has netting and ropes and a pirate flag on the centre pole. The tennis court was torn up sometime in the years Chloe was away, and now the playing field extends to the distant hedge. But she can still remember it all. The torn tennis net, the wooden castle where young couples went to have sex and take drugs. The day she and Amy sat on the old swings and the church tower dipped and rose, dipped and rose. Amy drank warm Diet Coke and talked about a party in Sennen. The old row of swings: red, yellow, black, wood, wood, pink, yellow, turquoise. Amy and Olly pulling their swings together, Chloe feeling the changes happening like the sudden chill of a summer twilight.

"Roundabout!", Evie says, and runs over to it.

"Hold on tight now." Chloe clamps Evie's hands to the rails and starts to spin it.

Saturday lunchtime and the park is busy. Kids on the swings shrieking, lads kicking a football on the grass where the tennis court once was, a father shouting up at a girl in the climbing frame.

Parks and playgrounds must absorb so many memories.

Chloe spins Evie slowly, and wonders if, in another life, she and Amy would bring their children here together to play, whether their children would grow up close as brothers and sisters.

Chloe often imagines the ghostly present-tense Amy. She'd still be slim and blonde, but she'd probably have cut her hair into a sleek bob. She'd change her Facebook profile picture every week or so.

Chloe hasn't called Olly yet. She's going to do it tonight. Saturday night. He'll probably be out with friends, out with a woman, won't answer. But she'll have tried.

"Mummy?"

"Sweetheart?"

"You've stopped pushing."

"Sorry, darling." Chloe pushes the roundabout again, and Evie yells with excitement.

"Hi there," says a voice behind her.

Chloe jumps, and grabs the roundabout.

"Hi Matt. How are you? Did you enjoy your holiday?"

"Yes, yes, it was fine."

He looks tired and depressed.

"Evie, Evie!" Luca races up to the roundabout and pulls Evie off. They run together, Evie wobbling on her shorter legs, to Zac, who's throwing a ball wildly.

Chloe's phone jingles in her pocket. She pulls it out. A new text.

Hi Chloe, we went to see Guy this morning. Very tired, but doing well. If you see Matt, would you tell him please?
H x

Chloe holds out the phone for Matt to read.

"He had his surgery yesterday," Chloe says.

"Oh bloody hell, I'd forgotten. I'll give Heather a call later."

"How's Millie?" Chloe asks, watching Evie and the boys stumbling about on the grass.

"Being Millie," Matt says, and turns and waves at the kids.

228

Evie comes running up to them. Matt swings her high into the air and she shrieks and pulls his hair.

Trouble in Paradise perhaps, Chloe thinks.

~

Most days Chloe saw little of Amy at the sixth form. They sat together on the bus, but they were taking different subjects, were in different tutor groups. Sometimes at lunchtime Amy and Olly would disappear together to Olly's house, if his parents were at work. When they came back, with moments to spare before afternoon registration, Amy was flushed and dishevelled, her kohl smudged; in the geography tutor room, Olly would grin at Chloe while Mr Kendall took the register, and she would find her face burning.

One breaktime Chloe was going to her locker by the library. She was about to open it when she saw Amy talking heatedly with another girl from St Michael.

"Don't be stupid! I'd know about that."

The girl said something back to Amy, and stalked off with a huge art portfolio under her arm.

Chloe left her locker and went over to Amy who was leaning against the wall by the study room.

"Did you hear all that?"

"I heard you yelling at Sarah that you'd know about something."

"She said—" Amy glanced around. "She said horrible things about Olly. D'you know Justine Abbott? From Penzance?"

"Yes, she does French with me."

Tall, curvy, spirals of dark hair.

"Sarah's in her tutor group. She said Justine told her she used to have a thing with Olly. But I'm his first girlfriend. He wouldn't lie, would he? Why's she making this stuff up about him? D'you think she fancies him?"

"Who? Sarah or Justine?"

"Either. Both."

"It's probably just bitching," Chloe said. "I wouldn't worry about it. Like you say, he'd tell you the truth. Why not ask him?"

"And where is he? He said he'd meet me here."

"Probably just with his friends. Come with me to get my history stuff?"

Amy looked round again, tearing a nail with her teeth. She followed Chloe to the lockers. Chloe scrabbled in her bag for the soft body of her frog key-fob. Amy flounced up to the window and stared out at the dark autumn afternoon. Chloe's locker was on the lower level, and she had to crouch down to reach in. Someone tugged her hair.

"Amy, don't." She stumbled up with her textbooks.

It was Olly.

"Hey, sorry, didn't mean to make you jump."

Amy spun round at Olly's voice.

"Ah, there she is," Olly said, and tweaked Chloe's hair again as he strode over to Amy.

Chloe kicked the locker shut, called a hasty goodbye to them over her shoulder, and dashed to the history room. She was first in there. She dumped her books on her usual desk, but couldn't just sit down to wait for break to end. She paced up and down the small room, to the window, back to the door.

Because when Olly said *hey, sorry, didn't mean to make you jump*, he'd smiled at Chloe and there had been something in his eyes, his green eyes: a question, or maybe an answer.

On the bus home Chloe didn't want to even bring up Olly's name, but she had to. She had to be normal, act normal, follow what Amy had been saying.

"Did you ask Olly about Justine?" Chloe mumbled, her face turned to the window as the bus reversed across the asphalt outside the school.

"Oh yes. It was nothing. Nothing at all. Apparently Justine used to live next door to him when they were younger. They used to play and stuff. I've a mind to tell *her*—" Amy jabbed a finger towards the back of Sarah's head a few seats in front, "to keep out of my business, and to stop spreading lies about people."

"Oh just leave it," Chloe said.

~

Chloe hasn't gone through Olly's five-hundred-odd Facebook friends. She's seen the ones they have in common – people from the sixth form, some from St Michael school – but that's it. Now she scrolls through screen after screen of photos. Grinning faces, babies, cats, dogs, a sports car. She's looking for one person.

Justine Kimberley. It's got to be her. Looking sultry in a skimpy top, dark hair caught up in a messy bun. She's Justine Abbott from the French group. Facebook says she lives in Oxford now.

Chloe remembers a day long ago by the lockers. Amy shouting about Justine, the things Sarah had said, the lies about Olly. And the tug on her hair – once, twice – and she knew even then that it was a moment to change everything.

"Let me find you something to watch," Chloe says to Evie, and flicks through the TV channels. "I've got to make a quick call. I won't be long."

She flicks past a drama with a lot of shouting, past an Arctic documentary – a polar bear stalking a seal – and finds a 1970s edition of *Top of the Pops*. Evie barely looks up from organising her dolls, Ears, a crayon tin, a cardboard box.

Chloe dials from her mobile.

"Hello?"

His voice is the same.

"Hello?" he repeats.

"It's Chloe," she says, and those two words are like lancing a boil. Her racing heart rate subsides. "If it's not convenient—"

"It's very convenient. How are you? How are you, for fuck's sake?"

"I'm all right," Chloe says. "What are you doing?"

"I'm just wondering what to cook for dinner."

Chloe tries to imagine him in some kitchen somewhere, in a flat or house in London. A little broader, lines at his eyes. Is there a girl? Is she there, mouthing *who is it?* to him?

"Thank you for the flowers. They were lovely."

"Were you surprised?"

"Definitely."

"Did you hope they were from someone else?"

"I didn't know who they could be from."

"I never got you flowers before."

"No."

"What are you doing this Saturday night?" Olly asks.

"Nothing. I'm at home with my daughter. What have you done today?"

This is crazy. This whole conversation.

"I've just been for a swim. Now I'm going to eat."

"I swim now," Chloe starts.

"You? You're terrified of the water. You always said you were."

"I am. Was. Still am a bit. But I started lessons in the New Year."

"Wow. That's cool then. How is it going?"

"It's good. I think." She peers round into the living room. Evie's lining up her crayons. "Olly. This is really weird."

"Yeah, I know," he says, and his voice changes. "It's going to be weird. It's just…I know you won't believe me, but I think about you a lot."

"But—"

"I do. I always have. All this time I've wanted to talk to you, and I found you on Facebook ages ago but I didn't have the balls to add you. I didn't think you wanted to hear from me. I didn't know you'd tried to get hold of me before. Then."

"You could have got hold of me," she says, and sounds petulant.

"I'm sorry. About everything. If things had been different…"

"Oh, if things had been different."

"If things had been different, I think we could have been good together, don't you?"

"I don't know."

"Chloe, you do know."

"Yes. Yes, we could."

~

Chloe wakes before Evie on Sunday with a strange yet familiar feeling. Of excitement, expectation, of spring in the air, and new possibilities. It's a nostalgia that takes her back to her teens, when she'd wake some days and think *this is the day something magical will happen, the day my life will change.*

All because of a phone call. All because she'd talked for fifteen minutes to a man she'd last known as a boy. The elastic of times stretches back; Chloe lies there beside a sweaty, snuffly Evie, and walks her mind through it again. The drive from Penzance to St Michael in his car. The rain, the water on the road, the dark. How she jumped out of the car quickly into the night, so he could roar away, unseen. And, only a mile or so away, Amy's car tumbling off the saturated road, over the edge of the Bends, crashing through foliage and rain, to the stream below.

Chloe's mobile rings on the bedside table. She swipes it up, sure it's Olly again. Heather's name flashes on the screen.

"Hi Chloe," she says.

"Hi Heather, how's Guy?"

"He's OK," Heather says. "We saw him yesterday. Only briefly. We're going up after lunch. Would you still like Jas to look after Evie while we're swimming?"

"Please. That'd be wonderful. Evie's drawn her some lovely pictures."

Chloe sends her love to Guy, and hangs up. It seems like such a long time since she was in the pool. Maybe some of her nerves, her anticipation, is because of that. Maybe.

~

Kat punches in the security code, the door releases with a hiss and she runs up the wooden stairs, the hot chemical smell filling her lungs.

Christa's balanced on the edge of the deep end in her track-suit, one leg behind her in an arabesque as she demonstrates body and head alignment. Three heads bob like seals in the water below: two dark grey, one rusty. Jason turns as Kat looks through the glass window. He grins and waves, then points to the water surface and gives a thumbs-down. Must be cold. Kat pads through the wet footprints in the corridor to the changing room.

Only a few days ago she was here with Jason and the children. She'll get ready really quickly and be there on the poolside when he gets out, so she can have a few moments to talk to him.

~

"Please don't worry," Heather says to Chloe, as they slide on their seatbelts. "Jas and Evie will be fine. Jas is really capable. I promise you. If I thought she wasn't up to it I wouldn't let her do it."

Chloe glances back once more to Orchid Cottage. The curtains are drawn, tinging the window pale copper. She's left Evie's supper out in the kitchen, told her to eat up nicely for Jas. That

235

should take most of the time up. They can watch some TV or do some drawing or whatever. *It'll be fine. Of course it will.*

It's odd not to be driving to the Headland, to be sitting instead in Heather's passenger seat with her swimming bag and towel on her knee.

"Are you looking forward to swimming again?" Chloe asks.

"Yes," Heather says. "It's been such an awful couple of weeks. It seems so long since we were here. I feel a bit wobbly about it really."

"Me too," Chloe admits.

"So much has happened since I was here last."

And to me, Chloe thinks, but she doesn't say it. Compared to what Heather and Jas have had to handle, ringing up an old boyfriend is nothing. It doesn't even feature on the scale.

~

"Hi there," Jason unhooks his towel, and slings it round his shoulders.

"Hi." Kat gestures to the water. "What's going on?"

"Terrible, isn't it? Must have been us lot the other day."

"Hi Kat, it's a filter problem," Christa says. "I ran over to reception to find out. They said it was OK, that it's safe. It'll be sorted out in the week."

Tim and Rob are out of the water too, and the surface settles again, waves becoming ripples, ripples becoming shudders. But Kat can't see the lines of dark tiles on the bottom. The water is thick and green.

"I told Christa it was fine the other day," Jason says.

"I heard you two came swimming. How was it?"

Kat opens her mouth about to say *it wasn't "us two"*, says instead, "We didn't do much swimming really. The kids had fun."

"Thomas did some swimming," Jason says. "And Kat helped Flora to float."

"There now," Christa says. "I bet you never thought you'd ever be teaching someone to swim."

Kat shakes her head, laughs. Kathryn Smith would never have taught anyone to swim. Kat Glanville, on the other hand: she could do anything.

"How are Thomas and Flora?" Kat asks Jason.

"I nearly didn't come tonight. Flora's upset about school tomorrow."

That Sunday night feeling. Anyone who's had it knows it. Words are not needed.

"I'm sorry," Kat says.

"I'd better get back." Jason rubs at his hair, and it sticks up in a jagged tuft.

Kat slides her eyes over his arms and shoulders, the lines of muscle honed from digging and pruning. Water droplets on freckles. She thinks his skin would turn angry red under the sun. She wonders if he wears a hat for gardening in the summer.

"Give Flora my love," she says.

"OK, speak soon."

He leaves the pool room, trailing his towel in one hand.

"Why not get in, Kat?" Christa kicks off her shoes and re-ties her ponytail, ready to get in too.

Kat backs down the ladder. The green water is cooler than usual, cooler than it was on Wednesday. She thought it looked heavy and oily then; tonight she imagines it'll be like glue. But it's not. It's still the thin fragile water that somehow supports her body. She takes a breath and jumps forward into a float. She can't see the bottom of the pool, just green darkness.

Chloe slaps the water round her thighs. Her body ends at the waterline. Her legs are somewhere beneath that choppy surface, but she can't see them. She can't see her scarlet-painted toenails through the murk. It's disorientating, like wading through a flood. It feels like the bottom of the pool is sloping and sliding, even when she's in the shallow end.

She points her arms in front and puts one foot on the wall. Her heart is fluttering. As she ducks her head and pushes off, the dark water closes over her. She can't see the wall ahead. She can't see the tiles. She has no idea where she is. Her legs drift apart, her head jerks out of the water, and she's stumbling in the middle of the pool.

"Would you feel better going back to the float?" Christa asks.

"I think so," Chloe says.

Heather's in the deeper water with Kat. She's not enjoying it either. The water is like what she imagines being in the sea would be like: cold, dark, green. Kat's swimming widths and diagonals grimly, not as cleanly as usual. Even Kat is ruffled by this unearthly pool. Christa's helping Chloe with her float. Chloe looks miserable in the shallow end, like her confidence has been sucked away. Heather takes a few steps farther towards the deep end, and springs off the side wall. Instead of trickling bubbles from her mouth she inhales sharply through her nose. Pain flares through her airway. She thrashes a second in the deep green water, comes up again gasping, flailing for the edge.

238

"You OK, Heather?" Christa calls, and arrows through the pool towards her.

Heather hangs on to the rail. For those seconds underwater, when it felt like her trachea was flooding, she knew what Guy felt. His airway blocked, choking on fluid, straining for air.

"Hack it up, hack it up," Kat says.

Hack it up. Yes, Heather thinks. I can hack it up. At least I can always hack it up.

Chloe holds the float before her like a life raft. A small piece of neon pink plastic will see her safely across. She takes a breath and plunges forward. She's still looking for the tiles on the far wall, but there's nothing, nothing at all. The float smacks the side and flips up, and she's over. There's no way, no way at all, she'll be able to glide over without it tonight.

Later, on the way home, Heather says "That was horrible, wasn't it?"

"Awful," Chloe agrees. "If it'd been like that the first night I'd never have come back."

"I panicked. It's thinking about Guy, and his throat, and the tracheostomy. Now I'm always thinking of my airway."

Heather parks outside Orchid Cottage. They get out, drifting wafts of chlorine into the night. Chloe unlocks the door, her heart racing. Will Evie be OK? Will Jas have coped?

"Mummy!" Evie launches herself at Chloe.

"Hello darling. Hi Jas."

Jas comes out of the living room, still trying to untangle a doll's long yellow hair with a tiny pink brush.

"Did you two have fun?" Chloe asks, looking from one to the other.

"Yes, yes," Evie cries. "More fun than at Aunty Millie's."

Jas reddens. "I'm sure you have fun with your Aunty Millie, Evie."

Evie runs back to Jas and hugs her round the legs. "You look after me next time."

"Are things any better with your sister?" Heather asks as Jas puts on her coat and cuddles Evie goodnight.

"It's just family stuff. It'll sort out."

Chloe wishes in that instant that she could talk to Heather. Really talk. About what Millie said, about Olly, about Amy, about her worries for Evie. But she can't. She doesn't even know Heather that well.

"When will Guy come home?" she asks instead.

"Six to eight weeks, I think."

They'll get exhausted, Chloe thinks, after they've gone, as Evie shows her the drawings she's done, her empty dinner plate – "I even ate the tomato, Mummy" – and the dollies' tea party she and Jas set up on the floor. Chloe wonders if there is anything she can do to help them. Jas is coping with her pregnancy well. Chloe felt ghastly all the way through. She'd never have been able to hold herself together like Jas. But if she had to she would. Of course she would. Because you do.

~

Heather starts awake at the sound of the phone. The room is still grey-dark. A pale light bleaching the curtains. Her breathing subsides. The house is quiet. Just the usual ticks and creaks. No phone call. She jumps at every sound now.

~

Chloe fumbles awake, as though she's clawing her way up through that thick green water. She's not wet, not cold. There's no chlorine in her mouth. She can breathe. In and out. Beside her Evie giggles quietly. Chloe strokes her absently. She's left her dream at the bottom of that pool, and she's trying to reach down for it. Olly. Olly was there. He looked like he did so long ago. Tawny hair, green eyes. She was with him staring up at a huge black-and-white building. She can't remember any more. She can't remember if he spoke to her. If he touched her. Yet her skin prickles as though he had. As though she were still seventeen. He touched me in my dreams, she smiles. Perhaps he's dreaming about me.

~

"Amy's not in today," Chloe said to Olly in morning registration.

"Is she ill?"

"I don't know. She wasn't on the bus."

"You'll have to be her deputy then," Olly said, and Chloe flushed, and was overwhelmingly relieved when Mr Kendall started reading out the notices for the week.

That night she called the Langfords. June said Amy had an ear infection and had been to the doctors for some drops.

"I think she'll have tomorrow off too," June said, and called Amy to the phone.

"How are you?" Chloe asked.

"Horrible. It really hurts."

"Your mum says you're not coming in tomorrow, that right?"

"Yeah. How's Olly?"

"Uh, fine. I told him you weren't on the bus."

"You'll look after him for me, won't you? Don't let that Justine near him."

"Of course not," Chloe whispered.

At school the next day, Olly asked "Amy here today?"

"Haven't you called her?" Chloe asked, surprised.

"Well…no. I thought she was ill."

"She's got an ear infection. She's still off."

"OK," Olly said, and smiled at Chloe. The bell rang for the end of registration. "I'll catch you later." And he scooped up a length of her hair and ran it through his hands.

~

Lunchtime. Chloe stooped over by her locker, sorting out her history textbooks. She sensed him a second before the gentle tug on her hair once more. She stumbled up, dropped a tatty volume on Richard III.

"What you got last period?" Olly leaned against the neighbouring locker, one hand in the pocket of his jeans.

"History," Chloe said breathlessly, picking up the paperback on the floor.

"I've got a study period."

Chloe didn't answer. Something was happening.

"I thought I'd go and see Amy."

"Oh. Right. Yes." Chloe banged the locker shut, wiggled the key, concentrating hard on tugging it to make sure it was locked. She didn't want to look at Olly.

"I'll run home at afternoon break and get the car. Meet you in the layby on the road outside?"

"What for?"

"Give you a lift home."

"But I've got history."

"Not today you haven't. Layby. Be there." He swung off the lockers. "Hey, Dylan, wait up," he yelled at his friend, who was running up the stairs.

There wasn't any question about it. Chloe wasn't going to history. After English, when the bell rang for the start of break, she escaped the other kids, saying she had to find someone. The corridors were heaving with people on their break. She jogged up the stairs and along the upper corridor. She glanced across the quadrangle, and down, to the window of the history room. The grimy curtains swished back. A couple of people in there, sitting on the desks. Chloe ran on towards the art block, and the way out.

Outside it was cold and damp. She zipped up her jacket, and started across the tarmac to the road. Past the empty bus-park on the left, through a gap in the hedge, and she was on the road. The layby was a few yards down. Often there was a driving school car there, waiting for someone having a lesson in a free period. That's where Amy met her driving instructor. Chloe suddenly remembered Amy was taking her test the next week. She'd pass all right, and she and Olly would be all grown-up going off in their cars, while Chloe was still stuck on the bus, with its

243

bursting seats and damp windows, and the horrible smell of mildew.

She paced up and down, checked her watch. Only a couple of minutes until the end of break. Someone else was coming out of the bus-park. That fat girl again.

A little hatchback swerved into the layby. Olly reached over to open the passenger door. Chloe ducked inside. The fat girl stared, and walked on.

"I knew you'd come," Olly said.

The ashtray was overflowing with cigarette butts. A couple had lipstick on them, Chloe noticed. Amy's pink.

"So are you going to the Valentine's dance on Friday?" Olly asked.

Oh Christ, this car is where they first had sex.

"Of course not."

"Why of course not? Not your thing?"

"No. Well, I haven't got anyone to go with."

"Dylan'd go with you. He really fancies you. And he's a genius, remember."

"No thanks." Chloe tugged her hair over her face, stared out of the windscreen, realised Olly had taken the back road to St Michael, not the way past Langford's.

"If Amy's still ill, I'll take you," Olly said, and squeezed her thigh. She was wearing a short skirt, and his touch burnt her skin through her tights.

"Just think." Olly let go of her to change gear. "If you'd come to the party at Sennen I might be going out with you, not Amy."

"Olly, don't."

"Why not? It's true. Why didn't you come?"

244

"I don't like the beach," Chloe said, and it sounded limp as wet sand.

"You don't like the beach?"

"The sea. I don't like the sea."

"What's wrong with the sea?"

"It…scares me. I'm frightened of water."

"You swim?"

"Not at all. I've never been able to."

"Oh sweetheart," he said.

"I'm not your sweetheart."

The first houses of St Michael. Chloe was relieved and distraught. She wanted to get out of the car, with its lipsticked fag ends, and memories of summer sex. But also, she wanted to stay in that car until Olly parked in the middle of nowhere and took her in his arms.

"Where do I go?" he asked.

"Left here, round by the chippy. It's just after the cricket club."

The little Micra bumped down Barrow Lane.

"Here we are," she said. "Orchid Cottage."

"It's not a cottage." Olly switched off the ignition, unclicked his seatbelt.

"No."

"It's not a cottage, and you're not my sweetheart."

"Both true." Chloe fumbled for her seatbelt.

"Chloe."

"What?"

He ran a finger down the side of her cheek, and twisted a strand of her hair.

245

"I really like you, Chloe Johnstone."

"I must go. My sister will be back from school soon."

"OK," he sighed ruefully. "I'll go home."

"I thought you were going to Amy's?" Chloe asked.

"I don't think so." He was still watching her with those green eyes. "I don't feel like it."

"Thanks for the lift," Chloe gabbled, and flung open the door.

Of course Millie wasn't going to be home for some time, and Olly must've known it. The house was quiet. Chloe picked up the sheaf of mail on the doormat and checked the answerphone. Nothing. She looked out of the front window in case that little Micra was still idling outside, but it had gone. Rod was coming for dinner tonight. Everyone would be here. She trailed along to the room she shared with Millie, threw her bag on the floor, and dropped down on the bed. What if he'd come in? What if she'd invited him in? She wished so much she had.

"What you doing here?"

Chloe jumped awake. She didn't realise she'd dozed off. Millie was tugging off her school jumper.

"Lesson was cancelled," Chloe lied. "I got a lift back with a friend."

Is he a friend, she wondered, watching Millie search for clothes in her drawers. What is he to me?

Elaine came home from the solicitors' office at five, followed by Rod half an hour later. Chloe and Millie liked Rod. He was older than Elaine. Apart from his love of heavy classical music he was pretty cool. Chloe was already fond of him. She came into the kitchen. Rod was sitting at the table with a glass of red, talking to Millie about her chemistry homework. Elaine rattled a sheaf of spaghetti into a pan and turned to Chloe.

"How was today?"

"Fine." Chloe poured herself a tumbler of water, swallowed a mouthful fiercely to try to stop the perpetual fluttering in her guts.

"You OK?"

"She's been weird since I got in," Millie said. "She came home early. Cancelled lesson. Imagine having cancelled lessons and you can just go home."

"You get the bus back?" Rod asked.

"I got a lift."

"Oh, who with?" Elaine asked.

"No one you know. Someone from Penzance. They – she – was coming this way to see someone."

"I think she's got a boyfriend," Millie said. "What d'you think, Rod?"

"No, I haven't," Chloe snapped.

She hadn't. She hadn't even got someone else's boyfriend.

~

Next morning Chloe walked slowly to the Archangel, hoping the bus would have gone, and she could go home, and stay at home, and not have to face Olly or Amy or anyone. But the school crowd loitered outside the pub, and someone waved to her, so she had to keep on walking, and then there was the loud grunt of the bus approaching, and she was funnelled up the steps into the damp fug once more. She sat in the usual seat she shared

247

with Amy. The window beside her was wet and misted with condensation; there was green mould growing on the rubber seal. The stuffing was spilling out of the seat in front, more today than yesterday morning. The bus ground on out of the village towards Langford's Autos. Chloe wished that Amy's ear infection would keep her off school, but there she was in the layby opposite the garage, and the bus wheezed and stopped, and she leapt up the steps. The bus moved off while she was still in the aisle, and she staggered unevenly into the seat beside Chloe.

"How're things?" Chloe mumbled.

"Better today. The drops are working. How's Olly?"

Chloe had expected the question; still, it flared inside her like an ill-judged gulp of wine.

"He's fine."

He obviously hadn't been to see Amy the day before. Chloe wondered again if he'd ever intended to. She'd never know. She didn't want to know.

"I rang him last night. His mum said he was out with Dylan and that lot. He never rang me back."

"You'll see him soon."

"Yes, I can't wait."

The bus was late arriving at the sixth form, and registration had already begun. Chloe left Amy by the library, and ran to the geography room. Olly looked up as she opened the door.

"Hey Chloe."

"Hi Olly. Sorry I'm late, Mr Kendall. It was the bus."

She busied herself with her bag, fiddling inside, looking for things she didn't need, feeling, sensing, Olly's eyes on her head. Remembering the touch of his finger on her cheek.

248

At morning break she hid in the library. She didn't want to see Amy and Olly's reunion and, at lunch, she pretended she needed to go to the shop down the road. The wind was bitter as she walked towards the town centre. She'd have to get over this. She couldn't avoid them every day. She turned round before she'd even reached the corner shop, and started back to the college. There was a driving school car in the layby; a boy she didn't know was getting into the driving seat. She crossed the damp asphalt and, instead of going back into the building, walked to the sports centre entrance. Inside it was warm. There was a good-looking young guy on the desk. He ignored her; they were used to the sixth-formers coming in to buy chocolate at the vending machines. Chloe trudged up the stairs, the carpet soft underfoot, the warm chlorine smell of a swimming pool in her nose.

The upper gallery was empty. She sat down on one of the squashy chairs and watched the swimmers below, listened to the weird hollow acoustics, which she could hear even through the reinforced glass.

Later, at afternoon registration, Olly asked "Where were you?"

"I had some stuff to do," Chloe said.

"You're not avoiding me, are you?" he asked, more quietly.

"No. Yes. I don't know."

"Don't," he said.

~

Valentine's Day. Revolting, Kathryn thought, as she huddled over a radiator by the lockers. There was that ghastly Amy Langford from St Michael dripping around with a single red rose in a cellophane sheaf. Obviously from Olly Bradshaw. Who only three days ago was driving off with Amy's friend, Chloe Johnstone. Kathryn had seen her getting into his car in the layby. And she looked guilty.

There was a Valentine's dance that night in the school hall. No doubt Olly and Amy would be there, slobbering all over each other. Kathryn wouldn't be seen dead at anything like that, even if someone would ask her.

I'm just a fat girl leaning on a radiator, Kathryn thought. No one important, no one worth noticing. But I've got eyes. There's Olly squeezing Amy's bottom, while she flicks her hair, and simpers. And there's Chloe Johnstone, with a face like green cheese, fiddling about in her locker, pretending not to look at them.

~

Guy is sitting in his chair when Heather arrives. His beard is starting to grow back. The swelling round his throat is subsiding. He takes her hand, traces letters on her palm with an icy finger.

~

Chloe waits, checking her phone for texts or missed calls, for Facebook messages. There's nothing. She wants to email Olly. No, she wants to speak to him. What for? He's hundreds of miles away. He's out of her life.

~

On Sunday afternoon Kat's phone beeps. It's a text from Jason. She holds it a moment, before opening the message.

Just to let you know I won't be swimming tonight. Mum not well. Need to look after kids. They say hello. Jason.

But he needn't have said anything. She'd have known he wasn't there when she looked through those tall glass windows and seen only two heads in the water. But he chose to tell her. It matters to him.

~

The day after the Valentine's dance Amy rang Chloe.

"Oh God, it was wonderful," she gushed. "Olly said I was the most beautiful girl there. And he was definitely the most beautiful guy. And then afterwards we went out in his car for a bit, you know?"

"I know."

Chloe was furious at the raw, yawning ache in her heart. She shouldn't care. She shouldn't even be thinking these things about her best friend's boyfriend.

"Are we doing anything for your birthday?" Amy asked at last. "We could go into town, do some shopping."

"OK, let's do that."

"I've kept the whole day free," Amy added.

251

Chloe's birthday, the Monday of half-term. She wanted to cancel meeting Amy. Her mother and sister were both at home. She just wanted a break from everyone at school. No Amy. No Olly. But then Amy might turn up at the house. Better to go into Penzance. At least there would be shops to look at.

Chloe walked up Barrow Lane to the bus stop. She passed her old English teacher, Mr Lovell, turning into his drive with a newspaper in his hand. A couple of Millie's friends loitering outside the mini-market.

Amy flagged the bus down opposite her house. It was just like going to school. Chloe forced a smile onto her face. In Penzance they trailed round the clothes shops. Amy bought a tight red miniskirt. Chloe tried on some tops and a jacket. The changing room was boiling. She was sweating. The clothes looked hideous. She looked hideous. She saw in the mirror that the eyeliner she'd put on with such difficulty that morning had smudged. When she came out with an armful of rejected clothes, Amy was twirling and pouting in front of another mirror. She wasn't scruffy and sweaty. Her eyeliner was perfect.

"Let's go to the deli for some cake," Amy said.

Chloe saw him first. Coming down Market Jew Street towards them. She hesitated a moment, unsure whether to say *Amy, there's Olly*, or whether to just bunk into the deli and hope he hadn't seen them. But that moment of indecision was enough.

"Olly!" Amy screamed, and bounded up the pavement towards him.

Chloe followed more slowly, watching her feet as Amy and Olly embraced.

"Look at this." Amy hauled the tiny red miniskirt out of her carrier bag and held it up against herself, spinning around.

"Lovely," Olly said. He was looking at Chloe, but Amy didn't seem to notice.

"It's Chloe's birthday. We're just going in here for some cake. Come too."

"Happy birthday, Chloe."

"Thank you," Chloe mumbled. "Are you coming?"

"I'd love to," he said.

They took a tiny round table by the window. It was hot and steamy in the deli, smelt of coffee and bread, and something garlicky. Amy shoved her chair close to Olly's. Chloe was about to rub her tired eyes, and remembered her messy eyeliner just in time.

"I'll get them," Olly said. "Give us a hand, Amy." He shoved Amy gently to go first, turned round to Chloe, and blew her a kiss. *Happy birthday*, he mouthed.

Chloe scraped her chair round to look at the street outside. Anyone could have seen what he just did: the people at other tables, the people in the takeaway queue. Anyone.

A few moments later Olly and Amy came back with a tray of coffees and cakes.

"When will I see you this week?" Amy asked Olly.

He forked up Victoria sponge and wavered a second. "I've got quite a lot on," he said. "I haven't done any of my geography stuff, or my economics. I've got to get some work done."

Amy looked deflated. "It's my driving test on Friday, remember?"

"Oh. Yes, course. You'll be fine."

"We could meet up after? Or on Thursday? I've got a driving lesson. I could drop off at yours."

Chloe swallowed cake and coffee, and tried to blank out Amy. She was being demanding. Olly didn't like it. Whether he'd be so offhand if they were alone, without Chloe, she couldn't tell. The deli was monstrously hot. Chloe wanted to go home. She thought of the burn of Olly's hand on her leg in the car, the charge – like electricity – when he touched her face. She watched him drinking his coffee, and she knew, in that moment, that he, too, was remembering.

Amy sulked on the bus ride back to St Michael. Olly had excused himself, saying he was meeting Dylan. He'd kissed Amy goodbye, and tweaked Chloe's hair, which turned her legs to water.

"Why's he meeting Dylan if he's got so much work to do?" Amy grumbled. "Did you hear him going on about geography and that? D'you think he's seeing that Justine again?"

"No," Chloe said. "So when are you seeing him?"

"I don't know. I'll call him later."

Amy rang the bell, and the bus ground to a wheezy halt outside Langford's. Chloe waved as Amy ran across the forecourt to where Dave was working under a car bonnet. The bus doors hissed shut, and it rumbled on towards the Bends.

~

The next morning Chloe crept out of bed, careful not to wake Millie, and padded down the corridor to the kitchen. What was going on with Olly and Amy and her? Well, nothing. Olly was going out with Amy. He hadn't said anything to make her think that was going to change. *I really like you, Chloe Johnstone.* It didn't mean he was going to break up with Amy. And, if he did, and came to her, that would mean losing her best friend.

Amy had persuaded him not to apply for university straight after A-levels because she didn't want him leaving. She'd told Chloe she hoped that she and Olly could apply for the same university at the same time, get a flat, live together. When she first mentioned this, Chloe felt uneasy in a way she could not define. Now, the thought of them cosied up in a flat together made her nauseous. Then a little voice inside her said: *he won't do it.*

~

The water's clear again. Chloe can see all the tiny tiles underfoot, and the jagged gaps where they've come loose. Her heart thumps as she squats in the shallow water and inhales. She can see Heather and Kat hanging on to the rail in the deep end, waiting to swim lengths. Evie, Chloe thinks, Evie's on the other side. She shoots off. The tiles skim beneath her, and her outstretched hands grasp for the rail. Her head is a jumble: fear, exhilaration, pride.

"How's Guy?" Kat asks Heather, as she watches Chloe glide back across the pool.

"Doing well. I mean, he can't talk, or even eat anything at the moment, except through the tube, but they're really pleased with

255

him. He's having a swallow test this week to check all the plumbing's intact. Then he can have a go with a speaking valve, and eat proper food."

"That's brilliant. And Jas?"

"She's great. She's been so scared. Sometimes I almost forget she's pregnant, with everything else. That sounds terrible, doesn't it?"

"I expect she has too sometimes."

"The baby's moving now. Time flies. She's got another scan coming up. I think this is the one where she can find out the sex."

"Will she?"

"She keeps changing her mind." Heather waves a thumbs-up to Chloe. "Jas babysits Chloe's little girl while we're swimming. Getting her practice in."

"I really like Jason's kids," Kat says before she realises it.

"And what about Jason?"

Kat shrugs. "I really like Jason too," she says.

Chloe sits on the pool edge. Her skin is quickly chilling. Kat has done several lengths, easy and languorous. Heather floundered and splashed her way down, and came up gasping. Chloe kicks her legs in the shallows. She'll never be able to do it. She'll never be able to shake that fear. She's managed to glide over but, each time, feels like her heart might stop. Christa asked her to add in her arm pull, and she lost her buoyancy, thrashing and uncoordinated.

She's also sure that Kat was at the sixth form with her. If she's right, she can't even ask, because Kat won't thank her for reminding her of those days.

And, if she's right, Kat might remember something about her too.

~

"It's done," Heather says to Jas, hanging up her phone. "The swallow test. It's all good."

They're both in the gallery. Jas twirls round on her stool, her own mobile in her hands. "That's great. Fantastic. He can start eating now?"

"Yes, and speaking. He'll see the speech therapists. Shall we go up this afternoon? Nothing's happening here."

"Yes, I'd like that."

"Are you OK?" Heather asks. She must ask after Jas more. She's having a baby. An unexpected baby. Her head must be full of questions and fears. Heather's guilt swells inside. She mustn't neglect Jas.

"I just sent a message to Andrew." Jas shakes her phone. "About Dad and that. I said I couldn't deal with anything else right now. I'm scared he's going to want to be involved. When it's born. I don't want that."

"I know you don't."

"I look at Chloe and Evie, and that's what I want. Just me and the baby. No man interfering."

"I don't know anything about Evie's father. Is he around?"

"He doesn't even know about Evie." Jas says, looks like she's about to say more, then stops.

"They'll be friends, the baby and Evie," Heather says.

Jas smiles. "Evie can't wait. She keeps asking if it's come yet."

257

When they arrive at Guy's bedside, he's not there. The blankets are tousled; the locker hanging open. Guy's Boogie Board is on the tabletop. *Roast beef, two bottles of Shiraz*, scrawled on it. The curtains of the next cubicle billow and part, and Cassie comes out.

"He's gone for a shower," she says. "He's doing amazingly well." She gestures to the Boogie Board. "His first meal order."

Heather fusses with the bedding, fluffs up the pillow, pushes aside Guy's pump stand, with its half bag of sand-coloured food attached.

"Here he is," Jas says.

Guy walks slowly, unaccustomed to moving. His dressing gown flaps around his thin legs. His damp hair stands up in a crazy halo. Heather's legs feel unsteady. She so nearly lost him again.

Hello, Guy mouths silently, dropping his washbag and towel on the bed Heather's just tidied.

"Hi." Heather gives him a hug. His shoulders feel like chicken wings. She smooths his hair down with her hand, averts her eyes from the exposed hole in his throat. "You're doing so well."

Guy shrugs, takes her hand, starts to trace a letter. Jas hands him the Boogie Board. He erases the writing, picks up the stylus.

Phil leaving. Wants to see you.

"No," Heather cries. She knew Phil Rowan was only a locum, but this is unexpectedly soon. She wants him beside Guy a little longer.

He's around today. Keep eye out.

"Over there." Jas nods to the nurses' station.

Rowan's talking to Cassie, who gestures towards Guy's bed. He dumps a folder of notes on the countertop by her, and comes over.

"Heather, Jasmine, hello. Guy, looking good. Feeling OK?"

Guy gives a thumbs-up.

"He's had the swallow test. All went well."

"We heard. Yes. Thank you. Guy says you're off."

"That's right. I'm so glad I was able to get Guy this far."

"I wish you were staying," Heather says.

"I'll be handing Guy over to my ENT colleagues here. Everything's in the notes. He'll be fine." Rowan turns to Guy. "You really have done remarkably well."

"He can eat proper food now?" Jas asks.

"That's the plan. Starting very gently. Bit of ice cream, that kind of thing."

Guy scribbles on his board. *I hate ice cream.*

So do I, Heather thinks. Ice cream, sorbet, yoghurt, eggs, all the soft foods she tried to get him to swallow when he had oesophageal cancer. Now Heather wants the crack of nuts, stringy meat, crispy bacon, green apples. Food you have to physically swallow.

~

"You've been quiet," Millie says. "Your babysitter worked out OK?"

Chloe bristles. "It's Jas Lovell. You know, Guy Lovell's daughter."

"Is she old enough? Was Evie all right?"

"They had a great time," Chloe says.

"Right."

"Look Millie, you've been great having Evie and I do appreciate it, but I'm sure you want Sunday nights with your own family sometimes, and it works well with Jas because Heather and I travel together to swimming."

"OK, then."

Chloe isn't sure if Millie is glad to be free of Evie, or whether she likes Chloe needing her too much for that. She wonders what Matt meant when he said *being Millie.*

"Have you heard any more from him?"

"Matt?"

"No. Bradshaw."

"Of course not."

Chloe hangs up. She's been a little surprised that she hasn't heard more from Olly since their phone call. They've exchanged a couple of emails. She's told him a bit of what she's done, sent him a picture of Evie. He wrote about working in the bank, how he wants to start up as a financial adviser, about his marriage and divorce, his twins, how difficult his ex can be, especially about the boys.

Neither of them have mentioned Amy.

~

Kat is in the back room of *Imago*, moving some boxes. The kettle whooshes loudly. She doesn't hear the door chimes.

"Hello there."

Kat jumps. There's Jason Hosking, standing by the till, watching her. She dumps the stack of books she's holding.

"Hi." She comes out into the shop. He's in his work clothes: faded jeans with mud caked on the knees, a khaki fleece over a lumberjack shirt, heavy boots. "On your own?"

"They're at school. I was in town. How was Sunday?"

"Good. I did some decent lengths."

"It's amazing, isn't it?" Jason fiddles with a painted tin on the counter. "Something we thought was impossible. I was embarrassed to tell anyone I couldn't swim. Weren't you?"

"I just hoped the subject never came up."

Jason laughs. "Yeah, me too. What can I get for Flora? A little present."

Kat comes round the counter into the shop, shows Jason a suncatcher shaped like a butterfly, hair accessories, stickers.

"How's she doing at school?"

"She spends the weekend imagining what the kids will say the next week. So she gets in a state about going on Monday. It started off about Dawn not wanting to be with us and all that, but now I think they've just got it in for Flora. I don't understand it. Why do kids stick the knife into someone just because her mother's gone?"

Why do they if someone's fat?

"It starts as one thing, just one way someone's different, and then it goes on, and they probably hardly remember how or why they started."

261

"I'll take these for her." Jason chooses a pair of girls' socks with a flock of pink butterflies on them. "Will I see you on Sunday?"

"Of course."

~

"Hi, it's me. Chloe."

"Hi, you OK?"

"Can we talk?" Chloe rushes on. "I mean, properly."

"I can't right now. I'm about to go out."

"Oh. I see."

"I know we need to talk. But not on the phone."

"How else can we talk?"

"I'm coming to Cornwall. That was the surprise I was talking about. The surprise other than the flowers."

"What?" Chloe staggers against the door frame. Olly Bradshaw coming to Cornwall. To see her. After all these years.

"I'm coming down. I still visit, you know. My parents are in St Ives now. I come to see them. Mum's not so well these days."

Of course he'd visit his parents. Visit where he grew up. Just because he and Chloe were severed, it doesn't mean he's cut out the entire county.

"I didn't know. I've never seen you. You should have—"

"Should have what?"

"Looked me up."

"I didn't think you'd want to see me."

Chloe doesn't know what to say. So many years, so much water, so many bridges.

"When are you coming?"

"Not sure. It'll be a weekend. Are you around on Saturdays?"

"Yes," she says.

"Can I see you?"

"Yes," she says again.

~

Another week gone. Guy gets stronger every day. At least that's what Heather tells herself. She hasn't met Guy's new consultant yet. When she asked Guy about him, he shrugged. Not a Phil Rowan then.

Guy has seen the speech therapist. He's going to start learning to talk with a valve in his throat. He's being shown how to care for his tracheostomy, how to manage the secretions, how to clear the tube. He's starting to eat soft food: ice cream, jelly, mashed potato. He has lost so much weight he is still being fed from the pump. But the swelling is subsiding, the ginger stubble on his chin has grown into darker hairs and, though his bones protrude through his skin, he is getting colour back to his face.

~

Chloe laughs as Evie shrieks under the shower jet. They're jammed into the little cubicle together. Evie's hair streams over her shoulders, darkened to the colour of toffee. She picks up a sponge and wipes soap off Chloe's legs. Chloe pulls her close, feeling warm wet skin on warm wet skin. Without Evie she wouldn't have had the courage to move back to St Michael; without Evie she wouldn't have the courage to learn to swim.

263

She turns off the shower and Evie stamps her feet in the cooling soapy puddles. Sharing a shower is her current favourite treat. Chloe wraps them both in towels. Evie stands on tiptoes, wet hair in her eyes, to look at them both in the clouded mirror.

Later, Chloe lies beside Evie on the double bed. Evie, soft and scented with shea butter cream, flutters her eyelids, quiet at last. Chloe sighs. Olly is coming to Cornwall. He wants to see her. But she doesn't know what she can do with Evie. She needs to see Olly alone. She can't ask Heather and Jas. They have too many worries, and she doesn't want to tell them what she's doing. But, even worse, is the prospect of Millie finding out. She can't ask her. Chloe wishes, yet again, she knew more people. But the village has changed so much since her teenage years. Many of the people she once knew have gone, and those that remain still remember a wild October night and a dead girl.

The phone rings and Chloe slides off the bed to get it. It's her mother. Elaine has never mentioned Olly after Chloe's birthday. They talk a few moments about Evie, about Rod's arthritis, about the new kitchen Elaine is planning.

Elaine says, "Have you seen much of Guy Lovell's family lately?"

"Not a lot. I swim with Heather. Jas looks after Evie for me."

"You should get out more, Chloe. I worry about you, living down that lane with Evie, never seeing anyone."

"It's kind of hard," Chloe snaps. "I've got a three-year-old. I can't just leave her alone here. And I can't go out and see people with her. It doesn't matter anyway. Evie's what matters. She's more important than anyone else."

"I know it's hard. That's what I wanted to talk about. Rod and I would be happy to have Evie come to stay over sometimes. Give you a night off. Time to go out or do whatever."

Chloe isn't expecting that. When only moments before she was worrying about how she could meet Olly.

"That would be good," she says at last. "Thank you. And I'm sure Evie would love it."

"We thought perhaps Saturday night? We'd pick her up in the daytime, return her Sunday lunchtime. What do you think?"

"I think that would be great. I would—" Chloe lowers her voice. "I would like a bit of time for myself sometimes. I love Evie, God knows I do, but we're together all the time."

"It's not good for either of you really. She needs to learn to be happy with other people. I know she sees Millie and Matt and the boys, but she needs other people too. We would look after her, you know that."

"Of course I know that."

"She's a super little girl. You've done fantastically with her on your own. I should have said it before."

Chloe smiles. "You have said it before."

"It's not what I wanted for you, especially after what happened to me, being left with two little ones all on my own, but you've taken it all in your stride."

"You've said that before too," Chloe says. "And anyway, I wasn't really left. I left him before he knew."

"It was all you could do in the circumstances."

The circumstances. Tony's wife and children. Circumstances.

"Evie'll be fine," Elaine says. "Now, you talk to her tomorrow about my idea."

Chloe rings off and goes back to the bedroom doorway. A warm pink glow from the bedside lamp, Evie's damp ruffled curls, the duvet moving up and down so gently as she breathes.

Elaine has answered her problem. Chloe hates knowing she'll be deceiving her mother, by not telling her about Olly's visit, but she simply can't say anything. Her time with Olly was built on lies and deceit before; it stands on those foundations still.

~

The path along the front of the sports centre was edged with blossom trees. Pale petals scuffed under Chloe's feet as she walked. There were a couple of benches; kids sat on them, eating packed lunches; one girl lit a fag.

Amy was away on a geography trip, and Chloe had escaped from the main school to avoid Olly. That morning in registration she'd felt his eyes on her, thinking, perhaps, as she was, that Amy was miles away in Dorset.

Chloe went through the glass doors into the sports centre. The smell of chlorine and rubber. The guy on the desk glanced up, nodded. Chloe jogged up the beige staircase, the carpet soft under her feet. Voices from above. When the stairs opened out into the gallery she saw a group of sixth-formers, including Sarah from St Michael and Justine Abbott. They turned to Chloe, chorused hellos. Below on the left the staccato thuds of a squash ball, the squeak of trainers on wood, a breathless curse. To the right, beyond the kids, the electric blue streak of the pool.

Chloe jammed coins into the machine, pressed the code for a ginger cookie, glanced under her lashes through the thick glass.

Swimmers churning the bright water. The dark lines of the lanes refracted jaggedly. The depth unknowable. The fear again, and something else: a pulling, a drawing. Chloe wanted, so badly, to swim.

The machine released the cookie. It landed with a thunk in the tray. Chloe scooped it out. It had broken into russet shards. She punched in the code for a bar of Highland toffee.

"Take a pew." Sarah hooked a spare chair with her foot.

"I'm going outside," Chloe said.

She didn't know where she was going, on her own with time to spare. The sunlight was bright when she stepped outside, dazzling her a moment. She turned left, followed a narrow flagstone path round the side of the pool. The water was on her level now, through floor-length glass panes. She heard the weird high acoustics, a loud splash. Dipping her head she could just see the upper window where she'd been moments before, and the blurred movements of the people up there.

Chloe walked on in the sunshine, biting crumby mouthfuls of ginger. She'd never walked this far behind the sports centre before. There was no one else around. She stopped a moment, gazing out across the fields, at the blue-mauve of the sky.

She didn't hear the footsteps until they were beside her. She turned, startled, and Olly threw a handful of pink blossom over her.

"Hey," she started, blushing, awkward, still clutching the cookie.

"I've been following you," Olly said, and pushed her up against the cold stone wall.

The bricks were rough on her neck, she dropped the remains of the cookie, a petal fell from her shoulder, and none of it, none of it, mattered, because Olly Bradshaw was kissing her, and raking his hand through her hair and, though her brain hardly knew how to respond, that didn't matter either, because her mouth and her tongue and her hands knew how.

~

"Do you still have Wednesdays off?" Jason asks Kat.

They're on the poolside. The air is thick and humid. Condensation drips from the ceiling. Jason whips his goggles off his head with a pop.

"I do." Kat says.

"Would you like to come here again with us? After school on Wednesday?"

"I'd love to," Kat smiles.

~

"Tomorrow we find out the sex," Heather says.

"Already?" Christa says. "Time's gone so fast. What does Jas think it'll be?"

"She thinks a boy."

"Evie hopes it's a girl," Chloe says.

"You must let us all know," Christa says. "Promise. Granny."

"I promise," Heather says.

Chloe's working on keeping her head under. Christa has given her half a dozen coloured sinkers to throw down and collect off the bottom of the pool. It should help her hold her breath, stop her inhaling when she's underwater. As she ducks her head, the pressure changes, and it feels thick round her ears, also so soft and peaceful. She snatches the last sinker and comes up, spraying water crystals.

"Come away from the edge," Christa says.

Chloe wades a little uncertainly into the centre of the pool.

"Watch me." Christa lowers herself gently, face-first, into the water, suspended like a star. She doesn't move, the water is still.

Chloe spreads her arms, lowers her head, lifts her legs. It's crazy. There she is, Chloe Johnstone, floating, suspended in the cool blue, watching little tiles below her.

After the lesson, they stand around the edge, wrapped in towels. The roiling water calms to a gentle surge, then becomes as smooth as glass, only broken by the odd drip from the damp ceiling. Chloe feels that pull to the water again; she wants to slide back in, to break that still surface.

Christa's talking to Heather about Guy. Kat's starting for the door. Chloe calls after her.

"Kat!"

Kat turns. Chloe's sure, then not sure.

"Kat, did we know each other a long time ago?" Chloe blurts out.

"I don't think so," Kat says.

"Oh. Right. Sorry. I just thought I knew you, and I'd been meaning to ask you, but I couldn't think where from—"

"No, don't think so," Kat says again.

Liar, Chloe thinks, watching her walk away. She's lying. Her name wasn't Kat Glanville then. Chloe can't remember what it

269

was, something much more usual. But it is her. She wishes she hadn't said anything.

~

"Tell him then." Heather shoves Jas forward.

"I had a scan," Jas starts. "It's a girl. Well, they think it's a girl."

Guy gives her a thumbs up.

"So we'll be off buying pink things." Heather puts her arm round Jas.

"Maybe not too much pink," Jas interrupts. "They said they weren't quite sure."

"How are you?" Heather asks Guy.

He writes on the Boogie Board: *Saw speech therapist.*

"Can't wait to hear you talk, Dad."

Guy scowls.

Paddy came yesterday. After you left. Everything sorted now.

The will. He's written a will. Heather doesn't want to talk about wills.

"How's Paddy?"

Better shape than me. Says he'll come again.

"That's good. Shall I ask some of the radio people to come and see you now? I've put them off because you were so poorly."

No.

"Wouldn't you like to see them? Rick perhaps? He'd like to come."

No one from radio. Guy wipes the board clean. *They say I'll be home by end of month.*

270

~

"We can't cope," Heather frets as they queue to leave the car-park. The barrier lifts for the car in front; Heather rolls forward, arm out holding the ticket. "We don't know what to do."

"They're showing him, aren't they?" Jas flicks the little sheet of photos, strokes a finger over her baby.

The red and white barrier jerks up again and Heather swings out. "He won't be able to do it all by himself. And what if he gets ill? We need to know. How to clean that trachy, all the kit he needs, the swabs and the tubes and all that."

"I thought he was doing OK with it."

"I think he is, but it's one thing doing it there with people to help out. It's different doing it at home on your own. I don't think he'll be ready to come home then. He needs to be able to speak. We can't leave him alone if he can't speak. What if he needed to call 999?"

"I hadn't thought of that," Jas says. "We need to find the new consultant, speak to him."

"I wish Phil Rowan was still here."

"Yeah, he was good."

"We can't have Guy home until he's safe on his own," Heather says.

"Will he ever be safe on his own?"

Heather wrestles the gearstick and doesn't answer.

~

Chloe didn't take in a word of anything the rest of the day. Her left hand was grazed from the sports-centre wall; she licked the dried blood, and opened the cut again to taste more. She thought everyone was staring at her, right into her mind, her heart, that they all knew. Her pulse raced and she couldn't calm it.

A few snatched moments, that was all, then some guys had come round the corner, dribbling a football, and Olly was gone, leaving Chloe breathless and alone. At afternoon registration Olly was already in the room when Chloe arrived. He was talking to his friends, but he looked over at her and smiled, and she turned her face away, and willed the moments to pass before she betrayed herself.

She ran to her locker at break, and then into the library, to hide between the cool stacks of books. Glass windows looking out onto the corridor and locker area. She saw Dylan's red hair, and then Olly. They threw a textbook between them like a rugby ball. Olly never looked towards the library, and Chloe shrank back against a spinning carousel of horror fiction.

~

"How long are you going to come to the lessons?" Jason asks Kat.

They're holding onto the rail, side by side, halfway down the pool, legs drifting in the water, while Thomas and Flora play catch with a half-deflated ball they'd found drifting by the ladder. There's only one other guy in the pool, surging up and down the other side.

"I'm not going to stop coming," Kat says.

"I mean you're really good. You could just swim on your own."

"Not good enough," Kat says. "And I like the lessons."

She doesn't say that Chloe Johnstone makes her uneasy, that Chloe has worked out who she is. She doesn't want to have to tell Jason about Kathryn Smith.

"What about you?" Kat asks. "Are you going to come a bit longer?"

"Oh yes," Jason says. "It's my treat, to do something for myself."

"Good," Kat says.

"Flora, back to the shallow end." Jason launches off the wall, and wades to the children, and Kat doesn't know if he heard her or not.

~

"I'm coming down. Not this weekend, but the next. Can I see you?"

"Yes," Chloe says, and her heart and her brain are churning.

"Is the Saturday OK?"

"Yes," she says again.

"We will talk, Chloe. About lots of things."

When Olly hangs up, Chloe calls Elaine.

"About Evie coming to yours this Saturday," she starts.

"We're really looking forward to it."

"Thing is, I was wondering if it could be the next weekend. I'm hoping to meet up with some friends that day."

"But Evie thinks it's this weekend," Elaine says. "You said she was so excited."

Chloe swallows a flare of panic. "I know, but she wouldn't mind—"

"So let her come both Saturdays."

"Thank you." Chloe almost cries with relief, and is disgusted at herself for lying to her mother and disposing of her daughter so easily, just so that she can spend a few hours with the man who broke her heart.

~

A free period. Amy had geography. Chloe felt lost. She hadn't been alone with Olly again. In registration she talked to other girls, even girls she hardly knew, or read. Sometimes Olly came to her and sat on her desk; once he lifted a strand of her hair, and made as if to reel her in to him, but he never said anything about that wonderful day. Chloe could no longer bear to be with him and Amy, and she took to hiding in the library, or in the study room. Amy, she was sure, did not miss her. Olly – she didn't dare guess what he thought.

He was taking his A-levels that year. Then he'd be gone, blazing out of school and into the summer. Chloe wouldn't see him again. The thought made her nauseous. She should go back to hanging out with him and Amy at breaks. At least then she would be near him. But the pain of seeing him with his arm round Amy, kissing Amy, was too painful. Chloe had even cried in the early hours one morning when Millie slept.

Amy had told Chloe that Olly was going to get a job when he left school and find a flat of his own in Penzance. Somewhere she could visit and stay over. He will still be around, Chloe thought. I may still see him sometimes.

Chloe went into the common room. Olly was lying across one of the soft chairs, a book open on his knee. Beside him Dylan was tipping a bag of crisps to his mouth. Olly glanced over, caught her eye. She bolted out of the common room. She didn't know where to go for the next hour. She stumbled out onto the path to the sports centre. The swimming pool. She would go up to the gallery and watch the people swimming below.

There was no one up there. She peered down into the squash court. Empty. She bought a Diet Pepsi from the machine and snapped it open. Cold liquid down her throat. Footsteps running up that beige staircase. She stood still. A tawny head appeared, green eyes. And Chloe realised that she knew Olly would follow her.

She put the can down on one of the tables, moved towards him, strange uncertain steps, like she was wading. By the squash-court window he caught her in his arms.

"Chloe, Chloe, I'm sorry I haven't…"

"It's OK, it doesn't matter."

"It does. I'll sort something out."

"What do you mean?"

"Ssh, don't worry."

He kissed her again and again, his hand inside her T-shirt, wrenching aside the lacy cup of her bra.

Kathryn was hungry again. It was so bloody unfair. She'd been trying so hard, so very hard, but she was always hungry. She was miserable too, and that made her even more hungry. She hurried past the blond Adonis on the sports club reception desk. He knew she wasn't going to swim or play squash or use the gym, she was only going to plod upstairs to the vending machine for chocolate, crisps, cookies, and sweets.

The stairwell hadn't changed since that first time when she and Davy and that girl with a plaster cast bunked off swimming. A ginger cookie, Kathryn thought, and perhaps a Mars bar.

~

"Someone's coming." Chloe shoved at Olly, her heart now racing with fear.

They turned together to where the stairs opened out into the gallery. It was that fat girl. The one Olly booted off the badminton court. When Dylan and Amy laughed, and Chloe was embarrassed because she felt sorry for the girl.

The girl – Kathryn something – stood there at the top of the steps, looking from Chloe to Olly, and back to Olly. He fidgeted his hands in his pockets. Chloe stared at her feet, her face flaming.

~

Kathryn wasn't expecting that when she went into the sports centre. Olly Bradshaw and Chloe Johnstone, flustered, hot-faced. Guilty. Olly slid his eyes off Kathryn. No *Earth Tremors* today. No. No insults. He pretended to search in his pockets. Chloe Johnstone hung her head, let her fair fall over her face.

"Isn't one girlfriend enough for you?" Kathryn said. She didn't know where that voice came from. "You know, her friend, Amy."

"Uh…Kathryn," Olly started. "It's not—"

Kathryn felt light, buoyant. She had waited so long, so many years, to get the upper hand. It was intoxicating now it had finally happened.

"Things rarely are what they appear," she said. "Excuse me."

She walked past him, almost gliding to the vending machine, shoved coins in with a trembling hand, and selected a bottle of Evian. She didn't need cookies or chocolate; what she had was so much sweeter.

~

"I'm going." Chloe's voice was odd, high, strained. "I've got to go."

"I'll come with you," Olly said.

Chloe ran down the stairs, her foot almost missing a step. The guy on the desk downstairs looked up from whatever he was doing behind the counter. Olly caught her arm at the glass doors, steered her round the back of the building.

"Will she tell Amy?" Chloe felt sick, so very sick.

"There's nothing to tell her."

"She saw us, she saw you kissing me."

"No, she didn't," he said uncertainly.

Chloe looked at him. She's never seen Olly doubtful.

"She doesn't like you. You were rude to her. Remember, when we played badminton."

Olly sighed, looked away.

"I've always been shitty to her."

"Why? Because she's big? That's not nice."

"I know. It started years ago. At secondary school. She was fat, awkward. Easy to pick on, you know. People thought it was funny. It went from there."

Chloe paced up and down the flagstones. She didn't want to think of Olly as a bully, picking on an unhappy girl. That wasn't the boy who kissed her, whose hands made her skin jump.

"I shouldn't have done it. I'm not really like that."

Chloe stopped pacing. "I guess you won't be nasty to her again, will you?"

"No." He smiled crookedly, embarrassed. "I don't want to talk about her. Not now. Please. Come here. There's no one around. I can't stop thinking about you."

When he let her go, her lips were tender, and her face was scratched from his stubble.

"What about Amy?" she said.

"I like Amy a lot," he said. "I just...it's you, Chloe. I don't want to hurt Amy. She's lovely."

"She's my best friend."

"She told me you two go right back."

"To nursery school. My mum and her parents...What's going on?"

"I've told you how I feel about you. But you haven't said anything about me."

"Christ, you know."

This time it was Chloe who reached out for Olly.

~

Kathryn skipped down the steps, the bottle of water cold in her hand. Olly Bradshaw's face. She might be fat, but she wasn't a complete idiot. She knew what was going on. Olly Bradshaw groping Chloe Johnstone in the gallery, where they thought they were alone. And then she'd turned up. Earth Tremors herself. They must have been really engrossed in each other, not to hear her dinosaur footsteps approaching until the last minute, when Chloe Johnstone hissed *Someone's coming*, with real fear in her voice.

The cold water was much fresher than the sticky threads of a Mars bar. Perhaps it wouldn't be so hard to lose some weight after all. Surprising things could happen. Like Olly Bradshaw being afraid of her. Kathryn knew she'd not hear *Earth Tremors* again.

~

Chloe shuts the door behind her and Evie, and pockets the key. They're going for a walk into the village to buy a few bits; Chloe wants to visit Amy's grave too. She doesn't know why – well, she does, it's because of Olly coming – but it feels like something she should do. It's a warm day, a spring day. The sky is blue, not the recent rain-sodden pewter, and the puddles are drying out in Barrow Lane.

"What's that way?" Evie points to the right. The lane slopes gently down past the last houses towards the copse at the end.

"A few more houses, and a wood. The country."

"We never go that way."

"It doesn't go anywhere. A footpath. Anyway, we have been that way. I took you down in the buggy when you were little."

"I don't remember."

"You were very little."

Barrow Lane was bumpy, and the buggy had jumped over the ruts and cobbles, and Evie had grumbled. Beyond the last bungalow was a rough turning space, half choked with weeds, then the lane became a track, winding into the wood. Chloe had turned the buggy round and wheeled a grumpy Evie home again. She couldn't bring herself to go into the wood, to find the stream, the bridge.

She still hasn't been that far.

"Come on." She takes Evie's hand, and they start up the lane towards the village.

Heather's gallery is closed; there are no details about revised opening times. Chloe wonders what's happening; if Guy has had a relapse, or maybe Heather and Jas are just taking a break for themselves.

After they have bought some milk and eggs and washing-up liquid, they walk on to the cemetery. Evie's complaining: she's tired, her legs ache, she's hungry, can she have an ice-cream?

There are flowers on Amy's grave. Daffodils, just turning limp and brown. Chloe lets go of Evie's hand so she can run on the pale mown grass.

"Amy," Chloe mutters. "I don't know what to say to you. I never have. So much."

She looks up to find Evie. She's scampering on the meadow below the rows of graves, the grass that will, section by long section, be cut open to receive the coffins of those living and breathing today. Chloe shivers.

"Evie, come back here."

Evie whoops, and starts back to Chloe.

"I'm sorry, Amy. For everything." *And for what is to come.*

"Who are you talking to?"

"My friend."

"She's underground. You said she was underground. Can she hear you?"

"I don't know. I hope so." *And I hope not.*

Chloe glances over the wall to Millie and Matt's house. There's no sign of life. She hopes Millie isn't watching her.

"Let's go home, Evie."

"Can we go in the car?"

"The car's at home."

"But my legs hurt. Get the car, Mummy."

"I can't get the car, silly. Come on, we'll be home in ten minutes."

"Why's your friend underground?" Evie asks as Chloe tugs open the heavy wooden gate, keeping her hand off the splash of bird shit.

"Because she died. When people die they go underground."

"Are you going underground?"

"Not for a long time. Hey, you're going to Granny's tomorrow night for a sleepover. That's fun, isn't it?"

Chloe wonders whether to see if Heather and Jas would like to meet up, or whether she'll just have a quiet evening on her own. Completely on her own.

~

"Can I come and see you? At yours?"

Chloe ran her eyes round the tutor group. Mr Kendall talking to some guys. The girls at the window. No one was looking at her and Olly.

"At home?"

"At Orchid Cottage. Which isn't a cottage. Orchid Bungalow."

Chloe smiles, remembers. "When?"

"This weekend?"

"But what if—"

"They won't," he interrupts.

"I didn't finish."

"You were going to say *what if someone sees?*"

"What if they do?"

"I'll be very careful. When can I come?"

Chloe shrugs. "Whenever. Saturday afternoon?"

"OK."

"I might not be on my own. Mum, Millie, I don't know what they'll be doing."

"Do they know anything about me?"

"They know you're Amy's boyfriend," Chloe says.

~

On Saturday afternoon Elaine arrives to collect Evie. Evie's over-excited, and keeps shoving extra ridiculous items in her overnight bag: a neon pink baseball hat, an old crushed Toblerone box, cotton wool. Chloe gently removes them and checks once more for the necessities of Calpol, toothpaste, and Ears.

"I've just been over at Millie's," Elaine says.

"I haven't seen much of her lately."

"I was going to ask you if everything was OK."

"What d'you mean? I think so." Chloe remembers Matt in the park. His words.

"Just that…I don't know. She was very on edge. No sign of Matt. She didn't seem to know where he'd gone."

"Perhaps to a patient?" Chloe hazards.

"Maybe. Oh well. Are you doing anything tonight?"

"No, just having some quiet time."

"It'll do you good. OK, Evie, ready?"

They walk out, the three of them. Elaine opens the back door and Evie scrambles in clutching Ears, and jumps into her seat.

"Bye, bye, sweetheart," Chloe says, swallowing hard. "You have a lovely time tonight, and I'll see you tomorrow."

"I'll bring her back just after lunch. So you have some time with her before swimming." Elaine's about to open the driver's door, then says, "I think Rod knows a friend of Guy Lovell's. A solicitor from Helston way. He was in hospital with Guy last time he was ill. I'm so glad Rod gave up smoking when he did."

Chloe watches the car all the way to the top of the lane. It turns right, but she can't catch a glimpse of Evie in the back. She's suddenly very alone.

And this time next week? Would he come? Would he really?

283

He won't come, Chloe thought.

The St Michael bus was in its angled space, doors open, smelly engine thrumming. The driver was on the tarmac, smoking. She climbed on board, headed for her usual seat. The bus filled up; the driver hauled himself in and settled behind the wheel. Just as he was about to close the doors, Amy came running across the carpark to the bus.

"I thought he'd go without me," Amy said, plonking down beside Chloe.

"Where were you?" Chloe asked, and wished she hadn't.

"Just with Olly."

Chloe breathed in and out, as the bus reversed and swung round. She said, "Won't you see him at the weekend?"

"Probably not. I'm meeting some guys from biology tomorrow. We've got a project to sort out. We haven't done anything yet."

"Where you meeting them?" Chloe asked carefully.

"Newlyn. At Rosie's house."

"You driving there?"

"Yeah, of course. Hey, what is this?"

"Only asking."

Amy fiddled with the buckle on her rucksack. "I know we don't do as much as we used to," she started. "It's just—"

"Olly."

"Well, yes. I really love him."

The bus stopped, let off some kids, and growled on to Langford's. Amy shouldered her rucksack.

"I'll see you Monday," she said.

The little Mini her father had found for her was parked out-side the bungalow. Chloe realised Amy hadn't offered to take her for a ride since passing her test. That's what a friend would do, wouldn't she? But I'm not a good friend, Chloe thought. Not at all.

He won't come.

~

Chloe woke on the Saturday, nauseous with trepidation. She hadn't said anything to Elaine or Millie. She didn't know how to. They knew Amy had a boyfriend called Olly. What could she possibly say if he turned up at Orchid Cottage?

He wouldn't come.

"Can we go this afternoon? Please?" Millie asked Elaine.

"Go where?" Chloe came into the kitchen.

"Penzance," Millie said. "I want those red Converse."

"D'you want to come?" Elaine asked Chloe.

"No, I'm all right. I'm there all week," Chloe said, and walked out of the kitchen. They were going out. She would be alone.

"OK," Elaine said to Millie. "But we'll have to go to Tesco on the way back."

"That's cool," Millie said.

Chloe heard all this, standing in the hall, and her heart swooped.

But he wouldn't come.

~

The house was both serene and forlorn without Evie. Chloe spoke to her on the phone before Elaine put her to bed. Rod had been teaching her to play cards, Evie bubbled. He'd shown her a magic trick too.

Chloe hangs up from Evie and finds Olly's number in her contacts. It goes to voicemail; she doesn't leave a message. She keeps the phone beside her while she flicks channels on TV, and eats an Indian ready meal off her knee. About nine a text comes through.

Hello beautiful. With the boys this weekend. With you next weekend! Not long now xxx

~

On Sunday evening Jas arrives holding a large carrier bag.

"I've brought some of my favourite dollies to show Evie," she tells Chloe. "The ones I liked best."

"That's sweet." Chloe glances into the bag, and sees twists of crimson and gold hair, pastel dresses. "Evie, you must be really careful with Jas's dollies."

"When Guy comes home," Heather says, as they walk to the car. "I think Jas will have to stay at home with him when I'm swimming. I'm sorry. I know Evie loves having her, but Guy can't be left alone."

"It's fine. I understand. I'll speak to Millie. Or Matt. Perhaps Evie and Jas could still see each other at some time?"

"Of course."

"You must both be so happy to have him home soon."

"I'm terrified," Heather says.

286

"Well done!" Christa says as Chloe reaches for the rail. "You've really come on tonight. It's starting to look like front crawl."

"I doubt that," Chloe says, but she can't help the grin cracking on her face.

"Well, I think so. Keep it up. Then we can start thinking about breathing. I'm going up to Kat and Heather, but you're fine to carry on on your own."

Christa starts to swim away towards the deep end, turns round, and says, "You can swim now, Chloe."

Chloe Johnstone can swim. The girl who was afraid of water, afraid of the sea. Who let that fear stop her going to a beach party so long ago.

Stop it, Chloe snaps to herself. She can't really swim, not like Heather, and certainly not like Kat. She's managed a few widths, with her leg kick and her arm pull, and she's stayed afloat, and she hasn't inhaled a lungful of blue water, but she hasn't yet turned her head, her chest, her hips, to take that breath. Until she can do that, she can't really swim. If she's not breathing, she's drowning.

She kicks off the wall once more, into the blue. Ahead of her is the dark line marking the far side. It slopes suddenly to the left, as the floor falls away. Next time she wades further down the pool, to where the water laps at her chest. Her heart thumps as she launches herself forwards, but the floor skims under her as before, and she feels her arm breaking the surface and curling over, and there's the sloping line below her, and her hand is on the rail.

"That was great," Christa calls. "Come and do it down here."

Chloe doesn't want to fail in front of Kat. She hangs on to the rail and hauls herself to the deep end. The water lifts her up. Christa comes beside her, shows her how to hold on to the rail with one hand, the other outstretched, how to place both feet on the wall, how to lean into it.

Chloe's heart races. They are all watching her: Christa, Heather, Kat. And, oh shit, a couple has just come into the pool: the woman is creaking down the steps into the water. Chloe's about to say *I can't* and then, suddenly she realises this is the last time she will be in the water before Olly comes – if he comes – and she must leave on a high. She sucks in a breath, and kicks off. She thinks she's going down, kicks furiously, hears the splashes behind her. She's in six feet of water, and she can't stand, she must, must, must, reach the other side. Her outstretched gliding hand touches the side. The surge of relief, and something else too: it felt great. It was exciting. It was frightening. She was frightened but she'd done it.

~

"Can I help? Are you looking for anything in particular?" Kat asks the woman in *Imago*.

She has wandered round the shop two, three times, not really looking at anything. She's probably about sixty, with a pale blonde bob. She's wearing slim navy jeans and a patchwork jacket.

"I'm just looking." She slides a book off the shelf, fans the pages, and puts it back.

Kat's puzzled. She doesn't look like a shoplifter. She doesn't seem very interested in the merchandise, but she doesn't want to leave. Perhaps she's hiding in the shop, avoiding someone on the street. Kat glances to the door.

The woman adjusts the handbag on her shoulder, and starts for the door. She's just about to put her hand on the knob, when she hesitates, and walks back to Kat.

"I'm sorry," she says. "Are you Kat?"

Kat studies her. She has no idea who she might be. Not someone from *before* though, she's certain.

"Yes, I'm Kat," she says. "Do I know you?"

"No. You know my son. I'm Anne Hosking. Jason's mother."

"Is—" Kat's about to say *is Jason OK?* but stops herself. "We're in the same swimming group," she says instead. "Well, we were. Now he's in the earlier group." She's rabbiting; she stops.

"Thomas and Flora enjoyed going swimming with you and Jason."

"Yes, it was fun. They're great kids." Kat's uneasy.

"Flora's especially pleased her father has found a lady friend."

"Oh, but I'm not a lady friend. Not like that. I mean, we're friends." Kat's face is hot with embarrassment.

Anne Hosking looks awkward. "I'm sorry," she says. "Flora said…I shouldn't have taken her word for it, should I? I am so sorry. I've embarrassed you. It's just that Jason's…the children's mother…she made Jason very unhappy. I'm sure you know all this?"

"No, I don't. It's nothing to do with me. I know she left them. That's all."

"Yes. She left them. It was almost the end of Jason. And he's been on his own since that day. Then he started talking about you, and you all went swimming together, and Flora was so happy, so I just assumed. I wanted to meet you."

The door-chimes jingle, and two young women come in. Kat is both relieved and disappointed. She knows one of them, calls out a hello.

Anne Hosking glances over her shoulder. "I'll get out of your way," she says, but she smiles at Kat. "I'm glad to meet you. I hope I'll see you again."

He talked about me, Kat sings to herself, as she unlocks a jewellery cabinet, as she hands out necklaces for the women to look at. *He talked about me*, as she wraps one of the pendants in pink tissue, as she slips some cards into a paper bag.

He talked about me.

~

Chloe brushed her hair again, and raced to the front window. Nothing. Of course. She trailed into the kitchen where the wall clock ticked noisily, biting off the minutes Elaine and Millie were gone. The doorbell rang. She jumped, and raced to the hall.

"I said I'd come."

His car was parked outside the house, where anyone could see it. If Amy changed her plans and decided to walk down to see Chloe she would see it straight away.

"It's OK," Olly said. "She called me this morning and said she'd be meeting up with her mates."

"Good. I mean, that's good to know. OK to know." There was no point pretending she wasn't an absolute shit any more, a heartbreaker, a Judas.

"Can I come in?" Olly asked. "Or shall we go for a walk?" He nodded down the lane. "Where does that go?"

"A wood, fields. Nowhere."

"Let's go to nowhere then."

"I'll get my keys."

Chloe fled inside and grabbed her keys, checked her face in the mirror – flushed, panicky, guilty.

Olly was still waiting on the step. As Chloe pulled the door to, he spun her round and kissed her.

"Are you pleased to see me?" he asked, when he let her go.

"Yes," she said. "You know I am. I just…I don't know…it's Amy."

"Yeah, I know." He took her hand, and they walked together down the garden path, past his car, and into Barrow Lane.

There were foxgloves in the hedgerows, poppies, pale wild roses. The mud underfoot was dry and baked hard. Summer had come.

"What's happening?" Chloe asked.

"I don't know," Olly said, and she thought she had never known him sound so serious and honest as when he was talking about her. "I really like you, Chloe, you know that. I always have. I wish…I wish you'd come to that party. Then I'd have met you first."

"I wouldn't have got a look in with Amy there."

"You would. You would."

"But you like Amy, don't you?"

291

"Yes. She's lovely and I think she loves me. But I never intended it to go on so long or be so heavy. I knew she wasn't the right girl for that kind of thing. Shit, she even got me to postpone going to uni. I shouldn't have done that."

"What are you going to do next year?"

"I've got a couple of jobs lined up for after my A-levels. I want to get a place of my own. I want to be here with you."

"And Amy? What about her?"

"I don't want any hassle now. A-levels are important. I can't do anything right now."

Do anything. Dump Amy for her?

Barrow Lane ended in a messy turning circle, straggled with weeds and litter. The track became a path.

"It's called Bernard's Wood," Chloe said.

"Who's Bernard?"

"I dunno. The guy who owned it, I guess. There's a stream."

Under the canopy it was cooler. Olly stopped her with his arm, and kissed her again. She was startled by his intensity, gasped for breath. The stream gushed beside them, over mossy rocks, and half-submerged ferns. The path crossed the water with a tiny wooden bridge. Its railings were crumbly and rotting. Chloe felt the sharp, damp wood in her back, as Olly kissed her, and wound his hand in her hair, and shoved her T-shirt up as though to tug it over her head.

"This is…it's all a bit fast for me," Chloe said.

She knew people her age were having sex. She knew Olly and Amy had been for almost a year, but it always seemed something other people did. Not Chloe Johnstone. And here was Olly tearing at her clothes and shoving himself against her and – inexperienced as she was – she did not misunderstand the tense hardness in his jeans.

"I'm sorry." He dropped his hands, adjusted her clothes, and she staggered a little on the bridge, more bereft than relieved.

"It's not I don't want to. I do want to."

"It's OK."

Chloe turned away miserably. She did want to, she wanted to so much she didn't have the words for it, and she was scared. It might hurt; there might be blood. It might be embarrassing, horrible. No, not with Olly. It couldn't be horrible.

"You've never?"

"No."

Olly wrapped his arms round her again, kissed her neck this time, gently, softly.

"The first time you do, it'll be with me," he whispered.

And when could that be? When would she have the chance to be with him like this again?

"Not here. Not on this bridge."

She tugged him across the stream. Sunshine came through bigger gaps in the trees. The dry grass of a field beyond.

"What? Here?" he asked her. "Wouldn't you rather go to yours?"

"They might come back." Chloe's breathing was ragged. "Please. Here. Today. With you."

~

OMG. So so sorry about my mother. Jason.

Don't be sorry. It's fine.

Was she really embarrassing?

No. Nice. I like her. She was just looking out for you all.

I guess. She can be a bit full on. With me and the kids. But I couldn't cope without her.

Sounds like you all get on great living together.

She loves the kids. My sister and her husband moved to New Zealand, so she doesn't see their boys.

Will you stay living with her?

Not sure. Perhaps when the kids are older we'll get our own place. I'd like a bigger garden. And more space. See what happens.

This is great, Kat thinks. We're talking on text. If only I could take it that stage further, ask him over for a drink. But she knows she'll have to be very careful with Jason. Careful and discreet. Especially now his mother knows about her.

~

The ground was hard and uncomfortable, and Chloe knew there was dirt and soil in her hair. She felt a little drunk, lightheaded. She couldn't exactly remember how her T-shirt and jeans came off. Despite the sun, the air was chill on her skin. Olly took off his shirt. He was broadening out into a man. He knelt over her to undo her bra, and she suddenly thought of him doing that with Amy, and felt sick.

"Are you OK?" he asked, dropping the scrap of lace onto the grass.

She nodded, saw the bright blue sky behind his head, the green of his eyes, the gold and red lights in his hair.

"You're beautiful," she said.

"So are you, Chloe Johnstone. Chloe Johnstone of Orchid Cottage."

She smiled. "Which isn't a cottage."

He pulled a packet from the pocket of his jeans before he tugged them off. Chloe hadn't even thought of that. He was so much older, more worldly, than her. So much more like Amy.

"Look at me, Chloe," he said.

~

They are booting me out end of week, Guy writes on his Boogie Board.

"I thought they said Easter? That's a week away. Not that we don't want you home," Heather amends. "It's just – are you ready? You can't speak yet."

New cons says ready to go. Says will still have speech therapy appts. And radio in couple of weeks.

Phil Rowan wouldn't be booting Guy out yet, Heather thinks. He's so thin and pale. He has eaten some soft foods, but he's still making up calories with the feeding pump. And more radiotherapy. Oh shit. Guy hated radiotherapy before. It left him weak and exhausted, coughing up blood. Burnt skin.

"Is it daily radio again?"

Guy nods, holds up six digits.

"Six sessions? No, six weeks?"

Another nod.

Six weeks of daily radiotherapy. As if he hadn't had enough.

They want to clear ward for Easter.

"Yeah, well they could keep you till Easter then, couldn't they? I'm scared. Scared how you'll cope at home."

Just have to, won't I? I don't get a choice.

~

Chloe stretched out for her clothes, dropped them over her. She felt dizzy, too close to the ground, to the earth's pulse.

"Was it all right?" Olly asked.

"Yes, yes."

"So why won't you look at me?"

"I think…I think you're going to hurt me terribly."

"I won't. I won't hurt you. I promise. That was wonderful. Amazing. Please look at me."

Chloe turned her head.

His eyes, green and searching. "You did want to?"

"Of course. It's just now I think you're comparing me to her. To Amy."

"I'm not even thinking about her. I'm not comparing anyone to anyone."

Chloe sat up, started to untangle her T-shirt, turn it the right way round.

"Amy told me about the first time she did it with you. In the car."

"Chloe, please don't. Don't spoil this."

"I'm sorry." She sat cross-legged, her jeans in a ball on her knees. "I've ruined everything. I was so happy when you came to see me."

"You didn't think I would."

"No. But you did."

She smiled at him, and he kissed her again, on the mouth, and the cheek, and hair, knotted now with grass.

"You'll always remember me now," he said. "You always remember your first time."

"So you'll always remember Amy in the car." She said it before she could stop it; as she spoke, she knew, for more than one reason, she should have stayed quiet.

"That wasn't the first time for me," he said. He said it openly, honestly.

"She thinks it was."

Olly shrugged, buttoned up his shirt.

"Who was it? Justine?"

"She was the second. Chloe, don't look like that. It was before I even knew you. The first one was a girl who's left Penzance. It doesn't matter now, does it? I'm here with you. It's you I want."

"Really?" she asked him.

"Really. Can I see you again?"

Chloe laughed, a laugh of relief and happiness and sadness. She threw her arms round him, and buried her face in his chest.

"I couldn't bear it if you didn't. Not after today."

He smoothed her hair, flicked out a leaf. "You look a right state."

"I feel a right state."

"In a good way?"

"In a very good way." She glanced down at Olly's watch. "They'll be home soon. Mum and Millie. I'm sure of it."

"You'd rather I was gone?"

Chloe bit her lip. "Yes."

"Are you going to tell them anything?"

"Not yet."

"OK." He stood up, hauled her to her feet.

Hand in hand they walked back into the copse, over the frothing stream, and out into the bottom of Barrow Lane. Chloe's heart thumped fiercely. If Elaine and Millie were back, what could she say? Olly's car was on the lane outside the house. They were returning from the field, stained with soil and grass. Happiness. Guilt. She wouldn't even need any words.

But Elaine's car was not there.

Olly dug his keys out of his pocket.

"I can't wait to see you next week," he said.

"We must be very careful."

"We will."

He kissed her once, deeply, intensely. She swallowed the taste of him: something fresh, almost salty, with a breath of tobacco underneath. He drove up the lane, and she waved once, then ran into the house.

In the bathroom she tore off her clothes. Stray grasses fluttered to the floor. She looked to the mirror and could not meet her own eyes. She threw her clothes in the laundry bin and turned on the shower.

In the space of an afternoon everything had changed.

~

"Perhaps it's better he's coming a week early," Jas says to Heather as they put away the supermarket shopping.

"How so?" Heather empties a carrier onto the worktop: biscuits, rice, spaghetti, cereal bars.

"If they chuck him out just before Good Friday we'll have the whole Easter weekend, when the surgery's closed. If he comes home the week before we can get anything sorted out before. Any problems."

Heather considers this. It is true. It would be terrifying to bring Guy home on the evening of Maundy Thursday. And, though Heather doesn't say it, and though she hasn't been in a church for years, she doesn't like Easter. She's always uneasy on Good Friday; it's a day of foreboding to her.

"We should start getting his room ready. Make space for the pump and that."

Jas curses as a bag tears and a pack of tomatoes falls out. "We haven't even changed the bed," she says.

"We'll do it next," Heather decides. "We'll get everything ready."

~

Chloe woke early on Sunday, earlier than usual. Only one more day and she would see Olly at school. And Amy on the bus. And then she'd see them both together at break times. Amy and Olly, the glamorous couple of the sixth form. And she felt crazy jealousy towards Justine too, who'd had Olly before either her or Amy. She didn't want to speak to Justine again.

Elaine and Millie had returned as she was coming out of the bathroom the day before. Millie had bought some Converse boots and a couple of T-shirts. They'd been to Tesco. They had bumped into one of Millie's friends and her parents in town. They were talking and banging kitchen cupboards as they put away the groceries, and Chloe wanted quiet. Quiet to think, to remember every moment of the afternoon. One she would cherish for the rest of her life.

Chloe slid out of bed and left the room, careful not to wake Millie. In the living room she curled onto the sofa, hugging a cushion. She had hardly slept. She had come to a decision.

Olly must not dump Amy. If he did she would lose her best friend. Everyone would know what a bitch she was. She couldn't bear that. People in St Michael would talk about her, and Millie would hear it all at school. Chloe Johnstone nicked her best friend's boyfriend. Chloe Johnstone of Orchid Cottage. Orchid bloody Bungalow.

She wanted Olly. She wanted Olly so much it squeezed her up inside. She wanted Olly and she wanted Amy. If Olly wanted to see her again – and a little cold voice asked if it had just been a game to him – then it would have to be behind Amy's back.

~

Kathryn was making little changes. Eating a bit less – not that she ate that much anyway; it was so unfair. Now it was lighter in the evenings she walked sometimes, even if it was just down to the seafront and back. She hadn't seen any difference yet in the mirror, but she felt marginally fitter. The hill back up to her house wasn't quite so exhausting, her legs didn't tremble quite so much, her pulse didn't thunder quite so fast in her ears. She wore make-up too now. Not the perfect black kohl lines of Amy Langford, which Chloe Johnstone had copied, so they now looked like two handmaidens painted on the walls of a Pharaoh's tomb. Just a bit of foundation to make her cheeks pinker, a swipe of mascara, pale lipstick. She kept her hair long and loose because she didn't know yet what she wanted to do with it. She would cut it, she thought. Probably colour it blonde or red. But until she was thinner, until her new body emerged, she'd wait. But she was changing. Changes were happening inside her chrysalis.

Early one evening she let herself out of the house, and started walking down the hill, past the long terraces of three-storey houses, with pointed roofs and jutting gables. Houses like hers. She wondered how long she would stay in Penzance. She needed to move, to start fresh somewhere. She could go back to Birmingham. She could go anywhere.

A group of kids came the other way towards her. She crossed the road quickly. People still whispered and sniggered as they passed her. She would love to say she was so used to it, it never bothered her, but that would be a lie.

She passed the phone box on the street corner – one of the newer ones, made of smoked glass – then the hill fell steeply to the seafront. She could smell frying from the chip shop. It made her stomach contract with longing. But, when she walked out she never carried money. That way she couldn't return home with a greasy parcel in her hands.

301

Chloe could not eat breakfast on Monday. She felt so sick she almost didn't go in, but she wanted to see Olly. Even if that was all it was: seeing him.

Amy bounced up the stairs of the bus in a haze of new perfume.

"Good weekend?" she asked.

"Yeah. Didn't do much."

They parted company at the lockers by the library and study room. Sometimes Olly waited there for Amy, but he wasn't there. Chloe walked slowly to Mr Kendall's room. Would everyone read her secret on her face? When she opened the door, would they all turn to her in a disgusted Mexican wave?

Of course not. Olly and two of the other boys were at the desk talking to Mr Kendall. The girls on the countertop were gossiping as usual. The others were sitting on tables or chairs, talking, or writing, or staring into space. Chloe shut the door quietly behind her, sat down at a table with some others, and pulled out her French homework to check. Or rather, to pretend to check. Because she was watching Olly. He hadn't turned round, he was still talking to the others.

Was he going to ignore her?

"All right," Mr Kendall called out. "A couple of notices to read."

Olly turned round, looked straight at Chloe.

She remembered the green of his eyes. The cold hardness of the earth under her. The blue of the sky.

As Mr Kendall read a boring announcement about the new roof for the music department, Olly came over to Chloe's table, and sat astride an empty chair by her.

"Hi," he said. "You OK?"

"I must talk to you."

"That sounds ominous."

"No. Yes. No, not really."

"OK. Later." He watched her a moment. "You haven't changed your mind?"

"No."

Olly grinned, and swung off the chair.

~

Guy slides down onto his bed, drops his Boogie Board beside him, and closes his eyes. Heather sighs. They have brought so much stuff back from the hospital. A feeding pump and a hefty box of food bags, a nebuliser, a ready-packed green emergency bag for the tracheostomy. A huge carrier bag of medicines: thyroid hormones, vitamins, antidepressants, calcium, cream for the J-peg, which is still in as well as the NG tube. Gauze covers and tubes, sterilised water and swabs for cleaning the tracheostomy. There's a wire brush for turning the speaking valve, the tiny white disc embedded in the back wall of Guy's trachea.

Heather piles it all up in the corner. She will have to clear some cupboards to fit it all in. She had no idea there would be so much. There is paperwork too. Leaflets and books about laryngectomy, learning to speak again, how to cope with the tracheostomy. Emergency procedures. A bracelet and car sticker marking Guy as a neck-breather. Heather feels despair swell. He shouldn't be home now. He can't speak. He's not ready.

"I'll plug in the pump to charge up," she says and unwinds the cable.

It looks pretty much like the ones Guy had at home before. Somewhere, in all the bags of kit, must be the giving sets – the sterile-wrapped tubes – to connect the food to the pump. And syringes for flushing it out. Oh shit, where are the syringes?

Jas comes up the stairs.

"Here's another one," she says in the doorway, dumping down a large cardboard box.

"Ah, there they are," Heather says. "The giving sets."

"And these." Jas hands Heather a sheaf of papers.

Instructions from the dietician about the food pump: when to feed, how much to feed, the flow rate. Guy's discharge summary. A note saying the district nurses must come and check Guy's thyroid and calcium levels.

I can't do this, Heather thinks, and watches Guy. He's curled over so his chin is pressing on his throat.

"Guy." She shakes him. "Guy, don't sleep like that. You're covering the trachy."

He rolls over and exposes his throat. He isn't wearing a cover on it, or a tube as far as Heather can see. It's just a hole in the red swollen skin of his chest and neck. An angry, dark hole. It rattles as he breathes.

~

Olly looked relieved. Chloe was confused. On the one hand she was relieved too; on the other she was disappointed he hadn't said *no no, I can't be with anyone else except you.*

They were round the back of the sports centre again, in a free period, hidden from eyes, but vulnerable too if anyone came round for a sneaky fag or a grope.

"I can't face it," Chloe explained.

"If only you and she weren't friends."

Chloe shrugged. "We are. And our parents. And they'll all hate me. Everyone will hate me."

"It's not your fault."

"They'll still hate me."

"This is going to be so hard."

"How can I see you?"

"I could come to yours. It's quiet down the lane. Do your mum and sister ever go out?"

"Not often together. And I don't know when they would." Chloe heard the desperation in her voice.

"OK. Look. You might be able to come to mine."

"How? Your parents like Amy. You said so."

"They're at work in the day. Times like now. Maybe. I don't know."

"People will see us disappearing."

"You know I'm getting a place of my own after the exams?"

"Is that definite?"

"Yes. I'm going to look at a couple of places. It won't be a proper flat. Just a bedsit kind of thing. I need my own space. I'm seeing a guy about a job this week."

"What's the job?"

"Bar work in the Mermaid. It's only part time so I'll look for something else as well. But I will have some time and a place. So let's be really careful for a couple of weeks, and then it'll be easier. I promise."

"You'll go off me."

"I won't. I promise that too." Olly kissed her and stroked her hair. "Are you walking back now? I've got to go to the library."

"You go on," Chloe said. "It's safer."

"OK." He lit a cigarette and started walking back round the square end of the sports centre, past the long glass windows of the pool.

Chloe watched him walk to the corner. He didn't look back. She stayed where she was, leaning against the wall. She felt so tired and so sad. So guilty. After a moment, she followed Olly's footsteps. She glanced in at the swimming pool. The bright water was choppy and surging. There were mothers in the shallow end, supporting babies with rubber rings. Chloe watched them a moment. Across the pool and up, and there was the high window of the gallery, where the vending machines were. She walked on, past the entrance, and along the path where the blossom trees once flowered. When she opened the door to the sixth form itself, there was Olly talking to some other guys and a skinny blonde. Chloe heard the girl say something about Amy. Chloe trudged past them, head down.

Later, on the bus home Amy said, "Olly's been weird today."

"Oh." Chloe couldn't think of anything else to say.

The bus growled as it reversed out of the parking space. Chloe gazed out of the window at some kids running for another bus.

"D'you think it's the exams?"

"What's the exams?"

"Olly. Being weird. Do you think he's stressed?"

"Probably," Chloe said. "Stressed. Yes."

"I can't wait for his exams to be done. He's getting a job at the Mermaid, you know, and a flat of his own."

Chloe couldn't find any words. She knew she had to be normal, talk to Amy about Olly, do nothing different to give herself away. Because giving herself away was simply not an option.

~

Heather roots out an old pill box. It's dusty from the memory of other ancient drugs. She washes it, dries it, and sits down at the table with Jas, Guy's drug sheet, and the array of boxes and bottles supplied by the hospital.

"These are only a few weeks' worth," Heather sighs. "We'll have to get them all on repeat prescription."

She punches out Thyroxine tablets, tiny white pearls, and drops them into the seven morning squares. Some of Guy's supplements, to be dissolved in water, are so huge she can't fit them in. She'll have to remember them. Make a chart. It's overwhelming.

When she's finished a week of medicines her fingers smell foul from the tablets. White, red, burgundy, they rattle in their compartments, when she picks up the box.

"I'll go and see if he's finished dinner."

Heather leaves Jas stacking up the remaining tablet packets, and throwing out the empty foil blisters. Please let him have eaten, she prays, as she climbs the stairs. It's been so long, so very long, since Guy left an empty plate. Please.

She shoves open the bedroom door. The bedside lamp is giving off a queasy glow. Guy is hunched on his side. The tracheostomy is still open. He should be wearing a cover. She must get him to wear one. His dinner plate is on the floor. He's taken a few forkfuls of mashed potato, hardly touched the fish.

"Guy." She leans over him, shakes his shoulder, still so thin under his shirt. "Can't you manage any more?"

He opens his eyes blearily, shakes his head. Heather picks up the plate and carries it back downstairs, tears jabbing her eyes.

~

Amy's geography group was on a field trip for the day. Mr Kendall was taking them in the bus, so one of the PE teachers took morning registration. Olly wasn't there. Chloe was deflated, desolate. The one day Amy was away and he wasn't there. But then he came in late, and Chloe wondered if he'd been seeing Amy off on the bus.

One of the girls from Chloe's history group was talking to her about the essay they were working on. Chloe nodded as she jabbered on about the Armada and Elizabeth's foreign policy. She couldn't get away. Olly was watching her. He wanted to speak to her. He knew, as she did, that this day was a chance.

The bell rang to signal the end of registration. Chloe loitered outside the geography room, pretending to repack her bag. The tutor group spilled out. Olly came last.

"I'll pick you up at lunchtime," he said. "In the lay-by."

308

And then he was off, catching up with his friends, and Chloe had not even had the chance to answer him, but it didn't matter because he knew she would be there.

~

"Hi Matt. It's Chloe."

"Hi. How you doing?" Matt sounds frazzled, tired. One of the boys is shouting in the background.

"Thing is, Matt. I need to ask a favour."

"Sure, what is it?"

"Evie. Is there any chance she could come to you again on Sundays? Guy Lovell's home now, as you know, so Jas has to be at home with him when Heather goes swimming. I don't know who else to ask. Otherwise I'll have to give up swimming."

"No, no, don't you give up. Of course we can have Evie. She's a sweetheart."

"Thanks so much, Matt."

I am so alone, Chloe thinks, as she hangs up. Evie's prancing around the living room in a sparkly tiara, waving a felt-tip pen like a wand. Other than Heather and Jas, what other friends does she have in St Michael? None.

Chloe often wonders if it was a mistake to come back to the village. Millie and Matt were already there, in their shiny new house. Millie'd been so smug about reclaiming St Michael for herself. The wounded party, who'd been forced to flee her childhood home, leave school in the middle of exams, lose her friends, because of her sister's unspeakable behaviour. These days there are many new faces in the village. Some nod at Chloe and smile at Evie, and Chloe knows she'll meet them again at the school gates when Evie starts in eighteen months' time. The older families, the ones she remembers from childhood – the Roses, the Gilberts, the Trewins – well, probably some of them don't even recognise her. But some do, and some remember.

~

"Where are we going?" Chloe asked, clicking her seatbelt in.

"Somewhere I've found. Somewhere quiet."

Somewhere he's been with Amy, Chloe thought. Or with Justine. Or that other girl, the one before, the very first, who disappeared. Did he still think of her?

Olly drove out of town and into the country lanes. Chloe opened the window; green tendrils and leaves bumped the car, and a scattering of fluffy seeds fell onto her lap. The sky was a bright, clear blue, the hedges were splashed with the colours of poppies and foxgloves. She felt, for a crazy instant, that they were on holiday together.

They hardly spoke. Olly pulled into a lay-by to let the car behind pass. When it had gone round a bend ahead, he turned sharply across the road, where trees hid a secret track. It wasn't a road, just a grassy lane, with two tyre grooves. Weeds and grasses grew long on the ground. The trees dipped overhead in a dappled canopy. Olly bumped along until the way was barred with a half-fallen branch, green with bright lichen. He turned off the engine, and reached for Chloe.

"What do you think of this place?" he asked.

"How did you find it?" she asked, and she knew she sounded petulant and jealous.

"I was driving home from the beach, stuck behind a tractor, and I saw this lane. You'd never see it unless you were going slowly. And I thought it could be a place for us."

"Just for us?" Chloe asked.

"Just for us." He tugged at her clothes. "Now, please, stop talking."

Later, Olly found a chocolate bar in the glove box, soft and sticky, and shared it with Chloe. She drank from her water bottle, and offered it to him. A car zoomed past on the road behind them.

"Are you ready for your exams?" Chloe asked.

"I think so." He handed back her water.

"Are you going to university? I mean, in a year's time?"

He sighed. "I don't know. I don't really know what I want to do. What I want from life."

"Nor me," Chloe said.

But at that moment, all she wanted from life was Olly Bradshaw, and the green shadows of the secret lane.

~

She didn't see him much for a while. He was taking his A-levels. Amy monopolised him when he was at school. Chloe went to the library or the study room. She knew Amy saw Olly sometimes at the weekends, and she was regretting her decision. Sharing Olly was beyond unbearable. She thought about the two of

311

them all the time. What they were doing, how they kissed each other, what plans they were making.

One Friday morning, near the end of the summer term, Amy wasn't waiting at the bus stop opposite the garage. While Chloe was at her locker before registration, Amy came up beside her, leaned on the neighbouring locker.

"Did you drive in?" Chloe asked.

"Yes. I'm doing something this evening."

Chloe quickly put her head back inside the locker, flicked through a textbook. Cool pages under her fingers.

"What you doing?"

"I'm staying at Olly's new flat."

Chloe's hands froze. She didn't know he'd actually got a flat, that he had moved in, that Amy was staying over.

"Where is it?"

"Newent Terrace. Up the hill behind the station."

"Oh yeah. I know it."

"You don't sound very interested," Amy snapped.

"I was trying to find something. Newent Terrace. Has he started at the Mermaid?"

"Yes, and he's got a job at Head Boy too."

Something else Chloe didn't know. Head Boy and Head Girl were two clothes stores, side by side on the main street. Clothes shops for trendy young people. They had blue and pink plastic bags, with silly prefect badge logos. Chloe didn't know Olly had applied for a job there. But she hadn't seen him for so long.

Amy peeled herself off the locker. "I'll call you when I get home on Saturday," she said. "Tell you all about it."

"Great." Chloe slammed the locker and twisted the key. "Have fun."

"I will."

Amy sauntered off to her tutor room. Chloe picked up her bag, which felt too heavy to carry, and started towards Mr Kendall's room. The upper sixth students had all left. Registration was flat now without Olly. Chloe trudged up the stairs. She felt sick. She'd feel sick all day. And all night.

Chloe was sure her mother and Millie knew something was amiss. She was miserable at home. It seemed to her the hardest thing on earth to nail a smile on her face, and talk about the little everyday things that made up the weekend. Rod coming over. Millie wanting to make a cake.

But I would rather be me than Amy, Chloe thought fiercely. If I were Amy I wouldn't even know Olly was seeing someone else. At least I know. He has no secrets from me.

Amy rang up on Saturday afternoon. Olly's flat was only a room, she told Chloe. A ground-floor room, with a single bed. He had a tiny cooker and fridge. You could hardly get round the bed without bumping into the kitchen worktop. The bathroom was next door, and he shared it with others. On the street outside there was a telephone box. Olly had given her the number, and said she could always ring it, and someone from the house would come and answer it. It clearly wasn't what Amy had been expecting.

~

Chloe saw Olly in passing when he came in for his exams. One lunchtime she opened her locker, and found a folded piece of paper. It must have been pushed through the vent. It was a Penzance telephone number.

This is outside my new place, the note said. *Ring it to speak to me.*

Chloe shoved it into the pocket of her jeans. She would learn the number, and throw the paper away.

She couldn't call that number from the house. Even if she were alone, Elaine had itemised bills. Early one Saturday morning, Chloe walked up to the phone box by the village hall. The red paint was chipping off, revealing a dull grey undercoat. The door was heavy to open, and it smelt inside. Chloe shuddered. Cigarette butts on the floor, a scrunched-up tissue on the shelf. She picked up the receiver, wincing at its greasiness, and clanked twenty pence into the slot. Mr Lovell walked past on the opposite pavement, on his way to the village, and Chloe hunched round, trying to hide.

The line rang out and out. She wondered how long she could let it ring. She was just about to hang up, when someone picked up.

"Hello."

"It's Chloe," she rushed. "Is that you?"

"It's me," Olly said. "Do you want to come over?"

"Today?"

"I'm not working till tonight. In the pub."

The line beeped. Chloe fumbled another twenty pence in.

"What about...?"

"It's cool. She's doing something with her Mum."

"I'll get the bus."

Chloe hung up and ran home.

~

Kathryn and her mother drove down the hill towards the supermarket. They turned into the top end of Newent Terrace. Tall,
narrow houses, like Kathryn's. Pointed gables. Bay windows.
Parked cars on both sides of the road. A guy swaggered out of
the phone box as they drew level. Olly Bradshaw. He went into
a house on the right. Kathryn twisted her neck back to look. Yes,
there was his car parked on the road. Newent Terrace was bedsit
land. Perhaps he'd moved into a room there. Somewhere to
string along his girlfriends.

"Anything wrong?" asked Kathryn's mother.

"Nothing important," Kathryn said.

~

Millie was in the kitchen rattling cereal into a bowl.

"Where you been?" she asked.

"I couldn't sleep."

"So where you been?"

"Just for a walk."

Millie poured milk and shrugged.

"Is Mum up?"

"Nope. She's having a lie-in."

Chloe hesitated. She wanted to make herself look better, put
on some make-up, but she didn't want Millie asking questions,

315

trying to stop her, saying she'd like to go into Penzance too. It was so hard, so very hard, when your life was a deception.

"I'm going into town," Chloe said at last.

Millie was still in her pyjamas, eating breakfast. There was a bus in fifteen minutes. She wouldn't be ready in time.

"Who is he?" Millie asked.

"No one." Chloe felt her face flame.

"Whatever." Millie turned on the TV, and Chloe raced out of the door again.

She bumped into Mr Lovell coming back the other way, holding a paper and a flimsy carrier bag.

"Morning Chloe. How are things?" he asked.

"Oh. Not so bad."

"A-levels going OK?"

"Yes. I think so. Hope so." She was almost at the bus stop, and she heard the bus grunting up the road. "I've gotta run," she said. "See you, Mr Lovell."

"See you, Chloe," he said.

When she got off, Chloe crossed the road outside the bus station and started up the hill. The houses were tall, thin, and grey, the roadsides lined with cars. At the T-junction she turned right up another hill. She glanced over her shoulder at the town below her. The railway line, the bus station, the winding streets. The next left turned onto Newent Terrace.

~

Fucking hell, Kathryn thought, as her mother drove back past the phone box at the bottom of Newent Terrace. There was

316

Chloe Johnstone, looking harried and guilty, outside the house Olly Bradshaw had gone into.

Again, Kathryn turned as they drove on. Chloe was knocking on the front door.

"What are you looking at now?" Kathryn's mother peered in the rear mirror. "Who lives there?"

"Someone I don't like."

~

Olly answered the door straight away and closed it quickly. The hall was narrow and dark, with two doors on the left, and one at the back. He led Chloe by the hand to the second door on the left. His room was tiny, but bright. A window looked out over the jumbled back garden. There must have been a basement or cellar built into the hill, because the ground fell away steeply making the window seem like one on an upper floor. Chloe gazed round. It was like she had already seen inside the room from Amy's description. There was a single bed and a tiny bedside cupboard, a few bookshelves, the kitchen worktop with the fridge and cooker. A desk and a straight-backed chair.

"What do you think?" Olly asked.

"It's great," she said.

Amy stood here. Amy looked out of that window. Amy lay in that bed, entwined with Olly, as darkness fell over the far west and the stars came out. Amy woke in this room, sticky and bleary, and turned to Olly beside her.

~

"So I'm here. At my parents'. Shall I come to yours tomorrow or would you rather meet at the pub?"

"The pub," Chloe says. "The Archangel. Let's meet there."

"When's your mum picking up Evie?"

"Lunchtime. Shall I text you when they've left?"

"Good idea."

"OK, then. Till tomorrow."

"Chloe?"

"Yes?"

"I'm so looking forward to seeing you."

~

Heather jerks awake. There's something odd, something new to remember. Guy is home. That's what it is. Heather holds her breath, listening to the house. It's quiet. So quiet she can hear the strange noises her ears make, feel the thud of blood in her vessels.

She slides out of bed and puts on her robe. It's 4.15. She'll just check on Guy, make sure he's not curled over the trachy.

The bedside lamp is on in Guy's room. That horrible dirty light. The light of a sick room. The bed covers are thrown back. The food pump is disconnected, with a half bag of pale slop attached to the stand. No Guy. Heather walks softly past Jas's room, and downstairs.

Guy is watching TV, with the sound down. Something about farm equipment. Heather sits beside him on the sofa, squeezes his cold hand. There are bruises along his veins. When he turns to her, she sees dried black blood coming from his nose where the NG tube hangs out. Under his pyjamas is the other feeding tube, the J-Peg, that goes straight into his bowel. She doesn't know which one he connected the pump to. Wasn't he supposed to finish that bag of food? She can't remember. There are so many instructions, so many drugs. Someone has to twist the speaking valve tomorrow, by sticking the wire brush into his trachea. Should she do it, or should he do it himself? She hasn't even looked at all the kit yet; she doesn't know what it's for.

"Are you all right?" she asks.

"Never better," he whistles.

Not a voice, hardly a sound.

~

No one knows. Once again, no one knows that Chloe is meeting Olly. She checks her face one last time, and steps out into the lane. She looks the same, and different. The same because she has kept her hair long and unruly, and the same gold-brown colour. Different because she's older, and there are crows' feet at her eyes, and because that gold-brown hair now glitters with stray silvers.

Her nausea subsides a little as she turns right at the top of Barrow Lane. A man she doesn't recognise is coming out of the red phone box outside the village hall. She notices because it's unusual these days. That was the phone box she used to call the one outside Olly's flat, the one Amy used that stormy Hallowe'en.

Chloe goes into the bar at the Archangel. A couple of old blokes. One nods hello to her. A young couple on a wooden settle, their table a mess of dinner plates, glasses, and sauce bottles. She orders a white wine, and sits where she sat with Heather and Jas. He's five minutes late. She takes out her phone to see if he has texted her. Nothing.

"Hello stranger."

Chloe drops her phone on the beery table with a clatter. Olly bends down to kiss her cheek. He smells the same, she thinks, incredulously, without the tobacco but it's the same citrus-salt smell of his skin. She watches him at the bar, taking a bottle of lager from the landlord. Like her, he's changed, and he hasn't.

He comes back and sits opposite her.

"Cheers, Chloe Johnstone of Orchid Cottage."

"Which isn't a cottage." Chloe clinks her glass on his bottle, and suddenly her eyes well up with tears. For times past, for people lost, for the passage of time, so relentless, so cruel.

"Hey, come on. I know it's hard."

"It's good," she says. "It's really good."

"I owe you an apology. I had no idea you'd been trying to get hold of me. I thought you'd want me out of your life for ever."

"No. No. But. Christ, it was so awful. The worst time of my life. Amy. You. Everything." Chloe drank wine. It was cold and thin. "I loved you, Olly. So much. I went out of my mind, knowing you were with Amy. I know I said not to do anything, and I didn't see how you could, but I felt sick all the time."

"I'm sorry."

"How did you think it would end?"

"Not like it did."

320

Chloe looks up sharply.

"I'm sorry," he says again. "Look, I was going to call it off with Amy. I knew that afternoon, that fucking afternoon and evening with you, that I had to. I'd stood her up, and I'd been lying to her, and when I was with her, I wanted to be with you. I couldn't even call you at home or come over because your mum didn't know what was going on. I had to do something. I knew you'd lose Amy as a friend. I didn't want that. I couldn't talk to anyone. Not properly. Not my parents. Dylan knew."

"Dylan?"

"Yeah, you know, Ginger Genius. The one who fancied you."

"He knew?"

"Kind of. I said I was in a mess. He said I should stop shagging around behind Amy's back. But he would say that, wouldn't he?"

"What happened to him?"

"He's in the States, works in AI."

Chloe drinks again. "Tell me about your boys."

Olly smiles. "They're fantastic. I love them so much. Their mother is always screwing me over with them. Changing plans and so on. It's upsetting them too."

"Who is their mother?" Chloe asks.

"Someone I met at work. We were together nine years."

"And then?"

"I did some investigating on her phone and email, you know. Let's just say she had other interests."

"That's shit."

Olly shrugs. "Just wish I could see the boys more without all the buggeration. Sounds like you've got it right with Evie. No one else involved."

"He was always married. It's hard work sometimes."

"Are you happy, Chloe?"

"I think so."

"Is there anyone in your life at the moment? Other than Evie, I mean."

Chloe laughs. "I'm sure I told you before. No. And that's fine. It'll happen one day, I guess. What about you?"

Olly shrugs. "No one important. I've had a few girlfriends, of course."

"I can't imagine you not."

"Do you want another?" He lifts his bottle.

"Not really."

"Let's go. I'm in the carpark over the way."

"By the cemetery?"

"I've been a number of times, you know."

"To see Amy?"

"Yes. In the early days. Sometimes I thought about going down to yours, to look at the house, find our field."

Outside the pub Olly puts his arm round Chloe and squeezes her to him.

"It's been far, far too long," he says.

They cross the road together. Chloe holds her head up. Let anyone see them, let anyone recognise Olly. Whatever.

"Shall we?" Olly asks, and gestures towards the wooden gates beside the carpark.

Chloe hesitates. It would be wrong, and it would be right.

"OK."

They stand together in front of Amy's headstone. There are fresh flowers there.

"I came once, and Jim was there," Olly says. "So I went before he could see me."

Chloe's hair blows into her eyes. She hooks it behind her ears, and glances over to Millie's house. She can't see if Millie is at any of the windows, watching her and Olly at Amy's grave.

~

"Are you all right?" Heather asks Jas.

Jas is sitting at the kitchen table spinning her phone round and round.

"Fine. Yeah."

"You don't look fine."

"It's nothing. I just had a text from Kelly. She said Andrew's going out with a girl in Heamoor."

Heather pulls out a chair, and sits down.

"I thought you didn't want him around?"

"I don't. It's weird though. Feels a bit weird."

Heather takes Jas's hand and rubs it. It feels warm and strong, so unlike Guy's, which is so fragile she thinks it might crack if she presses too hard.

"How's Dad now?"

Heather shakes her head. "I can't cope. He's just lying there, not speaking."

"Well, he can't speak."

"I mean, not communicating then. Not acknowledging I'm there. Not eating or drinking. That supplement thing, calcium thing, he hasn't touched it."

"Should he be back in hospital?" Jas asks.

"I don't think they'd take him."

~

They drive from the cemetery car park through the village to Barrow Lane. One of Chloe's neighbours peers at the shiny black Alfa bouncing over the ruts and stones.

"I've never been inside here. Ever," Olly says, as Chloe unlocks the front door.

~

Olly never came to Chloe's house. They met sometimes over the summer holidays, at his flat in Penzance, or they'd go to the secret lane. The only way Chloe could get in touch with him was by ringing the phone box. Sometimes he would answer it, sometimes someone else from the house would – and either fetch him out or say he wasn't there – and sometimes it rang out and out. Once a man answered and said *this is the phone box in Newent Terrace.* Chloe asked him if he could bang on the door of number one, and ask for Olly, but he hung up, and the telephone gulped her fifty pence with a happy clang.

And all this time Amy went to Olly's flat and stayed over. Chloe imagined her Mini parked possessively outside by the phone box. She tried to keep up to date with Amy so she knew when she'd be at Olly's, knew when it was safe to phone.

One day Chloe went into Penzance and loitered outside Head Boy and Head Girl. They shared an entrance, left for the boys and right for the girls. She looked into the boys' half, her eyes adjusting to the darker interior, and saw Olly, smart in dark jeans and a bright shirt, shuffling some clothes on their hangers. She glanced behind her once, and walked in. Loud music thumping, teenage boys in a fug of Lynx and tobacco. And then, hell, Amy came floating across the from the girls' side, swirling a nebulous mauve dress in front of her, and Olly grinned and said something, and she spun around, and obviously she'd been in there with him all along, and Chloe ran out into the street again. The sunlight burnt her eyes, and the thudding bass still hurt her ears.

~

"What do your parents think you're doing today?" Chloe asks.

She had changed the bed that morning – why? why? – and the sheet still feels crisp under her. Olly's arm is round her, and her head rests on his chest. If someone came in and snapped them, they'd look like a couple in a film, drowsy after sex, sweat drying on their skin.

"Catching up with friends."

"You said your mum was poorly?"

"Yes. Problems with her diabetes. And heart. So I come down more now. And I'll carry on coming. It's not too bad from London."

"It's a long way." Chloe hates driving out of the county.

"I'd love to come back for good," he says. "You can be a financial adviser anywhere. But it's Jeremy and Isaac. I'd never see them."

"Do you hate London?"

"No, but I've been there too long now, and I think you get to a point when you want to go back to your roots."

"I came back to St Michael."

"Exactly."

"It was hard."

"Must have been. But Evie'll go to the schools you went to and all that. The twins' school…there's always drugs…some kid got threatened with a knife. I'd much prefer them to be at school here."

"That's horrible for you."

"When Caitlin and I were together, I sort of hoped we could move as a family before the boys went to secondary school. So, Evie. Is she ever going to meet her father, do you think?"

"I doubt it. He wouldn't want to know. I don't know what to tell her."

Olly laughs suddenly.

"Jesus. Here we are. In bed. In Orchid Cottage. And we've got children. Who'd have thought it?"

"Did you ever think…" Chloe stops, awkward.

"What?"

"Did you ever think we might have children?"

"To be honest I wasn't thinking about children with anyone then."

"Amy wanted children with you."

"She'd have been a terrible mother." He says it affectionately; Chloe doesn't know how to respond.

"If I'd done the right thing," Olly goes on. "She'd be here now. I shouldn't have been so weak, so lazy. I hate the thought she died knowing I'd been a shit to her. I do hate that. She didn't deserve it."

"She died knowing I'd been a shit to her too," Chloe says.

"I'd told her I was at the Mermaid that Saturday working. That was so I could see you. Then I'd come over to the scarecrows in the evening. She rang the Mermaid, asked them if I was still there, and of course they told her I'd never been at work that day."

"Then she called the phone box."

"Yeah, then she called the phone box."

"Who the fuck was it who told her?"

"It must have been someone else in the house. There were six, seven bedrooms. Someone knew about you."

"I think about her," Chloe says. "I think about her driving off, knowing her two best friends had ruined her life."

"That's why I let you go," Olly says.

~

Kat recognises them through the huge glass windows. She's never seen them before, of course, but she can recognise them, knows them for who they are. A few moments later, they come into the pool. A skinny girl in a microscopic striped bikini. Two guys, both dark and swaggering. They stop a moment by the pool steps. Kat and Heather are in the deep end treading water.

Christa is showing Chloe how to elongate her arm pull in the shallow end. The three prance off disdainfully towards the hot tub, and climb in. It starts foaming with a roar. One of the guys has his back to the pool, but he turns round, rests an arm on the edge, so all three are watching the lesson. Oh yes, Kat can recognise them all right. They're the sort who'd snigger and point at Kathryn Smith.

You can't do that now, Kat thinks, and jumps forward into the water. She swims away down the pool, her arms strong and sure. To her right she sees Heather's ghostly legs kicking to stay afloat. Ahead, Chloe and Christa. Kat stops, drops her feet to the bottom. She knows the three in the tub have been watching her. That just as she can identify them as predators, they can smell her out as prey. But they can't quite work out why. Not now.

~

Chloe is having trouble concentrating. There's that group in the hot tub, watching her, there's the horrible roar of its grimy bubbles, and always, always, the memory of the day before.

"What now?" she had said as Olly left her in the evening. "What happens now?"

"I'm going back to London tomorrow."

"And then what?"

"I'll come down again. It'd be lovely to see you. If you can. If you'd like to, I mean."

"Of course I'd like to," she rushed.

Snapping her out of her reverie, Christa asks "Chloe, do you get what I mean? Do you understand about stretching your gliding hand, rolling your shoulders?"

"I'm sorry," Chloe says. "Please show me again."

"Are you all right?"

"I had a...weird day yesterday."

~

The water level is high tonight, and Heather can only just touch the bottom with her toes. As she kicks her legs to the sides, she feels herself sinking inch by inch, and there's a blue horizontal line across her goggles as her eyes go under. She pushes herself up off the bottom, and flops forwards, tries to swim off as Kat did, but, though the water lifts her, she can't get moving. Her legs are thrashing about behind her, and the water suddenly seems so heavy, she can't drag her arm free and into the air. She inhales chlorine and gasps, flounders to the side, and clings to the rail.

One of the guys climbs out of the hot tub and throws himself into the deep end. Water splashes Heather in the face. The other guy and the girl stand up too, get out of the tub, but don't turn off the motor, so the roaring continues. The second guy jumps in; the girl poses on the poolside, fiddling with her bikini straps, before sliding in with them. Even underwater, Heather can hear the shrieking behind her. She can't get her breath properly, and stumbles upright after a few strokes. She wonders how Guy is doing at home.

~

Kat isn't going back to the deep end now. Heather has come down to the shallow water too. Those three are showing off. One of the blokes is upside down; the other has the girl on his shoulders. Kat isn't impressed. She isn't interested. She hates the way that, even now, she fears these hunting packs: cool people, thin people, glamorous and confident people. They're not doing much swimming down there. She can probably swim as well as them now, but they still threaten her. They always will.

Jason would never have been that kind of person. She is sure of that. She would never want to be close to someone who had once, even for just one day, treated someone as she was once treated.

She'd only had a moment to say hello to him before getting in the pool. After tonight it's Easter holidays and she won't see him for three weeks. Unless she texts him and suggests meeting up.

~

Heather turns the corner and imagines the flashing blue lights and neon paintwork of an ambulance outside her house. Green paramedics wheeling Guy to the back doors; Jas fretting on the pavement, peering up the road, looking for her coming home.

But there is nothing like that. The house looks quiet and calm.

Jas comes down the stairs as she opens the front door.

"How is he?"

"I made him some soup but he only ate half of it."

"I'll go and see him."

"I think he's asleep."

Heather drops her swimming bag and towel on the floor. She's suddenly so tired. She sees weeks, months, ahead of Guy hunched over in bed, leaving plates of untouched food, in the half light of that queasy lamp.

"I need to turn that valve again," she says.

The day before she tried to twist the valve to keep it loose. It was dreadful, poking a wire brush into Guy's throat, hooking its end into the centre of the valve, which she could hardly see. Heather doesn't think she even managed to do it, but Guy was spewing phlegm from the open trachy, and she was scared, so she stopped, withdrew the brush

"Shall I try today?" Jas asks.

"OK," Heather says. "We both need to be able to do it."

"D'you think he'll start speaking soon?"

"I don't know. I hoped he would."

"Maybe he should try one of those handheld things?"

"If it was me, I'd just want to talk," Heather says.

"Me too."

"It's like he doesn't want to. Like he wants to retreat into himself more and more." Heather gathers her stuff and takes her damp costume and towel to the washing machine before Jas can see her tears.

~

It's just like it was before. Chloe can't tell anyone. She flaps the wet bedding out of the washing machine, and hooks it over the drying rack. She's put Evie's favourite pink set on the double bed again. Evie is sleeping now. Chloe hasn't drawn the blind in the kitchen, and she looks out, past the blur of her own reflection, to the darkness beyond. The tangle of garden, that she does so little with, the crumbling wall, then fields. Somewhere to the left, the smudge of Bernard's Wood, where the frail bridge still spans the stream. Probably some of the same boulders are there, greener and furrier with more moss. Or maybe the stream has altered its course slightly. Everything changes, moves.

Chloe ticks off the people in her mind that she cannot tell: Elaine and Rod, Millie and Matt, Heather and Jas. She should feel happy – or at least lifted, high, weightless – but she feels sad. Olly is going back to London. He has a life up there: an ex-wife, two boys, work, a gym, girls he goes on dates with. If he does come back down again it will be to see his mother above all else. Will he want to see Chloe again? And, really, what is the point? If Chloe had been looking for some kind of absolution, closure, whatever, she has not found it.

She puts away the laundry basket, pours herself a glass of water, and turns off the light. What she needs right now is a cuddle with Evie. Sometimes that is the only remedy.

~

They all crowd into Guy's room: Heather, Jas, and Matt Sinclair. Guy is sitting up in the bed, scowling, the remains of fractured sentences on his Boogie Board. Heather called the surgery and asked for a home visit as Guy wasn't eating, and wouldn't move from the bed. She didn't tell him Matt was coming until he was there.

"It is normal to have some scarring from the surgery," Matt says. "That's probably why you are finding it hard to swallow, Guy. And, you know, that may get worse with the radiation. Have you got a date for that yet?"

Guy shrugs.

"No," Heather says.

"OK, I'll chase that up for you. You're seeing the speech therapist later this week, right? Mention to her that you are having trouble, and she can get ENT to take a look. Was it like this in hospital or just the last few days? Since you've been home?"

That's what Heather wonders. Guy was eating small amounts of soft food on the ward. She has tried her best to get things he could manage – mashed potato, white fish, jelly, sorbet, soup – but he is hardly swallowing any of it. Is it because he's home? And how much was he really eating on the ward? She wasn't usually there for meals, and he was always topping up calories with the feed.

"Yes." That awful high whistle of breath again. Guy speaking with his mouth alone. He gestures wildly, then grabs the board and stylus. Heather moves forward to see what he writes.

Getting worse last few days.

"It would be about this time," Matt goes on. "The scarring would be at its most swollen." He starts to pack his stethoscope and thermometer into his bag. "And how are you doing, Jas?" he asks. "Definitely starting to show now."

"I feel less sick," Jas says. "I've got the midwife tomorrow. I want to ask her about having a Caesarean."

"Is that what you'd like?"

"We talked." Jas indicates towards Heather. "It seems better to know when it's going to happen. With Dad and that. We need to know."

"That's very sensible," Matt says. "If you're happy with that, Jas. Ask Diana to refer you. Any trouble give me a call."

"Thanks," Jas smiles.

Heather follows Matt out onto the landing, leaving Jas talking to Guy.

"Is it all OK? Really?"

"After you down the stairs."

In the hall Matt puts down his case. "Probably yes. We need to keep an eye on that swelling though. If Guy really is having trouble swallowing – and it's not just anxiety – we should probably get him in for a scan soon. Just to put our minds at rest. And he needs to keep that trachy covered." Matt takes out a pen and a receipt from his pocket. "Look, here's my home number, and my mobile. Call me. Any time. I mean it."

Heather takes the scrap of paper, and whispers her thanks. She watches Matt drive off. Idly she turns the receipt over. It's a restaurant bill. A place in St Ives she's heard of. Expensive. She takes it into the kitchen and pins it up on the noticeboard. None of her business if Matt takes his wife to a fancy restaurant for lunch.

She can't imagine ever being able to do that with Guy again.

~

The holidays had gone. September had crept in at the back end of summer. The early mornings were cooler, mistier. The tourists had gone home.

There were new kids waiting for the bus outside the pub. The year below Chloe from St Michael school, starting their first day of A-levels.

When Amy got on the bus a few moments later, Chloe realised she hadn't seen her or heard from her in days. It was her eighteenth in a couple of weeks. She and Olly were going to see a band, and she'd stay over at his flat after.

"If you keep staying there with him," Chloe ventured. "Will it stay special?" She felt sick as she spoke; she'd love to stay just one night with him.

"Of course it's special," Amy huffed. "We've been together over a year. We love each other."

"OK," Chloe said.

"We saw Dylan the other day. He wondered if you'd like to hang out sometime? Before he goes to Oxford. Shall I give him your number?"

"What? No. God, no."

"What's wrong with you? You can't be a maiden aunt for ever. He's a genius, you know."

"So everyone says. Hey, I'm starting my driving lessons soon."

"Ah great. I love being able to drive myself. You do all the manoeuvres round Olly's place. I remember doing parking on Newent Terrace."

Chloe was starting to form a plan. Once she knew when she had free periods, she could see when Olly was around. She could try to book her driving lessons at those times and maybe go to Olly's after. As long as Amy didn't have free periods at the same time.

If Chloe had a moment that day she would try to ring the phone box and see if Olly was there.

It was bleak at school, without even the possibility of Olly coming round the corner. Amy said she was walking into town at lunchtime with some of her friends from biology. Did Chloe want to come?

"No, I'll stay here," Chloe said.

She crept behind Amy and her two friends, watched them leave the carpark. Even if Amy was walking straight to Olly's – and why would she do that with two other girls? – Chloe had fifteen minutes. She hurried to the payphone outside the school office. It was up a short flight of stairs, and had a vast sunflower-yellow hood. She dug out some change and lined it up on the ledge. She knew the number of the Newent Terrace phone box. The receiver was sticky. She held it away from her ear and di-alled. A boy she didn't recognise bounded up the steps behind her and knocked on the office window; the receptionist slid back the glass. Chloe tried to listen to the distant line ringing out and out, rather than the boy complaining about his locker, and the group of kids below her shouting.

At last a guy picked up.

"Hello," he said.

"I'm trying to get hold of a friend at number one," Chloe said, her usual script. "Olly Bradshaw."

"I live at number one. Is this Amy?"

"Uh no. I'm a friend. Could you go and see if he's there please?"

"He's at work," the guy said, and hung up.

Chloe stood there, the sticky receiver in her hand. He had sounded hostile, like perhaps he knew Amy. She didn't think she'd spoken to him before. Perhaps she had; perhaps he'd recognised her voice.

"Hey, you finished?" demanded a girl with pink streaks.

Chloe dumped the receiver and slid past her. Probably Amy was taking her friends to meet Olly in Head Boy or in the pub.

She went out the front entrance, and through the carpark, then along to the sports centre. The same blond guy was on the desk. She padded up the beige steps to the upper floor. It was empty. She sat in one of the squashy chairs by the window, and watched the swimmers below. How could they do that? How could they move forwards, suspended in water, without sinking? It was impossible. Everything seemed impossible.

She missed Olly. She never really had him, but she missed him. She wanted to see him so badly. And then she had an idea.

~

That evening, Elaine and Rod were going out for drinks with someone straight from work. Millie lay on her bed, with her Walkman plugged into her ears. Chloe walked swiftly to the phone box outside the village hall. This time, she didn't dial the other kiosk.

"Hello, Mermaid, Louise speaking."

Bar noises. Clinks. A man's voice.

"Hi, could I have a quick word with Olly please?" If he wasn't there, she'd ask when he was next in. The woman in the bar wouldn't see the hot embarrassment on her face, even if she sensed it in her voice.

"Olly! For you. He's coming."

The clack of the phone being dropped down, then Olly said, "Hi, it's Olly."

"It's me. I'm sorry to call you at work. I just...I just wanted to see you."

"Tomorrow morning?" he asked. "I start at the shop at twelve, then I'm here in the evening."

"Tomorrow," Chloe said. She'd have to miss history. She didn't care.

The phone-box door clanged shut behind her. She hugged herself. She'd gone from desolate to happy in just a moment. A car honked, and she turned. It was Elaine, on her way home.

"What were you up to?" Elaine asked, as Chloe opened the passenger door.

"Just went to the shop. How was your evening?"

Elaine checked the mirror and pulled out onto the road. "Pretty dull. We didn't stay long. Rod's got a lot of work for court tomorrow."

If I'd been a second later coming out of the phone box I'd have been caught, Chloe thought. And I wouldn't have had a clue what to say. It would be so easy to tell her mother. So easy, and yet, like everything else, impossible.

~

When Olly opened the front door and ushered Chloe in, a girl was coming down the stairs from the upper floors. She had short black hair and a nose ring. She stared at Chloe. Olly wasn't touching her, wasn't doing anything suspicious, and yet inviting another girl into his room was surely suspicious, when the others in the house must have known about Amy.

"What would you do if Amy came round when I was here?" Chloe asked.

"I wouldn't go to the door."

They lay together in the narrow bed, Olly's arm round Chloe, his face in her hair. She watched the white slice of sky through the window. The front door opened, and someone ran upstairs, and then, Chloe thought, on again to the top floor. Then a shout from one of the upper rooms. She eased herself off the bed, and tugged on her T-shirt.

"Are you going?"

"Only to the bathroom."

She unlocked the door quietly, listened a moment. Nothing. She ran into the bathroom at the back of the ground floor. The suite was a bright turquoise. There were no personal belongings in there. No bottles or creams, no toothbrushes or razors. Just a half roll of peach-coloured lavatory paper, and a bottle of liquid soap. No towel. She dried her hands on her T-shirt and ran back to Olly's room.

~

"What were you up to?" Amy's voice at Chloe's shoulder.

They were outside the library, by the lockers. Chloe hadn't seen Amy appear.

"Up to?"

"Sam said you weren't in history. She asked if I knew where you were."

"I didn't feel well," Chloe said. "I went to the swimming pool."

"Why'd you do that?"

"Just to sit up there and watch the pool." Chloe opened her locker, fiddled inside.

"She thought you'd gone off to meet someone," Amy said.

"Hardly." Chloe slammed the locker and straightened up. She wondered if Amy could smell Olly on her.

"I told her you wouldn't be doing that," Amy said.

~

Kat's watching yet another of those house programmes. An impossibly thin presenter, who doesn't look like she knows anything about property, simpers at an older couple, awkwardly clutching hands. Shot of a stone cottage. The clop-clop of the presenter's heels on parquet flooring. The oohs and ahhs of the couple. Kat sighs and reaches for her phone on the table beside her.

How are you all? Any plans for the holidays?
   Swimming probably at some time. Are you up for it?
Definitely!
   Wednesday best for you?
Yes, if OK with you.

Heather might as well not exist. She's sitting on a chair in the corner of the examination room. The speech therapist has hardly acknowledged her.

"Are you turning this valve?" the speech therapist says to Guy. He clears the Boogie Board screen, starts to write.

"No, no," the speech therapist says. "Use your voice. Come on, Guy, like I showed you."

Guy puts his hand to the trachy, and air whistles.

"We've tried," Heather says. "But it's very hard."

"Let Guy answer."

Fuck you, lady, Heather thinks.

Guy whistles some more, and coughs. He pats his pockets for a tissue; Heather hands him one from her bag. She hates this woman.

"The GP came round the other day," Heather says. "Guy's got a lot of trouble with swallowing again. He said we should tell you and you could ask ENT to take a look."

"It's only swelling." The speech therapist doesn't even look at Heather. "It happens after surgery. There's a lot of scarring to settle down."

A knock on the door. One of the dieticians. Heather smiles a hello. She remembers this woman from the ward. The dietician starts talking to her, asking about Guy, and how much he is eating for himself, if he still needs the pump overnight.

"He's hardly eating," Heather says. "I've just told…" – she can't even remember the speech woman's name – "the speech therapist. Our GP said ENT should have a look."

"It's to be expected," the dietician says. "Everyone gets swollen after a laryngectomy. What sort of food is he managing?"

A knock on the door before Heather can reply. A nurse comes in.

"Guy Lovell? I've had a call from radiotherapy. Can you go straight down after you've finished here? They want to make your mask, and get a start date sorted out. Do you know the way?"

A strangled laugh from Guy.

"Thank you," Heather says. "We've been there before."

An hour or so later, and they're walking back to the car. Guy coughs and coughs. His whole body shakes with it. Heather shudders. It's like he was before he went into hospital.

Neither the speech therapist nor the dietician have absorbed Guy's problems. They didn't want to hear it from Heather and, instead of letting Guy write on the Boogie Board, they nagged him to use his voice, that thin gasp of air, but they didn't listen to what he was saying.

He told them he was afraid the cancer had come back.

In the car he whips off the tracheostomy cover the speech therapist strapped on for him. Before she starts the car, Heather looks at the site. It's red and puffy round the actual hole, that dark eye into his airway. White bubbles of fluid gather in the trachy and drip down to his shirt. She hands him a tissue. He can't seem to clear his chest, or his trachea, or whatever. He scrunches the wet tissue on his knee. Heather starts the ignition.

"Good they're going to get on with radiotherapy soon," she says.

If she can just keep afloat, buoyant, perhaps Guy will bob there with her.

"What would you like for lunch?"

Guy gasps something, but she can't hear over the engine because his voice is so weak. He probably said *nothing*. It doesn't matter what she serves for him: the plate is hardly touched.

She decides to call Matt later.

~

"I'll be back in a couple of weeks," Olly says. "Can I see you?"

"Of course," Chloe says.

"It was fantastic. The other day. I mean it. We should have done it years ago. I don't know why I didn't find you sooner."

Chloe hangs up, bereft.

~

Ice. Heather hates ice. She wraps a handful of cubes – welded together in that sticky way – in a tea towel and smashes them with a hammer. A few cold shards slide out and onto the floor. Heather drops the crushed ice into a bowl, finds a clean spoon.

Guy has dropped off again, in the few moments she was away. There's a trail of fluid leaking from the tracheostomy.

"New ice." Heather puts the bowl down and picks up the old one. She hates, hates, hates, that shallow pool of cold meltwater that sloshes in her hand. "Anything to eat?"

"Just ice," Guy whispers hoarsely.

Downstairs Heather dials Matt Sinclair's mobile. He picks up on the third ring, sounds harried.

"It's Heather. You said I could call. Do you have a moment?"

"Of course," he says, then mutters *give me five* to someone he's with.

"Guy's certain it's come back," Heather says. "And he should know. I mean, he knows what cancer feels like. They don't listen at the hospital. They say it's just scarring. But I don't think it is. He's only eating ice today. That's all he can manage. He had such trouble with his tablets this morning. I think tonight I'll have to crush them and put them down the tube."

"OK, well, remember how easily those tubes can get blocked. So make sure you syringe it really well after."

"I will. Matt, is there anything you can do? Can you speak to them at the hospital? If Phil Rowan were there he'd listen, I'm sure. All they're fussing about is Guy speaking with the valve, and there's no rush for that. They won't even consider he might have a point."

"I'll call them tomorrow," Matt says. "I'll see if I can get a CT sorted out. To reassure you all, if nothing else."

Heather exhales. She didn't realise she'd been holding her breath, as though she were under the blue pool water.

"Thank you," she breathes. "That'd be brilliant. To reassure us."

To reassure us, she says to herself again after she's ended the call. *To reassure us.* Or to devastate us.

~

Chloe started her driving lessons. Her instructor – not the one Amy had – picked her up in the lay-by outside the college.

Within a couple of weeks she was in Newent Terrace, trying to do a three-point turn, without hitting the kerb, or any of the parked cars. She was farther up the road than Olly's house, farther than the phone box, but she could see his car out of the corner of her eye, as she brought up the clutch and stalled. She fumbled with the keys, and her feet were shaking.

"OK, let's drive down the hill now."

Chloe started down Newent Terrace. Olly's front door opened. Olly and Amy came out together. Chloe thought Amy was at school.

"This side of the road."

"Sorry," Chloe muttered, straightening the wheel.

In her mirror she saw them kiss, then Amy skipped away and Olly disappeared inside.

~

"I've managed to get Guy a CT," Matt says. "After Easter, of course."

"That's brilliant, thank you so much." Heather writes down the day and time. "How did you manage it?"

"With difficulty," he says. "Scarring and swelling is very likely, but I want to be sure."

The front door opens, and Jas comes in with her pregnancy folder under her arm. Heather gives her a quick thumbs up, mouths *Matt Sinclair* at her.

"He's arranged a scan," Heather says when she's said goodbye to Matt. "How did you get on?"

"Fine," Jas says. "Diana's going to send me to the obstetrician to talk about a Caesarean. I told her Matt thought it was the right thing. And easier for us, given…everything."

"I'll go and tell Guy about the scan. I'd better take some more ice, I suppose."

~

Evie doesn't stay with Elaine and Rod on Easter Saturday. Instead they come down on Sunday afternoon to Millie's, and Chloe and Evie drive over. She has two small eggs for Zac and Luca, and boxes of Thornton's for the adults. Evie grumbles, says she feels sick.

"Because you've eaten too much chocolate already," Chloe says, locking up the Golf, juggling carrier bags and keys.

Matt answers Evie's thump on the door, ushers them in. Chloe can't remember when the whole family were last together.

Millie's had a new haircut, shorter and choppier than before, and a lighter blonde. Matt seems quiet, subdued. He's talking to Rod, but Chloe notices he's chewing his fingernails, and she doesn't recall ever seeing him do that before.

~

I've got some amazing news. You won't believe it! I'll tell you when we meet. J

Kat's stomach drops. Amazing news. Dawn's come back, clean of drugs, and metamorphosed into wonder-wife-and-mother? Or he's actually been on Plenty of Fish or Tinder or

346

whatever and secretly been dating women, and now he's found The One?

Kat glances at the young couple sifting through the T-shirt rack, and wonders what the hell to write back. A woman bursts into *Imago* with a jangling of bells, and asks Kat if the necklace she ordered is in yet. Kat puts down her phone, and goes out the back to fetch the black velvet box. She talks about the mother-of-pearl wings of the butterfly, and where she first found the jewellery range, and tries to smile naturally at the customer, but inside she's burning up, certain that Jason's amazing news will not be amazing for her.

~

Amy's eighteenth passed. She spent it with Olly. Chloe didn't faint, or vomit, or die. She plodded through the hours, keeping her mind in stasis, knowing that it would come to an end eventually. Amy gushed about it at school the next week and Chloe muttered silently *past tense, past tense, it's happened, it can't hurt me now* over and over in her head.

"Would you like to come over on Saturday afternoon?" Amy asked.

"To yours?" Chloe didn't mean to sound so surprised.

"Well, yes. We could watch a film or something."

Chloe didn't want to. She didn't want to be in the house with Amy's parents and her brothers. Not with what she was doing. But to refuse would look even worse.

"That'd be great," she said.

On the Saturday Chloe got off the bus at Langford's, and waited for it to wheeze off before crossing the road. She noticed Amy's Mini was missing from its usual place. The garage was officially closed, but Dave had his head under a bonnet, and a radio blared from inside the workshop.

"Hello Chloe," June Langford said, as she opened the door. She looked puzzled. "We haven't seen you for ages…but Amy's not here."

"Oh." Chloe realised she'd known it as soon as the bus pulled off, and she saw the empty parking space.

"She's gone to Olly's…had she arranged to meet you here?"

"I…I must have misunderstood."

"Oh, that's no good," June said. "She's stood you up. Come and have a cup of tea and Pete can drive you back."

Chloe hovered, awkward. "I can get the bus. Don't worry."

"The bus isn't for ages. Come on, I haven't seen you for so long. I am sorry about Amy."

Chloe stepped into the house she'd been into so many times before, yet not visited for so long. Jim was sitting at the kitchen table with the paper and a beer. Pete was doing something in the garden. She just wanted to go, but she had to sit with Jim and June and drink tea, and talk about A-levels, and how she wasn't sure what she wanted to do about university yet. June asked if she thought Olly was good for Amy, and Chloe almost burst into tears.

"Don't put her on the spot like that," Jim growled. "He seems decent enough. That's all we need to know right now."

Pete slammed into the kitchen and washed at the sink.

"Pete, would you be a love and run Chloe home?" June asked. "Amy's stood her up, gone off with Olly."

In the car – a black estate – Chloe glanced at Pete under her lashes. Amy once said he fancied her. He'd broadened out, his sandy hair was longer, more dishevelled. If Amy'd been telling the truth then, he'd probably long since moved on. Certainly he didn't give any impression of that as he swung the car onto the road and roared off towards the Bends.

"I don't like him," Pete said suddenly.

"Don't like who?" But she knew.

"Olly Bradshaw." Pete whooshed past a cyclist. "Everyone else thinks he's fucking marvellous, but not me. No. There's something. I don't know. He'll hurt Amy. I know he will."

Chloe twiddled her fingers in her lap.

"What d'you think?" Pete asked.

"Amy likes him a lot," Chloe started.

"Hmm," said Pete. "I bet I'm right. You wait and see."

"Just drop me in the village," Chloe said. "I need to buy a couple of bits."

"You sure? Here OK?" Pete stopped in the parking bay opposite the pharmacy.

"Thanks for the lift. Sorry I put you out."

"No worries, Chloe. See you."

~

They're the only people in the pool. Kat is amazed: she thought it'd be busy in the Easter holidays, but it's just the four of them. Thomas is on the poolside, almost falling into the large chest of

349

floats, rubber rings, and toys. Jason is cuddling Flora in the shallow end, bouncing up and down in the water. Flora shrieks.

"Kat! Catch!" Thomas chucks a couple of bright sinkers towards Kat, and scrambles back down the steps.

"We must tell Kat our exciting news," Jason says, lowering Flora onto her feet.

Our exciting news.

Something that affects all of them. Dawn is back. Someone else has come. They're moving.

I don't want to hear it, Kat thinks, wishing she could dive underwater where her ears are muffled with the cool blue, and she wouldn't have to listen.

Jason grins at Kat.

"It's incredible. You wouldn't believe it. It's crazy. I've met someone. Someone famous."

Kat hunkers down in the water, one eye on Thomas diving for the sinkers. Jason's met someone famous.

"I've got this client up the back of Marazion," Jason says. "And she told me a while ago the big house next to her had sold. Huge pile. Massive garden. All gone to wild of course."

"And I'm going there," Flora interrupts. "I've got a new friend."

Kat looks from Jason to Flora and back again.

"The other day I got a call. The new owners need help with the garden."

"Well, that's good," Kat says, confused. "I'm sorry, I don't get it."

"It's who the owner is," Jason says. "It's only Tessa Francis."

"Tessa Francis?" Kat gulps. "As in the Olympic swimmer?"

"Well, ex Olympic swimmer, yes. She and her husband have bought this house. Their daughter's starting in Flora's class after Easter."

"Oh wow, Oh God." Kat laughs. With relief, with happiness, with the sheer craziness of it. Tessa Francis. Olympic medallist.

"They've moved from Bristol," Jason says. "They want a quieter life. Their daughter, Lucy, she's been poorly or something. Anyway, Tessa—" He grins. "My mate, Tessa, wants me to go up and look over the garden, and she's asked Flora to go and meet Lucy so she'll know someone when she starts school."

"That's so cool. That's amazing."

Thomas and Flora are splashing each other by the steps. Jason steps closer to Kat.

"It'd be so lovely for Flora to have a new friend. Someone she's met all by herself, you know."

"And someone with a famous swimmer for a mother. Did you tell your mate Tessa about our swimming group?"

"I did, actually," Jason grins.

~

Heather stands in the bedroom doorway as she so often does, watching Guy. He's still sleeping, though it's getting on for noon. He's in the same pyjamas he's worn for days. They are damp with phlegm. His hair is wild and wiry. He looks shrunken. Each time she looks at him, he seems to have curled more into himself.

He won't see anyone. A couple of people from Ocean FM have asked Heather if they can come and see him. So has his friend Paddy. Guy refuses everyone.

His breath rattles through the trachy. Is this what a death rattle sounds like, Heather wonders. The room smells stale, sweaty. A bowl of melted ice on the floor. Swabs and tissues on the duvet. The Boogie Board, dark and silent. Heather picks it up, starts to write.

Going to the gallery for a bit. Jas is here. She'll check up on you. Please try to eat some lunch. H x

Guy doesn't stir when she places the Boogie Board by his hand.

He's got the scan the next day. The one Matt somehow got for him. The one to reassure us, Heather reminds herself, as she pads quietly down the stairs.

~

"It's none of my business, I know," Jason says, "But why didn't you learn to swim when you were a kid?"

They're sitting on a wooden picnic bench in the hotel grounds. Thomas and Flora are running on the lawn. Waves break on the rocks below the hotel. The sea is a hazy blue-mauve. Kat's spiky hair is still wet and she shivers. It's just too cold to be comfortable outside.

"It didn't work for me," she says slowly, and lifts her teacup to buy time.

"Did you have lessons at school?"

The poolside changing rooms, the turquoise swimsuit, Jonathan Roberts and his mother. *Blue Whale.*

Kat swallows Earl Grey, and swallows the memories with it.

"I wasn't very sporty," she improvises. "The school weren't interested unless you were good. That was before we moved down here." She replaces her cup on its saucer. "What about you?"

"I was the opposite," Jason says. "I loved sports. I played football and cricket. Cross-country running. But I just couldn't swim. And people couldn't understand it. They seemed to think because I was good at other sports I was just pissing about, but I wasn't. I was really scared."

"Those other sports don't involve putting your head in water," Kat says. "Hey, I've had an idea."

"What's that? Thomas! Back where I can see you!"

"You should ask Tessa Francis to come and give us all a special lesson. I bet Christa would be up for it. You must text her and tell her what's happened."

"Mmm." Jason pours himself another cup of tea.

"You don't think?"

"I've had an idea too," he says, quickly, dropping a white sugar cube into his tea. "Would you like to do something with me one day? I mean, just us. Without those two? I mean, I understand if you don't want to."

"I'd love to," Kat says.

~

When Heather sees Guy with other people she can really see how ill he looks. She's almost supporting him in the waiting-room chair. Under the hard fluorescent strip lights, his skin is waxy and grey. There's a terrible dullness in his eyes when he opens them. Heather got him to cover the trachy hole to go out, but in her head she can still see that dark red mouth in his throat. The muscles of his chest heave with each breath. His jeans are huge and flappy; she had to punch a new hole in his belt. Heather reaches out to stop the Boogie Board sliding off his knee.

There's a clanking and raised voices, and two orderlies shove a patient on a bed into the waiting room. The girl on the desk jokes with one of the porters, takes the notes from him. A man with a walking stick shuffles up to the table beside Heather, and pours himself a giant glass of straw-coloured cordial. Rustling as a woman flicks through a stack of *Hello!* magazines. A man and a boy sit down opposite Heather, both hunched over a mobile phone. A child shrieks from the other end of the waiting room. A radiographer in a white tunic, her trainers squeaking on the lino, taps the entry code on a door and disappears inside.

The difference between Guy and everyone else here is that they all look more alive than dead, Heather realises with a jolt of fear. Guy looks closer to death than to life.

~

The Hallowe'en scarecrows in St Michael were well-known. They'd go up a couple of days before, or on Hallowe'en morning. Like toadstools they would simply be there, standing, pointing, watching. There were stalls in the evening selling burgers and treacle toffee, gingerbread and parkin and steaming baked potatoes. There was a disco in the village hall for the youngsters; the adults spilt out of the Archangel into its chilly beer garden, lit with the burning toothy grins of carved pumpkins.

When she was a kid Chloe spooked herself with the scarecrows, with their masks, slashed mouths, vacant eyes. *His eyes moved*, she'd call to Amy. *His hand touched me.* But it was still fun, like watching bad horror films with the light off. As she got older, Chloe found a new darkness, a new sadness, to the scarecrows. The sense of time marching on, of harvests cut and stored, seasons turning onwards, ever onwards. The decay and dark nights of autumn. The veil between worlds thinning and stretching.

"Olly's working in the Mermaid Saturday afternoon," Amy told Chloe. "But he'll come over to the scarecrows and the disco in the evening. Are you coming?"

Chloe shrugged. "Might do. Don't know."

Hallowe'en was on a Saturday. The weekend at the end of half-term. Millie was meeting up with schoolfriends to go to the disco. Elaine and Rod were going to a private view in Truro. Chloe could hide in her bed, under the covers, safe from the noise and the fireworks and the music, hidden in the dark, wishing away another night of her life.

On the Thursday afternoon, Chloe huddled into the phone box outside the village hall. It was raining. The panes were misted. There was a slug sliding across one of them. The phone box smelt of piss, tobacco, and damp. A straggle of weed pushed through a crack into the corner of the concrete floor.

"Come over on Saturday afternoon," Olly said.

"I thought you were working."

Olly hesitated. Chloe shoved another coin into the slot.

"No, I'm not. I want to see you."

"Amy said…"

"I want to see you. Can you get here?"

"You know I can."

~

The house is disgusting. Heather hasn't done any housework for weeks. There is dust everywhere – and that must be bad for Guy's trachy. A huge tumbling pile of correspondence – bills, catalogues, receipts – slides across one end of the dining table. The last curve of Jas's Easter egg in lumpy gold foil. A bad smell drifts from the vegetable rack. Probably some potatoes that have turned. *Just do it*. Heather flaps open a Tesco bag and fumbles in the fruit bowl. The apples have wrinkled like desiccated hearts. Bony pears with blue mould smudges. Perspective is warped. This is not spring; this is autumn's decay. Heather shivers suddenly, as she drops a grey-blue lemon into the bag, with a puff of spores. She thinks of autumn, encroaching darkness, the night of the scarecrows, when she first met Guy.

She scrunches the bag of dead fruit into the black bin sack and ties the top. As she carries it to the front door she hears that sound from upstairs. That ominous sound. The hollow clink of a teaspoon in a china bowl, scooping up half-melted ice.

Heather's really spooked. She washes her hands in the kitchen, dries them on a damp towel that's been hanging there for ages. Her ears or her brain or her heart senses the ring of the phone a second before it happens. She knows who it will be.

"Heather. It's Matt Sinclair. How are you?"

"I'm OK." She shuts the kitchen door softly.

"Has anyone from the hospital called you about the scan?"

The scan. The scan to reassure us.

"No one," Heather says. She thinks she ought to sit down at the table, by that toppling pile of flimsy papers, should ground herself for the moment that is coming, the moment that will not reassure her, will wreck her.

"Would you like me to tell you?" Matt says, and his voice is gentle, and awkward, and – she also hears – deep with real sympathy.

"I think…I think you had better," she says, and she doesn't sit down, just stands where she stood moments before, and stares into the glazed whorls of the now-empty fruit bowl, still dusty with mould and a dried leaf, as Matt's words punch her over and over and over.

Extensive cervical tumour recurrence.

Inseparable from large volume nodal recurrence.

The floor of the mouth.

The hypopharynx.

The recurrent disease narrows the trachea around the tracheostomy.

The proximal cervical oesophagus.

Multiple lung metastases.

"Heather. Heather."

"Yes," she whispers.

"I'm so sorry. So very sorry."

"Is this it, then?" she asks. *Is this it, then?* She cannot pluck better words from her vocabulary. There are no better words, or worse words. Words are words. She has them. Guy does not.

"Probably," Matt says. "Is Jas with you?"

"Jas? Uh, no. She's at the gallery. She'll be back soon. Yes." She's gabbling, wasting those precious words she still has.

"I can come over," Matt says. "In an hour or so. I can talk to Guy if you'd like."

"I'll tell him. It should be me."

"Of course. But I can talk to him too if that would help. I emailed the oncologists before I called you. They'll want to change their plans for his radiotherapy, redirect it to these other areas. Probably add in some chemotherapy."

"You mean they'll be able to do something?"

"They may be able to buy time, Heather. But that's all it is. Time."

"How much time?"

"I don't know."

"I'll tell him. I'll tell him you've written to them."

"I'll be round later."

Heather sits at the table after Matt's voice has gone. The kitchen is the same, full of crap, and papers, and the dusty remains of rotten fruit. The vegetable racks still smells. The clock ticks. Every second that passes the cancer is growing and swelling inside Guy. Lung metastases. Five dull syllables like the hammering of nails.

Guy was awake spooning ice. He'd have heard the phone. He'll be wondering why she hasn't come up to say who it was. Very slowly, she gets up from the chair, adjusts the slippery pile of papers, walks to the door and opens it quietly. She's about to start for the stairs when the front door swings open.

"Hey, I sold two paintings." Jas shuts the door. "Kelly texted me and said could I meet up with her tonight? What is it? What?"

Heather takes Jas's arm and leads her to the kitchen doorway.

"Matt rang. Just now. It's bad. It's very bad. It's everywhere. He said all they can do is buy time."

"Buy time?" Jas's hand on her abdomen. "How long?"

"He couldn't say. Or wouldn't. He's coming round. We need to talk to Guy. Tell him first."

"How? How can it be back? He's only just had the surgery. Perhaps the scan's wrong."

"Come with me."

Heather goes first up the stairs. *Jas sold two paintings.* The words tap away in her brain over and over. She wants to ask which two. She's running through the paintings in the gallery, wondering which. What the fuck is the matter with her?

"Guy." Heather eases open the door.

Guy's in bed, propped up on a pillow. He looks uncomfortable. His eyes are open. Heather realises he never wears his glasses now. She can see the blue of his eyes unobstructed. The bowl of meltwater on the floor.

"Guy. Matt just called us about the scan."

"It's bad news," Guy wheezes through the top of his voice.

"It's bad news." Heather sits on the bed, reaches for his hand, his thin, pale hand, blotched with bruises. There's a jagged cut across his knuckles. She doesn't know how he did it. "You were right. It's back."

"Where?" A thin whistle, hardly a word, hardly even a sound.

"Everywhere."

Guy stares ahead. His hand does not respond to her fingers. Jas sits on the other side of him. Guy reaches for his Boogie Board.

I'm not afraid.

"I am," Jas cries.

"Matt's written to the oncologists. He's coming round this evening to see you."

Guy erases the Boogie Board and writes *ice.*

"I'll get it." Jas gets up, leans over to kiss Guy's thinning hair. She runs from the room without picking up the ice bowl.

Heather sits beside Guy not talking. Now they are equal, and she has no words for him.

She hears Jas downstairs crashing the hammer down on lumps of ice. She imagines Jas's fiery tears as she brings it down again and again on the chopping board and the frozen shards.

~

Two in the morning. Time has rolled over into the next day. The second day of this new shuddering pain. Heather's in bed with her laptop on her knees, staring at the blue screen.

Guy and Jas are sleeping. She checked on them both just fifteen minutes ago. She left the table lamp on in Guy's room. She doesn't want him to wake alone in the dark.

She's sent an email to Robin in Australia. She's sent one to the people at Ocean FM, to Paddy, to Carol, who introduced her to Guy so long ago. She's told a couple of her own friends, her parents. She can't keep writing these words. The battery is about to die on her, so she turns off the laptop, and slides it into its case. She's freezing cold, and wraps her robe round her shoulders. On the landing she hears Guy's wheezing breath.

When Matt came round he wrote a prescription for steroids. They'd helped with Guy's breathing before surgery; they should help again with his narrowing airway. Narrowing airway. Two of the most terrifying words put side by side like that.

Downstairs she pads into the kitchen to make tea. Her face pale in the dark window. She forgot to draw the blind. There's a white moth on the glass outside, not fluttering, just resting there.

The house feels different at night. More space in the living room. She puts on the TV, turns the volume down and flicks through the channels. Live roulette, *Countryfile* repeat, something with guns and shouting, something about the pyramids, do up an old car on the cheap, the Himalayas. She turns the sound up a tiny bit, watches the soaring aerial shots of the mountains. Rocks and snow and ice. Ice. God, how she hates that sibilant sound. She'll never take ice in a drink again. Not as long as she lives. A chemical-blue river thundering down a mountain gulley.

Guy in the doorway, holding his food pump. Thin liquid travels along the tube from the pump, disappears up his nose. The plaster holding the tube to his nose has almost fallen off.

"Can I get you anything?" she asks.

Guy shakes his head, sits down on the other sofa, puts the pump down on the coffee table.

"I looked in on you a while ago. You were sleeping OK," Heather says. She doesn't know what to say.

Guy is dying. He knows it, she knows it, Jas knows it. The last few years have been beyond terrible. The oesophageal cancer, the radio and chemo, the surgery. And while they were still reeling from that, it crept back, crab-like, and was slashed out once more. But now, there is nowhere to run, nothing to try. There is simply no way out.

Together in the half-light, Heather and Guy watch the Himalayas – snow, blue sky, prayer flags, Sherpas, scarlet and orange climbers, ice – while the liquid food drips steadily from its plastic bag into Guy's feeding tube.

~

Chloe is bleakly disappointed that Olly rarely gets in touch. Sometimes he texts her; once he called her. He sends her an email saying he will be down again for a long weekend. Would she like to meet up? Her downcast heart soars. She snarls at herself, but can't help it. He does want to see her again. He tells her he will come over again on the Saturday afternoon. He'll take her out for dinner.

Chloe wonders how many other dinners he's been to in London. How many girls he's gone out with, flirted with in bars, bought drinks for, gone to hotel rooms with. She's pretty sure he hasn't been celibate these last weeks, waiting for her.

There may once have been a time when he thought she was the girl for him, but that moment has gone, dissolved by time and tragedy, love and age, and she wonders if she is pathetic trying to grasp it back from thin air once more.

~

The times before. So many times. Days, nights, that simply weren't important. I should have kept them safe, Heather thinks. I should have preserved them, remembered them. So many hours with Guy, and soon all she will be left with are memories, and yet she has so few of those to show for the years.

She lies in bed alone, as dawn bleaches the sky through her curtains. The night she met Guy, the morning she woke with him, the hot blue August day of their wedding. Yes, she remembers these. She remembers Guy in the delivery room when Jas was born. It was November, stormy outside, but she was so hot, and Guy opened the window, and cold rain spattered inside.

And then other days, more hazy nebulous days she can't quite place in time. Guy singing Elvis hits, Guy meticulously masking round light switches when he was repainting a room, Jas tottering after Guy on the lawn, Guy saying something on a beach walk one evening that made her laugh so much she thought she'd pissed herself. Heather smiles. She can't remember the comment, but she remembers the bladder pain. Guy smoking. Guy drinking. With a start she realises he hasn't had a drink for weeks. He hasn't even said anything about it. Does he even care now? Holidays: Scotland, France, Greece, Norfolk, Spain. Guy and Jas splashing in a hotel pool somewhere. Where was that? She can't remember. Where was it? Guy coming out to rescue her when her car broke down. Guy helping her write difficult letters when she couldn't find the words. Sitting with Guy on the hard stone benches at Minack theatre, squally rain slashing down. What was the play? *Much Ado*? Or was that another time? Guy hustling a tiny Jas out of B&Q one Saturday afternoon when she'd had enough and started screaming. That must be eighteen years ago. Where does the time go? Guy trying to teach Heather chess, playing with only half his pieces to give her a chance. Guy shaking a bottle of Cava in the garden and spraying the sticky bubbles everywhere. What was that for? Would he remember if she asked him?

Heather lets the pain submerge her and throw her up again. If she rolls with it, she can bear it. All those days. There must be a day, a specific day, when the cancer first bloomed in Guy's oesophagus. When, the day before he'd had no cancer, and the next day he had. A hinge, a semi-colon, of his destiny. She will never know that date.

All those memories, and so many more. And she never sensed that foretaste of dread, that black edge to the day. To life.

Heather half-stirs. She wants to tiptoe across the landing to Guy's room, and lie down beside him, food pump and all, and feel the heartbeat through his thin chest. She's about to stumble out of bed, stops herself. She knows he would not want it. They will never lie together in bed again.

"Hey, how are you?" Chloe keeps her voice neutral. She's still wary of Millie, wary that she might say something about Olly, and Chloe doesn't know how to respond if she does.

"I'm OK," Millie says. "What are you and Evie up to today?"

"Nothing much."

"I thought I'd take the boys out somewhere. We've done so little over Easter. Matt never seems to be here. Have a day out before they go back to school." Millie hesitates. "Do you two want to come?"

"No, you go with the boys. Have some special time."

"If you're sure. Perhaps we'll go to the beach."

"I don't much like beaches," Chloe says.

She's unsure of this quieter, less assertive Millie. She wonders suddenly if Millie wants to see her, wants to say something. It's so hard over the phone to guess anyone's motivation. Chloe's still stung by Olly's indifference.

But he's coming down in just over a week.

"Sorry, what was that?" she asks Millie.

"I said, have you seen much of Matt lately?"

"No," Chloe says. "Is he OK?"

"I'm sure he is," Millie says brightly. "Just I never seem to see him these days."

As Chloe hangs up, perplexed and unsettled, her phone beeps with a new text.

Hi Chloe, sorry I haven't been in touch. Very bad news. Guy had a scan. Cancer back everywhere. If we're lucky we can buy some time, that's all. Maybe see you at swimming Sunday, maybe not. Hope all OK with you. H x

~

Hi Kat. Great news about date with Jason! Hope it goes really well. I'm sorry I haven't got back to you sooner. Awful few days. Guy had scan. Cancer everywhere. Seeing oncologists Monday to see if they can do anything. Probably not. Might see you Sunday. Not sure yet. H x

~

Jason isn't looking when Kat comes into the spa. She stops by the glass windows, and looks into the pool, but he's facing away from her talking to Tim. Christa's on the side by the hot tub, crouching down, gesturing with her hand. She's had her hair lightened to blonde. Below her Rob copies her gesture, and snaps his goggles down. Kat walks on into the changing room.

There are wet patches along the corridor, and an abandoned hair scrunchie. The air is so hot. She finds her breathing is shallow. She's actually scared of seeing Jason, now he's asked her out. There's still time for Dawn to have come back, for his mother to advise against it, for some beautiful woman to drift into his life.

One of the cubicle doors shows the red engaged line. A rattling inside, then the bolt draws back. It's Chloe Johnstone.

"Hi Kat. Did you have a good Easter?"

"Yes, not bad, thanks. You?"

Not bad? Not bad? Jason Hosking asked her out and it's *not bad*?

"Yes, good." Chloe shoves her belongings into a locker. "Have you heard from Heather?"

Kat stops. "Yes."

"Me too."

"Terrible," Kat says, chancing that Chloe knows about Guy.

"Poor Heather. She never gets a break from it."

"I've known other people," Kat volunteers. "And it takes over every part of their life. Nothing's left unscathed. For the person and the family. It's so destructive."

"I don't know if she'll come tonight."

"Can't blame her if not. I'll see you down there."

~

Chloe slaps through the wet puddles to the pool. Heather's coming in to the foyer. She looks exhausted, thin and drawn. Her hair shows its grey roots. She waves to Chloe and smiles sadly.

"How are you all?" Chloe asks.

Heather drops her swimming bag on the floor.

"We're...I don't know. We're seeing the oncologist tomorrow. They'll be changing Guy's radiotherapy now."

"I'm so sorry. If there's anything, anything at all, just ask."

"Thanks," Heather whispers, and shoulders her bag again. "Jas told me to come tonight, to get out, and do something for me. She's with Guy."

"Jas is very capable," Chloe says.

Heather nods. "I'll get ready."

~

"How about next Saturday evening?" Jason asks Kat, as he towels his bright hair.

"That would be lovely," she says.

~

Heather stands on the poolside, dazed. Kat and Jason standing close. Already their posture, their expressions, have changed, like they're sharing a secret. They'll get together, Heather thinks. They'll probably stay together. Chloe's climbed down the ladder into the pool. She's wading across the shallow end, ducking deeper and deeper to get her shoulders underwater. Tim's hauling himself up the steps. Rob's talking to Christa, with her new pale hair, by the towel pegs. Voices through the glass and a couple of girls go past to the changing rooms, towels under their arms. The smell of the chlorine, the hot thick air, the voices, the half-dressed bodies, frozen for a second, out of time. Heather panics. It's all too much. She can't cope. She can't breathe.

She kicks off her flip flops and grips the sides of the ladder. The metal is hard and sturdy under her fingers. She takes a step down, then another. The first cool lick of the water after the heat above. Down, and down, and down, and her feet find the chipped tiles. Heather doesn't wait for Kat to get in, for the guys to leave, for Christa to call them together at the rail to start. She takes a huge warm lungful of air, puts her head under, and shoots forward from the shallow end. She feels the bubbles leaving her mouth, the water in her ear as she turns to breathe, sees the floor falling away to the deep blue depths. There's a sinker down there, a red fish shape far below her. She swims on, fiercely, angrily; she feels like Jas smashing the ice cubes until they were nothing but chippings of frost. Her gliding hand touches the far rail, and she bobs up, stunned.

"Beautiful," Christa calls.

Heather turns back to the others. The guys are waving, as they leave. Kat's in the water now. Chloe's got the neon pink float. Heather just hangs on to the rail at the deep end, letting her legs trail below her in the soft, calm water.

The best she's ever done. And she can't remember one second of it.

~

"I'm going into Penzance," Chloe said.

"What for?" Elaine asked, puzzled. "It's horrible out there. They say it'll get worse tonight."

"I told you," Chloe lied, turning away, and shuffling through her bag. "I'm meeting Amy. She wants to do some birthday shopping for Olly."

Lies, all lies.

"Oh. OK." Elaine seemed unsettled. "I don't remember. Sorry. You're going to the scarecrows tonight, though, yes? You'll both be back for that?"

"Sure, yes. Are you staying at Rod's?"

"Yes. But I'll be back before lunch."

"Enjoy the gallery tonight." Chloe opened the door before her mother could delay her.

369

Rain spiked her face. Thick brown water gathered in the ruts of Barrow Lane. The wind was chill. A scarecrow peered over a garden fence: a bloodstained skull face wearing a battered fedora. The red paint was streaking in the rain.

The whoosh of traffic on the main road. Chloe shivered. The day was distorted already. Hallowe'en. Samhain. The Feast of the Dead. She felt it more acutely this year. Like a buzzing in the air, a shift of perspective.

~

They sit in a row: Heather, Guy, and Jas. Guy in the middle. The nurse, used to patients only bringing one person with them, had to fetch an extra chair.

"This is a serious recurrence," says the oncologist. "Some very aggressive spread."

Heather watches his face, searches for giveaways. But there's nothing. She wants to ask the question, but it must come from Guy, and she doesn't know if he will ask it. The Boogie Board slides on Guy's knee; Heather steadies it.

"I understand from Dr Sinclair, your GP, that you would like to try anything available?"

Guy nods.

"I won't lie," the oncologist says quietly. "It is very serious."

And? Heather waits. Waits for a figure, a number. Months, weeks, days.

"I want to rethink your radiotherapy," he goes on. "As you know it was going to be more of a clear-up job after surgery, but now we need to target the areas of recurrence. I'm going to send you to the technicians in a moment to see if your mask needs redoing."

Guy grimaces.

"Because that will take a bit of time, I want to start you on some chemotherapy straight away. I've booked you in for Thursday this week."

"Thank you," Heather says.

"The chemo will help with the head and neck disease, as will the radio. It should also help with the lung metastases. These will grow back after treatment. We'll have to look at the options as time goes on."

Options. Heather exhales at the word. Chemo, radio, options.

The oncologist shakes their hands, and leaves. The nurse goes off for consent forms.

"That's good, isn't it?" Heather says. "Chemo and radio."

Guy shakes his head.

"I know it's horrible." Jas squeezes his arm, and he flinches. "But you have to do it. You have to." She puts his hand on her bump. Heather bites hard on the inside of her mouth. "And he said there would be options for the lungs later on," Jas goes on.

Guy grins at last and mimes smoking.

"No! That's what got you here," Jas scolds him. "Anyway, you'd have to smoke through the trachy."

"That's cool," Guy wheezes and writes on his Boogie Board: *lary pipe.*

The door opens and the nurse comes back in with a stack of forms.

Just sign the bloody things, Heather thinks. Sign them now before anyone can change their minds.

~

Hallowe'en. Another day for cool people. Thin people. Glamorous people. Kathryn huddled into her padded jacket, which made her look even fatter. It was only afternoon but already the sky was dark and heavy with rainstorms. The sea in the bay was choppy like whipped cement. Kathryn had already seen witches and fairies on the streets of Penzance, careless of the rain and the cold. Probably heading off to a cool, glamorous party later. Or to that scarecrow thing in St Michael.

A girl crossed at the lights in front of her. The girl's hood blew back, and a tumble of gold-brown hair spilled out. Just for a second, then she bundled it back into the hood, but it was enough for Kathryn to see who it was. Chloe Johnstone. And she was heading up to Newent Terrace. The way Kathryn was going.

She let Chloe walk on ahead of her. Yes, that was the same bag bouncing on her back that Kathryn had seen at school. Rainwater streamed down the gutters. The hems of Kathryn's ugly, baggy jeans were soaked. She tracked Chloe up the hill, then right and left. Kathryn was breathing heavily and stopped to catch her breath. Chloe wouldn't see her. She was skipping up the path to number one. Kathryn started walking again, hood down. As she passed the gateway, the front door opened and she saw a sideways slice of Olly Bradshaw tugging Chloe into the hallway. Then the heavy door slammed shut on Kathryn, and the rain, and the darkening sky.

~

Heather drops Guy and Jas back home, then drives round to the Spar to pick up some bits and pieces.

The radiotherapy mask did not need any adjustment. Guy had another scan so the oncologists could calculate the new doses for him. Every moment, every second, where nothing is happening, and those tumours – because it is now tumours, not a single tumour – are growing, multiplying, swelling. Snatching the few calories Guy can get in through his liquid feed, draining his energy, turning him, cell by cell, into a living corpse.

Heather puts some potatoes in her basket, wonders if there's any point offering Guy some mash. Wondering whether he'll ever eat again. Wondering how long – really – he will be here?

Bananas. Tropical fruit juice – Jas's craving. Butter.

A bubbling laugh over the shelves. A voice saying *Evie, that's naughty*, but a voice full of love. Heather pokes her head round the corner. Yes, Chloe and Evie at the chocolate counter.

Chloe looks up, sees her.

"How did it go?" she asks.

"He's starting chemo on Thursday. Radio some time after that."

"That's good. That's really good."

"I don't think he's got long," Heather says.

"I'm so sorry."

Evie drops a chocolate orange into Chloe's basket and hoots with laughter.

"Look, look, Mummy."

"Yes, a chocolate orange." Chloe ruffles Evie's hair. Evie's clearly disappointed Chloe hasn't told her off, or acted shocked, or put the square blue box back on the shelf.

"Anything I can do…" Chloe says. "If he'd like a visit or anything."

"Thank you." Heather says. "I don't think he wants to see anyone, but thank you."

"Give him my love. And Jas."

~

Rain cracked on the window glass. Olly's curtains were open; no one could see in from the back of the house, not on that slope. Chloe watched the rain surge down the pane. The afternoon sky was the colour of dirty pewter. A streetlamp glowed an eerie orange.

"I don't want to go," she said.

"Stay here with me then." Olly nuzzled into the back of her neck.

"What?"

"Stay here. Be my trick. Or my treat."

An ambulance siren from somewhere. Chloe stared at the window. Could she? Elaine was at Rod's that night. But there was Millie. And suppose Elaine decided to come back early because of the storm? And she was meeting Amy for the scarecrows. Oh fuck.

"I can't," Chloe said at last. "I need to be home for Millie. The scarecrows." She turned round in the narrow bed. Olly's face right beside her. "Are you coming?"

"No."

"No?"

"I don't want to see Amy. It's not right. It's not fair. You go back if you want to or need to or whatever. I'll take you back in the car, but I'm not staying."

"What do I tell Amy?"

"Nothing. You haven't seen me."

"She's expecting you."

"She'll have to expect. I'm not going."

"OK, OK."

Olly was getting angry. At Chloe, at Amy, she wasn't sure. She loved the thought, just for a second, of staying in the flat with him overnight, while the rain surged and the wind shrieked. The pair of them wrapped together under the duvet. But if Olly didn't go to the scarecrows Amy would come to his flat. Chloe knew that. She wasn't going to say it, but she knew it.

She'd have to leave Olly tonight and go to the disco with Amy, and listen to Amy fretting about where Olly was, and how he'd promised to come to St Michael. Chloe could do that. It was hardly the first time.

I don't like myself, she thought, as she reluctantly staggered out of the bed and reached for her clothes to go to the bathroom.

Olly watched her dress.

"Do you want a lift now?"

"Please." Chloe felt like she should be apologising, but couldn't he see that her staying with him was impossible?

"I will make things better," he said, watching her tug on her jumper. "I promise."

Heather senses the difference. Like the metallic zing in the air before a thunderstorm. When Guy had chemotherapy for his oesophageal tumour, she was surprised, shocked almost, at the atmosphere on the day ward. The nurses were cheerful. Patients' relatives sat calmly beside the reclining chairs, talking, reading, tapping phones, doing puzzles, or just staring out of the open French windows to the little garden beyond. At lunchtime the sandwich trolley came round and, on cue at that moment, everyone opened lunch boxes and bags of crisps. It was more like a communal picnic, even with the shrouded drip stands and the shiny bald heads. People seemed happy, euphoric almost. Fuck you, cancer. It wasn't what Heather had expected at all. Just once she saw a patient cry, and the nurse whipped the curtains round her, and the sobbing subsided.

Now Guy is in a private room on the oncology ward. He'll be staying in after the chemo is finished, as his feeding tube needs re-siting. The view from the window is of another grey wall, part of some wing of the hospital. Heather can't work out where it is. He's coughed up a lot of thick phlegm. Heather can't help wondering if there are cancer cells in the discharge.

~

After lunch on Saturday Chloe waves Evie off with Elaine and Rod. They're taking her to an animal sanctuary and out for tea. Chloe feels the painful tug, watching Evie's little face through the car window. But Olly is coming. She runs back inside to get changed, do her face. And what is the point of all this, she asks herself. He's not really going to move back to Cornwall, is he? Not with his boys so far away. She knows what being a parent does to you. Suddenly, no one, nothing, can compete with that. It is quite simply another sphere.

~

Kat laughs as the waiter puts her dessert in front of her. She can't even remember the last time she ate anything like this. A tall clear glass, filled with layers of dark cherries, and chocolate and vanilla ice-cream, and chocolate sauce. A crest of whipped cream on top, and a flake. It's disgusting and wonderful and exhilarating, and Kat can't explain even how she came to order such a thing.

"Flora'd kill for that," Jason says. "I think I chose badly." He gazes gloomily at his pineapple upside-down cake, and they both laugh.

"I don't...I haven't..." Kat starts.

Jason waits, fork in hand.

"I mean, I don't usually eat anything like this," she says.

"Well, how boring for you."

Kat removes the flake and bites. It crumbles into her hand, and onto the tablecloth. She can't tell Jason. Not yet. Maybe not ever. Just this once won't matter. Not if she starves tomorrow. And swims really hard. Her mind drifts over the peppered steak and chunky chips she's eaten. And now this pudding. Fucking hell.

"Flora's really happy," Jason says.

"With her new friend?"

Jason laughs. "Yes. Who'd have thought it? My daughter's friends with an Olympic swimmer's daughter?"

"I think swimming's changed all our lives," Kat says.

"I'm so glad I went. I mean, if…"

"What?"

"If I hadn't gone…this sounds shit, but we wouldn't be here now, would we?"

Kat grins. She can't help it. "If you hadn't gone. If I hadn't gone." Jason shoves aside his empty plate. "Kat, I really like you. The kids really like you." Kat flushes with heat, scoops up ice-cream. She's not quite the ice queen she pretends to be.

"There's a *but* then?"

"No. No but. Not really. Just that I need to take things gently with this. I haven't done the internet dating stuff. After Dawn it's just been me and the kids, and that's been great, but it's time to move on now. Time for me to do something for me and all that. But I'm a bit wobbly, and I need to take time. Is that OK?"

"Of course it's OK." Ice-cream drips from Kat's spoon onto the table.

"You're dripping." Jason hands her a paper napkin.

She wipes up the brown and white blob, and she doesn't know where to look, what to say, what to think. He wants to take time. That means he wants to see her again. That means this is something for their futures. Kat never expected to take Jason back to hers tonight. She knows him well enough. That's not him. It's not her. And that's fine.

"That's fine," she says.

378

She looks up as a couple walk past. The man has his hand in the small of the girl's back. The girl has long hair tumbling down to her waist. Kat stares. They reach the door. Olly Bradshaw opens the door and Chloe Johnstone steps out into the cool mauve evening.

"Kat, you all right?"

"Chloe. That was Chloe. Just leaving." Her voice is staccato, weird, distant.

Memories. *Earth Tremors*. Kathryn Smith.

"Chloe from swimming? With that guy? Sorry, I wasn't looking. Was that her boyfriend?"

Kat drops her spoon into the tall glass. Through the restaurant window she sees Olly put his arm round Chloe, and they walk off together. Like a fracture in time. Kat glances down her chest and front. No, she's still slim, but she moves away the remains of her dessert. Too sweet, too sticky, too everything.

"In a way, I suppose."

Jason glances over his shoulder, but they've gone.

"You're not making any sense," he says.

Kat folds and refolds the sticky tissue.

"We were at sixth form together. Here in Penzance."

"I didn't know you two knew each other before."

"That guy she was with. He was at school with me too. The year above. Secondary school and sixth form."

"Was he your boyfriend at school?"

"No!" Kat yelps. "More like my nemesis."

Kat can see Jason is puzzled and not that interested, but suddenly she needs to talk, needs to tell someone.

"Can we go now?" she asks. "Can we just walk, and I'll tell you things?"

"I'll get the bill." Jason nods to a waiter, and reaches for his wallet.

I shouldn't have started this conversation, Kat thinks, offering her bank card. Jason waves it away. Why did I start this tonight? Why did they have to be here tonight? Tonight of all nights?

Jason opens the door that Olly opened moments before. Kat steps outside. She can smell the sea, hear the rattle of the boats' rigging in the harbour. A cold bony sound.

"So, there's a story about you and Chloe then?"

"I was a different person then." Kat starts walking, head down. "That guy, Olly Bradshaw. He had a girlfriend from St Michael. She was Chloe's best friend. I wasn't a nice person."

"I don't understand. What was that to do with you?"

"Nothing," Kat says. "That's the thing. It was nothing to do with me. But he – Bradshaw – had been such a shit to me."

"Why?" Jason asks. "You had a hard time at school. Was it him?"

"Amongst others."

"Oh Kat, I'm so sorry. Why? I mean, why you?"

Thin ice, thin ice, and a heavy weight. Deep black water underneath.

"I shouldn't be putting this on you. Let's forget it."

"I don't think we can. Not now. That guy was Chloe's friend's boyfriend at school? And was horrible to you?"

"He was also horrible to his girlfriend," Kat says. "Because he was seeing Chloe behind her back. And now I've just seen them like they're back together."

"Maybe they are?"

Kat doesn't answer for a moment, scuffs her toe on the pavement.

"I'm telling you this because I just know I can," she says. "It's all fucked-up stuff, but I want to tell you. I want you to know – I need you to know – I was a very different girl then."

"We all change."

"I wasn't a nice girl."

"It sounds like other people weren't very nice to you."

"They weren't."

"What happened to the girlfriend? The one he was cheating on?"

"She died."

"When was that?"

"When we were at school."

"There's more to this, yes?"

"Come back to mine," Kat says. "Just for a drink and I'll tell you about Kathryn Smith. And you can think about whether you ever want to see her again."

"If Kathryn Smith is the same person as Kat Glanville, then I do." Jason reaches out to her, puts a hand on her shoulder.

"She was a very different person."

"The answer's still the same."

~

Heather straddles Guy's legs and flinches as he coughs. Thick fluid seeps out of the trachy. His NG tube has been repositioned, and attached with fresh tape. He's home from hospital again.

"OK, put your head back."

Heather peers into the dark, gaping red mouth of the trachy. She can just see a flash of white. The speaking valve. She checks the end of the tiny brush in her hand, to make sure the bristles aren't loose. She's terrified a stray wire will fall into the trachy, and down into Guy's lungs. She slides the brush into his trachea, tries to feel her way down to the valve, tries to hook the end of the brush into it, so it can turn. She can't see what she's doing. There's no biting point of brush meeting valve. Just nothing. Her hand trembles. Guy wheezes. In fright she withdraws her hand and the brush immediately. Guy coughs up more phlegm. Thick ugly yellow stuff.

"You do it?" he rasps.

"I don't know." Heather's sweating, in despair.

The valve should be turned every day. Guy can't possibly do it. She and Jas have both tried, and it seems impossible. It's terrifying poking a foreign instrument into a man's airway, jabbing about blindly, trying to hook it into a tiny hole.

Heather slides off Guy's knees. She can't do any more. She's too frightened. Jas can have a go tomorrow. Someone has to be able to do it, or the valve will get jammed, or grown over with skin.

The trachy opening looks sore, swollen on Guy's left. Heather wishes there was something she could put on it to ease that redness. It'll get worse with the radiotherapy. She winces at the thought of that thin, frail skin being burnt, blistered.

Chloe's frustrated with herself. Each week she drifts back to the float. It buoys her up, in more ways than one. But she's here to swim, not to trail along behind a pink square.

"I'm not using this anymore," she says to Christa, and slams it down on the poolside.

"You don't need it," Christa says. "You can swim."

Chloe springs off the wall, and arrows across the pool. She arcs her arm, then the other, remembers to make a long stroke. If she could just get her breath, she'd be there. Her hand touches the far wall, and she surfaces. Everything changes, she muses, taking a side-step to where the floor slopes sharply beneath her feet. She can swim, well, sort of. Olly's in her life once more. And Kat is being friendly to her today; her terse sentences have softened and she actually smiled. Chloe inhales water, her mind not on the swimming, and stumbles up coughing. She's drifted into deeper water; she feels a little unsteady.

Kat shoots down the pool, fast and elegant, followed by Heather, more slowly, more awkward, more jerky, her head bobbing above the surface.

"I can't breathe at all," Chloe hears Heather say to Kat in the shallow end. "I just keep thinking about Guy and the trachy and his breathing."

Chloe doesn't catch Kat's reply, but she hears Heather again.

"It's like he's also having to learn to breathe in water."

Heather and Kat stand in the carpark, watching Chloe's Golf bump out of the hotel grounds. Heather's sorry she and Chloe don't travel together any more, but she can't let Jas look after Evie; Guy can't be left alone. She shakes her head, enjoys the cool wind through her wet hair.

"I'm glad last night went so well."

"I don't think it ended much like a date. Me telling him all kinds of shit about my life before."

"People tell people things."

"Not these things." Kat tosses her car keys from hand to hand. Heather thinks she's about to say more, but she doesn't.

"You'll see him again though?"

"Oh yes," Kat smiles.

"And you like his kids."

"They're lovely. Did I tell you Flora's new schoolfriend is Tessa Francis's daughter?"

"Yes, you said."

"Jason's going to ask Tessa to come to our class one week, give us a lesson. Christa's desperate to meet her." Kat jabs her keys at the car. "Anyway, you must get back to Guy."

"I must. Yes."

"Radiotherapy starts this week?"

"Hope so."

"Good. Things are moving then."

"But too little and too late," Heather says.

As she drives out of the carpark behind Kat, she realises it's almost her birthday, and she hasn't even thought about it. There seems little to celebrate right now. Somewhere at the back of her throat, her nose, there's some pool-water.

Past Langford's, through the Bends, and into St Michael. She turns into her road, and there, outside her house, is a neon-yellow ambulance. Sirens silent, blue lights off. Sinister silence.

~

Millie opens the door to Chloe's knock. She looks tired and unhappy.

"You OK?" Chloe asks. "Evie hasn't worn you out?"

"Of course not," Millie smiles thinly.

"Is everything all right?"

"Everything's fine." Millie straightens her shoulders and calls for Evie.

As Chloe waits on the doorstep for Evie – she can hear her voice from the kitchen – Millie scuffs her foot round and round on the carpet. She's wearing tatty grey slippers. Her sleeve has rolled up, and Chloe can see the raw flash on her forearm. Something's amiss, Millie's eczema always flares up when she's stressed.

~

Heather swerves the car into the kerb and leaps out, leaving her swimming bag and wet towel on the passenger seat. The front door is open and she runs in.

Upstairs, the frightened staccato of Jas's voice, the measured metronome of a man's reply.

"I'm here, I'm home." Heather stumbles up the stairs.

Jas comes out of Guy's room. Behind her Heather can see the two green-suited paramedics, an older man and a girl. They are blocking her view of Guy.

"What's happened? Is he OK?"

"I didn't call you. I knew you'd be back. The trachy. It started foaming. I was so scared. I called 999."

Heather shoves into the room and gasps. The front of Guy's shirt is soaked dark with fluid. White bubbles and froth cascade out of the tracheostomy hole.

"His saturations are better now," the male paramedic says. "And he's feeling calmer now, aren't you, Guy?"

Guy shrugs, and bubbles spew out of his neck.

"What is it?" Heather asks, and tastes again that chlorine in her throat.

"It's that swollen bit," Jas says. "The bit we saw the other day. It's like it's burst."

Heather puts her arm round Jas. "You did really well," she says, then, to the paramedics, "Are you taking him to hospital now?"

"Yes," says the girl.

"I'll pack you a bag," Heather says to Guy, already finding the litany in her brain: Boogie Board, pyjamas, toothbrush, laptop, socks, shirts. "Are you coming, Jas?"

"I'm coming."

Guy manages to stagger down the stairs and out to the ambulance. Heather and Jas walk behind him. Heather shivers. Her hair's still damp. Oh Jesus. She smells of chlorine, her hair needs washing, she needs a shower. But she must go with Guy now.

"We'll follow you up," she calls.

"I just went in to see him," Jas says, "and the liquid, the fluid, whatever, it was spewing down his front. I don't think he'd realised. I gave him a tissue to clean up, and then I was looking, and I saw more coming out of that swollen bit…it had like a hole in it, like a spot that's burst, but bigger. And suddenly it was gushing, just gushing out, and we couldn't stop it. He was frightened; I was frightened. I called 999 and sat with him, just trying to clean him, keep him calm. I was so frightened." Her voice breaks.

Heather hugs her. "You must have been. Are you up to coming in?"

"I want to come. I'm sorry I didn't call you, but I knew you'd be back soon and he needed me."

"You did everything right," Heather says.

~

Kathryn turned out the lights in the front room to discourage the trick-or-treaters. Her parents were out at a neighbours' Hallowe'en party.

"You're on the invitation too," her mother had said, but Kathryn shook her head. She didn't do parties.

Kathryn thought of all the cool people at Hallowe'en parties, at the St Michael scarecrows. She thought about Olly and Chloe just down the road, and of beautiful Amy Langford who had no idea what was going on behind her back.

Kathryn heaved up from the sofa in the darkened room, and trailed into the kitchen. She was hungry. Hungry and miserable and angry. A potent cocktail. She opened the fridge: salad, cheese, ham, yoghurts, half a pack of beetroot, a jar of red jam. She unscrewed the lid of the jam and found white spots on its surface.

She wanted comfort food. She wanted fish and chips. Even though that meant a walk in the pissing rain. She imagined the chip shop at the bottom of the hill. Bright lights inside, neon signs in the window. The curling posters, dampened by grease. Rows of chunky brown fish in the cabinet, and the rattle and hiss of vats of chips out the back.

She threw on her puffy raincoat and shoved her hair inside the hood. She'd just keep walking, not looking up at anyone, and hope the gangs of kids would ignore her. Or think she was in fancy dress, dressed as some kind of freak.

~

"I must go." Chloe hopped from one foot to the other by the door.

Olly was taking forever to find his shoes, his car keys. Her heart-rate was galloping. She should be back in St Michael. Amy would go to the disco in the village hall and Chloe wouldn't be there. She might go down to the house and find it dark and empty. She might bump into Millie and her friends, and Millie would say Chloe had gone to Penzance. To buy Olly's birthday present with Amy. Oh Jesus. Lies, lies, lies. Where did it all start? And where would it end?

At last Olly rattled open the door. Chloe scuttled out into the hall, zipping up her coat. Muffled music from the floor above. Chloe was frightened to step outside the house, certain Amy would be there, like a pale screaming banshee, like one of the scarecrows. But no. Nobody. Just rain.

Rain sluicing down from the gables of the house. Puddles on the path. A pumpkin in a front window opposite grinning into the night.

Olly drove out of Penzance, the wipers arcing through the downpour. There were kids hanging around in groups – witches' hats, pumpkins, cloaks – and a few loners striding home, heads down against the wind and rain.

"It's a proper Hallowe'en, isn't it?" Olly said, his voice strangely hard in the silence, as he took the back lane to St Michael. The road that did not go past Langford's.

The weather only swelled Chloe's unease. She was late. Amy would want to know where she was. She would look guilty. Olly said he was going to finish with Amy. Chloe felt she couldn't breathe, and opened the window a crack. Icy rain splintered onto her hands.

They met few cars on the dark lanes to the village. Once, Olly's headlamps flashed on a pouring dark river of water, spewing off a field and into the roadside. Chloe watched, eyes wide, through the wet black glass, for the landmarks she knew – the bent tree, the five-barred gate, the cottage on the corner – and counted them off in her mind.

"Where shall I take you?" Olly asked.

"Drop me on the main road. I'll walk down the lane."

He pulled in to the kerb. Despite the rain, there were people straggling along the pavement, the smell of burgers and onions, the soulless gazes of scarecrows.

"I'll see you soon." He kissed her once quickly, then she threw open the door and stepped out into two inches of water.

Olly roared off before she could cross the road. Soaked already, she stumbled down Barrow Lane. The house was dark. Elaine's car was not there. Chloe let herself in to the dry warmth and sobbed with relief. She just wanted to have a bath and go to bed. But Amy would be up at the disco waiting for her. Could she stay here and forget it all? She flicked on the hall light and saw her face in the mirror. She looked like a scarecrow herself, hair matted like wet straw, streaked make-up, shadowed eyes. She heeled off her sodden shoes and padded to the bathroom. A quick shower, then she'd have to go out again, into the storm.

She stayed under the hot jet just long enough to wash off the rainwater and the smell of Olly Bradshaw that she was sure clung to her like a new skin. As she stepped out of the bathroom, one towel round her body, another round her hair, she heard the scrabble of the front door, and Millie's voice.

"Chloe, Chloe, you're here. Is it true? Where have you been?"

Millie ran towards the bathroom, almost cannoned into Chloe. Chloe steadied her hair towel.

"Is what true?" she asked.

"Are you fucking Olly Bradshaw? Amy's distraught. She's been looking for you, looking for him."

Chloe's towel slipped from her head to the floor. She didn't move to retrieve it. Her wet hair slid down her back.

"Chloe. What the fuck's going on? Everyone knows."

"Everyone?" Chloe croaked at last.

"Yes, everyone. I heard it at the disco. Amy called the pub where Olly works and they said he'd never been in today, but he told her he was working, and then she called the phone box at his place and someone there told him he was with you, that he was always with you."

"Everyone?" Chloe whispered again. How did Millie know about the phone box?

"Even Mr Lovell."

"Mr Lovell?"

"Yeah, he was outside the phone box when Amy came out." Millie stopped, gulped. "It's true, isn't it?"

Chloe bent for her towel, held it crumpled in front of her, still clutching the other round her chest.

"It's true."

"Jesus. How could you?"

"I...I don't know. I couldn't help it."

"She's your best friend."

"I know."

"Everyone thinks you're a slut and a bitch."

I am, she thought.

"And you *are*," Millie shouted.

Composing herself, Chloe asked "Where is Amy?"

"She ran off. Or so I heard. Ran off to get her car and go round to Olly's and see what the hell was going on. I think Dave and Pete went after her, to calm her down. On their motor-bikes."

"Will you let me get dressed?" Chloe asked. "And I'll talk to you."

"I'm going back to the disco. Back to my friends." Millie ran back to the front door.

"You won't…" *Let anyone know I'm here,* she finished in her head.

Cold air sucked into the house and Millie surged out again. The door banged.

Chloe grabbed the phone and dialled the number of the phone box. She had to tell Olly. He might just be back now. She must warn him Amy had found out everything and was on her way over. The line rang out and out and out. No one answered.

Chloe hung up. There was nothing she could do. She checked the front door was locked, and turned off all the lights, then she huddled under her quilt, like an old spinster afraid of trick-or-treaters.

~

Heather can barely keep her eyes open to drive home. Beside her, Jas is quiet, and Heather thinks she may have nodded off, her hands clasped over her growing bump. Guy is back on the ENT ward, back in the same bed he was in before. Even the stain on the curtain is the same.

In A&E some old guy complained to the nurses about Guy's foaming tracheostomy. Heather almost cried. *Stupid old bastard.* Guy was left on a trolley for hours. At last someone came from ENT to see him, and admit him to the ward. He had the fluid suctioned out of the hole, but more kept coming. He changed into a hospital gown; it was soaked in moments. He was given a nebuliser. Cassie was the night sister. She promised to keep an eye on him all night.

Heather still smells of stale chlorine. She must wash before she falls into bed. She is so tired, but doesn't imagine she'll sleep. Old chlorine, sweat, and hospital grime. She must remember to take her swimming bag and towel off the back seat where Jas threw them. The seat will be damp and smelly by now.

Jas stirs, flexes her hands.

"Will he be here?" she asks, so quietly Heather barely hears her over the engine.

"You mean…?"

"Will he meet the baby? Will he still be here?"

Heather shakes her head, can't speak.

"Mum?"

"I don't know."

~

When Heather wakes the next morning she is lying on a soaked pillow. She hardly bothered drying her hair when she showered the night before. Her neck is stiff from the damp, her hair knotted. She calls the ward.

"He had an unsettled night," the nurse tells her. "But he's nebulising now, and we've got the food pump going. He should be going for his first radiotherapy later this morning."

"What's going to happen?" Heather demands. "That hole by the trachy. What's going on? Is he going to get that sewn up?"

"I think the plan at the moment is to manage it with suction and nebulising. See how it goes."

"What is it?"

"The doctors on the ward round think it's a fistula. A hole that's broken between his trachea and oesophagus. So whenever he drinks or sucks ice, or if he were to eat anything, it bubbles through into the trachea and out the hole."

"So he can't drink water? He can't have ice?"

"Not at the moment."

Heather slams down the phone and rushes into Jas's room. Jas is still sleeping, her dark hair tumbling off the pillow.

"Jas." Heather shakes her arm.

"Uhh." Jas jumps awake. "What? What?"

Heather curses herself for waking Jas like this again.

"I just rang the ward. He can't even have ice. He can't even have fucking ice any more."

~

"Are you coming down again?" Chloe asks Olly. She hopes it doesn't sound too needy.

"Sometime, yes," he says.

Chloe can hear the muted sound of the TV down the line. He probably is simply sitting at home, alone, with a beer, like he said.

"Do you...know when?"

"Not right now. But I will."

Chloe takes a gulp of Pepsi from Evie's Disney Princess beaker.

"What's happening?" she asks. "Like, you and me. I'm confused. What am I? What can I be? You're not really thinking of moving here, are you?"

"I'm really thinking about it. Whether I can or not…I don't know. I do know I want to be in Cornwall a lot. There's Mum. You. It's just the boys are here. And I can't walk away from them. I'm thinking maybe get a place and come down as often as I can…still work here…I don't know. I need to get my head round it."

"Because, you know, if you don't want to see me again, you can say so."

"What's brought that on? I never said that. I'm trying to work out something that suits everyone."

"I'm sorry." Another gulp of Evie's Pepsi. "It's just…it's hard."

"It always was," Olly says. "It always was."

~

"I'm thinking about speech therapy," Jas says.

"I don't think he's up to it at the moment." Heather drives down the acceleration lane to the main road.

"I mean, as a job. For me. I thought maybe, when the baby's older, I might look into becoming a speech therapist. A good one. One who really understands."

Heather glances briefly at Jas. "You'd be fantastic. But…could you cope if Guy…if things don't go well?"

"Whatever happens, I figured it'd be good to maybe help other people. I wondered if Rick might let me go on the radio and talk about loss of voice and stuff. Not right now. I mean later. When we know what's going on. What do you think?"

"I think it's a great idea," Heather says. "Guy would be so proud of you. Will be, I mean, will be so proud of you."

When they walk onto the ward Heather sees Guy straight away. Each time, he seems smaller, more fragile. The nebuliser has slipped from his throat.

"Guy." She brushes away a loose strand of hair from his face. His hospital gown is saturated with dark fluid.

One of the nurses comes over, a tall skinny man with sandy hair.

"He had radiotherapy," the nurse says. "But it was very hard for him, lying down for it. He was choking."

Jas winces beside Heather.

"Can't he sit up for it?" Heather asks.

"The oncologists calculate the radiotherapy for a specific angle. They would have to rescan him and recalculate if he were going to sit up. It would waste a lot of time."

"He must have it. It's only for a few moments, isn't it?"

"Yes," the nurse says, uncertainly. "We've been suctioning him a lot. You can do that yourselves."

He unhooks the thin tube and directs it into Guy's trachy. With a loud whoosh, thick streaks of white shoot up the pipe. Heather's eyes follow its length to the canister on the wall. It's almost full with a dark and white lacy network of phlegm.

"If you need to clear the tube, fill a cup of water and suck up some water. But don't let Guy drink anything. He mustn't swallow anything."

"Can he rinse his mouth?" Heather asks in despair.

"Only if he spits. Every last drop." The nurse nods to a spitting bowl beside the bed.

Heather and Jas look at each other and at Guy. He hasn't moved. The Boogie Board is on the blanket. There's writing on it. Heather wonders when he wrote it.

What am I? the board reads, the writing becoming smaller and wobblier with each letter, and then dies to black.

~

Heather and Jas return to alternate visits. At night Heather's ears strain for the sound of the phone. She jolts awake, sure she has heard it, but the house is quiet. Every moment that ticks by is another moment Guy still lives. She has started measuring Guy's life in moments, not weeks, or months, or years.

Sometimes Guy doesn't even open his eyes when they are there. He has been given sedatives to get through the trauma of radiotherapy.

On Thursday Heather arrives on the ward, wondering if he has already gone to chemo, but he's propped up on pillows, eyes open. The nebuliser is discarded on the bedcover. Bubbles froth out of the fistula. Heather reaches for the suction catheter and clears them. It's oddly satisfying to see those deadly bubbles destroyed by her hand.

The food pump still drips its grey sludge into Guy's feeding tube. He is still nil by mouth, but he swills out his mouth with water. He asks her to bring ice; she refuses.

"I'll swallow, you clear it," he rasps, and his words, from the depths of that red-black hole, are like the voice of a corpse.

Heather is afraid of what will happen, but how can she deny him water? She tugs the curtains round the bed. Guy swallows and, as soon as he does, liquid slides through the hole from his oesophagus and into his trachea. Heather drops the suction catheter in, and the water disappears into the tube.

"This is how we do it," Guy says, and coughs and coughs.

His face goes dark with the effort, and Heather yanks back the curtains but the tall sandy nurse is already there, and he bundles her out, and she hears his voice reassuring Guy, saying something about deep suction and getting the chest physios up to see him. Another nurse disappears behind the curtain; hissing and whooshing sounds. Heather paces up and down by the nurses' station, looking at the same thank-you cards, the same postcards, the same notices, glancing every few seconds at Guy's curtains, which bulge and sway as the two nurses move.

At last the sandy-haired nurse pulls them back and gestures Heather over.

"We've given him some deep suction. I'm going to get on to the chest physios, get them to come up this evening to see him. He's having chemo tomorrow, by the way. A day late doesn't matter."

Heather smiles her thanks, goes back to Guy.

"I'll let you rest now," she says. "Jas will come tomorrow. Love you."

Heather's never been a *love you* sort of person. Now she vows to tell him every time she leaves, even if he's asleep.

~

Jas comes home from the hospital the next day tear-stained.

"For you. For tomorrow." She holds out a creased white envelope.

Heather takes it, uncomprehending. There's no writing on the front. She pulls out a card. It's a modern abstract in blues and greys.

Happy memories, Guy has scrawled inside it. Nothing else.

"I'm sorry," Jas says. "I thought you'd like a birthday card from him. I chose it. I thought he'd write something, but he was so bad today with the chemo and just falling asleep it took an hour to get him to write that."

Heather studies those two words, in writing that no longer even looks like Guy's. Not happy birthday. *Happy memories.* Happy memories for who? Him in his hospital gown, stained with sputum and blood, remembering happier days? Or is it for her to open and look at in the years to come? To help her find happy memories?

Jas is watching her with tears smudged on her cheeks. Heather puts the card in the centre of the mantelpiece, shoving aside the other cards that have already come, some from friends who don't even know how ill Guy is. She knows it's the last birthday card she'll have from him.

Happy memories.

~

Heather feels so guilty. The warm water laps round her shoulders. Kat and Chloe and Christa have told her she must not feel guilty: she is entitled to an evening for herself. Jas said the same. But Heather can't help the guilt, and the terrible symmetry or asymmetry or whatever it is. She is choosing to immerse herself in water, to exhale under its blue surface, and Guy is choking on his own watery secretions.

A figure on the other side of the glass. Jason going home. He stops and waves at Kat, and grins at her, and Kat waves back, smiling. Their story is just beginning, Heather thinks, and mine is ending. There's nowhere to run now, no rabbit to pull out of a hat. The medics have said there is nothing they can do for the fistula. Guy can carry on with the radio and chemo while he is strong enough, but that is all. When his strength gives out, that will be the end. It could be any day.

Heather gulps air and puts her head underneath. The pool is clear and she can see all the way down to the shallow end. The blue is soft and gentle. She lets herself float there, holding her breath, suspended between living and drowning.

~

"I can't come next weekend. It's May Bank Holiday," Olly says. "But I'll try for the next one. Is that OK?"

"Yes," Chloe says, and her heart surges, then falls again because, despite the happiness, there's sadness too.

I'm wasting my life again, she thinks, when she's said good-bye and hung up. She can remember the day, so clearly, when she first met Olly in the village with Amy, and they went to the park to sit on the swings. Sometimes she fancies she knew that day was going to change her life, that it was the start of something that could end only in heartache; other days she is beyond astonished that a simple meeting in a village street could have come to this, and left Amy lying long and cold in the earth.

"Who was that?" Evie asks.

"An old friend. We were at school together. A long while ago."

"You went to school?"

"You know I did, silly. Everyone goes to school."

"Am I going to school?"

"One day, yes."

"When's one day?"

"Not for over a year."

What will have happened by then? Chloe plays with her phone for something to do. She has a new email from Christa.

Hi everyone,
Next Monday's Bank Holiday. The hotel suggested we don't have our groups on the Sunday as it will be busy. Sorry about this. Hope you're all well and I will see you the week after.
Christa

~

Kat's phone beeps under the counter. She's adding up a customer's goods on the till, but she glances down and sees the screen flash ice-white with a new text. Once she has handed over the carrier bag, she grabs the phone.

Hi there, have you seen Christa's email? No swimming next Sunday. I thought perhaps we could do something? Do you fancy Heligan or somewhere? Let me know. J x

The days spiral on in a choking haze of phlegm and suction, that pale dripping food, the beeping of Guy's monitors. Each day he is weaker, stranger, farther away. A couple of times radiotherapy had to be cancelled because the sedatives made him too drowsy to be safe in the linear accelerator.

Heather sits on a hard plastic chair by his bed. He's asleep or – at least – he's not awake. He's on antibiotics for a chest infection. There won't be any chemo this week. Heather's eyes rove round the bed space: the Boogie Board, the tatty notepad and pens, a paperback he doesn't seem able to read. The spitting bowl with bloodstained sputum. The wires and cables everywhere: the feeding tube and pump, the monitors, the suction catheter.

Heather's heard of patients plucking at bedcovers and she's never understood what it really means until today. Guy's fingers scoop and pinch as though he's trying to pick up something tiny. He opens his eyes and squints at his fingers, like he's checking if he has picked it up. He points suddenly at something on the curtain, makes a gun with his hand and shoots at Heather.

She gulps down her tears, takes his roaming hand and steadies it under hers. She squeezes it, feels the bones just there beneath the skin.

"Squeeze me," she whispers, and he does, just gently, but he does. "Shall I send your love to Jas?" she asks, and again he squeezes.

His gown has drifted apart; she stares at the pattern of moles on his chest.

He jerks upright with a spasm of choking. Frenzied beeping. His saturations on the monitor tumble down the nineties. Heather grabs the suction catheter and draws up the bubbling fluid from the fistula. The hole beside his trachy seems bigger, redder, stretched. More fluid spurts out. She sucks it up, then rinses the end of the sticky tube in water. The saturations climb once more and the machine quietens.

Guy scrabbles on the bed cover for his Boogie Board. He has trouble unclipping the stylus; Heather releases it and hands it to him.

Where are the scarecrows? he writes in that strange script, drops the board and stylus. On the screen his vital signs are stable, but Heather cannot rouse him to say goodbye when she has to leave.

She erases the sinister words on the board and writes *I love you.*

~

Jason pulls up in a parking space just along from Kat's flat. He turns off the engine, and unclips his seatbelt. Kat clicks out of hers too; they face each other over the gearstick.

"Today was brilliant," Jason says.

Kat nods and smiles. "It was."

They went to Glendurgan gardens. Kat hadn't been before. She never realised how much Jason knew about plants and land-scaping. She enjoyed listening to him describing things. She didn't mind when he said he had been before with his mother and the children.

"Your choice next time," Jason says.

"That's good," Kat says. "Not that it's my choice, that there's a next time."

"Lots of times, I hope."

Kat hesitates. "Would you like to come up?"

"I've got to get back," Jason says. "I'll have to relieve Mum."

"Sure. Of course." Kat scrabbles for the door release.

"Hey." Jason reaches across to her, and pulls her mouth to his.

"I must let you go." Kat opens her door, steps out onto the pavement. She waits for Jason to start the ignition and drive off, but he doesn't.

She opens the passenger door again. "Are you OK?"

He's flicking open his phone. "I'm just going to see if Mum can cope for a bit longer," he says.

~

"How are you feeling today?" Heather asks Guy.

Jas has come with her; she stands on the other side of the bed, hands him the Boogie Board.

Terrible.

"You've got this infection."

So they say.

"It's just a temporary setback," Jas says fiercely.

Guy laughs silently.

~

"I'm really pissed off with the people at Ocean," Heather says on the way home. "It's like he doesn't exist any more. No one's asked after him for ages."

"I guess they don't know what to say," Jas says.

"They don't have to feel awkward, do they? They know, whatever happens, he won't be coming back to work."

"The listeners have been asking after him," Jas says. "I've looked on Ocean's Facebook page. People have been asking. Rick just writes that he can't give any details. I didn't know whether to say anything. Thought it best not to."

"Don't say anything," Heather says.

~

"I was just ringing to say I could look after Evie when you and Mum go swimming on Sunday," Jas says.

"How's your dad?" Chloe asks.

"Not good. He's having chemo and radio when he can, but he's got this infection and he seems out of it sometimes. The radio makes him choke because he has to lie flat. I don't think…I don't know."

"Jas, I'm so sorry." Chloe knows her words are inadequate. She's heard of people with cancer, yes, of course, she has, but she's never, ever, heard of anyone suffering like Guy Lovell. It's beyond her imagination.

"I'd love to see Evie, if you think she'd like it."

"I know she would."

~

Heather rings the ward before setting off to the hospital. The nurse tells her Guy tugged his NG feeding tube out during the night, and his J-Peg has become dislodged. There's no way he can eat safely. He can't swallow anything for himself.

She leaves immediately, with a crushing dread in her heart. Jas stays home, exhausted and nauseous from constant heartburn. The fear, Heather thinks, as she drives. The fear never goes. Not for an instant.

On the ward Guy is comatose. He has no nebuliser, no feeding tube. The pump has been shoved to the back corner of his cubicle.

One of the nurses comes to check his vitals.

"When's he getting the tubes back?" Heather asks.

The nurse fiddles with the monitor. "The J-Peg has to be done down in radiology. None of the ward doctors will put the NG in."

"What?"

"We'll try to get one of the specialist nurses to do it tomorrow."

"So he's got no food at all?"

"Not at the moment."

"Did he have radio this morning?" Heather knows the answer already.

"No, he couldn't tolerate it."

No food, no chemo, no radio.

Heather grips Guy's hand in despair. It's freezing cold, blotchy and bony. Like a dead hand.

I'm going to miss you so much, Heather thinks. Then: I already do.

"What do you do when I'm with Granny and Grandad Rod?" Evie asks.

"Not much. I do the housework. I do shopping. I have a bath. I read."

And sometimes, Chloe adds silently, I have sex with Olly Bradshaw, who broke my heart so long ago, and is all set to break it again.

"I've brought you some stuff from the farmers' market," Elaine says when she arrives for Evie.

Chloe watches her unpack her wicker shopping basket. A crunchy-burnt loaf, a chocolate cake, a square of white cheese, some speckled eggs.

"Thank you," Chloe says.

Elaine pulls out a chair and sits down. "Something's wrong with Millie," she starts.

Chloe slides the packet of cheese into the fridge. Without Rod, Elaine could talk for hours, and Olly will be coming shortly.

"I haven't seen much of her," she says.

"You live in the same village."

"Yes, but, we're both busy, I guess."

"Do you think she and Matt are having a rough patch?"

"I don't know." Chloe remembers Matt in the park. There was something. "I don't think she'd tell me if they were. Anyway, none of my business, is it?"

"Are you ready, Granny?" Evie wheedles, tugging Elaine's sleeve.

Chloe feels that two-forked flash inside her again: relief that she will be alone, sadness at Evie's excitement about going with Elaine.

~

"I've got a surprise for you," Olly says, when he finally lets go of Chloe.

"What's that?"

"I told Mum I'd be staying with a friend tonight."

"You mean me?"

"Is that OK? Is Evie staying with your parents?"

"Yes. Yes, that would be lovely."

"I'll go whenever you want me to. First light, before the neighbours up are, twitching the curtains at the Orgy of Orchid Cottage."

Chloe smiles. "We're still creeping around telling half-truths."

"I probably always will be," Olly says, and Chloe feels the surge of the sadness that is never far from her.

~

Later, something jars Chloe awake. It's Olly's phone ringing from the pile of his clothes in the corner. He shuffles in his sleep, but doesn't wake. Chloe lies there next to him, as the ringtone dies away, and studies his face. The same face, yet different. The boy's face that has become a man's. His phone starts up again and he stirs. Chloe's about to say something, but he shifts his arm, pulls her tighter to him, and settles again.

Chloe's awake now, and she checks the time. Gone six o'clock. Olly said he would take her out for dinner again, but she'd rather just throw on a robe, and make something at home. Some pasta maybe. She has chicken in the fridge she could cook, and the new cheese and loaf her mother brought. She has wine, white and red.

"Olly." She nudges him. "Let's eat in tonight."

"OK," he says, opening his eyes.

"Your phone's been ringing," Chloe says.

"Sorry. Should have turned it off."

"It might be your mum, do you think?"

"I doubt it. She was fine today."

No. Of course not his mother. Some girl from London, no doubt, hoping to catch him on a Saturday evening. To suggest cocktails, or whatever people in London did. Chloe wishes she'd never mentioned it.

Her bladder is bursting and, now she's awake, she can't ignore it any more. Her stomach feels raw because she hasn't eaten. She tugs her robe from the bedpost and slips her arms in. As she crosses to the door Olly's mobile rings again. She can just see the illumination of the screen under his jacket.

"You'd better get that."

She grabs the phone, sees the name *Caitlin* flashing on the screen, and a photo of a sharp-faced woman with straight dark hair. Chloe throws the phone onto the bed and closes the door behind her when she goes out. His bloody ex. The twins' mother.

Chloe washes her hands in the bathroom and checks her reflection. There's a tangle in her hair where she was lying beside

Olly; her mascara has smudged under her eyes. She tries to wipe the shadows, and wonders how long she should take before going back to him. With the tap turned off, and the cistern quiet, she can just hear his voice, though she can't pick out any words through two closed doors.

She unlocks the bathroom door loudly, and walks back to the bedroom. As she opens the door, she sees Olly, wild-eyed, trying to get his shirt on, with the phone to his ear.

"No, don't do anything like that. I'll be there...look, I'm leaving now...Ring me if anything...OK, OK."

Olly throws down the phone, and snatches up his jeans.

"I'm so sorry. I have to go. Isaac's in a coma. Knocked off his bike."

"Jesus. What happened?"

"I don't know. Caitlin's hysterical. Jeremy's in shock. A white van or something...he's got other injuries too...legs and spine. Oh fuck, fuck."

Chloe stands there, wrapping her arms round herself. She feels superfluous, in the way.

"Call me," she says. "When you can. Tell me how he is."

Olly pats his pockets. "I have to go. I'm sorry."

"No, no, I'm sorry." She reaches out to hug him. He's rigid in her arms.

"I'll call you later," he says, and then he's gone, and she's left there in the hall, in her dressing gown, with a lumpy tangle in her hair, and a half-vision of a dark pinched woman, and a twelve-year-old boy on the cusp of life and death.

Chloe trails back to the bedroom and lies down in the sweaty covers. She wishes Evie were with her. At last she struggles up and rips the sheets off the bed, balls them into the laundry basket. She'll have a bath, and then eat that new loaf and cheese.

She knows, knew as soon as Olly answered the call, that she won't see him again. He probably won't even text to tell her how Isaac is. She's lost him because he's a parent, and she knows she would be the same with Evie. Because that love is all-consuming.

~

Chloe's chilly after her bath, and puts on jeans and a jumper. She's wiped off all traces of her smudgy make-up, unhooked her earrings.

In the kitchen, she saws off a rough chunk of the bread, surprised that she's hungry, and revises her thoughts. She will see Olly again. They're bound together, always were. It won't be in a couple of weeks' time, it won't be later this year, it may not be for years to come, when their children are grown up. Evie, Jeremy, and Isaac. Please Isaac too. She can't bear any more grief for Olly. But they will meet again, Chloe and Olly, and they will probably be lovers again. It's the turn of the seasons, the wheel of life, destiny, whatever. Since the day they first met in the village they've been tied as one. Chloe gouges some of the crumbly white cheese and tastes it. She feels almost calm, almost free. Olly has gone, but one day he will return. It is a certainty, like the sunrise.

Half an hour later, Chloe's on the sofa, one eye on the TV. She is still dry-eyed and strangely content knowing Olly has gone, and the interlude is over for now, but it's a little like doing a dead man's float: she can stop her breathing, hold still on the water surface, and everything is OK but, one wrong movement, one tilt of the head, or inhalation, and she'll sink and stumble, coughing and eyes streaming.

Over the TV she hears a car coming down Barrow Lane, then the engine dies. She sees headlights through the thin curtain fabric. For a stupid, confused second, she thinks it's Olly.

She stands up to answer the door. A man outside in the half-light, with a bottle of wine in his hand.

"Matt," Chloe says. "Is everything OK?"

"Not really," Matt says. "Can I come in?"

"Is it Millie? The boys?"

"They're fine."

Chloe shuts the door behind Matt. He stalks into the living room and chucks down a rucksack beside the sofa.

"Drink?" He waves the bottle of red at her.

"What's going on?"

"Millie's not fine actually." Matt sinks down on the sofa, pulls his phone out of his pocket and glances at the screen, then shoves it away again.

"What's happened? Is she hurt?"

"She's thrown me out."

"What?"

"I wondered, could I crash here tonight? I won't disturb Evie."

"Evie's with Mum and Rod. Why did Millie throw you out?"

"It'll be OK," Matt says. "I'll sort it out tomorrow. But some space tonight would be better. I'll sleep here. On the sofa."

Chloe reaches out and takes the bottle off him. "Why did she throw you out?"

"She found out I'd been seeing someone else," Matt mumbles at last.

"Who?"

"No one."

"Well, that's ridiculous. It can't be no one."

"No one you know. No one she knows. Someone in St Ives. It was hardly anything."

"How long?" Chloe puts the bottle down on the floor, wanders into the kitchen for glasses.

"Couple of months," Matt calls through. "On and off. I mean, I didn't see her that much. A few meals, a few drinks, her place...Do you want me to go?"

Chloe hands him the glasses, and twists off the top of the bottle. "Not really," she says. "I think I could do with some company."

"Missing Evie?"

"Yes, and...well, whatever."

"What?"

"Nothing. Are you and Millie going to sort this out?"

"I hope so."

"Does this woman...your girlfriend...know Millie knows?"

"I think Millie made sure she did."

Chloe winces, and slugs her wine. It's cool and rough. She thinks she's feeling wobblier than she did before Matt came.

"I can go." Matt puts his glass down on the floor. "You're probably massively pissed off with me."

"I'm not," Chloe says carefully. "Jesus, you know I'm not perfect. You know why we left St Michael."

"Yes, but you were only a kid."

"The story didn't end there."

"What d'you mean?"

"Olly Bradshaw." God, his name sounds so odd on her lips again, now his bright comet has fled the skies.

"That guy you were seeing."

"I've been seeing him again," Chloe says. "He was here today. If things had worked out how I...we...intended we'd probably be out for dinner right now. But he had to race back to London. His ex called and said their son had been knocked off his bike and was in a coma."

"Shit."

"And I won't see Olly again, because his kids matter more than anything, and he'll be with Isaac now, and it could take ages for him to get better, if he does. And Isaac's got a twin brother who saw the whole thing. So Olly won't be coming to Cornwall any time soon."

"That's...dreadful for him," Matt says. "I'm sorry. I don't want it to be like that. I don't want to get some call from Millie saying something's happened to one of the boys. I don't want to be the last to know."

"You won't be." Chloe tops up their glasses. "You'll sort it out. I know you will. D'you want some cake?"

"Yeah, thanks, I'll have it and eat it."

~

Kathryn heard about Amy Langford on Sunday's local news. She had her Walkman on but, through Whitney Houston, she caught a few words from the newsreader: *scarecrow festival, St Michael Bends, flash flood, eighteen-year-old woman.*

She whipped off her headphones, the tape still playing.

"Who was that?" she asked her mother.

"They said she hadn't been named yet. A girl from St Michael. Maybe someone you know."

Kathryn stopped the tape, and twiddled the headphone cables. She didn't need the eighteen-year-old woman to be named: she just knew straight away who it was.

The next morning at school, the first day back after half-term, the whole of the sixth form was called to an assembly. The head, who was only ever a fleeting presence in a dingy brown suit, confirmed the dead girl was Amy Langford but, by then, Kathryn had heard the shocked whispers at the lockers, seen a few blotched faces, and knew she had been right.

As the head went on about a counsellor being called in for people to talk to if they were upset or angry or confused, Kathryn scanned the lines of tense faces around her for the one she sought, but Chloe Johnstone was not there.

~

"Bye sweetheart. Have fun with Jas." Chloe kisses Evie's head and hauls her swimming bag onto her shoulder.

To Jas, she says, "Evie's been so looking forward to seeing you again."

Jas smiles uncertainly. Chloe almost says something about remembering to look after herself and the baby, but thinks better of it, and runs down the path to where Heather is waiting with the engine running.

"How's Guy?"

"Terrible. I went up this afternoon and he didn't open his eyes at all. Not even when I was suctioning him. Every day he's farther and farther from me. I think he's gone too far for me to ever bring him back."

"He was always one of my favourite teachers." Chloe winces at her past tense, but Heather doesn't stiffen, and anyway, Guy was her teacher half a lifetime ago. "It's lovely for Evie to see Jas," she goes on. "I wouldn't have been able to take her to Millie's tonight."

"Are they away?"

"No, she threw Matt out yesterday."

"What?" Heather sounds genuinely shocked. "Not Matt? He's lovely."

Chloe hesitates a moment, wonders how much she can say, but Heather's so stressed, it might take her mind away from Guy just for a second or two. "He's been seeing another woman in St Ives."

"Oh shit. And Millie found out."

"Yes, the usual. Texts on his phone. So he turned up at mine to sleep on the sofa."

"That's awkward."

"Well, Millie doesn't think I'm that important to her as I haven't heard from her at all. If Matt hadn't told me I wouldn't have known. He's trying to sort it all out today."

"I'd have thought she'd have called you straight away."

"Not Millie. She wouldn't want me to ever think their lives aren't perfect."

Heather indicates right and swings into the drive of the Headland. Kat's just getting out of her car, checking her pockets, locking the door, walking across the tarmac to the spa.

"I think I've got a piece of evidence," Heather says, reversing into an empty space beside Kat's car. "Matt wrote his mobile number down for me on the back of a receipt for some swanky restaurant in St Ives. I thought *lucky Millie* being taken out there."

"Unlucky Millie," Chloe says, clicking out of her seatbelt.

~

Everything is changing for all of us, Chloe thinks, as she wades into the middle of the pool. She saw Kat and Jason hug each other briefly at the changeover; Guy is fading from Heather; Olly has fled back to his family. He sent Chloe one text at Sunday lunchtime, just saying how ill Isaac was, how traumatised Jeremy was. Nothing about her, nothing about their times together. Just one kiss. Chloe read the message twice, and deleted all the texts between them. His number is still in her phone. It'll rest there quietly, amongst the others, until their orbits collide once more.

Chloe lets the water lift her into a float. She's disconcerted with the depth beneath her. Her body drifts forwards, she snatches for the rail, but it's not there. Her legs drop, and she's in deeper water, up to her shoulders. She's inhaled some, and it clogs her airway like a wet sponge. She coughs and splutters, and Heather turns instinctively to the sound.

~

Heather's had her shower and put her towel and swimsuit on the pile of laundry by the full washing machine. Jas is eating a sandwich in front of the TV. She looks tired. Heather knows she's not giving Jas enough attention at the moment. She's written the proposed date for Jas's Caesarean in July on the calendar, but she's not asking after her enough. Not about the pregnancy or Andrew or any of it.

"I'll call the ward before I get some dinner," Heather says.

Her fingers find the numbers by themselves. She sees in her mind the nurses' station, the whiteboard, the thank-you cards, the telephone, which is ringing out and out and out. Eventually one of the nurses answers.

"I was going to call you," she says. "Guy's not so good tonight. He's still got the chest infection and the urinary infection, but he's very tachycardic, in atrial fibrillation at about 160. The doctors have given him some Digoxin and they'll review him again in a couple of hours."

"Should I come in?" Heather whispers, feels Jas nudging her arm.

"Come in if you'd like to," the nurse says, "but until this AF has been sorted out I don't think he'll respond to you. I'll call you when he's been reviewed again."

"Please do. And if anything changes."

Jas finishes her sandwich, swallowing woodenly. Heather doesn't eat anything. She checks her mobile for battery, and plugs it in to charge. Her own heart rate feels fast and jagged in her chest. She stands by the phone, watching its single red light, waiting for it to flash and shriek. Nothing. She wanders into the utility room, unhooks the washing basket and opens the washing machine. Guy's socks spill out – grey, black, navy. A set of his pyjamas. A hoodie she'd brought home covered in blood and phlegm.

She carries the basket to the rack and starts hanging up the items. *Happy memories.* Can memories ever truly be happy? A memory is only a loss. Guy whisking eggs for an omelette with a fork; Guy mowing the lawn, with the red cable thrown over his shoulder, half moons of sweat darkening the armpits of his shirt; Guy making up silly songs and poems for Jas; Guy leaning into an open car bonnet, wiping the oil dipstick carefully on a folded piece of kitchen paper; the damp smell of his shower gel drifting across the landing from the bathroom; the sweeping embrace of the capital G when he signs his name. Heather throws down a sock. All her memories are still in the present tense. Guy still has a present tense because his things are still in the house, his washing is still drying on the rack. His post still falls on the doormat. He's here, but not here. He's suspended, like Heather floating in the pool, caught between the worlds of air and water, held on the finest of membranes. He could breathe or he could drown.

The nurse rings back after two hours. Guy has been reviewed again and given more Digoxin. He is still in fast AF. There has been no change.

"We noticed there's no DNR in his notes," the nurse says. "Perhaps you should—"

"No," Heather interrupts loudly. "You are right. There is no DNR. That's how it should be."

~

"I'm going to bed," Jas says soon after. "Let me know anything."

Alone downstairs Heather sits in the dark with the TV off. If she scrunches up her eyes she fancies she can see Guy sitting on his sofa, the way his legs crossed, the way his arm rested on the cushions.

He won't ever sit there again. He won't ever sleep in his bed again. He'll never come home.

Heather's stomach is raw. She finds a packet of Hula Hoops and eats them quickly. She makes tea. She's frightened to ring the ward. They'll start bullying her about the DNR again. They went over all this when Guy had his oesophagectomy. Guy believes his life is worth something. He wants to live it at all costs.

She lies back on the sofa and wraps a soft throw round herself. She's too tired to walk upstairs. The salt from the Hula Hoops makes her throat dry. If only Guy's throat could be dry, not that foaming, frothing gaping hole. Tracheostomy, she sounds the five syllables silently in her mind. A life-saving slash of the throat. That will kill Guy.

She startles awake. The phone. Her neck's on fire, jammed into the corner of the sofa. Grey dawn light in the room. She stumbles to pick up the handset before the answer machine kicks in.

"I think you should come in," the nurse says. "He could arrest at any moment."

When they arrive on the ward, they can see the curtains pulled tight around Guy's cubicle. The shift has changed over, and a young male nurse leads them to an office.

"The oncologist is coming to see you," he says, offers them tea.

"No thanks," Heather says.

Jas is sucking fiercely on a mint. She was almost sick before they left the house.

Heather cranes her neck back to see through the door. She winces at the tightness in her muscles after sleeping in a twisted ball on the sofa. Beyond the nurses' station, beyond the metal breakfast trolley, she sees the curtains swish aside. Cassie and the oncologist step out of the cubicle, leaving the drapes half open. Heather can just see the trachy trolley at the end of Guy's bed, the swabs, the bowls, the spare suction catheters.

"We seem to have the atrial fibrillation under control now," the oncologist says when he comes in, "but the next forty-eight hours will be critical."

"Should he be in Intensive Care?" Jas asks, unwrapping another mint.

"Not at present," the oncologist says. "You realise, with Guy as he is, he won't be able to have radio or chemo at the moment."

They stand, one on each side of the bed, looking down at the husk of a man between them. Jas is crying, stroking her father's thinning hair on his forehead. Heather can't find tears. Here, in the very space where she is sure Guy will die, she cannot even summon her memories. All she can do is see, note facts. The thick dried sputum on Guy's neck and chest. The navy hoodie draped over him, half pushed off. The damp bloodied gown. The mole on the side of his face. His hands, once bony, now swollen and dark. The rasp of his breath, the judder of his chest as he inhales. The thin blue lines of iris beneath his closed lids.

Fluid froths in the tracheostomy hole. Jas reaches for the suction and clears it gently. Heather does not know which sound is worse: Guy's gasping breath, or the wet gurgle of the suction catheter.

~

Heather and Jas travel together to see Guy for the next few days. As they walk across the asphalt, through the automatic doors, along the corridor, and up to the ward, Heather's breathing falters, and nausea rushes at her. The walk along the short passage, past the abandoned wheelchairs, laundry trolleys, and tea trays, past the washbasin with the squirty soap, and into the ward itself. Heather's eyes go first, as always, to the visible swathe of stained curtain around Guy's bed. Sometimes the curtains are pulled closed, bulging with human shapes from inside – a nurse suctioning fluid from the trachy, a chest physio rattling Guy's ribcage to loosen the phlegm, a healthcare assistant checking his vital signs on the flickering screen – and sometimes the curtains are pulled back, and Heather can see the metal trachy trolley at the foot of the bed.

And *he's still here*, she thinks, and the nausea judders and settles.

~

It's just past midnight, and now it's Saturday morning. Jas has gone to bed. Heather turns off the TV. It's a programme about the weather. When she fell asleep on the sofa it was something about art history. She's been sleeping for over an hour. The house is cold, even though summer is fast approaching. And with it, Guy's birthday.

Heather fills a glass with water at the sink, picks up her paperback where she left it on the kitchen table. There's a dirty mug there too, and a plate, which she missed when she loaded the dishwasher.

She walks out into the hall and time does something, speeds up or slows down, and she has a feeling, a bad feeling. She glances at the phone and its red light is still and steady. I'm tired, she thinks, that's all, and takes a further step towards the stairs. The hall explodes with the shriek of the phone. Heather spins round. The red light is flashing, the handset lit up. She's holding her glass and her book and, for a second, cannot think what to do with them. She drops her book to the floor and snatches the receiver, knowing that the next few seconds will change her life.

"Heather, it's Cassie. You need to come in. Guy's very unwell."

"What d'you mean, *unwell?*" Heather thinks she may be shouting, but she's not sure.

Movement at the top of the stairs. Jas.

"He's very poorly. His heart's stopped."

"There's no DNR."

"I know that. He's having resus. But he's really not good."

423

Jas runs down the stairs.

"I must go," Cassie says, and the line goes dead. Flatlines.

"I'll get dressed," Jas gabbles, and turns to go back up. She stumbles on Heather's paperback.

Heather's still holding her glass of water. She feels very cold. Her own heart is skipping.

"I don't know what to do."

"Is he going to die?"

"I don't know. He's having resus, she said. Cassie. His heart stopped." Heather gulps her water. "I can't drive."

"I can. Let me get dressed."

"Jas. Wait. There's nothing we can do. It'll be over before we get there. One way or another."

They sit, opposite each other at the kitchen table. The dirty mug and plate are still there. Heather drains all her water and refills her glass. Jas is restless, holding in her tears. Heather knows Jas thinks they should be in the car, racing towards Guy, but she can't do it. After all this time, she can't. She has to know what she'll find when she arrives.

Again, the phone fractures the night. Heather looks at Jas, and picks it up.

"Heather, we've got him back," Cassie says.

~

Jas has gone up to bed. Heather has promised to wake her if there is any news. She sits downstairs in the hard light of the kitchen. When she goes to the sink to fill the kettle, she sees a huge brown and cream cockchafer on the sill. A spider scrabbles

424

in a corner cobweb. Heather suddenly wants to stand out there in the garden, hearing the rustles and sighs of the night creatures, feeling the soft brush of a moth on her arm.

Instead she makes tea and sits down again, rereads the same page she's been reading over and over. At four, her eyes hardly focussing, she calls the ward. The healthcare worker answers and fetches Cassie.

"I'm watching him all night," Cassie tells Heather. "Let me just go back to him a sec."

A clang and a squeak, then quiet for a moment.

"I asked him if he had any messages for you, and he wrote on the board: *why would I have messages? Why's she ringing at this time?*"

"That's more awake than he's been for ages," Heather says.

"Get some rest. Come and see him tomorrow."

~

"Do you know what happened last night?" Heather asks Guy.

He shakes his head.

At least his eyes are open. In some ways he looks better than he has for a while, but he has no feeding tube in his nose or abdomen, and the food pump is once again pushed into the corner. The window is open a crack, and a cool slice of air hits Heather's bare arm. The revolving fan on Guy's bedside table whirrs softly as it turns.

"You had a cardiac arrest," Jas says.

Guy fumbles on the bed cover for his Boogie Board. The stylus has unclipped. Heather reaches for it.

Scared.

"Just another temporary setback." Jas smiles at Guy.

He clears the screen. *Could do with non-temp setback.*

"No," Heather and Jas say together, their eyes meeting over Guy's bed.

~

Heather doesn't go swimming on Sunday. She wants to, she'd love to feel the cool water lapping at her shoulders, to watch the tiny tiles swooping by beneath her, to breathe in that intoxicating smell, but there's another story too, and the fear of inhaling water, of her airway blocking, of choking on fluid has transfixed her.

Jas goes to Chloe's to play with Evie, and Heather waits at home, her ears straining for the phone. She dozes off on the sofa, starts awake at the sound of ringing, but it's on the telly.

~

On Monday Heather goes alone as Jas is feeling sick. Her legs are starting to swell, Heather has noticed, and her heartburn is worsening by the day. She gulps down foul chalky spoonfuls of Gaviscon, which does little to help. She's tired, beyond tired, as Heather is too.

Guy is sleeping, still with no food pump connected, no tubes in his nose or bowel. Froth spews out of the tracheostomy like lacy lava. Heather reaches automatically for the suction. It sucks listlessly. She checks the nozzle. It's blocked with pale sticky deposits. She finds a paper cup on Guy's trachy trolley and fills it at the sink; then she dips the end of the suction catheter in till it whooshes itself clean. She turns back to Guy and the cascade of fluid. It's pooling on his chest, soaking his gown, making the skin raw. He has shoved off his hoodie, which she can see is also drenched. The fan still whirrs on the cabinet. The monitor beeps as his saturations fall. Heather sucks up the liquid, one eye on the pulsing screen; the figures slowly climb as the airway opens once more.

A young man arrives and introduces himself as a chest physiotherapist.

"Guy's going to have a transfusion of platelets," he explains. "The deep suction he has to have is causing trauma and bleeding." He gestures to the canister on the wall. Heather sees the bubbles are laced with dirty blood. "His platelets are low. I can give him some physio now, then he'll have the transfusion, and then more physio later. This infection has really made his chest thick."

"OK," Heather says. "Thank you."

"We want to get him back to radio and chemo as soon as possible."

Heather nods. "And food," she says.

"I believe they're doing the NG tube tomorrow."

Tomorrow and tomorrow, Heather thinks, and hears Guy's voice, before it broke and cracked, before it was cut from him. He loved *Macbeth*. Loves.

~

427

When Heather and Jas arrive the next day the first thing they see is that the NG tube is back, with a fresh tape attaching it to Guy's skin. Food is dripping from the pump. Guy opens an eye and watches them. He chokes on something, hacking and hacking. His face and eyes flush dark. Grey-red liquid splatters his gown and the bed. Heather runs out of the cubicle but the sandy-haired nurse is already coming.

"I think he needs deep suction," Heather says.

Jas is trying to clean the trachy with the suction catheter, but Guy is still gasping.

Is this how it will end? Heather cannot bear the thought of Guy drowning in his own bloody fluids on this ward.

"It's still blocked," the nurse mutters, after the deep suction.

Guy's face is blotched purple. His eyes are streaming. Jas backs out of the cubicle. Heather wants to follow her, but she can't. She must stay. The nurse removes the laryngectomy tube.

"A lump," he says, and replaces the tube.

Guy wipes his eyes on his hands, taking shuddering breaths through his neck. His chest heaves.

"He does seem sticky today," the nurse says.

He washes his hands at the sink, and Jas creeps back into the cubicle. Guy is writing on the Boogie Board. He holds it out.

Will I ever have juice again?

Heather glances at Jas, doesn't know what to say.

"When this fistula gets better I'm sure you can," she starts.

Guy laughs silently, wipes the screen.

It's all fantasy.

~

428

In the morning Heather calls the ward, and is surprised when one of the junior doctors answers. Since Phil Rowan left, the medical staff have melted away whenever she and Jas arrive.

"We can't put the J-Peg back," the junior says. "Guy wouldn't survive the anaesthetic. We've tried to put the NG as far into the bowel as possible to avoid regurge. We also took a CT scan to have a look. The lymph nodes are very bulky, the metastases in the left lung have increased, and the right lung has partially collapsed under several abscesses."

"But...but that's so much," Heather falters.

"I've told Guy," the junior says. "He does understand."

"I'm coming in now."

~

Guy writes: *It's not going to get any better.*

"No, it's not," Heather says.

~

A hot day. A sunny day. Blue sky. Chloe and Millie are sitting on the plastic chairs on Millie's terrace, drinking Pepsi, and sharing a bowl of crisps. On the lawn Evie is rolling on the grass, picking up stray petals, chasing a Red Admiral into the flowerbed.

Chloe hears a rumbling noise from over the wall. She sucks on her crisp, not wanting to crunch and make any sound. She knows what the noise is.

"Back in a moment." She scrapes her chair back and pads into the house, checking the perfect cream carpet behind her for mud.

She runs quickly upstairs and into Millie and Matt's room. The huge double bed with its blue Madras covers. She pads to the window. There's Evie on the lawn, tugging down her floppy sunhat. Millie laughing. Chloe angles her head to look over the wall and into the cemetery. The squat yellow digger is there, grumbling loudly, as it scoops up mouthfuls of earth.

Chloe backs away from the window before Evie can see her face at the glass, and goes back downstairs and into the garden. Evie has found one of the boys' footballs, and is dribbling it uncertainly at the far end under the apple tree.

"Are you and Matt coming on Thursday?"

Millie lifts her sunglasses. "Of course." Then, "Have you heard from Heather?"

"Not much. She hasn't been swimming."

Millie puts her glasses back on.

"I should have said before, thank you for having Matt that Saturday night."

"Oh." Chloe's confused by the sudden change of subject. "It's nothing, no problem."

"You stopped him going to her place. I hope you hadn't got plans that got ruined."

They were already ruined, Chloe thinks. Olly has texted her a couple of times. Isaac is still in a coma. Jeremy is ill with fear. All he wants is his parents to get back together. Chloe didn't reply to that one; shortly afterwards Olly deleted his Facebook page.

430

Heather and Jas and Guy. Alone together for the first time in so long. Bright sunlight outside the bubbled glass. The smell of candles and oak. Heather reaches out to Guy's face, strokes the sparse hairs of his beard.

Guy's wearing one of his favourite blue shirts and his black jeans. A white cover hides the terrible fistula, stopped now, dry and silent.

An engine coughing once, twice, then starting, in the carpark outside.

Heather puts her arms round Jas, holds her close.

Guy's body falls away beneath his ribcage. Heather is glad his hands rest there, so she can't see how thin he really is. His pale cold hands, mottled with bruises.

Jas presses her bump into the side of the coffin to bring her baby as close to Guy as she can. Heather turns away, and back again, still hoping it's a trick, a lie, and Guy will have opened his eyes, be smiling at her.

Just the smell of candles and oak.

A strange unearthly peace.

~

It's another glorious day. Foxgloves and poppies in the hedgerows. Butterflies. Inside the church it's cool. Sunlight through the stained glass.

Heather sits at the front with Jas on a pew that's almost a thousand years old. The carvings have worn to blurry lumps. Heather rests her hands on the cool-warm wood.

When they came in, behind Father Geoff, behind Guy, Heather saw dark rows of people, filling the pews, standing in corners. She couldn't take in who any of them were, kept her eyes on the coffin, on the roses and lilies heaped on top of it.

She knows the sonnet word for word. *A summer's day.* A day like today.

Father Geoff looks at her, and she stands. Her heels are hollow on the old stones. She opens her folded paper, even though she knows the words, will always know them. *Thy eternal summer shall not fade.*

And now, at last, she looks down on the upturned faces before her. Jas, arms wrapped around her bump, her parents down from Norfolk. Radio people, teachers, Carol who brought her to Guy, ex-pupils, the postmaster, the pharmacist, the grocer, Jim and June Langford, Guy's friend Paddy. And more. Chloe with Matt and Millie Sinclair. Kat and Jason. Christa with Tim and Rob. They're all here, her friends from swimming. These brave people who have learned to breathe air through water.

So long as men can breathe.

~

Heather and Jas beside the gaping chasm in the ground. The undertakers' men lower Guy's pale coffin into the darkness.

In sure and certain hope.

There is no hope.

432

They cast their flowers into the grave. Soft thuds on wood. They'll lie here, trapped beneath soil for centuries, these roses held by Heather and Jas on this hot blue and gold day.

A helicopter buzzes overhead. Heather wonders if the pilot can see down into Guy's grave, to the metal plaque on the coffin.

Jas's black maxidress drifts in the wind, silhouetting her bump.

Heather glances behind them. Stragglers on the cemetery path, those who didn't go straight to the Archangel for the beer and sandwiches. They're waiting for us, Heather realises. They're waiting for us to move.

"We must go," she says to Jas.

~

Chloe, Millie, and Matt stand on the path. Just a few yards away is Matt and Millie's house, the bedroom window where Chloe stood a few days ago. Chloe's hot in her black dress, tights, boots. She was relieved when she saw Jim and June Langford get into their car after the service. She never wants to encounter them in the cemetery.

The sun shines on Jason and Kat's bright heads together. Chloe peels away and walks back to the earlier graves. She steps carefully, not treading on anyone, and stops beside Amy. There are fresh flowers in her vase. The angel is still mossy and rain-stained.

"Amy," Chloe says.

Someone comes up next to her. Chloe blinks in the sunlight. It's Kat. She's wearing a smart trouser-suit, and has green eye-liner.

"Chloe," Kat says.

"Kat."

They stand together, side by side, looking down at the patch of grass covering Amy's bones.

"I'm sorry," Kat says. "For everything. It wasn't your fault. What happened to Amy. It was mine. Me."

Chloe turns to her.

"It was my fault. Mine and Olly's."

"Yours, Olly's, and mine then. It was me she spoke to that night. I answered the phone box. I'd gone for fish and chips. I was so angry and upset."

Chloe doesn't speak.

"Olly...you won't know this, but he was horrible to me at school. For years."

"I remember," Chloe starts. "I remember the badminton court."

"I'd had years of it. And I knew he was seeing you as well as Amy."

"You saw us in the sports centre." It seems like only days ago, when they heard footsteps coming up that beige staircase, and sprang apart.

"I saw you going to his flat too," Kat says. "I only lived round the corner. I knew you were there all the time."

"I didn't know you liked Amy."

"I didn't. I thought she was stupid." Kat stops, embarrassed maybe, as she is standing on top of her. "Stupid about Olly Bradshaw. As you were. And he was just doing whatever he wanted. He was unfair to you both."

"Why did you upset her on the phone?" Chloe asks.

"I was angry. I'd seen you go up to his place earlier. I didn't know it would be Amy on the phone. I just answered it for the hell of it. I realised who she was. She was going on about her boyfriend who lived at number one, and she'd been trying to get hold of him, and his work said he hadn't been in, and something terrible must have happened, and could I go and bang on the door and find him. So I told her he was with you, as he had been for months."

"I think I knew all that," Chloe says at last. "I knew it was you at swimming, but you didn't want to know me."

"I've changed a lot."

"I don't think I have."

Chloe looks over to the path. Millie and Matt are hovering, waiting for her. Jason's loitering by the gate. Everyone else seems to have gone. To the Archangel or back to their cars.

"Let's go for a drink with Heather and Jas," Chloe says.

~

Evening. The sun is slanting in the sky. Heather stumbles back into the cemetery alone. Her heels crunch on the gravel as she walks to Guy's grave. The sections of grass have been replaced on top of the earth mound, the flowers arranged on top. She stoops to look at some of the cards attached to the blooms:

435

Robin and family; Chloe and Evie; Kat and Jason; Carol, Paddy, All at Ocean FM.

Heather straightens. She's had too much wine. Her head spins. She turns round, her back to Guy's wooden cross, to the dead of St Michael. She gazes down the slope of the cemetery to the old wall at the bottom, tangled with nettles, valerian, and honeysuckle. Over the wall to the fields. To forever.

She stretches her arms out like she's about to fly or dive. Like a crucifixion. The wind ruffles her hair.

She thinks, for an instant, that there's a noise behind her. The dry whisper of Guy's voice through his trachy but, when she checks over her shoulder, there's just the flowers and the raw earth, and a butterfly spiralling across the graves.

Acknowledgements

My father was the bravest person I have known. Time after time cancer came back for him, but he refused to give in. He was a true warrior to the end. I have never seen such courage and dignity before and I know I will not again. Many of Guy's experiences are similar to those my father went through, but I spared Guy some of the worst times. I'd like to mention two other men – Doug Crew and the late Geoff Read – who showed us all so much support and kindness in the darkest of times.

Thank you both.

Thank you to Kimella Pope for being the kindest of nurses in ENT. You were there at the terrifying start, when you were so cold in the scanning department he gave you his blanket; you were there – full circle – at the very end. Thank you also to Rose Bryan, who made the impossible possible, and turned me into a swimmer. You changed my life. Learning to swim as an adult is rewarding and exhilarating, exciting and terrifying. I have picked up a whole new vocabulary (Push and glide! Arm pull! Dead Man's Float!) but most of all I have made some lifelong friends.

Enormous thanks to Sarah Hembrow of Vulpine Press for believing in me and helping me realise my ambitions, and the same to Robin Ash, whose fantastic editing and sharp eyes for awful lines has made this book so much better.

Please do not ignore any symptoms of hoarseness, change in voice, sore throat, or breathing difficulties. Get checked out immediately. Here are the links to some head and neck cancer websites.

www.laryngectomy.org.uk

www.cancerlt.org

Lucinda Hart grew up in Cornwall and has been writing fiction since the age of three. She has a BA in Fine Art and Creative Writing and a MA in Creative Writing, both from Bath Spa University. The themes in Lucinda's books are often of great relevance to her. Place is also important; she uses her favourite locations in novels and hopes they will interest the reader as much as they have inspired her. She lives in Cornwall with her two daughters.

Please join her FB page Lucinda Hart – Author, where she shares news, extracts and short fiction. She would love to know what you think about this book, and how it has touched you. She hopes it might help anyone who has to face the situations in it in some small way.